THE BOHEMIAN

MICHAEL DE STEFANO

Night to Dawn Magazine & Books LLC
P. O. Box 643
Abington, PA 19001

www.bloodredshadow.com

Copyright © 2023 by Michael De Stefano
Paperback ISBN: 978-1-937769-80-2
Ebook ISBN: 978-1-937769-81-9

Cover Artist: Pawel Radomski
Editor: Barbara Custer
Published in the United States of America

For Kathryn

TABLE OF CONTENTS

CHAPTER ONE
MY POOR LINGUAL FRENULUM

I have had a devil of a time deciding how to dive into this narrative. Should I begin with yours truly, the protagonist of this hodgepodge of a tale; the improbability of how I came to meet and eventually wed Gabby; the wickedly carnal transformation of cousin Molly; my scare-the-living-shit-out-of-me femme fatale sister-in-law, Nina; the asexuality of the ever-kooky Harold and Jane, the all-time headscratcher of a couple, Warren and Ursula, or my wildly eccentric next-door neighbor whom I have dubbed Miss Havisham and suspect is a murderess? Amid such quirkiness, how can one choose?

I couldn't choose. So I decided to shove aside my merry band of bohemian friends and begin by describing an exercise. It may not possess a liberal measure of relevance but does have some, and a story, after all, must start somewhere, and this soon-to-be-revealed exercise would be good a place as any to begin, though the term "journey" might be more fitting. But first, allow me to state, for the record: I am a bicycle enthusiast, and to be even more precise, I am not a "tour" cyclist or rider of notable talent; I am merely enthusiastic. Unlike my friend, Warren, who is somewhat brutish and thumps his chest in honor of the acquired expertise he claims to have ascended to on behalf of his collected hobbies and after-work pursuits, I tend to maintain a more grounded perspective. Not Warren. He believes, and is hardly alone in taking ownership of such faulty self-appraisal, that because his level of enthusiasm is high, so too must be his proficiency, and he drones on and on about his many hobbies and pursuits with nauseating authority. We have all known our share of Warrens. But, if for some reason "a Warren" has eluded you, I recommend finding one. Your IQ will receive a positive jolt, as will your perspective concerning your etiquette and sophistication.

Keeping to the abovementioned, Warren has become part of an ever-growing sect: those who, if not already downsized or out-sourced, are bored, disgruntled, or disillusioned in their jobs, voca-tions, or professions and accordingly have gone in search of some-thing aside from their livelihoods upon which to hang their hats, and it has led to many attacking their chosen hobbies and weekend pur-suits with uncommon vigor and placing upon them an unbalanced premium. In other words, nowadays, for the sake of our fragile egos—and when I say "our," I'm referring to men—many take them-selves far too seriously in areas where it matters least. In that respect, I, too, nearly crossed the line. Fortunately, I reined myself in, holding my thirst for recreation above any lingering needs I had to pass my-self off as a competitor. Besides, with the ever-increasing challenges of menopausal sex as part of my routine, who needs the pressure of maintaining a certain speed over a given distance when pedaling a bicycle? Happiness begins when one has allowed room for perspec-tive, or so I recently was informed.

More often than not, I begin a cycling adventure from my driveway, and never have I pedaled beyond my block, failing to create a stir. Why? I shall be frank and admit this so-called stir has little to do with the swiftness of my cycling thrust or sleek posture that I tend to exaggerate when attractive females are afoot—no man wants to appear slumped over his handlebars and laboring when short-shorts and sandals are in the vicinity—and everything to do with my riding apparel and, more specifically, my top, which does tend to command attention. You see, I have a fondness for bright colors, and when spotting the likenesses of Bert and Ernie on a riding jersey hanging on a rack, I couldn't fish the plastic out of my wallet fast enough. Delightfully conspicuous, the jersey's depiction sees the typically snickering Ernie sticking a bright yellow banana into the ear of the typically scowling Bert. Who isn't a sucker for the Muppets? Be it new mothers, mothers-to-be, and young children pointing excitedly from the back seat of automobiles, their reactions are priceless: *Hey, there goes an adult wearing a Sesame Street jersey!* Occasionally, I'll pedal past a male whose scowl I managed to convert to a smile. Thus far, thank goodness, I have yet to encounter an imbecile subscribing to the theory Sesame Street uses Jim Henson's famous Muppet duo, subliminally or otherwise, to promote alternative lifestyles. Those poor Evangelicals are always looking to spot trouble where there isn't any, nor ever was in the first place. That aside, it is a joy to wave to the children in my neighborhood and hear them call out, "There goes the Bert and Ernie guy!"

Off I go, cycling down Sussex Pike, waving to neighbors, including Mr. Finnegan's fearsome-looking Akita, who, if not, thankfully, secured to a stout chain attached to an equally stout hook anchored into concrete, would chase me down the pike and tear off my scrotum. Mr. Finnegan has never intimated as much that his Akita would attack me in this fashion; it is simply a feeling I get when pedaling past this leaping, barking, and abundantly muscular specimen.

Next, I cycle down Arbor, then Perry Lane, where I skirt along the lush grounds of a Presbyterian Church on the way to scenic Meetinghouse Road. Situated on both sides of the country lane are multi-million-dollar mansions, horse farms, and agriculture farms. It's like Kansas meets the Hamptons, except it is suburban Philadelphia providing the scenery. Bells Mill Road is seven miles into my trek, where I take my first rest and swig of water. That's generally about when Gabby begins to stir—I can sense her arousal. So, back up onto my bicycle, I climb. Three miles down the road is Willoughby's Farm, where baked and churned are the county's best apple pies and soft-serve ice cream. Who doesn't love a farmer's market with a built-in bakery and creamery? More importantly, it is there, at Willoughby's Farm, after ten miles of pedaling, Gabby finally, and thankfully, climaxes.

I am hardly insensible to what the female reader must be wondering: *What kind of deranged lunatic imagines his Sunday bike ride while pleasuring his wife on Saturday night?* But before you judge too harshly, is there any among the female sect who, in their wandering minds, has not planned a menu for a holiday dinner or ran through a vacation checklist because their man was taking his sweet, ol' time climaxing? Yep, that's what I thought.

It was not always like this between Gabby and me; our lovemaking was once spontaneous and imaginative, and, if anything, our exploratory journeys of idyll were too swift. Then came the hot flashes, cold spells, mood swings, and all the other joys a hateful condition known as menopause levies upon interested couples. Early on, when ambushed by this cruel trick of nature and—as might a typical male—selfishly appraising it as "my" inconvenience, I imagined not a Sunday bicycle adventure. Instead, I would attempt to remember every best picture, best actor, and best actress award winner beginning with the year of my birth up to the present. I thought it was clever on my part to use the time spent at Gabby's vagina to engage in a memory exercise; I am a real multi-tasker. Anyway, it made perfect sense to me, though I could not reconcile that *Shawshank Redemption* and *Pulp Fiction* were each edged out by Forrest Gump, *Network* by Rocky, or that *Shakespeare in Love* was ever nominated! I did not, however, let my internalized harangue interfere with Gabby's pleasure; I'm not a selfish brute entirely.

Well, now that I have gone and introduced my wife's vagina to you, I suppose it is about time to move forward in our narrative and introduce myself. The name's Mitch—Mitch Morningstar. I never cared much for my name; it's not Morningstar that displeases me—Morningstar, however uncommon, works fine—it is Mitch that I never appreciated. I was born back when, aside from a human being, expectant parents did not know what they were getting, much less getting in*to*. Anyway, my father was hoping for a girl he would promptly claim "my Michele," but I dashed his hopes, having the audacity to arrive brandishing a penis. How inconsiderate! Meanwhile, my mother decided the world already had suffered too many Michaels, so I ended up with this ridiculous hybrid of a name: Mitchel, though my friends, thankfully, and with me encouraging them to the point of pleading, call me Mitch.

Incidentally, I am a novelist by trade. My genre? Serial killers! You see, I have had a decades-long fascination with, of all people, Jack the Ripper, and for two reasons: First, he never got caught; second, they were not even sure his name was Jack; all along, he might have been Nigel the Ripper and his ability to evade the efforts of Scotland Yard has shielded us from a century-old truth.

I had only known our neighbor, Warren, a short time when he made it his business to tell me, "You know, Mitch, writing about serial killers is sorta like cheating."

It was one of those absurd remarks that can cause a man's face to twist into a comical distortion. I could not imagine where Warren was going, though he did satisfy my curiosity when he explained: "These worst of deviants, who make up such a minute percentage of our society, are inherently interesting by virtue that they're deranged." Warren made a courageous effort to be tactful, but he more or less informed me any moron in possession of pen and paper could make a serial killer sound interesting. He also worked into what had chiefly evolved into a one-sided conversation: "Many years ago, my cousin, Albert, from Toronto, wrote a novel. The protagonist was an achondroplastic dwarf with a speech impediment who rescued a pregnant woman from a burning building, and afterward was pressured into an on-the-scene news interview and later a television appearance." Warren did not close by adding, *try turning that into a novel, hotshot,* but he may as well have. I, in turn, told Warren to go fuck himself if not a stuttering dwarf and, in the process, was courageously tactful. So, as it stands, I am known as "The Bert and Ernie guy" to the children in town and "The serial killer guy" to the adults.

We're kinda-sorta friends, Warren and me, though, if truth be told, our wives keep us together. I believe that's how it is in many cases. It has been my experience that when men reach a certain age, aside from family and work, they begin edging toward becoming lone wolves, only to find themselves forced into friendships by the women who have selected them. Sometimes I feel Warren and I have fallen victim to that dreadful late-twentieth and early-twenty-first-century phenomenon known as playdates. However, I cannot blame Gabby for her efforts, for novelists tend to lapse into spells of reclusion, and she wants to ensure that I remain a social creature.

"Don't forget, we're going rafting with Warren and Ursula tomorrow," Gabby reminded me. Then, after twisting my neck back into shape, I let out a telling groan as I had been feasting upon Gabby for a good twenty minutes. Gabby knew my groaning had little to do with my neck cursing her menopause and everything to do with the weekend coming and going, and the only cycling I would do was what I had just finished imagining.

"Rafting is every bit as exciting as cycling," Gabby maintained. There was no need for Gabby to defend rafting as a worthy activity. I was perfectly aware of the excitement it can provide; however, when cycling, I slip into an alternate universe, and when immersed in that universe, I develop characters and storylines. Negotiating rapids while dowsed by cold river water is not conducive to my needs.

"Warren isn't all that bad, you know." Gabby's tone was somewhat chiding. "And he isn't nearly the dunderhead you, at times, imply."

"I never implied that Warren was a lunkhead, just Canadian." Gabby frowned at that remark, then wondered aloud whether I had an equally lofty appraisal of the British (Gabby was a Brit). I wisely responded, "Perish the thought; you Brits practically invented irony." We both returned to the goblets of wine poured before we began a Saturday night menopausal interlude which saw Gabby receive the lion's share of the attention. I winced when the wine hit my mouth, as once again, I tore that fleshy piece of tissue that anchors the tongue to the floor of the mouth; neither Gabby nor I knew the name of that fleshy oral gadget. Then, one day, Gabby remembered to ask Ursula—Ursula's field was to make sense of the messiness that tends to accumulate between our ears but also is a whiz at anatomy—who promptly informed us while unable to resist a smirk: "Mitch, I'm afraid you've torn your lingual frenulum." It was clear that Ursula took enormous pleasure in sharing this information, not because it afforded her an opportunity to show off her anatomical acumen but because she correctly assumed why a man would suffer a tear in such a place. Afterward, she seized upon the opportunity to coquettishly wink in my direction, then later informed me, "Gabby is a lucky woman." From that moment forward, I have not stopped wanting to bed Ursula but have developed a peculiar sense: should Ursula decide to stray from her vows, it would be to show Gabby the true meaning of an inexhaustible tongue.

One year and many lingual frenulum tears later, I still obsess over Ursula. During this period, I have received more flirtatious winks and overtures carrying ostensibly sincere messages; yet, Gabby has received what I would purport are the more meaningful glances. I am unsure whether Ursula is truly bisexual or a woman who, since turning a certain age, is looking for new experiences. Whatever the case, her beauty, regardless of one's taste, is undeniable; her long flowing hair, tall willowy form, sharp features, and husky bedroom voice nearly makes Warren tolerable—even on Sundays—though it has become somewhat of a sore subject with yours truly that my Neanderthal neighbor, doubtless due to some twisted sense of cosmic justice, has been awarded the privilege of bedding such a glorious creature. At least, I assume he does. Where couples are concerned, Warren and Ursula are my idea of "a real head-scratcher." Incidentally, I am still very much in love with Gabby; and also, allow me to state for the record my desire to bed Ursula does not stem from any deep-seated deviance, for example, wanting to stick it to her blustery husband by wearing a telling smirk for the duration of a rafting trip; it is simply one of those "healthy" obsessions that creep up during the course of a long-sustaining marriage.

Some months ago, following a Saturday night session that resulted in another torn lingual frenulum, I approached Gabby with my suspicion of Ursula. She was quick to dismiss the notion, perhaps too quick, and it led me to theorize: either my British bride was insensible concerning Ursula's overtures or wholly agreeable to the idea of the long, slender beauty having a crack at her happy place. Whichever, I decided not to press Gabby concerning my suspicion. Not that I lacked inclination or interest, but I was fearful of revealing myself as a shameless wanton owning a secret desire to witness two women discovering one another, even if one of the women happened to be my wife. The last thing I wanted concerning a matter of this nature was to seem too eager; doubtless, it would lead to Gabby and Ursula snickering behind my back, and I couldn't begin to guess Warren's feelings on the subject. So I let the matter pass without another word.

"So, how's the new novel coming along, Mitch?" Gabby asked. It wasn't a thoughtful inquiry; it was more like Gabby's version of small talk—a post-climax oh-by-the-way initiative. You see, Gabby is a fan of my novels—it was what brought us together—but she is not the least bit in favor of my latest effort.

"Fine," I told her. "I can state, with confidence, it's coming along better than expected." Haughtiness to offset Gabby's meager appreciation of my latest work was not the intention; I simply stated a fact.

"Good for you, Mitch," she said. "But the real test will come when your readers get their hands on it. It's pretty damn bold of you to write a serial killer spoof; I'm surprised your agent went for the idea."

"I wouldn't necessarily say that she 'went' for the idea, but after all these years, she owes me a little latitude." Gabby sighed that I was correct but was no more appreciative that I shattered my mold by writing a spoof. *Hey, you're supposed to be "the serial killer guy," remember?*

We finished the contents of our goblets, with me occasionally wincing but offering nary a complaint, then crept into bed. Sleeping next to Gabby is a joy; so soft are her body's luxurious curves, and she is always delightfully scented. I truly am in love with my wife.

Just as Gabby began to doze, I inadvertently let slip a chortle. When she asked what was so humorous, I lied and said I must have been dreaming and couldn't remember. The truth? I decided that a spoof should have a disingenuous or "spoof-like" dedication. When nearly having dozed, only one person came to mind: Warren. Indeed, my friend and neighbor would suffer the cruelest of fates in this dark and bizarre parody.

CHAPTER TWO
FUNHOUSE

Around the time my career was getting off the ground, my cousin Nicholas Morningstar was preparing to join the United States Air Force. Unlike me, Nicholas appreciates his name. Who wouldn't want to be named Nicholas? It's a smart-sounding name, a real man's name. Nicholas was a few years younger than me and, growing up, resided on the other side of town (Philadelphia). So age and geography marked the prevailing reasons we were not close. There were others: Aside from sharing an unusual surname, we had little in common. In high school, I was in the drama club, wrote for my school newspaper, and when winding down my senior year, clamored to attend Amherst if not some other fancy liberal arts college where I would take up all sorts of impractical studies bound to make me sound brilliant but keep me broke. My father wished me luck and sent me to Temple. From the position of a middle linebacker, Nicholas chased down and tackled ball carriers, made an occasional interception, sacked quarterbacks, and forced and recovered fumbles. And when the offense was on the field, he paced the sidelines, grunting, spitting, and head-butting teammates. Of all the cousins, Nicholas and his athleticism, time and again during holiday dinners, received top billing; not once can I remember receiving an "atta-boy" for a particular article I wrote or a challenging role I played. And poor Molly; she was accepted into the University of Pennsylvania with a partial scholarship and still had to languish in Nicholas's shadow. But, as I have stated, Nicholas was a few years younger than Molly, me, and our other cousins, and none of us relished the role of spoilsport; thus, we did not dare give voice that we begrudged the spotlight that always seemed to shine so generously on our younger cousin.

When Nicholas announced that he would be leaving the bosom of his family "to serve my country," this decision was met with nauseating praise. Uncle Lambert, Uncle Peter, Aunt Belinda, and Grandpa Alexander projected him as a war hero—assuming a war would break out—if not the next Eisenhower. It led Molly and me to dub our young cousin "Boy Wonder," a name we kept between us. Three months later, in San Antonio, Texas, where his superior athleticism served him well, Boy Wonder became Airman Morningstar. "Someone in our family has finally earned a title," I heard my father blathering.

Sometime during Nicholas's transition from citizen to serviceman, I had my first novel, *Funhouse*, published. As a ten-year-old, when carted through The Wacky Shack—a haunted house amusement on Hunt's Pier on the boardwalk of Wildwood, New Jersey—I can recall thinking: If you were someone inclined to commit murder, this would be just the place to do it. Thus, The Wacky Shack—an amusement long ago dismantled—became the first seedling for *Funhouse*. In *Funhouse*, Davey Coyle possesses a psyche similar to that of Dostoevsky's Raskolnikov in the novel *Crime and Punishment*. He is destitute, suffers from bouts of isolation and alienation, and feels utterly discarded by a society for which he has contempt, and it drives him to kill. However, the similarities end there. Raskolnikov's murder of a pawnbroker, thought to be unscrupulous, thus serving a utilitarian end, was a contemplative and targeted act that afterward left him tormented, whereas Davey Coyle's multiple murder victims were chosen arbitrarily and were acts yielding no shred of remorse.

Orphaned by way of his parents perishing in an automobile accident which Davey survived, he got passed around until he reached age eighteen with nothing but a long, lonely, and uncertain road ahead of him. He traveled the countryside, taking whatever odd jobs his limited skills permitted, and come the evenings, he slept in flophouses. Occasionally, Davey found steady work, but the income was always meager. Often, it was stocking shelves in grocery stores or pumping gasoline in autumn, winter, and spring. Come the summer, he landed a job working a wheel of fortune at an amusement ground. The job was simple: spin the wheel, collect money, and hand out prizes five days a week from noon until ten in the evening. Fifty hours a week, Davey Coyle stood on a platform surrounded by three walls and a countertop that came up to his waist. The corresponding numbers and letters of the wheel were on the countertop—it was also where the bettors placed their money. Similar structures flanked Davey's station. One was set up for a water pistol game that saw contestants shoot streams of water into the mouths of clowns, which filled balloons; the first balloon to burst was declared the winner, the outcome announced by a bell; another structure accommodated a game of beanbag toss. All day and night, Davey was enveloped by the collaborative smells of popcorn, cotton candy, funnel cake, roasted peanuts, pizza, and machine oil while enduring the constant serenading of whirring motors, grinding gears, and raucous arcades, and all for the right to perform a mindless task for low-end pay. But what choice did he have? Davey Coyle was not a young man who knew from making choices, much less blessed with any to make. He did not choose to lose his parents, get passed around, then tossed into a world that held for him little in the way of prospects if not offering contempt. Getting cut from a team can be devastating for a young man still navigating through boyhood. Davey Coyle was not let go from ballplaying; life made him a castoff. Then, one night, staring back at him was the answer—a pathway to latch onto a team and prove to all who had discarded him that he could not only belong but triumph.

The funhouse was a hotspot: day or night, it never failed to draw a crowd. Perhaps the ghoulish figures leering from the blood-smudged and well-cobwebbed windows of the two-storied structure lured the multitude of fun-seekers and enticed them to enter. Despite its share of startling props and eerie effects, teenage boys dismissed the funhouse as silly. Still, they would enter with the notion they were protecting girlfriends who would cling to their arms throughout what often proved an eventful experience for everyone. The protection of masculine arms aside, the girls screamed, and their shrieks were exaggerated when accosted by the animated props and effects the funhouse offered; to anyone forced to listen, like Davey Coyle, whose wheel of fortune was in close proximity, one might imagine genuine torture was taking place within those walls. Davey found the girl's shrieks irksome—an odious assault that tore at his senses with a ferocity similar to a pack of ravenous wolves gathered around a kill. "Why must they scream so loudly; it's a funhouse!" he would seethe under his breath.

They were girls in the autumn of youth—high schoolers, mostly—only a few years younger than Davey; spirited damsels coddled by knights in shining armor who chose to scream; it was also their choice to enter the funhouse, have boyfriends, wear skimpy colorful summer clothes that drove their male counterparts to distraction, and brashly delight in what seemed a moment-to-moment life with each moment joyfully introducing the next. How Davey begrudged such an existence and the unabashed manner he saw it collectively celebrated; to someone strenuously familiar with loss, abandonment, disillusionment, and despair, these girls owned an embarrassment of riches and an overabundance of choices; the unfairness and disparity were too great.

The moment Davey Coyle was overtaken by an impulse to kill, he knew the place and that the victim must be a young woman. All that remained was the *when* and *how*; there was no wrestling with indecision. He would impress upon everyone an understanding of what it truly means to have a say in the world.

Gunfire would alarm not only everyone inside the funhouse but outside as well; it would ring out over the roar of the roller coasters and the music ringing from the carousel. Conversely, the screams produced by bludgeoning or stabbing, particularly from within a place such as a funhouse, might seem perfectly natural—or so Davey theorized. The night following his resolute decision, he made his way to the funhouse, stood in line for what seemed an eternity, and all the while ran through a gamut of nervous ticks beginning with the cracking of knuckles and ending with mindlessly taking inventory of the scant contents of his pants pockets. "'Bout time you came wandering over here," crooned Mr. Riggs, who ran the funhouse. "I was beginning to think you'd never give in to your curiosity!" Davey smiled somewhat sheepishly that his preoccupation with the funhouse had not gone as unnoticed as suspected. Upon entering, he permitted others to pass him so that he could methodically creep about. His objective was to familiarize himself with the order of props and effects—every twist, turn, nook, and cranny delineable in the darkness. A week later, he went through it again and repeated the effort the following week. "I'm flattered," said Mr. Riggs. Davey smiled as to intimate: *What can I say; the funhouse is the highlight of the grounds.*

It was mid-July: the nighttime crowds were growing denser, thus bringing forth the height of opportunity. "Next week," Davey told himself while operating the Wheel of Fortune across the way. He repeated the words while glaring contemptuously at the funhouse

The Bohemian

and those awaiting their turn to enter. The wheel zipped around and around, the pegs clicking by a pointer that would ultimately decide the winner. By night's end, the *how* and the *when* would also become a settled affair.

A worn yet inspired Davey Coyle ambled back to the place that served as his accommodations; it amounted to little more than a flophouse he shared with several other young men who, like himself, were vagabonds that managed seasonal employment and a place to put up for the summer. Scantily furnished was the house, and, if not broken, its meager offerings were threadbare, the worn material well stained. The bathroom reeked of urine, as often, over many years, it got victimized by drunk young men with faulty aim, who cared not to clean up after themselves—the result of this repeated carelessness had seeped into what became grotesquely discolored grout lines near a century old. It was a minute to the a.m. side of midnight when Davey slipped past the front door. Scattered about were several overflowing ashtrays with lit cigarettes beside those who had fallen asleep; several crushed beer cans were also visible at the feet of those who had passed out. The scene was all too representative of a shelter, come nighttime, that served as a dumping ground for a handful of the world's woe begotten. Davey looked them over and wondered who among them possessed the courage necessary to commit an ultimate act and, if summoned, could they grasp the core of its essence—the breadth of its power. His formulated answer caused him to sneer contemptuously at a mass of oddly positioned bodies. To a man, he believed they were made far too inferior for such a calling— such loftiness.

Mr. Riggs' nephew, Charlie, who worked at the funhouse as a ticket taker in the summertime, took Davey's ticket at just past five in the afternoon. At six o'clock came the changing of the guards; thus, Mr. Riggs had no way of knowing that Davey was already well entrenched in his funhouse, hunkered down and biding his time. Davey knew the precise spot where he could crouch down and remain hidden away—it was just beyond a bend where a life-sized skeletal figure recessed in the wall came lunging out to greet the fairground's fright-seekers; the unexpected thrust triggered flickering lights followed by blood-curdling laughter. It was a typical haunted house effect but never failed to startle those arriving at the bend unsuspectingly. For a while, the screams that rang in Davey's ears did not belong to high schoolers but to those younger, braving their way through the funhouse accompanied by a parent, if not flanked by two. Finally, after crouched in what amounted to a nook of an area and for a longer time than he planned to be cramped, Davey's well-adjusted eyes could delineate size, shape, gender, and age. As more time passed, finer details became apparent, and his improved sight led him to the anxious notion that he was equally conspicuous. *Hey, you're that wheel of fortune guy; you can't fool us!* Davey had himself all but convinced he was not only visible but equally ostensible were his evil intentions, which led to the paranoid delusion everyone was laughing at him. Thus, the ether within the funhouse seemed to twist and distort; it echoed the questions: *What are you doing crouched so long in a cramped space? What have you to prove, and to whom would it matter?*

Moreover, who was Davey Coyle? Was he a miscreant in his soul or a man playing the role of a malefactor, and were these theories mutually exclusive? His thoughts transitioning from decisive and resolute to twisted and distorted was an unexpected dilemma, as Davey never imagined that gaining the ability to see clearly in the dark would become a source of torment. Thus, he remained in a strained and nervous crouch ruminating an unforeseen vicissitude. At last, using bargaining and reasoning, he managed to compose himself and reconcile the notion those thirsting for fright had not the time to acquire his sense of sight; this renewed awareness hastened the restoration of confidence that it was he who wielded control and was the decider of outcomes. How Davey longed for control, to revel in its essence, to tingle with the sensation of owning the power to shape the destinies of others affords.

Night has fallen, and the darkening sky enlivens an already lively scene. In every direction, there are bright splashes of light—reds, yellows, oranges, and whites—pulsating, flashing, darting, and swirling, enticing a dense multitude to ride carousels and roller coasters, lick ice cream cones and candy apples, and play various games of chance and skill with the hope of walking away with a prize. Twenty-five cents a spin; twenty-five cents a throw; step right up; give it a try; it might be your lucky night! Bells, whistles, balloons, and laughter cascade throughout the park—it is a nonstop amusement ground where endless fun is had by nonstop folks milking every moment from a too-short summer: these fun-seekers will blink, September will be upon them, the amusement ground will transform to a ghost town that turns its back on childhood until next year but not without offering a parting gift in the form of lingering memories, but one memory will linger more impactfully, it would overshadow all others following the summer of '72, thus leaving the good folks of Sandusky, Ohio in terror.

Davey became aware that outside darkness had fallen, for no longer seen were innocent children clutching the arms of trusted adults. The funhouse now belonged to the dreaded screamers, laughers, and aspiring young lovers, those whom Davey reviled, who night after night served to heighten his sense of isolation, his inadequacy; he would show them, every one. But there were so many: who among them should he choose; who was most deserving, and how could he, a mere mortal, make such a judgment? But why should it matter; tonight, he was omnipotent: The All-Powerful, down through the ages by way of decisive measures unfair when juxtaposed to human frailty, had whisked away countless multitudes; was he not permitted to commit a single ultimate act? Indeed, Davey Coyle would point his finger at will, just as God Himself had when arbitrarily pointing a finger that left a young boy orphaned alongside a randomly chosen road. How Davey had called to his mother but was helpless to spark life back into her dead eyes; silent, too, was a once loving and heroic father. No God, who permitted such tragedy, would dare judge him less stand in the way of his triumph—his glory.

Her name was Cynthia Gibbs. She was sixteen years old and about to enter her junior year of high school. Unlike Raskolnikov's slaying of an unscrupulous pawnbroker, Cynthia Gibbs' exit from the world was not perceived by her slayer as a utilitarian act. Her death was simply the result of a young man who, over time, since pulled from a life-altering wreckage, had become deranged, thus crossing a threshold to an alternative reality—a realm where delusions reign as the conquerors of reason—where, deciding the fate of humanity, or a single link in its age-old chain, marked the only pathway to euphoria.

The life-sized skeletal figure came lunging out from the wall at three unsuspecting girls. Next came the instantaneous arrival of flickering lights, then blood-curdling laughter, synchronized events yielding what all summer long had been the typical reaction. The effects of the funhouse, and the shrieking that accompanied this well-wrought chamber of horrors, occurred with little variation; and Davey, crouched in the darkness, had witnessed the repetition numerous times—maybe a hundred times—it was as predictable as gravity, and, with the elimination of chance, so swelled his confidence, though upon him rose a moment of indecision when he saw the sparkle of youth flicker in the startled eyes of Cynthia Gibbs once she passed the skeletal figure. *Why did it have to be you?* But for whom was Davey lamenting? Why couldn't he have been a boy born destined to hold the hand of this girl who was to die? A moment that nearly blossomed into a bout of rumination dwindled to a mere flicker of regret, then passed altogether. The sparkle in Cynthia's eyes—her youthful vivacity—owned no dissimilarity; she embodied every girl, and they were all Davey's tormentors, individually and collectively.

She never saw it coming. In one instance, Cynthia Gibbs was a young woman filled with hopes and dreams that awaited her on a promising horizon; in the next, Davey Coyle showed the young women who flocked to the amusement ground what it truly meant to have a say and possess control; the power these feelings introduced to Davey's being would become his life's elixir.

Cynthia Gibbs did not depart, perish, or pass away—those are reconcilable terms that help mortals process death—her life instantaneously was snuffed out as though she was nothing more than a bug one thoughtlessly treads on. The two female friends at her side were rendered speechless, powerless to utter a sound, and frozen in terror; they clutched one another and trembled as some might when forced to interface with the consequences of a world capable of unimaginable realities. Their shock would last not for hours but days. The singular act of a madman with a whim could prove too much for anyone, much less two young girls, to comprehend.

Once the funhouse was declared a crime scene and taped off, homicide detectives arrived, asking all the predictable questions, including: "Did anyone notice a man bringing a knife into the funhouse?" The detectives spoke mainly with Mr. Riggs and the two young men who, along with their girlfriends, were the ones to discover Cynthia Gibbs' lifeless body and her two nonresponsive friends. "At first, when I saw the knife sticking out of her back, I thought it was a prop, but then…." The young man shuddered when reliving the gruesome discovery.

Davey hastened his steps until he reached those who had gone before Cynthia and her friends. By the time Mr. Riggs was alerted that a killing had taken place in his funhouse, Davey had inconspicuously poured through the exit and circulated through what had been a typically dense crowd. After all the hours spent in a dark, cramped space, he was grateful to have his legs stretched and moving about in the open air; he would position himself toward the back of a throng already buzzing with curiosity. But, before long, what began as mounting curiosity, turned to horror; it swept through the crowd, and, for Davey, it generated a sense of euphoria he would savor. Indeed, it was like any other night at the amusement ground until Davey Coyle killed.

The following afternoon when Davey showed up to take bets and spin the Wheel of Fortune, what greeted him was a pang of remorse. However, his guilt-ridden spasm had nothing to do with the cavernous void he created by robbing Cynthia Gibbs of her life; the funhouse shut down pending further investigation was what robbed him of a clear conscience. It was not the scenario Davey had foreseen: putting Mr. Riggs out of business for an undetermined period.

"That hardly seems fair," Davey said to Mr. Riggs. "You did nothing wrong, and now you have to lose business."

"There's always collateral damage, and this time it's yours truly who drew the short straw," Mr. Riggs bemoaned. "But a few greenbacks are nothing compared to what that poor girl's folks must be going through. Imagine a murder at an amusement park: what's this world coming to!"

"No good, I suppose," said Davey before walking away.

The amusement ground was understandably subdued that day and remained so for several days afterward. Before anyone could realize it, Labor Day, the last big bash of summer, was upon them. The amusement ground would remain open on weekends and close altogether after September. With its closing would come the vanishing of hundreds of jobs: ticket takers, popcorn poppers, carousel barkers, rollercoaster operators, and the spinner of the Wheel of Fortune. Davey Coyle would depart Sandusky, Ohio, but not before purchasing a one-way ticket for a bus heading east. He would spend the year performing odd jobs, reaching for an opportunity wherever one presented; he would work hard for his employers, then move on, making his way east, until he arrived at Hunt's Amusement Pier on the boardwalk of Wildwood, New Jersey, just in time for the launch of the summer season. On Wildwood's famed boardwalk, he spent his nights dipping dough into hot oil; the finished product was a dessert called funnel cake. Come the summer of '74, it was off to Norfolk, Virginia, and Ocean View Amusement Park. In '75, his destination was Myrtle Beach. On and on he went, and in each place, he killed; time and again, he proved he was a force—an entity for which the world must account, not the other way around. But like all killers who subscribe to the theory that murder is an art form and that the essence of their art is profound and brilliant, he craved recognition; no longer could he separate the *art* from the *artist*. In 1979, at age twenty-five, he returned to Sandusky, Ohio, for a curtain call; it would be his eighth and final performance. After the curtain went down on Gail Morrison, a seventeen-year-old cheerleader, Davey Coyle strolled into the nearest police precinct and announced: "I'm The Funhouse Killer." His words were expressionless, resonating from one bearing a crazed presence. In other words, Davey bore not the resemblance of one who committed murder but a deranged killer. He need not repeat his words or work to convince anyone of his claim. Nevertheless, several days of a thorough and later publicized interrogation followed, and upon delving into the psyche of a serial killer—a journey that both fascinated and horrified—one fact persisted as irrefutable: Davey Coyle knew details only the killer himself could, and despite turning himself over to the authorities of Sandusky, he was tried, convicted, and sentenced in Virginia, where, recently, the death penalty was resurrected. The parents of all eight of his victims were present to witness his execution. Before being put to death, he addressed the crowd: "It was my choice to come forward. It was my will that brought us together. What you are about to witness is suicide."

****

It came as no surprise—despite work, studying for her masters, and having not a moment to spare on fiction or any discretionary reading—that Molly was the first among my kin to rush out and purchase a copy of *Funhouse*.

Mitch, congratulations! she wrote. *Nothing this exciting has happened in our family since "Boy Wonder" intercepted a pass against Central. (I hope that little bit of humor made your day.) I'm sure, one day, I'll wiggle my way through this impossible thicket known as my seemingly endless college career, and when I do, my first order of business will be to remove Funhouse from my bookshelf, where I've made it a focal point, and read it. Although I must say, dear cousin, I never figured you, given your penchant for humor, as the serial killer type; however, judging from the endorsements, it looks quite promising.*

What *did* come as a surprise: Airman Morningstar, amazingly, was the first among my kin to turn the pages of *Funhouse*.

Dear Mitch, he wrote from Wright-Patterson Air Force Base in Dayton, Ohio—not all that far from where Davey Coyle murdered Cynthia Gibbs—*I just finished reading Funhouse, and I'm not just saying this because you're my cousin, but it's the best novel I ever read!*

I was not aware Nicholas could read. He was a typical jock who went out of his way to exhibit typical jock-like behavior on his way to typical jock pursuits; I was always under the impression that reading, disinterest aside, was a skill that gave him fits; though, being as I am, a novelist, I should know better than to make the mistake of judging a book by its cover. Nevertheless, Nicholas claiming that *Funhouse* was the best novel he had ever read would be akin to me, an only child, claiming I am my parents' favorite son. Anyway, I wrote Nicholas back to thank him for his glowing endorsement and warn him—assuming he failed to see *Funhouse* as a piece of fiction—that using a furlough to drive to the amusement ground at Sandusky could prove unwise.

CHAPTER THREE
THE DRESS REHEARSAL

It may seem that I lack a spark of fondness for my youngest cousin, Airman Nicholas Morningstar, given that I own a meager opinion of his acumen; but it was Nicholas, although unwittingly and indirectly, who years ago paved the way for what thus far has proved, for ol' Mitch Morningstar, a happy life. Naturally, being a military man, Airman Morningstar did his share of traveling. Fortunately for me, it placed him on a collision course with a young woman who, like himself, got a real charge out of a serial killer who used what, nowadays, would be considered retro amusement parks for his killing grounds.

On his way to a six-month stint in Nairobi, Kenya, Nicholas departed Dayton, Ohio, then was issued orders for a two-year tour in England. *Dear Mitch,* he began: *Shit is the one word that comes to mind, and best describes English cuisine. Cuisine, however, is a poor choice of words, but because it is safe to ingest, I suppose what they offer on plates in England still deserves to be called food. As for the beer? It's otherworldly!* It warmed my heart to learn my young cousin had not abandoned his lofty principles. The food in England was permitted to be lousy, not the beer.

Six months into his tour, lonely, homesick, and starving for affection, Nicholas and four other airmen wandered into Lord John Russell Pub in the Bloomsbury section of London. They were not yet shown to their seats, these five airmen once scattered throughout the United States, when Nicholas found himself drawn to a table where sat two women whose looks were in stunning contrast with one another. One was tall and slender; her bountiful locks were made a tasteful shade of blonde by a professional and tumbled to the middle of her back. By all accounts, she was a head-turner but, as Airman Morningstar alleged, had too much presentation in her appearance. Not to suggest that her appearance was artificial, just the result of painstaking effort; in other words, she seemed to the young airman a canvas that was toiled upon by an artist striving for perfection. The application of her makeup was beyond impeccable, and she was well if not over-accessorized, especially for lunch at a pub. One might suspect that she was overcompensating, but for what, the young airman could not hazard a guess. It was unimaginable that someone possessing such an overabundance of physical beauty lacked confidence. Moreover, it was anomalous for Airman Morningstar to have struggled to appreciate a creature so overly endowed with beauty.

It persists as a fascinating phenomenon that the lonely hearts of the world seldom gravitate toward the stunners; they tend, more often, to fall into the laps of those whose beauty is less threatening. Perhaps they think their overtures and affections would be better received and returned. The other woman in Airman Morningstar's sightline—the one who managed the lion's share of his attention—was much shorter; she could also be described as tufty-headed and slightly plump, though in a way many would consider pleasing. Her eyes had a smile all their own. As for her features in totality, they possessed warmth and a sense of invitation; in concert, they were nothing short of lovely. Moreover, her bearing represented a calm sea in a madding world; she was the woman a fellow runs to when "Beauty" has made confetti of his poor heart, and once illuminated to her often-overlooked essences, he will discover the vibrancy of springtime, thus a facility to make "Beauty" seem far less than ordinary if no longer beautiful. I would like to believe that Nicholas had an intuitive nature that somehow eluded Molly and me—that this never-before detected asset drew him to the lesser impressive of the two females, not the notion that she was assumed the easier conquest. It is upon this premise that we shall proceed.

"What are you waiting for, Morningstar; for her to flash you a nipple?" Nicholas's fellow airmen urged rather boisterously. "She isn't gonna sit around all day waiting for you to grow testicles!"

What is worse than being caught ogling? To begin with, getting egged on by colleagues who have made your sudden interest painfully clear to where it reached the ears of everyone in the vicinity, including the one who captured your attention. The way Airman Morningstar read the situation, he had two choices: He could excuse himself to the men's room with the hope that, upon his return, a matter which had yet to materialize fully would blow over—or, he could do the manly thing and stroll up to the table like a confident American airman. He chose the latter and was wise to do so; anything less would have resulted in his colleagues rowdily shaming him into action.

Airman Morningstar had not quite reached the table where sat these contrasting women when, abruptly, the taller of the two rose from her chair. Her intention was unmistakable; to exit from Lord John Russell Pub swiftly. With the swaying prance of a runway model, she wound her way between the rows of high-top tables; her lovely mane danced to the delight of the crowd; her sleek stilettos pounded gloriously upon the hardwood and had announced what for many, including Airman Morningstar's colleagues, was an unfortunate departure. As she wound her way toward the front door, the airmen jeered, "A real Prince Charming, aren't you, Morningstar?" Little did the airmen know, it was never the sophisticated beauty the pub-goers deemed a femme fatale for whom few were worthy that Airman Morningstar had intended to pursue.

"I hope you're not too disappointed she's gone. But, if you are, it's okay; I'm used to it by now." The woman punctuated her words with a warm smile and a nod toward the recently vacated chair. Both tacit gestures were a cue for Airman Morningstar that, if he wished to, he could join her at the table; the brief preamble, however, was farcical, as the woman suspected the airman's interest did not rest with her taller eye-catching companion; the evidence had occurred when, during her departure, every head in Lord john Russel Pub turned, save for the approaching airman's.

"Who's gone?" the airman returned. "And why on earth should I be disappointed?"

"Granted, she may not have been your type; still, it's okay to admit she grabbed your attention. Trust me," she added, as a sparkle formed in her smiling eyes, "it won't hurt your chances." For a woman who had no qualms admitting she was routinely overlooked in favor of her companion, her words sprang forth with surprising boldness and confidence and disarmed the airman. "And in the event that you plan to ask, my name is Gabby. Gabby Norwich." A grin, implying wickedness and delight, formed on Gabby's mouth.

"I'm terrible at this," the airman confessed. "Back home, when I was in high school, I played football, and in America, girls tend to flock around you when you play football. In other words, I never had to work at acquiring certain social graces."

The Bohemian

"And your name is?" The intonation Gabby Norwich wielded on the unknown serviceman served to make and mock his point. His head sank as one's might when perceiving themselves as a blunder searching for a place to occur. Eventually, the airman shrugged off his self-deprecating posture and blurted out a reply. The surname Morningstar triggered a reaction from Gabby Norwich. When the airman went on to further state, "This is one of those situations that makes me wish I was more like my cousin, Mitch; he's a real whiz with words," Gabby Norwich's mouth fell agape, and she intoned, "Mitch Morningstar, the novelist? *He's* your cousin?"

It was not too far of a leap that Gabby Norwich had taken; after all, how many Mitch Morningstars might an American generation supply? The answer notwithstanding, it was somewhat uncanny that a lonely, homesick, affection-starved airman entered a pub and managed to acquaint himself with the one woman who—because she owned an appetite for serial killers—made him feel less alone and homesick. Moreover, there were feelings pointing toward the prospect that romance rests somewhere on a not-too-distant horizon.

And there they sat, for three-plus hours, Gabby Norwich and Airman Morningstar, drinking and delving into the psyche and intricacies of Davey Coyle—two people who began the year an ocean apart, bonded over a fictitious serial killer: ain't love grand? The four airmen who had accompanied their well-occupied colleague to Lord John Russel Pub had long since gone. Their departure went unnoticed, as too did the turning over from the afternoon crowd to the night crowd, and still, they sat engaged: the girl who claimed a past that saw her routinely overlooked because of the company she kept and a lonely airman who admitted to struggling with social graces since leaving the bosom of his hometown. Then, as they were about to make their departure, it finally occurred to Gabby Norwich to mention, "Incidentally, that was my sister."

"Your sister?" replied Airman Morningstar, somewhat puzzled. At first, he suspected Gabby Norwich was alluding to a random woman walking hurriedly in the opposite direction on the other side of the street. Then, sensing the confusion, Gabby added, "The person whose seat you had taken..." Glancing down at her wristwatch, she further added, "...nearly four hours ago."

It seemed, to Airman Morningstar, an eternity ago since the over-polished, sophisticated beauty had made her departure from

Lord John Russell Pub. Then again, everything that had occurred in his life before the moment he got invited to sit across from Gabby Norwich seemed an eternity ago. So when the airman summoned the image of a woman whose departure from the pub sent every heart but his reeling, he looked quizzically at Gabby at first, then assumed she must have meant they were kindred spirits who considered themselves sisters, for no two siblings, could look so utterly dissimilar. He also considered the possibility that Gabby and her alleged sister shared only one biological parent—which was not the case—but decided it was best not to question her on a matter not yet his concern. On they went, strolling the streets of Bloomsbury, and even without the benefit of Davey Coyle, the conversation flowed. Their stroll ended at a lamppost beside a bench in Tavistock Square, where they shared their first kiss. The evening would continue doling out its delights. The next day Nicholas wrote:

Dear Mitch,

> *I met a woman who just so happens to be your biggest fan. What were the chances? Her name is Gabby Norwich, and she is lovelier than a jock like me could ever express. And the best part of all, cousin, you practically wrote me right into her drawers! I'm eternally grateful! I'll keep you informed.*

> *Nicholas*

Strange, but it seemed the further away Nicholas and I were mileage-wise, the closer we became as cousins. Life is full of surprises. First, I wrote Nicholas back to tell him I was glad to have been of service and that he should be wary of women who take too much pleasure in reading books about deranged killers. Next, I called Molly and enlightened her that the service has done "Boy Wonder" a world of good. Apparently—doubtless, due to self-improvement in numerous areas—he has graduated from girls who throw themselves at jocks with ogre-like manners to women of worth, their literary choices notwithstanding. However, Nicholas's following letter came a month later and was a bit disconcerting; its purpose was not to inform me that he and Gabby had *planned* to marry but *already had* married.

I suppose we should have seen it coming: a young man accustomed to adulation, thousands of miles and an ocean separating him from his home, working for a unit uninterested in who he was in his former life, was bound to get swept away by his first overseas encounter. As for Gabby: she had always been her sister's keeper, so to speak; it was a role she never begrudged and performed with honor, but it was also a role whose needs were diminishing, and with a reduction in responsibility, Gabby had more time for herself. Given the circumstances, you could say Nicholas and Gabby coming together represented the perfect storm.

"You're right, Mitch," Molly began over the phone, "it *was* the perfect storm, but storms have two things in common: volatility, and longevity, and this is one marriage that won't see a year before it hits the old scrap heap. Who in their right mind dashes off to the altar before the afterglow of a first fuck wears off? What the hell was our *Boy Wonder* thinking? He wasn't thinking; that was the problem! And I'm not wholly unsympathetic to the 'homesick, lonely boy, come to mama' scenario, but at least he could have called and allowed us to try and talk him out of it. And what's with the mysterious sister-in-law whom he's only met twice and uses two names: one for the daytime and the other at night; has he told you about her? I have more than a mild suspicion it's a strange lot that our young cousin has fallen in with."

Usually, I enjoy my conversations with Molly—often, she is a delight to talk to—but this was one instance when, not five minutes in, she had me worn out and wishing I had never picked up the phone. No wonder Nicholas was not particularly keen upon seeking advice from his fellow Morningstars. However, as it would come to pass, Molly's prediction of the ill-fated marriage of Gabby and the airman could not have been more accurate if foretold by Nostradamus. Yet it was not the accuracy of Molly's prediction that I found irritating; it was how she delighted in the correctness of her forecast. Though Molly is not alone concerning such matters as failing marriages, among us, some salty old souls root for poor results for the sake of crooning those never-welcomed words, *I told you so.* Speaking for myself: all along, I was rooting for the young couple to beat the odds and prove everyone wrong, that it was possible to marry on what seemingly was a whim and, by virtue of dumb luck, end up soulmates, but we cockeyed optimists rarely, if ever, see our horses come in first. Gabby and Nicholas, unfortunately, were not the Amazin' Mets, nor were they the 1980 U.S. Olympic hockey team; they were simply a young couple that did not know what the hell they were getting into, and the result was predictable … not desirable! To their credit, there was no animosity or blaming one another. Throughout their one-year marriage, including the months of decline, by way of written letters and odd-hour phone calls, I got to know Gabby Norwich, and in some ways better than Nicholas; she had a bright and lilting tone to her voice that made speaking with her a pleasure. "I've been bragging to anyone willing to listen that Mitch Morningstar, the author of *Funhouse*, is my brother-in-law. However, I'm afraid I might've gone too far when I told members of my book club there was a possibility I could persuade you to fly to England and give a book talk. Is it possible, Mitch?" she sweetly peeped. I promised her, upon completing my next manuscript, which I was plowing through with moderate success, off to England I would trek.

Never once did Gabby complain to me that her marriage to my cousin was not going as well as she had hoped. We kept our conversations mainly to novels, from both the reader's and writer's perspective, and from delving into literature, it was surprising how much we were able to learn about one another. Over the course of one conversation, I let slip some details of my current effort, *Somnambula*, and the misspeak led to hours of discussion, which saw Gabby interjecting her ideas for the plotline.

****

It was a few ticks shy of 2:00 a.m. when two Philadelphia detectives turned up at the home of an architect, Ted Truman. It had been the custom that whenever Laura, Ted's wife of fifteen years, worked late, Ted would drive to the downtown section of the city and pick her up, but on the evening in question, he, too, for the sake of a deadline, was forced to work late. "Don't give it a thought," Laura told him at breakfast. "For once, it won't kill me to take the train." At eleven o'clock, Ted walked through the front door expecting to find Laura or watch her soon follow in his footsteps. An hour passed, then another; during this time, Ted's demeanor shifted from laden with misgiving to frantic. Numerous times he had dialed the law office, but everyone had gone. Next, he began dialing every friend he knew Laura to have and was on his way to wearing a hole in the carpet when the doorbell rang. There are few things more ominous than a ringing doorbell at just shy of 2:00 a.m. Ted's trembling hand had difficulty twisting the doorknob. When the porch light revealed the grim faces of two detectives, Ted sank to the floor in an inconsolable heap.

It is an awful sight to see a man's worst fear realized: best as could be expected, Ted Truman was shielded from the gruesomeness and savagery of Laura's rape and subsequent murder, but his wife stalked, followed at a late hour to a deserted train station then left for dead, proved sufficient in preying upon his saneness. Ted's conjured images of Laura that night—her fright, how she must have struggled, the terror in the precise moment that revealed the unlikelihood of her survival—if not equal to or surpassing reality, traveled far beyond what he could bear. It was natural for Ted to blame those at the law office for failing to accompany Laura to the station and seeing her situated safely on the train. Moreover, regardless of how vehemently Laura may have rejected the notion of a co-worker going out of their way on her behalf, someone, Ted believed, should have emerged unwavering concerning the matter, if for no other reason than to afford themselves time alone to flirt with a woman who, in everyone's judgment, was attractive. Thus, what would have been a minimal effort hardly worthy of being called magnanimous on the part of a coworker, when juxtaposed to what became the consequence, Ted Truman would never reconcile.

Morose was the one word that could best describe Ted in the following weeks, especially at work. And come the evenings, he would drink himself unconscious. For days on end, he went with nary an exchange, never mind a conversation; he had gone so long without hearing the sound of his voice, when finally, he did let loose an utterance, it proved jarring, not so for those within earshot; it was Ted whose senses received a jolt.

Days spilled into one another; time and space became entities for which there was no delineation. Slowly but unmistakably, Ted Truman was receding into the one realm on earth sure to serve as a distorted refuge: his mind; it would allow him—late at night, hunkered down in a quiet, lonely domicile, while nearing the end of a bottle—the folly of imagining that he had saved Laura from her terrible fate. In this state, he was not a man indulging in fantasy, but a tortured soul whose teetering sanity straddled the divide of reality and the imaginary, a man requiring trickery to feel, if only for a fleeting moment, his life got restored. Those were the many sequential nights of Ted Truman until off he walked into the dark of night, a glassy-eyed disheveled man seemingly resolute in whatever may have been his purpose.

As Ted walked along the avenue, heading toward the train station, he would have given anyone the impression of a man fully conscious of his relationship with space, distance, and the animation of a world into which he was asserting himself. Yet, despite nimbly negotiating his way through the train station, when settling himself on a bench seat in the last car, he possessed the faraway demeanor of a wretch the world had discarded, if not a man whose wife had shown him the door. The reality of his vicissitude, when fully grasped, prompted a midnight ramble.

The train arrived at the center-of-town station. As might a man whose cognition was based strictly upon memory-aided premonition, Ted strode from the car to the platform, turnstile, then concourse before ascending the stairs leading to the street where he began ambling toward the law office where Laura had spent the last eight years of her life. From there, Ted assumed a more resolute march, walking the precise path Laura had taken every day on what, save for her final time, was crowded, bustling five o'clock sidewalks. Humanity was scarce tonight, as was the case when Laura Truman's feet last were set upon this path. Ted, undaunted, followed the killer while managing to keep Laura in his sight. The effort led him back to the train station where, with what any onlooker would have perceived as incoherent movements, he intervened at the precise moment Laura's attacker had struck. It was no great surprise to Ted that, come the morning, he had awakened in his clothes—the same outfit he donned twenty-four hours ago; nowadays, it had become a matter of routine to rouse fully clothed. What did come as a surprise: Laura was not beside him; the sensation that he had saved her was as palpable an event to him as any known reality, but it was a lie—the worst of deceptions—one whose realization was crushing. Similar nights would follow, many in succession. Off Ted would go—into the night—a somnambulant burdened with the impossible task of revising history. How kind, though, was the darkness of night and desolate train station, for neither failed to bring about a triumph. Conversely, unkind was the morning light; without fail, it would arrive bearing the harshness of truth and glaring reminders of one man's unbearable reality.

The Bohemian

Days became nights that morphed into new days; this unrelenting procession sent Ted Truman spiraling through space, repelling reality while embracing distortion. A "psychotic break" was what he was purported to have suffered: thus, a man who, nearly every night for weeks, went sleepwalking into the center on a mission to rescue his beloved became a stealthy killing machine.

Gabby and I debated mildly over Ted Truman's victims. Should they be those whom he alleged failed to protect Laura or those who, in his somnambulant state, were perceived would-be assailants of defenseless women? It led to a debate over whether the killings should happen in desolate midnight streets, downtown alleyways, or ominous late-night parking garages. Gabby relished the opportunity to thrust herself into the psychology of Ted Truman and had plenty to share, and much of it, I should confess, was worth a listen. She illustrated that Davey Coyle and Ted Truman were each damaged by events over which they had no control but that the former had a much greater period to evolve into something other than a killer; thus, in her estimation, the latter was the more sympathetic figure. There was one area, though, that was off-limits: the title; yet Gabby could not resist championing the name *Night Rider*, citing that the story, essentially, was based on a recently widowed husband of a slain woman who, by way of a midnight train, sleepwalks into town. I told her, "*Night Rider* sounds too much like the title of a classic rock song—The Allman Brothers' 'Midnight Rider'." She retorted by telling me, "*Somnambula* resonates similarly to a title The Who would use for an album—*Quadrophenia*." Despite both sounding like conditions or relating to diseases, I thought *Somnambula* to *Quadrophenia* was a bit of a leap. Ultimately, I decided to keep my title but promised Gabby the dedication.

Toward the end of our conversation, a few ticks shy of midnight, and for Gabby, 5:00 a.m., I decided there was no harm in wondering aloud about her sister, who Nicholas swore was avoiding him and kept two names. My curiosity caused Gabby to chuckle; doubtless, she sensed that I was expecting a worthwhile mystery behind her sister's use of multiple names. I chuckled too when learning that Gabby's sister was Bobbie Norwich by day and Nina Linette the two nights a week she sang in a nightclub. I should have guessed a stage name instead of loaning an ounce of credibility to Molly's suspicion there was something amiss concerning the Norwich clan. She, too, felt foolish for leaping to conclusions—spies and drug dealers were among her faulty speculations—before settling on the obvious. As for Bobbie Norwich or Nina Linette avoiding her brother-in-law? "She's awfully timid around men," Gabby told me. I found it curious that a woman possessing such physical beauty, who was comfortable enough to stand behind a microphone in a nightclub, would have difficulty around men. But, at such a late hour, my drowsiness overwhelmed my curiosity, despite my intuition screaming that, whether as Bobbie Norwich or Nina Linette, Gabby's sister would require nearly as much examination as the ill-fated Ted Truman.

CHAPTER FOUR
A FAIR REVIEW

One could easily allege that Airman Morningstar's final months in England were not the most pleasurable of his tour. Lonely, homesick, and divorced was how he had to finish fulfilling his military obligation; it was no wonder he was miserable—anyone would have been. But there was a light at the end of the tunnel, which came in the form of an Air Force Base (McGuire) on the east coast United States (New Jersey). It would not be long now. I wrote Nicholas and told him: *Keep your chin up, cousin; your ill-fated marriage was nothing more than a dress rehearsal for when the real thing comes along.* I also wrote Gabby and told her more of the same, and yes, I am perfectly aware that my words were analogous to a hokey song lyric accompanying a mindless melody written by a burned-out old rock star desperate for one last hit; being a writer, I should have been more thoughtful, but, when trapped in the moment, somehow those idiotic words resonated. Nicholas responded with a phone call not to inform me that I was hokey, but to complain that Molly had lambasted him by strongly suggesting that during his remaining months in England, he would be wise to "Stay out of the goddamn bushes!" and, "Don't be an idiot and go planting any seeds in foreign soil!" She also informed him, "It would be a sound idea, going forward, to add masturbation to your list of brainless hobbies." I told Nicholas, "Let it run off your shoulders. Molly is one of those rare birds who lead mistake-free exemplary lives, whereas 'we,' the mass majority—whether or not we realize it or care to own up to it—make up a cluster of dysfunctional screwups condemned to spend the majority of their time fixing and atoning." I went on to more or less add that this was a concept that he would be wise to embrace. In other words, life is messy, kiddo; get used to it.

Beyond the divorce, which saw Airman Morningstar arriving on American soil both sad and relieved, Gabby and I continued to correspond. Occasionally, one of us would take the initiative and dial a telephone, and despite the inconvenience that a five-hour time change presented, we never viewed our conversations as anything other than time well spent—the first few minutes of each conversation spent apologizing for ringing a telephone either at midnight or five o'clock in the morning notwithstanding; and whether by way of the written word or the pleasure of her lovely voice, Gabby never failed to remind me of a promised trip to England. "We can't wait to meet you, Mitch," she often gushed. By "we," she was referring to her and her sister. During one conversation, Gabby made it known that Bobbie Norwich, a.k.a. Nina Linette, had also become a fan and was looking forward to my coming to England. I found it curious that a woman who for months kept herself hidden away from her airman brother-in-law developed an anticipatory approach concerning someone who, save for some tidbits Gabby relayed and a work of fiction, was essentially a stranger. Indeed, it was curious. Had Bobbie by day or Nina by night suspected that somewhere well encrypted within the pages of *Funhouse* was an autobiography and that she wished to question me in person concerning certain matters? Or, perhaps the character of Davey Coyle hit too close to home, and it was counsel that Gabby's sister was seeking? As a writer of serial killer novels, I tend to possess an overactive imagination; there have been occasions when some accused me of delving too deeply into the psychology of matters, even when there was little, if any, psychology into which to delve. Now that I have made that admission, there is a door number three in the matter of Bobbie by day and Nina by night, albeit a far less compelling one: It's likely that Gabby's sister is involved in the same book club as Gabby and is looking forward to the talk I promised.

Somnambula debuted with a review that I would disappointingly describe as "fair." Erskine Hatch, a book reviewer for the "lordly" New York Times, did not necessarily pan it or praise it; what he did was question it. Initially, I was livid and inclined to write to Mr. Hatch and present him with a piece of my mind. Fortunately, I thought better of it, for had I taken up an angry pen to Mr. Hatch, it could have proved a career-ender.

Erskine Hatch alleged I traveled so deeply into the psyche and condition of Ted Truman that I "failed to present him sufficiently as a malefactor." Circa 1989, serial killers were supposed to be deranged psychopaths such as Albert De Salvo (The Boston Strangler), Jeffry Dahmer, Ted Bundy, Gary Heidnik, and David Berkowitz (The Son of Sam), not those who traveled beyond the ordinary breadth of perception to settle into a gray area where criminology and victimology overlap. To feel sympathy for a "malefactor," I suppose, was too unsettling a concept for Mr. Hatch; after all, some need their serial killers to be utterly monstrous individuals depraved to where they can only exist beyond any known human dominion, otherwise presented is the unsettling possibility that any one of us, at any time, could cross the line that transforms them into Ted Truman. Of course, getting a reader to consider this possibility was never the goal; I was simply a novelist weaving a story. Luckily for me, that Erskine Hatch questioned *Somnambula* worked in my favor: readers became curious. The minute Gabby, my muse and defender, finished reading the review, my phone rang... at 4:00 a.m. "Is he a moron!" she shrieked. "It simply isn't possible to be this dense!"

The moment it occurred to me that the phone was ringing— not in my dreams, in reality—I assumed it must be Gabby. If not my transatlantic phone partner, it must be Molly calling to inform me that some Morningstar, be it Uncle Pete, Uncle Lambert, Aunt Belinda, or Grandpa Alexander, had kicked the proverbial bucket. Upon reaching for the receiver, what greeted me was the abovementioned shriek. Of course, it is difficult, especially over the phone, at four a.m., to assign a person to a shriek, even if the person in question has a pleasing British intonation. Thus, when I heard the blood-curdling suggestion that someone was a moron and dense, I leaped to the conclusion that Nicholas had involved himself in another escapade and that Molly, in her typical fit-to-be-tied manner, could not wait until my preset coffeepot sent forth its aromatic 6:00 a.m. offering to inform me of the juicy details. But then came the less hysterical words: "And he calls himself a reviewer?" Then I knew, at once, that somewhere in Bloomsbury, at approximately 9:00 a.m., whether in pajamas at her kitchen table or dressed and sipping coffee at a nearby café, it was Gabby with her nose in the supplemental magazine known as The New York Times Book Review.

I would have preferred to have waited until later and read the review on my own, say nine o'clock eastern standard time, while upright and fully awake, but Gabby had worked up a head of steam;

thus, it was pointless to try and stop her, though, at some juncture, I ceased from listening, as her agitation caused her syntax to ramble such, it made grasping any nuance or subtext Erskine Hatch may have tried to convey difficult if not impossible. "Well, what do you think, Mitch," Gabby, despite near the end of her breath, managed to chirp. I sighed. It was the sort of sigh one discharges when forced to listen to more than one can bear. A moment of silence followed, and the inclination to dash to the nearest convenience store for a copy of *The Times* surged. I took a breath to allow the moment to pass and did not budge from my bed. Afterward, I asked Gabby to slowly and composedly read through the review. When she finished, I wished that I hadn't. In the days and weeks ahead, I went from livid, to morose, to having brooded to Gabby, "Oh well, *Somnambula* won't be the last novel I'll ever write." I further added, "In the States, sometimes art must suffer for the sake of decorum and our delicate sensibilities." Then, one morning I woke up, and sometime during the day, I became happy, for I learned that by questioning *Somnambula*, Erskine Hatch generated more interest than had he praised it. The next thing I knew, I was booking a flight to London, England, and my first-ever face-to-face with one Miss Gabby Norwich.

CHAPTER FIVE
THE JAZZ SINGER

Molly called with the offer of lunch and a ride to the airport. It was a considerate gesture on the part of my cousin, I thought. Not only had I transportation to the airport, but lunch would give us a chance to catch up, and I always enjoyed, despite the pomposity with which Molly often took ownership of the moral high ground, an opportunity to catch up with my dear cousin; however, no sooner had we the rims of our goblets, into which got poured crisp chardonnays, to our lips, Molly got *that look*. I am referring, of course, to the kind of look one gets when they have tricked you into agonizing through unwelcomed advice; thus, there, I sat, a man in his late twenties, making his own way in the world and a seasoned writer—the latter, my opinion—about to receive a life lesson based on the trickery of Molly's gender.

"Call it a gut instinct, Mitch, but I don't trust those Norwich sisters," she hissed. "I was hoping, by now, we had moved on from them."

I began glancing at my wristwatch, fussing with my collar, and doing whatever one does when forced to listen to counsel they would prefer not to endure. "It's just a silly book talk," I insisted. "Let's not read too much into it, shall we?"

Molly's frown made it clear that she was far from convinced I was flying to England for the sole purpose of discussing a novel with a bunch of strangers as a favor to someone with whom I had only a telephone relationship. "Who crosses an ocean to accommodate a book club?" she further pressed. "Really, Mitch, you must see this as excessive and to where it might put ideas in someone's head. And let us not forget that Gabby Norwich was but a mistake made by 'Boy Wonder,' and her people, you might well imagine, must feel the same. So be sensible; building bridges with the ex-wives of first cousins is in no man's playbook."

For whatever reason, I was having a helluva time convincing Molly that I was a "big boy" fully capable of looking out for himself. But Molly was intuitive; I was not crossing the Atlantic for the mere sake of a book talk; the very notion must and should be considered absurd. The truth: Gabby had gotten under my skin. Moreover, aside from the crude descriptions of her ex-husband, which came by way of a few lines in a written letter, I had only Gabby's voice to feed my imagination. I did not know what she looked like, and, oddly enough, it was a matter with which I had no preoccupation. Imagine, there I was, a red-blooded bourgeois American man, wholly unconcerned with a woman's appearance; either I had evolved far beyond the meager expectations of my bestial gender, or my hypothalamus was beginning to erode. Whatever the case: with each line of every written letter and with each midnight telephone call, I was falling more and more under a spell known as Gabby Norwich; there were times when I had all but forgotten she was once married to my young cousin and not an acquaintance I had acquired on my own, and that our ever-evolving friendship had no known origins and, concerning its value, exceeded all relationships past and present. And let us not forget the ever-intriguing Bobbie by day and Nina by night. Indeed, the Norwich sisters held for me far more than a mere measure of lure but enough to prompt me to fly across an ocean.

I explained to Molly that Davey Coyle was a literary invention, not the byproduct of a novelist with deep-seated desires that run far afoul of the boundaries of normalcy. "Can't my trip be a far-flung adventure whose purpose is to feed the spirit; must it be seen as erratic and bordering on lunacy?"

"Still, Mitch," she saw it fit to press, "that your mind travels to such dark places could signify that you're predisposed to derangement or erratic behavior. Anymore, we're always hearing about these men who for years were perceived by their family, friends, and co-workers as 'Average Joe's,' killing their wives and children, then turning the gun on themselves." Following the sort of sigh one lets loose when sensing futility, she added, "I'm not placing the crossing of an ocean for such a meager reason as a book talk in the same league as serial killing ... just ... just ... be careful."

The Bohemian

"One day, when I'm married with children and seem unbalanced, feel free to have me placed on the family annihilator watchlist. Meanwhile, I'm on my way to England."

I love Molly, but more and more, she's becoming impossible.

It was seven hours from Philadelphia International Airport to London's Heathrow; the plane touched ground at midnight; I lost five hours. After considering what I might have done with those hours, I decided it was no significant loss. During the seven hours I was airborne, I devoured a substantial chunk of *The World According to Garp*. Despite my conservative parents and at times overbearing cousin—seldom do they find themselves without cause to gaze down at their noses with narrowing eyes—it was titillating to wonder what it would be like to lead a life that reads like a John Irving novel. I had a sneaking suspicion that I was about to find out.

The plane was losing altitude and circling to land. For hours, I had been the picture of concentration, nose in a book, only to become a bundle of nerves surging through me and producing involuntary sighs of apprehension that were both visible and audible. I kept reminding myself: *It's just a book talk for a silly book club; I'll be rubbing elbows with a bunch of cackling women with charming accents; what could prove easier?* Not much, I suppose, except one can enjoy only so much success when the objective is fooling themselves. I repeatedly pounded into my head the well-known idiom: *You never get a second chance to make a first impression.* But would the expression apply when you have known someone for quite a while, with a measure of intimacy, but had not an opportunity to present yourself in the flesh? Nevertheless, a "genuine" first impression lingered on the immediate horizon and caused me to fret. I spotted a woman holding a sign: *Welcome to England, Mitch.* Despite the midnight hour, there gleamed an anticipatory sparkle in her eyes. It got met with a smile, not a nervous or contrived smile, but an involuntary reaction over having a terrific appreciation for what my eyes beheld. As I was advancing toward Gabby, we both did a remarkable job disguising that we were assessing one another's appearance— it was only natural that we do so—and this delicate feat was aided by expressing the thrill of finally meeting.

"Mitch Morningstar," Gabby crooned with delight. Never so much had I enjoyed the sound of my name; Gabby's in-person voice was even lovelier than her transatlantic. Next, we embraced as though an embrace was long overdue. Soft and frothing with loveliness would best describe Gabby—these assets were bountiful if not beyond compare—she was like an ocean one could dive into and not give a care as to whether they could swim. Everything that accounted for her essence screamed welcome; I was already too far gone—perhaps even in love—I just didn't know it. Sorry, Molly.

We took a taxi back to Gabby's flat in Bloomsbury, which she shared with Bobbie, though given the hour, it would be Nina. It was nearing 2:00 a.m. when we arrived.

"We won't be waking your sister, will we?" I wasn't so concerned about disturbing Nina's sleep as I was curious to know whether it would be tonight that I would meet her.

"She sings until 1:00 a.m. but doesn't usually leave the club until closing," Gabby told me. "Often, it's three or four in the morning when she comes creeping through the door, so for tonight, you'll simply have to settle for the company of the short, plump, older Norwich sister."

Gabby flashed a devilish smile; it was a tacit response to my making it abundantly clear that I did not favor her meager self-appraisal concerning her appearance. Next, she introduced me to my room, where we both sat crisscross applesauce—the newest term for sitting Indian style—atop the bed. To an onlooker, I imagine we appeared as eager children awarded the privilege of a slumber party than a man and woman destined to become lovers. As for conversing with Gabby: it was more effortless now that I was inches from her round, lovely face, and sparkling eyes than it had been during all our overseas telephone calls, and within our many held glances, not a vestige of innuendo was captured, only openness as glaring as the sincerest language had resonated. Then she reached for my hand. I was sure it was an impulse. Next, she began stroking it and said placatingly, "You must be exhausted, Mitch."

Gabby was right. I was exhausted but making every effort to conceal signs that I was faltering, for I was involved in a moment life seldom offers—a sublime connection with someone able to reflect in their eyes the past, present, and future. Nevertheless, every day must have a beginning and end, and I had reached the end. We embraced as might two old friends who had been apart too long, but lingering was a sense that we were embarking on a journey—a journey that had in store for us many splendors and delights, though we need not leap ahead and explore them tonight.

The Bohemian

You know you are in a good place, mentally, when exhaustion has set in, and it is not sleeping that prevails as a point of anticipation but the next day. I was there, amid all its keenness: it was accounting for my spiritual whereabouts; I was exhausted yet never more alive. Moreover, it seemed an eternity ago that I was sitting across from Molly, accompanied by chardonnay and Caesar salad, while she categorically droned on about why I needed to be wary of the Norwich sisters. Poor Molly, always so upright, so high-minded, never affording herself a moment of folly, much less exploring even the more conservative forms of human debauchery. When many of her peers seemed in a race to forfeit their virginities, Molly held onto her virtue as one would the holy grail.

"You do, at least, masturbate, don't you?" I once felt bold enough to ask my cousin. "And understand it's a normal activity, *not* a sin?"

Molly sneered at me. I was unsure whether she sneered that I had mocked her belief that masturbation was a sin or that she had no difficulty locating her vagina and, like anyone considered normal, hadn't any disinclination in pleasuring herself. "It's your vagina; you're allowed to do with it whatever you want, you understand," I told her.

My irony went unappreciated, which prompted me to bellow: "For crying out loud, Molly, there's no prize for becoming the oldest virgin in the ever-corruptible western hemisphere! It's one thing to wait until you're married had you planned on doing so at twenty-three. You're twenty-eight. And trust me, cousin, your virtue won't put a dent in the moral decay that is tightening its stranglehold on our country."

The above conversation took place several months before I jetted to England. When came the day that Molly dropped me at the airport, nothing about her nonexistent sex life had changed.

I am a year younger than Molly. At age twelve—in the sixth grade—I had developed quite a case of the hots for my dear cousin. We did not attend the same school, but I saw much more of Molly than I had of Nicholas and the rest of the Morningstar cousin clan. At Molly's thirteenth birthday party, I experienced my coming-of-age awakening. The girls in my grade were essentially boys with squeaky voices and long hair. What a difference a year can make! There I was at a party where males were scarce; everywhere I looked, budding womanhood had greeted me: round bottoms, sprouting breasts; I was basking in a garden of earthly delights! There was only one drawback: to hear Molly drone on concerning our respective ages would have given anyone the impression that the one year that separated us was a chasm that, on no level, be it physically or intellectually, I could span. Indeed, to hear her that day, for the benefit of her seventh-grade female contemporaries, one would have thought she was older than her mother and I was just out of diapers, but it was her party; thus, I refused to play the spoilsport. And why would I want to? I was in the garden of earthly delights! Surrounding me was enough fascination to help me overlook the denigration I suffered for the insufficiency of my age. And yet, it was Molly, my antagonizer—among her peers, Molly came endowed with the curviest figure—who reigned as most fascinating among this delightful array of creatures. Consequently, I willingly adopted the role of a loyal puppy dog to what my twelve-year-old mind had perceived as copious mounds of womanhood. So yes, my dear cousin became the object of my desire that night when I took to my bed and put an exclamation point on what had been the initial celebration of my awakening. Many would follow.

Eight years later—with Molly a junior at Penn and yours truly a sophomore at Temple—that unnavigable chasm had dwindled to an undetectable crease: thus, Molly and I were no longer held together by a thread known as kin; we had become genuine friends, and on Sundays, we would meet in Old City Philadelphia for an art film or at Wissahickon Valley for a hike—the latter was a place where we had many thoughtful exchanges, though often we would reminisce how Aunt Belinda use to complain when Grandpa Alexander cracked his knuckles at the dinner table, or when Uncle Pete hollered at Uncle Lambert for "salting the living shit" out of his dinner before ever tasting it. "You're gonna get arth-er-itis," Aunt Belinda would tell Grandpa Alexander. There was no convincing Aunt Belinda that "arthritis" had only three syllables. Grandpa Alexander would shrug and say, "I was born with arthritis." Uncle Pete used to warn Uncle Lambert, "You're gonna end up with high blood pressure," to which Uncle Lamber would respond, "What the hell would you know about high blood pressure; you're a Dallas Cowboys fan—a goddamn frontrunner." Anyway, we were twenty-one and twenty, respectively, when I confessed to Molly, "You were not only the first to inspire me to a climax but the first to inspire me to try." I had clung to the misguided notion that she would feel proud that, at age twelve, I worshipped her and thus would react accordingly. My admission, bawdry though it may have been, had quite the opposite effect.

"Mitch!" she screeched, alarming all that lived and breathed in the valley. "You wanted to fuck me, your own cousin? You lecherous fiend; that's incest!"

"No, no, no," I cried. "I was only twelve; I didn't dare imagine anything so bold as penetrating your vagina: I imagined that we were alone, and you, being older and naturally more perceptive, recognized the longing in my eyes—that I desired to see you naked—and so you undressed and allowed me to admire and touch you; I may have nuzzled a nipple a time or two."

There was some truth to my admission, which should have proved enough to defuse Molly. I was wrong. Thank goodness I failed to offer a full confession, for old Mitch Morningstar had a bold imagination. And it didn't dent my ego in the slightest that my worship of Molly's body was a source of revulsion. After all, we are cousins. Anyway, that was the day when I realized no one had gotten to Molly—no one had come close—and it was not merely sex with a deviant cousin that she found disagreeable but the very notion of sex itself.

Molly was one of those rare birds who, from as early as age eight, knew what she wanted, and her ambition was to attend the University of Pennsylvania; not even for the time it would have taken to offer up a free feel did she take her eye off the prize. Looking back, it was apparent: although Molly's body may have hit puberty—and rather gloriously, I might add—her mind either rejected the notion or possessed the discipline to ignore all those pesky but delightful urges and changes that accompany the onset of womanhood. Molly never tried out for a school play; she worked on set designs; she didn't write for her school newspaper; she edited; she engaged only in that which kept her safely tucked behind the scenes away from the spotlight, and the result was her never losing focus. In a way, I envy Molly but mostly feel sorry for her. Either way, she's my cousin, my friend, and I love her.

It was three-thirty in the morning, London time, when my head sank into a pillow surrounded by four dark and unfamiliar walls. Meanwhile, it was 10:30 p.m. on the east coast of the United States. My thoughts drifted to Molly, alone, curled up on her sofa, enraptured by something wholesome on a public television station: the development of an ancient civilization or the mating habits of some obscure species indigenous to some far-flung part of the globe. Poor Molly; dear, sweet, virtuous Molly. I heard a key unlock a door and a door pushed open by someone making an effort to be respectfully quiet. It must be Nina. Of course, it was Nina; who else could it be? I chuckled silently over the notion that if Nina could snap her fingers and transport herself to Hong Kong, she would already be Bobbie. It was inane humor on my part and hardly worth a chortle, but, in my weary 3:30 a.m. mind, it was the best I could do. Nina settled the door back into place as quietly as she had pushed it open: A considerate maneuver. But why, I wondered, did she bother making such an effort of her entrance and then fail to remove her heels? I found it curious, and Nina did not creep about the way you would suspect one might at such an hour; she pranced, and the points of her heels struck the floor with a measure of authority that was both precise and elegant, and this inspiring coalescence stroked my imagination such, I was unable to resist lustful thoughts regarding the feet, legs, and overall form that settled so gloriously inside those heels. Nina was a nymph announcing the arrival of her many delights—a femme fatale perfectly aware of her capacity to inspire a man without first being seen. So aware she was of the power and seductiveness of her prancing feet—or, it was just a case of a novelist's imagination kicked into overdrive. Whatever, I adored Gabby but was curious about Nina. Infinitely curious!

Nina's heels continued to strike the floor: precision, elegance, authority, audacity—they rang beautifully this synthesis of elements that converged and collaborated to create one dynamic creature. Nina was everything that Gabby said she was—or so I was imagining. Louder came the strikes upon the floor—nearer and nearer—then abrupt silence. All was still—eerily quiet and still. She posed herself, I could tell, just outside my bedroom door. I matched her stillness by barely breathing. Next, I heard the knob of the door turn—it turned with a similar thoughtfulness with which the front door was unlocked, opened, and settled back into place. It was all very curious. Why would she announce herself in a manner that sparked my imagination, only to invade my bedroom with such stealthiness? What were her intentions? I feigned sleep but managed to spy Nina's striking silhouette framed in the doorway. And what a pose she had struck: her head tilted in a fashion that saw every lock of her rich, luxurious mane fall to one side; perhaps all day long, Nina was anticipating me arriving in Bloomsbury—Mitch Morningstar, the author of *Funhouse* and *Somnambula*—and was making sure I was here; this would seem logical, but it was three-thirty in the morning, my imagination was in overdrive, logic was in short supply. No, it was unlikely that whether or not I arrived was the impetus for Nina entering my room; she already knew I was here; her intuition told her as much; I was sure of it.

Moreover, I was being watched or observed to be accurate. Nina was akin to a scientist peering into the cage at a lab rat dosed for the sake of human advancement and patiently awaiting a reaction; I felt strange, even violated, that someone was observing me in this manner. Had she spoken, made an utterance, it would have served to humanize her, and the strange feeling gripping me might have passed, but Nina never uttered a word or displayed any inclination that she would. Instead, she continued observing me from her well-advantaged position—a dimly illuminated doorway—while I pretended to be asleep, a lab rat in a cage. If there was a purpose to this wickedness, I could not hazard a guess as to what it was. Though, should I at some time become emboldened to ask, I would be admitting that I had faked sleep, ergo adding subterfuge to the wickedness that was swerving toward farcical. I wanted to believe that I was overthinking matters—that Bobbie by day and Nina by night was not a compelling mystery—but it was three-thirty in the morning, and I was a novelist.

Gracefully, Nina pirouetted on a heel—a maneuver that led to her taking her leave, and for that, I was grateful. She closed the door with the same thoughtfulness with which she opened it. Her footsteps were soft, then softer; they faded into silence as she walked away.

I had grown accustomed to the early rays of sunlight flooding through my bedroom window; it was what roused me and all the alarm I ever needed, but I was in England, the Bloomsbury section of London, more specifically, and, as I would learn, that big old ball of fire which has been illuminating our solar system for the past four and a half billion years, give or take a month, does not shout "good morning" as cheerily to the British as it does to us Americans, especially in the earlier part of dawn. One could go so far as to suggest the sun is quite stingy to the Brits. Anyway, I failed to crack an eyelid until the aroma of the coffee that Gabby was brewing meandered down the hallway and settled in my bedroom. It was already 10:00 a.m.; the morning had all but passed.

The morning is when I do the majority of my writing. One might imagine that a writer of serial killer novels would prefer the nighttime, that full moons and darkness would serve as mood enhancers, inspiring the flow of creativity. But it is the morning when I feel unburdened, as absent is all the weight one tends to accumulate throughout the day. Concerning that weightiness, it lurks about seemingly at a safe distance until all at once we feel bogged down by the culprits that create it: tension, aggravation, colleagues bitching about their significant others, significant others bitching how they go underappreciated, people taking on the establishment or powerbrokers of society, the powerbrokers or establishment kicking them squarely in the nuts to remind them that they are plebeians whose primary function is to obey, counterintuitive news angles designed to stroke the ire of the masses, the masses reacting accordingly, influencers disguising themselves as leaders, leaders conveniently misplacing their ideals, and then there's Molly to remind me of my corruptible soul. Blessed are those who deliver comedy to a madding world, for they are the truly benevolent. But then, as reliable as gravity, the gift of a new day arrives, and all our angst has been exorcised, our focus restored. And while we are on the subjects of clarity and freshness, those would be the two words that would best describe Gabby upon my entering the kitchen: delightfully clear and fresh! And how her cheeks glowed and eyes sparkled; with the very vision of Gabby, I had all but forgotten about the seductive heels of Nina and my three-thirty in the morning visitation.

"Were there any particular sections of London you wish to visit, Mitch?" Gabby thoughtfully asked. "I've been told I make a good tour guide. Incidentally, it will only be the two of us; Nina needs her beauty sleep."

My first inclination was to tell Gabby: *the only part of London I care to see is standing right here in this kitchen.* Thankfully, I thought better of it, for such words may have seemed too forward, especially since we had yet to embark on day one of what potentially could prove a romantic journey. Also, upon playing the words over in my head, I was sure it sounded like *a line*—the sort a fellow keeps in reserve for the right opportunity, such as picking up a bar floozie. I did not care to hand Gabby "a line," especially one that had the risk of sounding painfully artificial.

The Bohemian

"I'll go anywhere and do anything so long as it doesn't make me appear a bourgeois American tourist," I told her.

"In other words," she brightly chirped, "you wish to go slumming."

"Perfect!" I replied.

"Then it's settled; a slumming we shall go." Her smile was lovely. Gabby Norwich could lead me anywhere, and first up on the docket was Camden Lock Market. How to describe Camden Lock Market? A human jungle of nonconformity would be an excellent place to start. It is also safe to say that no place else on planet Earth has seen such a collection of honkytonk as Camden Lock Market. Most major cities in the United States have *a* street, if not *two*, designated for carnival-like celebrations for all things considered "alternative," and, if somehow, were combined into one menagerie, I'm confident it would fall short of equaling the totality of Camden Lock Market: it was a menagerie beyond anything I might have imagined—far beyond what a single pair of eyes could behold—thus it became necessary to keep my eyes focused in one area at a time, or else I would have become dizzy: So many colors, costumes, acts, smells, and sounds—there was no end to it! And because there seemed no end to this eccentric cityscape, I became what I hoped to avoid: a bourgeois American tourist. The notion made me frown.

"Mitch, don't you get it?" Gabby cried. "Do you not understand why I brought you here? Mitch, dear, take a good look around," she brightly urged. "It's your next novel. In a place such as this, with its mass of humanity, a clever serial killer could commit murder every day for months before getting caught. You could have them discovering bodies at the Inverness Street Market, Buck Street Market, Stables Market, the village, and alleyways—hell, you could even have them pulling bodies out of the damn canal!"

She was positively beaming, Gabby; I had never seen anyone so enthused over the prospect of a serial killer at large. "Fear not, all," I called out with outstretched arms, my voice mimicking a carnival barker, "it's only a novel, make-believe." I was acting farcically, naturally, with the notion of tempering Gabby's enthusiasm. I failed.

"Mitch," she continued to gush, "we could call the novel *The Phantom of Camden Lock*! He'll be more famous than Jack the Ripper, except that he'll be fictional."

Suddenly, I sensed myself swept away in uncharted waters, reaching for something to keep me afloat and finding nothing. Gabby had done it: she went and used that earthshattering, game-changing "we" word and did so in a manner that made it seem well within the natural order of affairs; she had gone from a fan of *Funhouse* to someone who, during its development, felt encouraged to discuss *Somnambula*, to someone I now envisioned would be right there at my elbow looking over my shoulder, and critiquing every page, paragraph, and ding-blasted sentence! Clear as a bell, I heard Molly's voice careening inside my head: *Did I not warn you about those Norwich sisters, Mitch?* Then Gabby begged, "Don't look so grim, Mitch." Putting a gentle hand on my cheek, she added, "I'm not looking to come between you and your art; I was only hoping I might inspire you in some small way; that's all."

I tried not to sigh as one might when experiencing a sense of relief. I failed. Angst came gushing out from every pore of my body. Of course, Camden Lock Market was an ideal setting for a killing ground; any moron could see that. All at once, I felt very much at home; no longer did I appear a bourgeois American tourist, or so I believed. Next, what came blurting out were the words, "The Case of the Camden Lock Killer." I was bracing myself, hoping Gabby would not feel too disappointed, when I told her, "*The Phantom of Camden Lock* sounded too much like a horror film: might as well call the novel *Gaston Leroux Meets Bram Stoker on the Way to Edgar Allen Poe's House.*" Gabby sneered at me; it was what I least deserved, but I couldn't spare a moment for concern, as my mind had already kicked into overdrive. I saw the narrative not as a psychological thriller from the viewpoint of a deranged killer but as a baffling day-to-day account from the end of law enforcement—driven, over-caffeinated, under-the-gun detectives, working sixteen-hour days with administrators and the media continually breathing down their necks; tensions on all sides would mount and escalate until an entire city got placed on its collective edge. It was perfect; I was inspired and could not wait to get started. Thank you, Gabby Norwich; you are a genius!

However, again I thought it necessary to brace myself: this time, it was because I told Gabby, "You're right; a clever serial killer could commit murder every day for months in a place such as Camden Lock Market without getting caught, but I'm guessing a murder every day might be, dare I say... overkill? If we space the killings at a rate of, say, twice a month, we'll give the story a fair chance to breathe; it's always helpful when you can work in subplots and other human-interest angles, especially if they're somewhat dysfunctional. For example, Detective A, we shall call him for now, put in charge of the investigation, is a stout, craggy fifty-two-year-old functioning alcoholic whose wife just left him and whose daughter hasn't spoken to him in over ten months. He has taken his coffee at the same diner every day for the past twenty-five years. He sits on a stool at the counter where Joe, the establishment's proprietor, has poured his coffee for all twenty-five of those years. Joe and Detective A have never seen one another beyond the diner's front door; that's a fact. Here is another: the two men could write one another's biography, and the day Detective A's wife splits, Joe, by default, becomes the longest-running relationship in Detective A's lonely, dismal life. Their relationship, which has never traveled beyond an old Formica counter-top, is unwavering, dependable, and, on some level, as fulfilling as a marriage. Joe pours coffee. He leans over the counter so that his ear is only inches from Detective A's mouth. Detective A is weary and frustrated; Joe can tell. He clears his throat so that he can speak effectively in whispers. 'Six damn weeks and still not one solid lead,' Detective A grumbles. He scowls and pinches his brow. 'Have you heard anything about Jill since she split?' Joe decides to ask. A heavy, throaty sigh reverberating from the detective would be all the answer that Joe would require. It was often that Detective A took Joe into his confidence; doing so was no less reliable than keeping case details and personal items to himself. After all, it was a marriage of sorts."

"Mitch, it's brilliant!" Gabby gushed, her eyes filling with those delightful sparkles I have become fond of seeing. "Positively brilliant!"

Camden Lock Market was a sea of brick and cobblestone, and floating in that sea was a multitude of tents and stalls in which was sold everything from tacky T-shirts to outlandish bric-a-brac. They were lined and positioned amid centuries-old architecture— structure after structure in which there were a variety of pubs, along with eateries serving everything from junk food to international cuisine; also, there was a multitude of clothing stores able to accommodate those who worship the alternative, and plain-old American bourgeois tourists like, for instance, yours truly. This dense conglomeration created numerous nooks, crannies, passages, and alleyways accommodated by a multi-leveled landscape. Indeed, Camden Lock

Market was perfect; and so I began the overwhelming task of familiarizing myself with every inch of the place—I needed to know where everything was in relation. That's when I saw Gabby reach into her pocketbook and produce a camera.

"So much for not looking like a tourist," I frowned.

"If it makes you feel any better, Mitch, we work for a company that creates brochures. The Monarch of Montage, if anyone is bold enough to ask."

"I like a woman able to think on her feet." I smiled. Gabby sparkled. We were both beginning to sense the quickly developing synergy between us.

She had a difficult time containing herself, did Gabby. Though, if truth be told, we were both giddy from the excitement a new project can bring. Gabby was especially drawn to the Goth style of the Stables Market. And a fascinating place it was: Everywhere we looked, there were bronze statues of toiling blacksmiths and forgers. So grim and determined they seemed in their bearing; distinct signs of heat and exhaustion overwhelmed their faces. The horses, how tall and regal many stood: some were on their hind legs, their front hooves flailing away like wild broncos, others had their noses pointed downward; they were beasts of burden pulling heavy loads. Also, bronze-plated scenes depicting stable workers and men pounding horseshoes on anvils were mounted on redbrick walls. The hues of the Stables Market were dark, and the mood it portrayed was deliciously grim.

"This place has murder written all over it," Gabby intoned.

"If you must mention murder," I whispered, "try not to do so with such fiendish delight."

****

We spent hours at Camden Lock Market investigating pubs, eateries, shops, alcoves, and passageways for their suitability. According to Gabby, no fewer than seventy locations could accommodate murder.

"A bit heavy-handed, aren't we," I said, once the count reached fifty. She shrugged and retorted, "We're not here to play patty cake, Mitch; we need to maximize the killer's possibilities."

The one place that she kept dragging me back to was the canal. "Murderous charm" was the term that she used to describe it, and it was a term that I had no difficulty reconciling. The water was still and murky—suitable for discarding a victim—the perfect burial ground for a deranged killer.

"I wouldn't be surprised to learn that there are bodies down there right as we speak." Gabby's eyes widened as though nothing would give her more pleasure than dredging the murky water in search of veiny, turned-blue, stiff-as-a-board cadavers.

Footbridges span the canal; stone stairways lead down to cobbled walkways that wind along the water; tall, stately willow trees rise from the cobbles on both sides of the water; behind the trees runs a ten-foot-high brick wall well-worn from a thousand seasons. Atop the walls are wrought iron rails, and gripping one is a stout craggy fifty-two-year-old detective—we shall now call him Granville Tovey—agonizing over an elusive phantom who has created hysteria throughout the city. Detective Tovey has not slept in days; it is apparent to all Londoners who have bothered to notice him. He stares down into the murky waters of a canal miserly in its inclination to offer up an answer. He goes home to an empty house, a bottle of scotch, and a telephone that refuses to ring. Indeed, as Gabby has already suggested, the canal was murderously charming.

Despite a confusing number of eateries and a wide range of foods from which to choose, Gabby decided that we should save our appetites for when we return to Bloomsbury and Lord John Russell Pub.

"Lord John Russell?" I began as though preparing to launch into a protest. "Isn't that where you and Nicholas...."

"That hardly makes it off-limits, Mitch," Gabby swiftly interjected. Then she smiled somewhat sympathetically. "You truly are a poor, bourgeois American; we'll have to work on that."

Gabby was right: I had a few issues that required tweaking. And having had specific protocols and etiquettes drummed into my middle-class American head, as Molly and my folks would see them drummed, perhaps there were more than a few issues that required modification. For example, the old rules of not dating a girl from whom your brother just detached himself, a girl not chasing a man who just scrapped her best friend, and not returning to the scene of the crime, be it a restaurant or motel, with a new love interest, was total nonsense—or, since we were in England: rubbish.

"Mitch, Nicholas was a blip on my radar, and I was no more than a blip on his. Naturally, nothing so insignificant as a blip should ever result in marriage, but our lives happened to intersect at a time when a blip seemed sufficient—if that makes any sense. Anyway, I've grown up a bit since, and I imagine Nicholas has too. I don't know if there's anything more to say of the matter other than I'm glad you're here. Now on to more important matters," she added brightly. "We'll be meeting two friends at Lord John Russell Pub. They also happen to be members of my book club, to whom I promised some private time."

"So you've gone and set me up, have you?" I was feigning indignation.

"I'm a wicked woman, Mitch Morningstar. A most wicked woman, indeed."

Harold and Jane were the two friends we met at the pub. Coming from a place where the aspirations of most men begin and end with acquiring a pricey car and improving their golf game, I found it odd for a man to involve himself with a book club. But, as I would soon discover, Harold and Jane were happily married and, to their credit, aspired to hobbies and activities for which they shared equal passion and were confident in possessing similar abilities. At first, I thought it was all very noble and admirable, but upon further review, I decided that their well-chosen hobbies and activities were the byproduct of their asexuality. It was not a rush to judgment on my part; it was clear that I was sharing a table with a married couple wholly devoid of any sexual presence yet were predictably "indie" concerning their hair, attire, and accessories. Next came the less predictable notion that Gabby had thrust her two oddest friends my way to see how I would react. Well, if Harold and Jane were indeed a test, then yours truly passed with flying colors.

For the sake of Harold and Jane, I spent the next two hours at an amusement ground in Sandusky, Ohio, and on a midnight train bound for the center of town while delving into the psyche of a deranged killer and a man who had suffered a psychotic break. At first, I found it a distraction, as I was well on my way to crafting my next killer, but eventually, I got caught up in the spirit of their enthusiasm.

"And guess what?" Gabby excitedly cried once we had exhausted Davey Coyle and Ted Truman, "Mitch's next novel will take place right here in London, and more specifically, Camden Lock! We just spent hours at the markets and canal concocting all sorts of spine-tingling scenarios."

The Bohemian

Nothing like spilling the beans before typing word one: "It's merely an idea in the infancy of its development," was what I told Harold and Jane with the hope of tempering Gabby's enthusiasm.

"Mitch is far too modest: *The Case of the Camden Lock Killer* will be his finest novel yet, I predict. But remember," Gabby warned her asexual friends, "neither of you has heard the title of Mitch's next novel for the simple reason that neither of you has yet to meet him. We wouldn't want the other club members to think you had a leg up going into tomorrow's meeting."

"What novel?" said Harold.

"Mitch, who?" said Jane.

"Perfect," said Gabby

Harold and Jane acted exceedingly proud in agreeing to unite with concern about being tightlipped. Having had the advantage of two-plus hours to observe them, I noticed the indie asexual couple had a habit of celebrating every concurrence—no act of solidarity, regardless of how insignificant, passed without some mild celebration or acknowledgment. It was peculiar behavior for a married couple: I was always led to believe married couples agreed to disagree and thus turned bickering into a sport. Perhaps Harold and Jane were not married long enough to invite the sort of backbiting that was awaiting them on the horizon.

"It's awfully kind of you, Mitch, to include Gabby in the process of researching a novel," said

Jane.

"I should say so," Harold was quick to agree.

"Perhaps," I said, looking Jane's way. "Although it seems more the other way around."

"Oh, Mitch," cried Gabby. Despite a frown, still evident was the sparkle in her eyes.

"So, tell us, Mitch, what do you do when you're not creating deranged killers that keep us turning pages?" To his credit, it was not small talk that Harold was attempting to spark; he seemed to have a genuine interest, but then Jane went and fucked it up by adding far more brightly than necessary, "Oh yes, Mitch, *do* tell."

I glanced down at my wristwatch—a universal sign to anyone paying attention that time, as it was currently passing, was beginning to wear—only to realize that it was still set for the east coast United States. Resetting my watch to 6:15 London time permitted me a moment to consider just how agonizing tomorrow afternoon could potentially prove, especially if Harold and Jane were in any way representative of the club, or worse, if they were the best the club had to offer. Just who in the hell is reading my novels!

Since Jane appeared so eager for an answer—it was apparent in her swollen eyes and the wringing together of her hands—I decided to enlighten her concerning my "doings" beyond creating deranged killers. "Monday through Friday, I teach AP lit at the local high school. There are eighteen students in my class, and it's almost worthwhile for the five who routinely participate in our open-ended discussions."

"I should say the opportunity to discuss great literature with even *one* person must be considered worthwhile," Harold could not help from interjecting. I leaned closer to the table and upon it rested my elbows. Harold made a fair point, and for its sake, I once again felt engaged. Thus, what I was sure would prove a dreadful book club meeting was showing signs of encouragement, but then Jane went and fucked it up by adding, in a parrot-like manner, "I should certainly say *so.*" Then the asexual pair turned their eyes upon one another to celebrate that they were yet again in perfect accord. I removed my elbows from the table and sagged against the back of my chair. Following a sigh, a devilish grin formed on my face, for I imagined the dedication of *The Case of the Camden Lock Killer* reading: *In memory of Harold and Jane, victims of a deranged serial killer.* However, my next thought was not nearly as amusing: I envisioned a novelist, tomorrow while orating in front of Gabby's book club, stabbing himself in the neck with a pencil, then bleeding to death on the floor of a stranger's living room.

"Discussing literature," I went on to add, "*is*, in every instance, worthwhile, I understand, but, in a forum such as a classroom, the hope—and perhaps I am a cockeyed optimist—is for maximum participation. This past year I introduced some gems: *Slaughterhouse-Five* and *Fahrenheit 451* among them." I nearly bit clear through my tongue, thinking: *what the hell was I doing sparking a discussion on the respective works of Kurt Vonnegut and Ray Bradbury; have I not endured enough?* I quickly segued from my vocation to one of my chosen activities. "On weekends, I go cycling. No motor—a ten-speed."

"So, you're a man with a vocation, a hobby, *and* a passion," Harold seemed pleased to illustrate. "All that's missing is a wife." His eyes shifted to Gabby, who, in turn, cringed. Not that she found the notion objectionable, but Harold's boldness was beginning to wear on her.

"You're so right, dear," Jane added, "a wife would be the cherry on top—the drizzle of chocolate syrup on a sundae already smothered with whipped cream."

God help Harold and Jane; by the time I'm through with *The Case of the Camden Lock Killer*, they will need all the help He can spare.

Next up was Tavistock Square: It was a square like any other city square; it could easily have been Washington Square in Philadelphia or any one of a dozen or so squares scattered throughout New York and London. So why was Tavistock so meaningful to Gabby? Who knows why a particular place holds more lure than another; often, such matters are based on a feeling—mostly impalpable ones not easily explained unless you're Gabby Norwich, who offered the clarification, "I like it best because I like it best." So off to Tavistock Square we went, and along the way, she apologized for my having to agonize through nearly three hours of Harold and Jane.

"The time flew by just like that," I told her, then snapped my fingers to indicate the speed with which the afternoon had passed. Gabby laughed heartily, then added, "Don't let anyone tell you that you're not a good sport, Mitch Morningstar. But they *are* my friends, Harold and Jane, and dear ones too. Funny, though, when it's just the three of us, they don't seem so odd, but with you present, their peculiarities—and I didn't realize they had so many—were quite glaring."

"Let me spare you the worry, Gabby: we're all dysfunctional in one way or another, or as my Grandpa Alexander is fond of saying: 'Comfortable in our own craziness.' We view the world based on our own reality shaped by personal experiences unique in their essence and perception. It explains why we're quick to judge and allege it's the other guy whose worldviews are misshapen and doesn't know his arse from a can of corn. But, of course, none of this applies to my cousin, Molly; not only is she dreadfully perfect but thus far quite immaculate."

"Does any of it apply to Melissa?" Gabby wondered.

"Who the devil is Melissa?" I assumed that I must have suffered a momentary blackout during the course of our conversation.

"She's Detective Tovey's daughter, of course. But now comes the all-important question: Has Melissa not spoken to her father in more than ten months because of how his alcoholism affects her, her mother, or both?"

"Ah-ha! My co-writer strikes again."

"Don't you approve, Mitch?"

"Melissa will do fine," I said. "And incidentally, I'm considering dedicating the novel to Harold and Jane."

"Mitch, you can't be serious!"

"Oh, I'm quite serious, Gabby. So many of us have found out the hard way that finding happiness in this world is no easy endeavor. But, whatever happiness means to Harold and Jane, they've found it, and it's admirable, and now that I've had some time to ponder, I can honestly say that I'm better off for having met them."

"Then perhaps we should make Melissa a Jane," Gabby suggested.

"Jane is too mature sounding for the daughter. So we'll change Granville Tovey's estranged wife from Jill to Jane."

"And Harold? Perhaps he could be the detective's confidant/coffee barista."

"Gabby, dear, no one named Harold has ever owned a diner."

"Point taken; Detective Tovey will have his morning joe served by Joe, but there's nothing to prevent us from making Harold the man Jane runs to when she leaves her craggy detective."

"Perfect," I said, and Gabby trumped my excitement when she added, "And they could have an affair that includes sexual relations!"

I ended the exchange, which developed in a crescendo-like fashion, by further adding: "And when they're all through with a session of passionate lovemaking, we could have the killer murder them in cold blood and have it as messy as the Whitechapel murders; we'll challenge The Ripper himself for sheer gruesomeness!"

"Mitch," Gabby frowned, "you've been toying with me all along, haven't you?"

"I have not," I resolutely maintained. "I most certainly have not."

****

Nine weeks. Six murders. No leads. Granville Tovey raised his eyes from the canal's murky waters to better survey the multitude that, in every which direction, was shuffling through Camden Lock Market. He had a keen sense the killer was among them, that his eyes were somewhere lost in the crowd and taking pleasure in his weariness and frustration. "You're toying with me, aren't you, you bastard?"

The Bohemian

The detective spent the past three weeks delving into cases both past and historically significant: in particular, H.H. Holmes and the killing spree that took place at the 1893 World's Fair in Chicago; David Berkowitz, better known as The Son of Sam; also, more times than he could remember throughout his career, he reexamined the case file of Jack the Ripper. Aside from the choice of weapon (a knife), there were no apparent similarities between The Camden Lock Market Killer and The Ripper. After the third killing, Granville Tovey was beginning to piece together nothing that resembled a lead but a profile: The murders were swift, not indicative of a hedonistic killer, and there was no evidence of rape, necrophilia, or signs that the victims were tortured before killed.

"Looks like we got ourselves a thrill killer," Detective Tovey whispered to Joe the morning after another night came and went without sleep; he had been up all night with a bottle of scotch and The Ripper file.

"You mean to say he kills for sport?" was Joe's whispered return.

"That's one way of putting it," said the detective. Then, following a sigh of frustration, he added, "He's a weak man, this sort of killer, and driven to feel powerful, and the way he achieves power is through the thrill of snuffing out the lives of fellow human beings." In a matter of seconds, Granville Tovey chugged his coffee. He let out a gasp, then cleared his throat. "Anymore, I'm finding it harder and harder to reconcile that we're all of the same God. Incidentally, that's a telltale sign a man's been on the job too long, but I'm a stubborn old sonofabitch, Joe."

The fourth and fifth killings each supported the profile that Detective Tovey strenuously pieced together; however, when a sixth body was discovered—the second to have been found floating in the canal—the profile began to unravel. Tovey and his partner, Detective Hellickson, who was ten years younger and a chain smoker, knelt beside the stiff, purplish body once it got fished from the canal. They let out long and dispirited sighs. "I'll take one of those," said the senior detective, and Hellickson handed Tovey a Pall-Mall.

"Something's not right," said Hellickson. "A serial doesn't change his M.O. in the middle of a killing spree."

Pinching his brow, Granville Tovey let loose a thoughtful rumbling sound that echoed from the base of his throat. "No, a serial does not change, but something has: Either he's evolving, or we're looking at another killer. Whichever the case, this wasn't a thrill kill; it was personal—as personal as it gets." He puffed on the Pall-Mall, then glanced down at the area on the corpse where once was a penis. Hellickson pried open the corpse's mouth and, with a gloved hand, retrieved the severed organ and placed it in a plastic bag. "This is a first for me," he said and lit another Pall-Mall.

By day's end, the identity of victim number six was determined. His name was Harold Halsbury, which proved an interesting development, especially for one Detective Granville Tovey. He had a closed-door meeting back at the precinct with Lieutenant Van Pelt.

"If matters weren't already messy enough, now we're really in the shit," grumbled the lieutenant. "But if there's a silver lining, we know we're still dealing with one killer."

"That's not a whole helluva lot to hang our hats on." It was clear the senior detective was both angry and distracted.

"Agreed," said Van Pelt. "And what's worse, Gran, he's on to you and has gone and proved it by murdering and de-cocking your estranged wife's lover. In other words, Gran, he's made you his business and has made no bones that he's gotten close to you—quite close, indeed; and what's more, he's of the theory that it's within his power to create a cloud of suspicion over you."

"Has he?" Detective Tovey gazed out at an edgy, overworked precinct through a closed glass door.

"Are you asking me whether everyday citizens, living in a country that has made the fiendish devouring of tabloid journalism a culture, would be willing to believe that a craggy, jaded detective, some would assert has been on the job too long, would castrate his estranged wife's lover?" The senior detective and the lieutenant shared a laugh. Then Van Pelt went on to add, "The murder of Harold Halsbury was our killer's ostentatious way of saying, 'Let the games begin.'"

"His game, his rules," the senior detective grumbled dispiritedly.

"Gran," Van Pelt called as the detective reached for the doorknob. "Somebody has to inform Jane that Harold Halsbury's body was fished from the canal this morning."

"And you think *I'm* the one best suited to perform such a courtesy?"

"Never mind," growled the lieutenant. "I'll send Barnwell and Thatcher."

"What was that all about?" wondered Hellickson.

"One of those 'perception is reality' pep talks," grumbled Detective Tovey.

"So, you've killed off poor Harold but decided to keep our dear Lady Jane. I like it, Mitch," said Gabby. "And I particularly like that the killer gets close enough to our Detective Tovey to where he can learn personal matters—a deranged killer playing mind games with a detective whose life is damaged; the intrigue is irresistible!"

Gabby didn't bother to mention the irony of Harold losing his penis. "I take in then, you approve," I said.

"Approve? It will be your best novel yet! And Harold and Jane, I have no doubt, will surely approve. Jane, leaving a craggy, jaded, alcoholic detective for, shall we say, a teacher? —indeed, we should make the ill-fated Harold Halsbury a school teacher—it won't get construed as scandalous but a matter of survival. It's perfect!"

"So, this is Tavistock Square?" I was not striving for irony upon our arrival, just stating the obvious: Like most squares, it was an oasis nestled within a bustling city; its boundary was a wrought iron fence, its partitionings were walkways lined with park benches, and there were lawns accented with lovely foliage and dotted with tall, stately trees. There was one tree, a magnificent cherry planted in memory of the victims of Hiroshima. In the center of the square was a circular garden outlined with boxwoods; within the circle were flagstones, and atop the stones was a four-tiered base upon which sat a pedestal. Atop the pedestal was a bronze statue of Mohandas Gandhi. It's a typical depiction of the Mahatma; he's sitting cross-legged, appearing quite meditative, and with a garment draped over his right shoulder.

"It's lovely, isn't it, Mitch?" Gabby intoned. "How this place bursts with vibrancy in the springtime; so lush and well scented it is in summer, and in the autumn, there's no more charming place in the whole of London! And over there," she pointed across the way, "was where Virginia Wolfe used to live."

Indeed, the square was lovely; any place capable of inspiring Gabby's charm to reach its pinnacle of radiance, where I was concerned, was Heaven on Earth.

"Oh, incidentally, Mitch," Gabby added—I could tell she was about to reveal a matter that slipped her mind— "Nina has requested that you go and see her sing tonight."

Nina? It had been such an eventful day that I had all but forgotten about the mysterious femme fatale whose 3:30 silhouette in the doorway I perceived as both inspiring and dangerous.

"When does she go on?" I asked, sensing the day was slipping away.

"She's the headliner; usually, it's not until 10:30 that she takes the stage."

I glanced down at my wristwatch. It was 7:30. As intrigued as I was by Nina, I was keener to begin pounding out pages of *The Case of the Camden Lock Killer*. I imagined my night would get spent at a keypad, accompanied by a bottle of wine with Gabby nearby, close enough to feel her breath on my cheek while enshrouded in the loveliness of her scent. I would read passages aloud, and we would mull them over with delight. Sometimes Gabby would read aloud. Then, we would go back and forth, bouncing between my creative energy and her input and inspiration; who knows to what heights we would ascend!

"What time would we need to leave?" I had difficulty feigning curiosity, then sensed reservation in Gabby's demeanor. Finally, she managed to squeeze out the words, "Mitch, it will be just you who's going." Before I could launch a protest, she added, regretfully, "Mitch, you must forgive me, but late hours in dark smoky nightclubs don't agree with me."

Alone, I would venture out at night to an unfamiliar place in an unknown part of town to meet my 3:30 a.m. visitor. I glanced upward at Mohandas Gandhi, but thanks to the work of a superbly capable sculptor, the Mahatma appeared to have more important matters on his mind.

It was 9:45 when I said goodbye to Gabby and was seen off in a taxicab. I had no practical reason to feel nervous: after all, I was going to see Gabby's sister sing; why should the younger sibling of a potential love interest set me on edge? If only Nina had spoken last night, had uttered anything: *hello Mitch, welcome to England*, or *fuck you*; any one of those would have worked, for had I heard her voice, I might have gained some insight into her persona; instead, all I had to go on was a silhouette in a doorway, and that she had preferred to remain a mystery was what had me on edge, though, if truth be told, that was always my mind's eye image of Nina—even far back as when Airman Morningstar was married to Gabby—a strikingly feminine silhouette posed in a doorway, a woman who was the very essence of feminine mystery, lurking in shadow, the irresistibly aloof Bobbie by day and Nina by night, and now this phantom-like woman had summoned me. And now that I've turned to the subject of my summoning: at precisely what point had Nina requested that I come to watch her sing? It was a question I wished I had thought to pose before Gabby ushered me to a cab.

The cab pulled up to the curbside of Doc Watson's a few minutes shy of ten o'clock. I chose not to enter the club just yet. It was not my design to walk in just as Nina took the stage. First, I wanted to exorcise Mitch Morningstar by adopting the persona of a stranger—one to be reckoned with—who just so happened into a strange place, and I decided a craggy, jaded homicide detective would do the trick. To accomplish this metamorphosis, I began pounding the sidewalk, circling clear around the block, each step urging on the manifestation of a fictitious character that sprang from my imagination. Indeed, I would enter Doc Watson's, not a timid soul with trepidation but in the shoes of Granville Tovey—a man capable of staring into the eyes of a deranged serial killer.

The detective's first introduction to Doc Watson's was a long bar around which hardcore-looking men were well engrossed in a soccer match. It was the World Cup: Czechoslovakia versus Costa Rica. I grinned the way one might when looking down their nose at a matter one finds trivial. Luckily, I caught myself: an American who has no time for soccer was not my role; I was a stout, glary-eyed English homicide detective, though no one seated at the bar took an appreciative notice of my presence. Czechoslovakia was leading the match 4—1. Mitch Morningstar knows little about soccer but enough to realize goals come at a premium; thus, three-goal leads often hold up. I learned later that the World Cup had already advanced past the groupings and had begun the round of sixteen: England, which figured to get past Belgium, would play Cameroon, who earlier in the day beat the Colombian team 2—1. Looming at the other end of the bracket, though, was the vaunted German squad, and the only team with a viable chance of knocking them out of the tournament, thus clearing a path to the finals for England, was team Czechoslovakia:

hence, the reason the men at the bar were so delighted by the 4—1 score. "God bless those Czech bastards," I heard one bellow.

I was skirting alongside the bar towards the stairs when the abovementioned man bellowed his sentiments. I kept my eyes pinned on the television. In living in the moment, an infusion of bravery came over me. "God bless them, is right," I added with a vestige of an accent. At the top of the stairs, I was greeted by a hostess, who inquired whether I intended to dine or was on my way to the third-floor lounge. "The latter," was what I told her before adding, "I'm meeting someone." She shot me a queer look. As I began to walk away, it occurred to me how idiotic it must have sounded to a London nightclub employee that I deemed it necessary to justify showing up alone at such an hour. So much for my Detective Tovey bravado. I stopped, turned toward the woman, and told her, "I'm sort of a friend of Nina Linette's and have been promising her that I'd come and watch her sing."

"A friend of Miss Linette's, are you?" the woman said. I sensed doubt in her tone but couldn't fathom why any association I had with Nina, real or imagined, was her concern. Then, of all matters, she smirked at me. "I'll bet you are," she added. I was inclined to demand: *just what do you mean by that,* but heard a cascade of applause, which prompted my swift ascending of the stairs. I entered into a sea of black leather and red velvet. Sinking into all that black leather and red velvet was a crowd already a few drinks in, anticipating the main attraction. On stage was an all-male band featuring a drummer, keyboard player, saxophone player, and bass guitarist. They played a strain unknown to me; its purpose was to summon their queen bee to the stage. I surveyed the lounge; there was not a stool or chair to be had. I remained standing toward the back, in shadow. In the darkened room, wine glasses, bejeweled fingers, wrists, necks, and ears reflect like stars zipping through a quasar, and from that darkness and starry glimmer emerges a jazz singer whose allure was beyond compare. She was nowhere until, at once, her sinuous swanlike form displayed for all to behold. Through a star-studded lounge, I watched Nina Linette take hold of her microphone—she cradled it in both hands; it was how a starving man would beg to be touched. She was wickedly delightful—an artist whose craft was to weaken men and turn them into groveling wantons. Gone was Granville Tovey; the craggy, jaded detective came seeping through my

The Bohemian

pores, leaving nary a trace. He was no match for Nina Linette; neither, for that matter, was Mitch Morningstar. There was a deft change of key; the introduction the band was playing was now familiar; it reaches a crescendo, then falls precipitously into silence. Longingly cradling it in her slim lovely hands, the vocalist brings the microphone provocatively to her mouth.

This may come,
This may come as some surprise
But I miss you
I could see through all of your lies
But still I miss you

Huskily, but owning the clarity of a bell, her voice hovers throughout the lounge—it is all around us, caressing us, seducing us; it is burning wood on a cold winter's night; it could not get close enough to us, or us to it. Her words were of sadness and longing and crept into our souls in wistful elegance. We belonged to her, and just as she held her microphone, she too was holding us; we lay breathless and paralyzed in her lovely cradling hands.

He takes her love,
But it doesn't feel like mine
He tastes her kiss,
Her kisses are not wine,
They are not mine

I remained tucked away in the shadows, yet she knew I was there. Nina knew; I could sense her awareness, and she communicated to me through a lyric Sade had made famous a few years earlier. Had I soared the span of the Atlantic for the express purpose of a book talk? Of course, I hadn't, and Nina suspected all along that I was in love with Gabby. I didn't require the instincts of Granville Tovey to recognize that Nina Linette was frighteningly intuitive, but tonight—if she believed the possibility existed, and apparently, she had—she would stake her claim. But why?

He takes,
But surely she can't give what I'm feeling now
She takes,
But surely she doesn't know how

Did Nina truly see her sister as unworthy or, through osmosis, or the benefit of a far-flung imagination, see us together as lovers on some lofty plateau? We had nary exchanged a word; Nina's thoughts were unknown to me, yet there was so much to her that I chose to assume. My thoughts, conversely, were not entirely strange to her, for much of Mitch Morningstar was subliminally encoded in both characters and narrative and could easily be extracted by one owning superior insight. *You know me, don't you, Nina?*

Is it a crime?
That I still want you…
And I want you to want me too

I crept out from the cloak of shadows. It felt no less threatened in doing so but reconciled there was no point in remaining. I wound my way to the bar, and once there, I carved out a spot and ordered a straight vodka over ice. "She's quite good, isn't she," I acknowledged once the barkeeper served up my order. He gestured to the crowd with the wave of his hand. "We don't pack 'em in like this just because the furniture's comfortable." He wasn't flippant, merely proud on behalf of the jazz singer. "I suppose not," I said.

My love is wider than Victoria Lake
Taller than the Empire State
It dives, it jumps
I can't give you more than that,
surely you want me back

The lounge erupted with applause, and why shouldn't it have; Nina had skipped over the appetizer and entrée and served up dessert—a delectable French pastry! She was gracious to the crowd, citing that a woman needs to feel desirable. She whipped her luxurious mane of hair from one side to the other—it was no longer blonde as it was back when Nicholas and Gabby were married; it was an alluring and gleaming chestnut—then glared at the crowd like a nymph welcoming all comers. Next came a swift change of character; the jazz singer abandoned her femme fatale persona and announced, "All you devotees of Doc Watson's, there's a special guest among you, and he has come all the way from the United States—clear across the Atlantic—just to hear me sing." *Please don't do it, Nina,* I was pleading inside. *I beg you, don't do it!* "Now *there's* a man who knows how to make a girl feel desirable. So, please, ladies and gentlemen, a warm welcome for bestselling novelist and friend Mitch Morningstar!"

The jazz singer pointed to where I was standing; her eyes must have pierced through the star-studded lounge, spied me in the shadows, and followed my winding path to the bar. A spotlight obeyed her authoritative finger; its harsh glare caused me to recoil—I may have even cringed—nevertheless, I managed a halfhearted wave to acknowledge the mainly polite applause I received. However, I could tell a few clapping hands had picked up one, if not both, of my novels: never let it get said London is a city unappreciative of a good serial killer. I nodded to Nina. It was a gesture to acknowledge her command and control over the room, me, and her right to wield it. Finally, the spotlight was taken away from my face: my five seconds of fame were over; all eyes returned to the jazz singer; the crowd was shamelessly pleading once again to be conquered by its seductress and her voice. I was among the shameless—the first in line—and wanted it known that I had submitted. The jazz singer placed her microphone back on the stand. She began to crowd it, to sinuously coil around it, like someone about to whisper words of sin. Next rang out a blues number sung tantalizingly unhurried.

Don't put no headstone on my grave
All my life I've been a slave
Want the whole wide world to know
That I'm the gal that loved you so
Mama, Mama, don't you cry
I'm gonna meet you in the by-and-by
Tell Papa I'm comin' home
God, it can't be very long.

I closed my eyes, allowing my mind to travel to places I had not foreseen venturing, only to acknowledge the notion as laughable: I had allowed nothing; it was all Nina's doing; it was the jazz singer's will that my mind got flung to profane places where sinfulness lived untethered and was free to flourish. Gabby, dear, sweet Gabby: your round face, sparkling eyes, and delightful plumpness seem light-years away—lost in space—a mere speck amid a star-studded cluster known as the galaxy. I had a fleeting desire to abandon my drink, the bar, and Doc Watson's and run off in search of Gabby. *Gabby, darling, I must find you before it's too late, and we're lost to one another forever.* But Nina ensured that I remained right where I stood: my mind open to suggestion—my soul, corruption.

With my eyes still closed, I lapsed into a reverie provoked by the mysterious strains of *Masquerade*; like a slow-accumulating fog, it crept down from the stage and mingled with the black leather, red velvet, sparkling wine glasses, and sea of jewels. Then Nina's voice grew effortlessly from the notes—in a similar tone and texture, it emerged and lent more mystery to the already mysterious. *Are we really happy in this lonely game we play?* were the satiny words first to echo. Who *was* "really happy" nowadays, I wondered? I opened my eyes, for a moment, to gaze out upon the cluster of stardust enraptured in the lounge, only to witness humanity's odds and ends desperately trying to fit together. Who longed for someone to conquer them, who needed saving, and who among them—even the "really happy" ones—understood the difference? Were we but a collection of souls drifting in space, hoping for a collision that would rescue us from *the lonely games we play*? It was a notion that sparked me to wonder: at the end of the evening when everyone got up to leave, would it matter whether they went home with the same person with whom they came? Moreover, how long would it take before they noticed, and how much would it matter once they had? I could feel myself falling in love with one Norwich sister but fascinated by the other—infinitely fascinated! It must be the mysterious strains of the song leading my mind into shadowy spaces; that was what I tried to convince myself; for some songs have such power. Though I could easily attribute the hours spent with Harold and Jane—some were spent in agony— to my confusion. Indeed, my favorite asexual couple's juxtaposition to my current vicissitude and society still in the throes of a sexual revolution may have steered me toward the shadows, for their life together was anything but a masquerade or lonely game; they—how dare they! —were "really happy."

Poor Harold. To have gotten himself killed as he had and such a sweet fellow beneath all the quirkiness. But wait: real-life Harold did not get fished from a canal with his castrated penis shoved into his mouth; that was fictitious Harold. Real-life Harold was home with real-life Jane, doubtless celebrating, having agreed upon something inanely frivolous. How bizarre, I thought, that it was the fictional version of Harold and Jane whose messy lives found a way to collide, whereas their real-life asexual counterparts were "really happy." Then again, bizarre or not, real life was not supposed to be as simple as real-life Harold and Jane made it seem. I took a moment to examine myself: I was not a craggy, jaded old detective but real-life Mitch Morningstar. *Masquerade* ended with the saxophone trailing away to a faint drumroll and gentle tap of a cymbal. Next up was *Angel Eyes*. It was clear that Nina was a talented singer; one need not possess an ear for the vocal arts to understand she was weaving spells and moods through the gift of voice; she was an atmospheric diva whose craft was making each song her own and making everyone feel that she was singing just for them: She could draw a fellow right into a song and hold him captive, spellbound; thus, I was no longer Mitch Morningstar or Granville Tovey, but a guy at a bar who had checked his wristwatch a thousand times and was praying either the hands were lying, or he had misremembered an appointment he made with a woman who had charmed him beyond all hope.

> *Try to think that love's not around*
> *But it's uncomfortably near*
> *My old heart ain't gaining no ground*
> *Because my angel eyes ain't here*

I was lost in the song and believed this time she would show, that I would not get stood up yet again—a lonely man dying a slow death one drink at a time in some lonely midnight bar in the loneliest part of town, with only a bartender's ear for a lifeline.

> *Need I say that my love's misspent.*

Nothing could make a sucker out of a man faster than a beautiful woman, and no one knew this better than Nina. I was getting restless and needed an answer to *why my angel eyes ain't here*. The music stopped playing. The room fell into stillness and silence in anticipation of how Nina would put the finishing touch on what had been the sultriest of saloon songs. First came a smirk, followed by a casual shrug, then she let out a barely audible but self-deprecating chortle. Next came the bell-like and satiny words: *'Scuse me… while I dis … ahh…pearr.* The final syllable lingered both beautifully and tragically until it trailed into silence. The spotlights went out on the stage; a moment later, when again illuminated, all that was visible was the band; Nina Linette had vanished, stolen away into the night.

The set had ended; the applause was resounding. I took a moment to regard my empty glass and wondered whether I should order another and stick around for the second set or call it a night. I checked my wristwatch; it was 11:15. If I left now, if lucky, I could be back with Gabby before midnight. The prospect was an attractive one; besides, I had a book talk tomorrow afternoon and wanted to appear reasonably alert and refreshed; I owed Gabby that much. I would have felt fine leaving after the first set, as I had fulfilled Nina's request and, in the process, achieved levels of arousal I had failed to anticipate. The latter, I suppose, was a bonus; therefore, had I stayed, I would have been risking Nina getting further under my skin and me losing all sense of reality. That was the last thought I could remember crossing my mind when, from behind, I felt a slender hand on my shoulder. I spun around, hoping to discover tufty hair falling about a round face accented with sparkling eyes, that Gabby decided a dark, smoky nightclub was less objectionable than a lonely flat. Instead, upon completing my about-face, who should be standing before me but the more lethal of the Norwich sisters, back from her disappearing act. Nina's eyes did not sparkle; instead, they pierced, darted, and threatened. Even in delivering a husky yet seemingly innocuous "Hello, Mitch," she had dissected me—I was oozing from each precise slice.

"Shall I call you Bobbie?" Since I was a guest at her home, I assumed it was a sensible question. Why call her by a stage name? However, Nina was quick to inform me, brightly and with nary a trace of regret, "Bobbie Norwich is long gone; nowadays, it's Nina Linette, all day and every day."

I didn't warn her of the dangers of giving herself over to a persona; I had no experience in that area, less the right.

"I'm glad you're here, Mitch," she added. The brightness in her tone disappeared; her words were satiny, sultry, and resounded in a lower register. Was she performing? "I'm glad that we could have this time together." She took a probing finger and, with it, located an opening in my button-down shirt. I felt her nail make a deep impression on my skin, then rake its way down my chest. It was curious, to say the least, but also strangely pleasurable, and it made Nina smile that I ostensibly found favor in a mild display of sadism. When her finger couldn't travel any further, she used it as a hook to pull me nearer to her. With Nina in heels, we were nearly the same height.

She lurched forward so that it became possible to place a kiss on my cheek.

"I know that you're in love with Gabby, Mitch. I've known it for some time, perhaps as early as when Nicholas was still in the picture. I want you to know that I approve. All I ask in return is that you keep an open mind. You can do that, can't you, Mitch?"

The warmth of Nina's breath in my ear; the loveliness of her scent, which had me dangerously enveloped: it was all quite intoxicating, even paralyzing; and her presence, at such proximity, proved every bit as hypnotic as the satiny notes that so effortlessly flew from her mouth. "An open mind?" I finally asked, feigning ignorance of what she had implied.

"What has Gabby told you about me, Mitch?" I snapped to a posture one might assume when about to rattle off numerous aspects meant to satisfy a long-expected entreaty; however, it occurred to me that a truthful offer would be to say: *not nearly as much as I would have liked*, though that, I feared, might have resonated with too much audacity, never mind encouragement. Despite the numerous occasions Gabby and I spoke over the phone and corresponded through letters, she failed to reveal much about Nina. Moreover, I developed a sense that Nina was a reluctant subject for Gabby. "Only that you went by two names, which is no longer the case," I began, "and that you are quite beautiful—or, in Gabby's words, 'a real stunner,' and she never failed to mention that you're a terrific singer. The latter two are overwhelmingly evident: you have quite a voice, inspiring, I would go so far to say, and, with the risk of sounding redundant, you're quite a pleasure to look at."

My last words were an immediate regret: Aside from redundant and flirty, which they were—the benefit of nuance notwithstanding—I was afraid they might lead me down a path I was unprepared to travel. In other words, for lack of a better term, I did not care for Nina and me to get *lost in a masquerade*. Or did I? Having her so near was an altogether different experience than watching her performing on stage: With the ever-present threat of her long, sinuous form dangerously looming, I felt cornered, trapped; she was all at once an irresistible force and immovable object.

"Is that all?" she asked. Nina was not fishing for additional compliments—that much, I could tell—but alluding to how little Gabby had revealed. "I truly love my sister, Mitch; a better friend I've never had or could I ask for, but you and I have so much more in common—we are so much more alike."

"How can you know that?" I wondered. I was not expecting a reply steeped in pragmatism: Nina was an artist; thus, an enigmatic ramble based on the magic that potentially occurs when kindred spirits encounter one another on an astral plane was what I anticipated. But, before she spoke, she again employed her finger to draw me nearer.

"You'll understand better, Mitch, just how alike we are when you go to touch me."

There gushed upon me a moment that seemed an eternity brought about by the reality of Nina Linette. When trapped in this period, all functions of my body were betraying me or had ceased. To begin with: I was succumbing to a creeping paralysis, and if my appendages were any indication, my blood was resting idly in my veins, and it was with equal certainty that my breathing, if not impaired, had stopped altogether. Then, with a start, I managed to recoil away from Nina and pirouette toward the bar.

"Is it necessary to act repulsed, Mitch? It is, after all, the gay 90s—or, perhaps, haven't you heard? Besides, a girl has feelings, you understand, and you are by all accounts, or so it has been told to me, a gentleman."

"A girl?" It was a throaty shriek that I managed to muffle when turning away from the bar to face Nina. My vicissitude aside, I kept a well-restrained deportment, as it was not my desire to cause a scene. Moreover, my intuition warned me of possible dangers, having theorized I was the only one in the lounge aware of what I had just come to learn of Doc Watson's superb headliner. So there I was, Mitch Morningstar, trapped within the pages of a bizarre novel and powerless to write myself out of the scene. Had this been a novel, I could have myself killed off in the next chapter, if not the next page, but it was not a novel; it was reality, and I, like never before, was *lost in a masquerade.*

"Tonight, I sang for *you,* Mitch, and while I sang, we were lovers of the most splendid kind. I could feel you surrendering to the passion that surged from within: Did you make love to me roughly, Mitch? Did you toss me about, and did it not thrill you? Or did you take me in your hands as you would a delicate flower and gently lay me down before gorging yourself? It's all right, Mitch; you don't have to say a word; I already have my answer."

Indeed, she had her answer; even after learning what I had of Nina Linette, it was difficult not to want her—impossible to conceal an ever-growing fascination.

"Must we become Echo and Narcissus, you and me? Look at me, Mitch," Nina implored. "Just look at me."

She was quite the rarest of creatures, Nina—a unicorn among beasts of burden—a phoenix in a henhouse. From head to toe, the essence of feminine charm and mystery came together as harmoniously as any Mozart symphony whose calms became storms soaring gloriously toward their riveting climaxes. It was undeniable, Nina was all woman—by far the most beautiful I have ever had the pleasure to behold—except where it mattered most.

Then something peculiar and unexpected overcame me: my feelings for Gabby aside, I felt strangely inadequate for my failure to see beyond Nina's only blemish—her one fatal flaw. Empathy for her burden came upon me in a sudden burst. Poor Nina: her only imperfection, which, in her mind, was purported a birth defect—a cruel trick of nature—that disqualified her to all men; I could ponder nothing crueler, sadder. Poor, lonely Nina: too beautiful for some men and unsuitable for others. Indeed, despite her wicked charms, of which there was an abundance, she was, unfortunately, disqualified.

"What is it you want from me, Nina?" My words were not curt but empathetically curious. Nina had not revealed herself to me without reason or for the simple thrill of acting the part of a playful vixen; her motives, I could tell, were quite sober.

"Hold me, Mitch, and I'll tell you," she said.

I did not consider it an unreasonable request, and I would be lying if I said that Nina's form felt anything short of delightful in my arms. "I wish not to be a nymph or siren, Mitch, always luring men, but to no end: Like everyone else, I want to matter to someone, to have it feel like life or death. Now kiss me, and I'll tell you the rest."

Unlike earlier, I did not throw myself into a recoiling lunge toward the bar but stood firm, keeping Nina nestled securely in my arms. "You should realize: for someone trying to shed the persona of a nymph or siren, you can be quite intoxicating." At first, Nina met my gaze with a schoolgirl's bashfulness, but then juvenile timidity gave way to the weightiness of unbearable sorrow. I brushed aside a tendril of hair that fell in front of her eye, then brought our lips together. I kissed her as she would have wanted. When our lips parted, she whispered in my ear, "I want you to write my story, Mitch. *That's* what I want from you."

It was a confession nearly as unexpected as learning the truth about Nina Linette. "You do understand what I'm asking of you, don't you, Mitch?" she added. "I don't want to be a character in one of your novels or have my life encrypted in fiction; I want you to write my story."

"I shall go out on a limb and claim that enlightening you to the fact I never once considered writing a biography won't dampen your spirit in the slightest."

"You see, Mitch," she said, "you're getting to know me already. But on a serious note," she added, "you're a writer and a damn good one, and I have a story worthy of your powers."

"But you *are* only in your mid-twenties," I reminded her. "Not yet a third of the way through your life; let us hope."

"So it shall be a running manuscript—a piece that won't get published for another decade or two. No matter, I promise you shall find me a worthwhile subject. But you should get going, Mitch. You have a big day tomorrow, or have you forgotten?"

The musicians were back on stage and summoning the jazz singer with the strains of *Black Magic Woman*. "Mitch," Nina called to me above the music, "do you think my life will be a tragedy, or will my story end happily?"

"We have years yet to work on a happy ending," I called back to her. She pirouetted brilliantly on a heel and went prancing toward the stage. Little did I know that Nina's life had already been a tragedy—one I would write about intermittently over many years.

CHAPTER SIX
PLEASE LET IT BE GABBY

I decided to walk back to Bloomsbury; I needed fresh air—
as fresh as London could offer—and a longer period than the duration of a cab ride to clear my head. Who wouldn't? Besides, it was
not that far a walk. However, of all matters, the moment my feet hit
the pavement and nostrils sensed the outdoors, I heard my dear
cousin Molly in my ear: *Did I not warn you about those Norwich sisters,
Mitch?* It was just what I didn't need on a midnight ramble in an unfamiliar city: Molly screaming the words *I told you so* in my ear. It had
been a mere thirty-seven hours since Molly and I shared lunch, some
mildly contentious words, and travel time to the airport. Somehow,
it seemed an eternity ago, and I confessed to the air, with humility,
that I was craving her company. Indeed, my cousin, the pragmatist,
always found a way to restore one's equilibrium whenever she decided it was necessary; however, it was far too often for my liking.
Poor Molly: always well-intentioned despite her efforts being unwelcomed or underappreciated. Tonight, though, would have marked a
rare exception. And what on earth was Gabby thinking sending me
off for my first-ever meeting with Nina unprepared? Not to suggest
that I'm a novice concerning dicey situations, but tonight, as they say,
took the cake. What was worse, I allowed myself to become angry
with Gabby. But my anger did not linger, for I decided to take the
high road and assume that Gabby had no knowledge that Nina
planned to reveal herself to me. As far as Gabby knew, Nina never
intended to do so; thus, had Gabby taken this delicate matter upon
herself, it might have landed in her lap as an unpardonable breach of
confidence. Anyway, that was what I kept telling myself as I went
ambling the lively midnight streets of London.

Poor Nina: cursed with more beauty than has ever come together in any one person, and the result was a sad and lonely life; how

desperately she longed to be understood—to be realized with acceptance and favor. But all was not gloomy; she had procured an agent, a confidant... a biographer? My mind was a whirlwind with the plotlines of three novels running through it at once: a serial killer was playing mind games with a craggy alcoholic detective whose wife had left him for a lover that would eventually fall victim to the killer himself; a jazz singer, who, if not for an unfortunate detail, could easily be considered the most beautiful woman on the face of the earth; and last, the vicissitude of yours truly, which seemed to hover above all matters with intriguing twists and turns.

Given the hour and my swerving state of mind, I was in no great hurry to get back to Gabby. Instead, I visited her favorite place, and Tavistock Square was delightfully illuminated—a more romantic spot one would be hard-pressed to find, with its numerous lamplights setting aglow flower arrangements, and the low-arching limbs of trees. The night air was close; it created a well-scented ether within the square. Saturday at midnight, save for yours truly, only couples had flocked to the famous square—aspiring lovers—and I would have otherwise felt out of place if not for my current preoccupation. I planted myself, with arms folded, directly in front of Mohandas Gandhi. "It's a remarkable likeness," I heard a woman remark to a man whose hand she held. The man agreed, but I could tell they were at a point in their relationship where he would have agreed to anything. Besides, even had he believed the likeness to be less than remarkable, there was no upside to stating as much. Where I was concerned, remarkable likeness or not, the Mahatma was no more helpful now than he had been at the onset of evening.

I wandered away from Tavistock Square with one lingering thought: for the sake of Gabby and all her eager book club friends, I needed to dwell less upon Detective Tovey, the Camden Lock killer, whoever he was, and a jazz singer who calls herself Nina Linette, and more upon Davey Coyle and Ted Truman. It was not an easy endeavor; the excitement of a new project and the complexities of someone such as Nina are difficult to dispel, and the more I tried to eclipse them, the more compelling they became, especially the latter. If *The Case of the Camden Lock Killer* was complex, Nina was impossible; I could devote more time than I might care to with concern to the psychology of Nina Linette, and still not unearth every aspect; she would prove every bit as compelling as Davey Coyle or Ted Truman. I was not, however, a biographer, as I tried to impress upon Nina, but any idiot could see that she was a writer's dream.

I walked in and found Gabby asleep, sitting up in a chair. On her lap was a copy of Somerset Maugham's *The Moon and Sixpence*—a novel that journeys through the mind and soul of a middle-aged stockbroker who abandons a life of conformity to pursue art. We're fans of Maugham, Gabby and me, and, on more than a few occasions, his novels became the subject of our transatlantic conversations. She must have sensed that she was about to nod off and marked her page. Catching up on her reading was not her only motive for remaining behind: Alongside the chair was a table; atop the table was a 14 by 11inch sketchpad; sitting on the open pad was an artist's pencil. I set aside the pencil and took hold of the pad. The opened page revealed a drawing of a man with a prominent mustache and eyebrows. Below his check-styled duck-billed tam was a well-furrowed forehead—the permanent condition was a cumulative result of years spent pondering—and eyes filled with wisdom and anguish; the lines in his face were not so much from age as they were from experiences. Indeed, this was a well-weathered and intense-looking man and one who caused me to stagger momentarily. Somehow, Gabby managed to reach inside my head and produce an astonishingly accurate image of Granville Tovey—right down to the minutest detail, I was staring at my craggy, alcoholic detective! I began flipping back through the sketchpad. First, I came upon Ted Truman: I immediately knew it was the tortured protagonist of *Somnambula,* as it was exactly how I had always imagined him to look. What was equally remarkable was the detail of the drawing: Ted was seated on a train; through the window were glimpses of a cityscape; in Ted's eyes was the look of a man who was once part of a vast ethos known as reality but had become unattached, adrift, and would never find his way back. I turned the page. Again, a remarkable likeness of Ted Truman: the image saw him slumped in a chair; beside him was a bottle; in his hand, a photograph; doubtless, it was of Laura, his recently slain wife. He appeared distraught—any man would—but more than that, he seemed a man who would have preferred to shrink his way out of existence. I flipped the page and was greeted by the world-weary eyes of a homicide detective who had made one too many midnight rambles carrying news that a spouse had just become widowed. Beside him was his respectfully disconsolate partner. In the foreground was the back of Ted Truman's bowed head; one of his hands was grasping for anything that would help him remain on his feet. The next drawing featured Laura Truman from the neck up. Her head was disproportionately large when juxtaposed with the deserted train station in the background. Her eyes were shifting warily as one's might when sensing danger. Next were the *Funhouse* sketches in full breadth, beginning with a frightened five-year-old boy clutching the hand of a first responder while looking back at a wrecked automobile and ending with a deranged man who walked into a police precinct and announced, "I'm the funhouse killer." There were six drawings in all: in each, Gabby managed to capture the essence of Davey Coyle; it was truly uncanny, her ability to pluck images from my mind and replicate them on paper, and quite surreal to hold what was a composite of images that represented my past and future literary output.

"Ah-ha, I see we're awake." Although Gabby was lovely in repose, it was delightful to watch her features come back to life, especially since I felt somewhat lonely.

"Ah-ha, I see we've been snooping," came her groggy retort, though there was not even a vestige of accusation in her words; it was all quite playful.

"I see we also have secret talents—remarkable talents, I should say."

"Remarkable? That might be a bit generous. Secret? Not anymore."

"But surely you can't mind me having discovered your art? You did intend to show me your work, did you not?"

"Of course, eventually," she said, which I took to have meant *not tonight*. Then it occurred to me: the Granville Tovey drawing might be incomplete, that there may be fine details yet to come—the sort that only an artist would know were missing.

"Gabby, you must know these are extraordinary drawings, but do you understand why? In each one, the subjects are just as my mind's eye had imagined them. So, my question to you is quite simple: How were you able to do it? And, more importantly, how is it possible?"

I peered in at Gabby like one expecting to find present on her mien evidence of witchery. But, instead, like myself, I could see that she was jogging her memory, recalling conversations in which core characters received detailed discussions: ages, demeanors, circumstances, motives, psychologies; these were the aspects we conferred upon as a matter of routine, but never had the detailed appearance of a given character become a subject, be it hooded lids, an aquiline nose, drawn cheeks, etc... And yet, in my hands, I held a sketchbook representing a near-flawless fusion of Gabby's art and my imagination.

Gabby rose from her chair and approached me. Despite a bothersome and unwavering nuisance known as the Atlantic Ocean, permitting only odd-hour telephone calls, Gabby and I developed a rare symbiosis. We each sensed it the first time we spoke, and thereafter it flowered but was never underscored; perhaps it is the sort of matter better left alone to enjoy instead of muddling with analysis. Anyway, it was for that reason that I hesitated to come to England. Seeing one another, spending time together in the flesh, could have put the kiss of death upon something I had placed a high premium. I had worried for nothing.

The sketchpad, I noticed, found its way back on the table. I'm not sure exactly how it got there: did Gabby manage to wrestle it away from me, or had I set it down myself? Whatever, the maneuver was lost in the gathering haze overwhelming the room's ether; the atmospheric shift seemed to coincide with Gabby rising from her chair; I could visualize the air, its hypnotic capacities, or so I imagined. What followed my noticing the sketchpad was Gabby's arms slithering around me; I found myself swathed in an embrace. What, if anything, hastened her initiative? Throughout the day, I pondered the sensation of a first kiss, imagined its delight, and the heights to which we would soar. But there loomed a competing variable or collaborative brainchild: in it, we immersed ourselves—the Camden Lock killer and his jaded alcoholic pursuer—thus, instead of behaving like aspiring lovers, we acted more as children embarking on a far-flung adventure who forgot what time they were told to come home for dinner.

No longer would I need to imagine the thrill of our first kiss, the joys of its sensations: I felt it, lived it, and thereafter would delight in its lingering effects. Indeed, with a single touching of our lips, Gabby and I were launched beyond a threshold into rarefied air—a place where we were no longer "the novelist and his muse" but the romantic aspirants we secretly dreamed of becoming. Our lips parted. Gabby gazed up at me. Her head tilted and eyes went aflutter—a coalescence of feminine charm that rendered me delightfully weakened. We were never at a loss for words, but all we could manage, immersed in a moment lush with reverie, was to stare at one another, intoxicated and bleary-eyed. It was Gabby who finally spoke.

"I want more, Mitch, so much more." Her breathy words floated upward in wistful puffs of air that caressed my chin. She buried her head in my chest as though no place else on earth was more reassuring. It was then that I realized "much more" would not come until later. I further realized it was for my benefit. I had lost hours flying, trudged all over London, endured three hours of real-life Harold and Jane, and had an eye-opening experience at Doc Watson's. Despite the bliss of being held in Gabby's thrall, I was quite done in; jet lag and exhaustion had crept into my legs; I was running on fumes, near-delirious, and wilting right before Gabby's eyes.

"We shall have a lovely day tomorrow, Mitch," she intoned. "I just know that you will be a hit with my book club." The tips of her fingers slid down from my face. I caught them and brought them to my mouth. "Goodnight," I whispered.

The loveliness of Gabby Norwich: it was the only thought I wanted to take to my bed as exhaustion finished overtaking me, and yet I could not keep my mind from drifting to my alcoholic detective who, while in pursuit of a phantom known as The Camden Lock killer, himself had fallen under some suspicion.

Joe poured Granville Tovey's coffee, just as he had on five-thousand mornings past. Twenty-four inches—twenty-four inches of counter space was all that separated these two men who had more conversations than they could begin to count, less remember, and yet their respective lives took place in vastly different universes. Joe leaned over the two-foot barrier, a black hole that had kept their universes from colliding. "Did you read the paper this morning, Gran?" he asked.

"Not a word," the detective's low, cynical rumble came. "I could well imagine, though, the claptrap that made it into print."

"They can't really like you for the Harold Halsbury killing, can they?"

"The law? Not a chance! But a homicide detective whose wife left him for a man just fished from a canal with his prick clipped off and shoved into his mouth is a journalistic version of a wet dream." Granville Tovey sipped from his cup, then cleared his throat. "Unfortunately, Joe, it's not law enforcement that's in a position to shape public opinion." The detective smiled paradoxically, adding, "I have every confidence the court of public opinion would have me tried, convicted, and hanged in the square by four o'clock this afternoon. And so it goes."

"I get it, Gran; their job is to sell newspapers, but anyone capable of critical thinking has to realize this is tabloid journalism with a painfully frivolous agenda." Joe rattled the newspaper, then tossed it aside as one would when owning the notion news was seldom worth the paper upon which it got printed.

"It's not what they know in their logical minds, Joe—logic is dull, humdrum—it's what they allow themselves to believe, and if a story is just plausible enough and can stir excitement into their humdrum little lives…." The detective let loose an anguished sigh. "But Hellickson is right; a serial killer doesn't change his M.O. in the middle of a killing spree, so it makes sense to consider that Harold Halsbury's murderer was someone other than The Camden Lock Killer."

"For example, a certain soon-to-be ex-husband?" Joe interjected.

"That would be *one* place to start. And speaking of Hellickson," the detective continued, "the poor bastard ended up with shit detail yesterday. Actually, he volunteered, which took Barnwell, Thatcher, and yours truly off the hook." Granville Tovey raised his cup and winked at his friend.

"Oh, I get it, Gran; poor Hellickson delivered the "good news" to the soon-to-be-former Mrs. Tovey because someone else was too chicken shit."

"I'd swim in me own piss before I'd deliver that sort of news to Jane. But all kidding aside," the detective continued, "I never caught a case quite like this one. And I'm not too proud to admit: that this madman has gotten close enough to me to know that my wife left me and for whom is a bit unsettling. And I can't wait until Jane puts two and two together and finds out her lover was nothing more than the collateral damage of a killer playing mind games with her estranged husband. Won't that be a day to look forward to?"

"Don't mean to put a damper on a chilly morning," Joe added, "but if Jane reads the paper, chances are, she's already done the arithmetic." Detective Tovey gulped his last sip and rose from his stool. Joe went reaching for his arm. "Gran, a minute ago, you mentioned the killer was in the *middle* of a spree."

"We have no leads, Joe. So, unless our killer conveniently puts in for retirement, there'll be more bodies." Thus far, the body count has reached six. Neither Joe nor the detective could imagine the hysteria that would sweep through the city were that number to double, less the level of pressure levied upon law enforcement.

****

I never heard Nina come through the door. Those stunning heels that drew my eyes to the stage floor, had they intended to announce their arrival like the night before, they went unnoticed; either I had drifted off to a satisfying oblivion, or, tonight, Nina thoughtfully removed her shoes. Whichever, I also failed to hear anyone, be it Nina or Gabby, enter my bedroom but sensed I was no longer alone. Concerning my intuition, it was with ambiguity, not keenness, that it received due appreciation. And since I was semi-conscious, the sensation was akin to a blissful dream, or what I hoped would evolve as such. *Gabby, my dear, sweet Gabby, you have come to me in dreams.* But was I dreaming? Was it a dream that someone peeled off my blanket, and with feline-like stealth, placed themselves in bed alongside me? *I want more, Mitch, so much more* was what Gabby had longingly intoned, but had I summoned my delightfully plump, round-faced angel or her long lethal sister? The answer? I had beckoned neither: I may have been asleep but was not dreaming.

I was lying on my side when I felt the warmth of a body alongside mine. I called out Gabby's name, but my voice, as is common in dreams, either failed to project or was barely audible. "Shhh," was the sound I heard the bold intruder make. I obeyed. At first, albeit faintly, I could feel breathing against my throat; it moved and trailed downward; gentle puffs of air were warm against my chest, then my stomach. I began to swell, was tingling, and my breathing quickened. Next, I felt my pelvis nuzzled delicately by a nose and soft cheek and met this nuzzling with gentle thrusts. It was all at once delightful, maddening, and bizarre, as this novel, from which there was no escape, was introducing yet another twist.

After sharing our first kiss, Gabby and I had said our goodnights; it crowned a lovely day, but who's to say she did not feel a spark—an irresistible flicker of lust that launched her from her bed? Or was this the work of the she-devil herself? Whichever, I was flying blind while hungrily devoured by an artist whose performance, in my experience, was unparalleled. How I desired to reach down and feel the tufty hair of my little round-faced angel. But what if my fingertips found themselves mingling among long silky strands; it would confirm that my first overseas blowjob was coming by way of someone with whom I was anatomically accordant. Inside I cried: *Let it be Gabby; please, let it be Gabby!* Yet was it *this* what I wanted for our first encounter? I resisted a reach, deciding it was best to fly blind instead of disturbing the potent sensations darting through me like electrical impulses. Indeed, it was only to honor selfish purposes that I would grant my middle-of-the-night intruder the anonymity they seemed to desire. Whoever it was that had me so wickedly engaged, I would learn in due course, or so I imagined. Dear sweet Gabby, of course, it must be you. Mustn't it? The next voice in my head belonged to Molly: from across the ocean—yet again—she emerged and warned me of those *wicked Norwich sisters*.

Despite my praying for Gabby and hearing Molly, it was Doc Watson's headliner whom I failed to pry from my thoughts, as she proved steadfast in her unwillingness to relinquish her place in the forefront of my mind; it was the vision of Nina on stage that became the prevailing image when keeping closed my eyes: the titillating manner she cradled her microphone before bringing it to her mouth, every move and tilt of her head that sent her lovely mane falling to one side or another, every kind of expertly executed gradation—it was all meant to leave men a tortured wreck; but what truly validated Nina Linette was not her possessing the sort of beauty that made men want to fall to their knees and surrender; it was the soulful and satiny voice launched from her mouth—a haunting voice echoing a vestige of sorrow from the road an unforgiving world had forced her to travel.

Everywhere, I was aflame: the burn was glorious; it crept upward into my neck and head, rising in measures until, like a rumbling boil, it engulfed me in totality and pushed me nearer and nearer to the threshold of inevitability, else a transcendental and pinnacle moment when I would burst forth like a river whose dam has broken. I was constricting: tighter and tighter, my fibers were coiling; soon, they would snap and unravel. *Gabby, dear Gabby, it must be you.* I heard a soft moan from whoever it was, welcoming an epic release of unimaginable pleasure. When it was over, I lay there quivering, unable to make a sound. It was more shock than afterglow I was experiencing, and while imprisoned in its throes, my intruder made a clean getaway—not even a silhouette in the doorway had I to glimpse. The intruder came, conquered, and vanished like a puff of air. I rolled on my back and stared upward into the darkness. There was only one thought—one bemusing, bizarre, and somewhat jarring notion racing around my head: Nina had just contributed an entry, if not an entire chapter, to her life's account. Nothing like blowing your biographer. I suppose it was Nina's idea of a down payment.

At eight o'clock in the morning, there came three taps on my bedroom door. "Mitch, are you awake?" a voice called.

It was Gabby. So lovely, refreshed, and lilting was her voice; it announced to me that a new day had arrived, and if she wielded even the slightest bit of influence, it was to be a splendid one.

The morning saw me whisked away to Ebenezer's, a nearby coffee café in Bloomsbury. So light of heart was Gabby as we went about our merry way—her presence was akin to a feather in a summer breeze; if she didn't float away, I was sure she would begin skipping. Celebratory would best describe her morning demeanor: but what was she celebrating? A new day? Our first kiss? Or the devil himself, having manifested within her in the middle of the night?

"You slept well, Mitch?" It was a typically polite question a hostess asks a house guest, but thoughtful nonetheless.

"I slept well at first, again later, but, in between, I had the most peculiar dream; perhaps you could help me to remember it?"

"I don't see where I could be much help to you there; perhaps it was a racy dream?" She latched onto my arm. On her face formed a mischievous grin; she seemed to welcome racy thoughts. I was inclined to call out, *Ah-ha! It was you!* but instead asked, "You don't, by any chance, sleepwalk, do you?"

"I don't believe so; why?"

"No reason," I lied, "I just thought maybe you had."

"I wouldn't rule it out entirely; anything is possible, but if I were Bloomsbury's version of Ted Truman, I'm sure Nina would have told me by now." Then she added a rather ponderous "Mmm." I could see her wheels turning; after coming to an abrupt stop, she took a firm hold of my hands. "Mitch, that's it; your peculiar dream: You must have gone to sleep with *Somnambula*, our first kiss, and *The Case of the Camden Lock Killer* all on your mind, and somehow they weaved themselves into one fantastical dream which saw me sleepwalk to Camden Lock, commit murder, toss the victim in the canal, and arrive home before daybreak."

The Bohemian

I searched Gabby's face. She did not appear even the slightest bit farcical, explaining why I suspected she had abandoned her bed in the middle of the night. Thus, it left me with the unsettling conclusion that Nina, currently tending to her beauty sleep, had paid me yet another visit.

We chose the alfresco section of Ebenezer's, which was the sidewalk. Before long, we were presented with two dark roasts—I learned that Gabby is a great appreciator of what she describes as "take no prisoners" coffee—and two blueberry scones.

"Mitch, we got so involved in my drawings and other matters..." Her eyes blissfully went aflutter at the mention of *other matters*, "...I forgot to ask what you thought of Nina's performance."

Given the latest turn of events, "performance" seemed a peculiar choice of word and caused an involuntary chortle on my part, which Gabby either failed to notice or chose to ignore. "I'm afraid that was my fault; it should have been the first thing I told you last night, but once I discovered your drawings, everything else fled from my head."

"Well, don't keep me in suspense," Gabby pleaded.

I took a moment to sip my coffee. During this time, I tried to determine how best to explain what it meant to watch Nina Linette perform without revealing that she was the most sexually potent creature with whom I ever acquainted myself. "On the merit of her voice alone, I'm confident she'll go far," I began. "Although her true gift is how she uses her voice." Upon the latter, Gabby's ears picked up. "Not to be crude," I added, "watching Nina perform is similar to receiving a lap dance at a strip club, not that I have experience in such matters. That is to say: she can take the whole—meaning the audience—and reduce it to as many slices as required; thus, everyone in the room feels she is singing just for them. It's a rare quality, for sure. On stage, your sister is a true artist." I was inclined to add that Nina's artistic endeavors extended well beyond the stage but thought better of it. Gabby was pleased that I had spoken so glowingly of Nina; my opinion, for she saw me as an artist of sorts, seemed to carry quite a bit of weight. With that being the case, I took the liberty of taking the subject of Nina beyond her ability to hold captive an audience.

"Nina is lonely, Gabby—terribly lonely." I reached across the table and took hold of Gabby's hands. "Perhaps she would feel less lonely, less tortured if she decided to live her life... *differently*?" I assumed using the term "differently" rather than "as a man" would resonate with more tact and seem less jarring. I was wrong on both counts; thus, Gabby fell against the back of her chair; the abruptness with which she fell caused her hands to rip free from my grip.

"I'm sorry, Mitch," she began. "I was unaware Nina, so soon, had intended to reveal herself to you." Last night, the nearness of Nina triggered an ephemeral yet affecting moment that saw me, like David, tiptoeing through a lion's den. I decided it wise not to rehash it; I saw no point. Gabby lurched forward in her chair and ensnared my hands. "Mitch," she whispered, "we're not talking about a drag queen— someone who can simply change her clothes and play another part— Nina is more woman than any woman I have ever known, present company included. Most women would kill to possess her beauty and feminine charms."

"But that's precisely my point: even a gay man possessing the keenest gaydar would never view Nina as a viable love interest. And where heterosexual men are concerned, she is—I'll use her term of choice— 'disqualified.' So where does that leave her?"

"It's more complicated than that, Mitch." Gabby's tenor and downcast eyes led me to understand that it was a long story but one I would learn in due course. "No doubt," I replied, before confessing, "There's also a minor twist to the story: I've agreed to become Nina's biographer."

"Come again?" Gabby's sneer was more than enough indication that she was not amused.

"I'm going to write Nina's story." I nearly cringed.

"That's your idea of a *minor* twist?" Gabby protested. "What about *The Case of the Camden Lock Killer*? Please, Mitch, tell me you don't intend to shelve our brainchild?"

The notion I could have both Norwich sisters competing over me was titillating until I imagined that Harold Halsbury's body would not be the only one fished from a canal. I assured Gabby that our novel would not get placed on the back burner and that Nina's story was a subject that would get worked on intermittently over many years. Still, I couldn't blame Gabby for her reaction; we were really on to something with *The Case of the Camden Lock Killer*; our excitement for the project ran parallel, and neither of us could wait to get all the ideas in our heads onto paper. But first things first: we had a book talk to get through; the deranged Davey Coyle and psychologically damaged Ted

Truman were each on tap this afternoon. Regarding my novels: I had remained mainly behind the scenes, as they say. Today would be the first instance I stepped out in front of my work, making myself fully visible and accessible, and, if I don't say so myself, it all went rather swimmingly. Moreover, I also did a plausible job, I believe, acting like I met real-life Harold and Jane for the first time.

Conversely, real-life Harold and Jane flubbed the charade miserably. When introduced, Jane giggled inanely, and Harold worked in a half-dozen of what he believed were cryptic but painfully obvious winks. Afterward, the two celebrated their agreement over the thrill of meeting their favorite novelist. Then it occurred to me that real-life Harold and Jane were an adult human version of Pixie and Dixie—a Hanna and Barbera cartoon mouse tandem from the 1960s, who appeared in every scene together and forever were echoing each other's sentiments. So they meandered about the room, joined at the elbow, did real-life Harold and Jane, appearing as though nothing short of complicated surgery could sever them. I managed to catch Gabby's eye, and she was intuitive to my prevailing thought, which was as follows: Harold and Jane both should fall victim to The Camden Lock Killer, and the more gruesome their murders, the better.

****

It was a few ticks to the tardy side of when the talk was slated to begin when Nina made her appearance. Several times, Gabby's nervous eyes had found one of the three clocks displayed in plain sight. She tried to conceal her mounting preoccupation, but it was becoming apparent. "Appearance," however, in this instance, must be considered a curious term, as Nina remained standing behind all others in attendance. I was standing in an archway dividing two rooms. Everyone was seated in front of me; some were on plush pieces of furniture; many were on bifold chairs arranged in arced and staggered rows; altogether, twenty-eight people came to ask questions, hear me blather, or both. After making yet another stealthy entrance, Nina stood behind the last row of chairs. Her luxurious mane was gathered prettily in a side ponytail and hung in front of her left shoulder; a silky lock was purposely let out to contour her face and graze her chin gracefully. She wore dark glasses, sported dark-colored clothes, and would have given anyone the impression she was a celebrity trying to avoid recognition. She flashed a devilish smirk meant for me, which I alone noticed, and she delivered it with a head tilt, exuding assertiveness that bordered on threatening.

Indeed, if you are in a room, Nina Linette, you are its most compelling figure. *How are we doing up there, Mitch; having a good day, are we? I should think nothing could bring you down after your impromptu wee hours of the morning experience.* Nina's thoughts could not have been more apparent had she shouted them. Somehow, I kept my poise and avoid stutters featuring painful pauses with inane gestures. Nina, in turn, nodded to acknowledge what we both viewed, given the circumstances, as more than a modest achievement. But then I noticed something peculiar develop: During what had evolved into a well-participated and engaging dialogue concerning the complexities of Davey Coyle, I noticed that Nina became restless, even agitated. So carefully modeled she was, in all her splendid elegance, it was unimaginable that anything could cause her to unravel. I could not claim to know Nina well, but well enough to know that her performances were not relegated to the stage. Nina Linette was no longer Bobbie Norwich's dominant and more intriguing persona; it was her only persona, yet something triggered her to reveal vulnerability—to expose a hidden crack in her armor. One among the modest crowd remarked that Davey Coyle would have become a serial killer regardless—that his parents perishing in an automobile accident, thus leaving him to get passed around from age five, merely hastened the process. True or false, I thought it was an astute observation and what seemed to spark the sudden change in Nina's demeanor. On some level, did Nina feel a connection with Davey Coyle; did *Funhouse resonate as* more than a piece of fiction—a psychological thriller that managed to fill three hundred pages?

She exited through the door with nowhere near the stealth she had entered. Posed on the walkway leading to the door, she hoped a cigarette would help compose her. With Nina outside yet still visible, not diverting my attention became more of an effort than it had in the moments following her silky entrance. However, I managed to carry on, but I was less than sure to what effectiveness. For the moment, the twenty-eight folks who remained seated seemed well engaged, though their robust exchanges failed to overwhelm my resolute notion that there was an aspect to *Funhouse* that struck something deep within Nina. But what? My prevailing thought as I commanded a room or oversaw a room essentially commanding itself: Nina Linette was a fascinating subject beyond her sexual complexities and doubtless would prove a biographer's dream.

The Bohemian

When Nina reentered the room, she did so not as a phantom or femme fatale delighting in her facility to create a stir but as someone who came to participate in a book talk. She even located and used the seat set aside for her designation, and this act of simplicity served to humanize her and snuff out what I had perceived as an ever-present threat. It was 1:30 in the afternoon; only fourteen hours had passed since I said goodnight to Nina in the third-floor lounge of Doc Watson's. Our first and only actual meeting lasted all of twenty minutes, yet prevailing was the peculiar sensibility I knew her more intimately than I had known anyone. Perhaps that she revealed herself so soon into our relationship brought forth this odd perception—or was it more a matter of being added to what I alleged were the "trusted and privileged few" granted a peek into the secret world of Nina Linette? There was, of course, a third option: Simply put, I could not stop myself from thinking of Nina, and this wave of constancy fed my mind, thus triggering all sorts of leaps and conclusions not necessarily in accord with the essence of her character. There's a scientific term for this condition: it's called *getting under one's skin*.

I did my best to see that Davey Coyle and Ted Truman received equal attention; however, it was the latter who sparked a more robust debate: half the room theorized it was his wife's murder that triggered a psychotic break and subsequent killing spree. Thus, he was worthy of some sympathy; the other half subscribed to the theory Ted Truman was unbalanced; therefore, had his wife's murder not occurred, another episode of similar or lesser proportion would have engendered a break and subsequent spree.

At the end of the talk, I signed fifty-six books, including the four owned by real-life Harold and Jane. I smiled somewhat ironically at Jane when handing back her books. She mistook my smile for one of warmth and friendship when, in fact, I decided right then and there to spare her life. The Camden Lock killer already made his point with Detective Tovey by killing poor Harold; it now occurred to me that killing Jane would be redundant. Besides, Jane would remain much more compelling to the story as a woman estranged from an alcoholic detective, minus a lover, and dangling in the world a fearful soul than she would have been as victim number seven.

"Congratulations, Jane; you get to live," I said before walking away. The perplexing look that passed between the "real-life" couple was priceless. Gabby and I shared a good chuckle over it while skimming through our menus at Lord John Russell Pub. When Gabby suggested the preferred haunt, we assumed Nina would leap to make it a three-some, but following the book talk came a resurgence of her stage persona—Nina Linette, mysterious femme fatale extraordinaire—and off she ran to an undisclosed destination. Gabby did not question Nina but, after kissing her on the cheek, warned, "Be careful." I found Gabby's cautionary tone curious. It was hardly typical of advice one would offer in passing, nor was it the sort of instruction a parent issues a child recently deemed worthy of having their boundaries extended; there was an unmistakable note of misgiving in Gabby's tone. I was inclined to question her on the matter but decided it best to wait until we separated from what was a familiar crowd with curious ears. By the time we arrived at Lord John Russell, asking was no longer necessary: with a novelist's acuity, I became enlightened that Nina, as she had many times in the past but to no avail, had gone in search of the proverbial needle in a haystack. In other words, she was hoping to encounter the one heterosexual male in a million hot for an experience and sensitive enough to overlook her one fatal flaw—throughout the experience, she could pretend she was genuinely cared for and appreciated—or unearth a bisexual male agreeable to unparalleled feminine charm with an unfortunate touch of masculinity together in one package. It was no wonder Gabby issued a stern warning: Should Nina, as they say, bark up the wrong tree—often, such trees were in the less desirable sections of town (not just London but any town)—the result could prove disastrous. Poor Nina: out there all alone in the world, hoping that there existed a gateway through which she might connect with another human soul despite her beauty and uniqueness. I could only hope.

With a sudden burst, I felt the full force of Gabby's presence; she snatched my menu, tossed it aside, lunged across the table, and devoured my mouth. It was all at once stirring and jarring, and what triggered this action was my staring blankly too long at a menu.

"Back from our little trip, are we?"

"Quite," I said, eyes widened and face flushed from being made an hors d'oeuvre.

"Good," said Gabby, "because now we must decide what to do about Jane and Melissa."

"Jane and Melissa?"

"Why, Granville Tovey's estranged wife and daughter, of course. Surely, Mitch, you haven't forgotten the names of our characters?"

Leave it to Gabby to dive in headfirst just minutes after our book talk.

Detective Tovey returned home after yet another day of reviewing forensic evidence and interviewing Camden Lock merchants, to meager results, only to find his wife and daughter—their combined estrangement equaled eighteen months—in his living room. First, he assumed each was there to issue separate grievances but thought it wise to proceed with the appearance of solidarity. Next, he expected unification over concern for a single matter which one would voice while the other provided moral support. Whichever the case, the detective had a good sense he was about to get double-teamed. Yet he could not say it displeased him to arrive home and find Jane and Melissa waiting for him. They were both, especially following the events of the day, a pleasure to look at, and aside from their appeal, it was a welcomed change to walk through the door and get greeted by something other than what four lonely walls had provided, even if that something were to prove hostile.

Granville Tovey was a bit bleary-eyed, and his appearance, for which he readily apologized, was quite ruffled. His apology was more for Melissa's benefit—why should Jane have any concern about his appearance? —as the detective assumed that his daughter, their deteriorating relationship notwithstanding, would not wish to see her father "go to pot" as they say. The detective went for his handkerchief and wiped his eyes, hoping it might help him appear more alert if not having restored him to the glow of someone far less burdened. Despite the effort, he appeared as out of sorts as might a woman whose mother-in-law paid her an impromptu visit when the house was in a state of chaos. The detective's eyes traveled past the archway of the parlor into the dining room and rested at a table. Atop the table were several sheets of paper and copies of newspaper clippings that made up the case files of Jack the Ripper and Henry Howard Holmes. The Ripper file was more a pastime or part-time obsession—aside from the weapon of choice, Tovey saw no relevant connection between The Camden Lock Killer and his infamous renowned predecessor—thus, it was the H.H. Holmes file that garnered the lion's share of his attention. Like the Camden Lock Killer, the Holmes murders were relegated to a specific location and, more specifically, a hotel that the locals dubbed "The Castle," which Holmes supposedly had built as a hostelry to accommodate those expected to flock to Chicago in 1893 to attend the World's Fair. Detective Tovey had considered the similarity in dynamic and dimension between a marketplace and an area designated for a fair. The ground floor of the hotel was reserved for commercial space. The rest was a labyrinth of rooms, with doorways opening to brick walls, odd-angled hallways, and staircases leading nowhere. Other quirks made it possible for a killer to isolate his victims; trap doors and chutes leading to the cellar made the disposal of bodies a less laborious task. But what kept Granville Tovey twisting, fretting, and agonizing to all hours of the night was not Holmes's killing ground but the man himself. What would drive someone born into privilege, who would one day become a medical student at the University of Michigan, to become first a con artist, then a bigamist, and ultimately a serial killer? The detective alleged the succession as inconceivable leaps, but his instincts were screaming that Mr. Holmes and The Camden Lock Killer had similar profiles.

After the detective's eyes traveled to where they rested in the dining room, he winced. The reason was not for the well-littered tabletop but the bottle of scotch three-quarters of the way empty standing next to one that had been relieved of all its contents. Scattered about the bottles were four empty glasses recently put to use. The detective tried to resist a glance in Jane's direction, as he was sure to see the estranged and soon-to-be-former Mrs. Tovey looking down her nose as if to say, *I see things haven't changed all that much, have they, Gran?* Nevertheless, he was unable to resist: perhaps he was looking for a rebuke, any sign that Jane still cared, but, to his surprise, what he anticipated, was not what he received: Jane Tovey appeared wholly unconcerned over the state of what was once her dining room turned into an area where an overtaxed and riddled detective drinks himself into a nightly stupor. Instead, evident in her mien was a woman racked with grief and concern: grief over having lost a man whom she cared for and became, in trying times, a haven; concern for her safety and her daughter's safety.

The world changed, and it had changed such that, without shame, less the need for humility, Jane Tovey found herself running toward the very man from whom she tried to escape, who for years

The Bohemian

offered little else than misery but the one man she knew was best suited to keep Melissa and her safe. The craggy detective did not dare bargain with fear to curry favor but comported himself graciously over being sought out and trusted.

"I'm sorry, Jane," the detective said. "I truly am sorry for Harold and that I failed to solve this case before it hit so close to home."

Jane was seated on a Queen Anne chair positioned at a forty-five-degree angle to an end table and sofa. The sofa and table lined a wall featuring a depiction of The Last Supper. The chair was facing the front door. How many nights over the past thirty years had she sat in that very chair and read popular fiction by the light of the same lamp while awaiting her detective's return? And how many nights over the same span had Granville Tovey shed his coat and hat and largely ignored his bride after offering a feeble greeting? The detective stood in the middle of the parlor with the weight of thirty years of mistakes baring down upon his shoulders; he saw them all at once—they were glaring and loud, these revealings of his failures. He made it across the room, where the wealth of that weight caused him to sag to one knee. He extended a hand to Jane, the other to Melissa, who was seated at the end of the sofa. Both women unhesitatingly reached for the craggy detective.

"Jane, this madman killed Harold, so I would come under suspicion."

"Are you?" Melissa interjected.

"Nowhere that it truly matters, so don't allow gossip journalism to bother you any—not that it's worth fretting over." The detective went on to theorize: "I'm guessing that Harold wasn't anywhere near Camden Lock, which means the killer ventured out beyond his killing grounds, or comfort area, which also means he went to an awful lot of trouble to prove his point, that he was able to get close enough to *me* to learn things about *us* without me knowing it. It isn't likely he'll risk that sort of boldness and effort again; he'll return to his pattern." The detective sighed before adding, "Nevertheless, I would have a much greater peace of mind while on the job if the two of you were under one roof; if nothing else, it would allow me to put a uniform on the house."

Jane Tovey's head inadvertently jerked such that her eyes fell upon the disarray on the dining room table in plain view. Still, she decided that a few empty glasses were hardly worth getting into a twist over, especially when juxtaposed with a deranged killer loose in London generating hysteria. Jane could only imagine the pressure, never mind the danger the detective was up against. It was all too sobering; thus, just as the craggy detective had experienced the weight of numerous failures, raining down upon Jane Tovey was an avalanche of similar proportion. In other words, no one put a gun to her head and forced her to marry an aspiring homicide detective; such a position is seldom enviable. Nevertheless, presently, a wife and daughter, estranged from a husband and father, welcomed a sense of being united.

"We'll do whatever you believe is best, Gran," Jane Tovey resolutely stated. On the subject of their safety, she had faith in his judgment.

Gabby and I raced home from Lord John Russell Pub and began pounding out page after page of *The Case of the Camden Lock Killer*. First, I typed while she remained at my side, thinking out loud, asking poignant questions, and calling all sorts of angles and possibilities to my attention. Then she typed while I dictated. We went back and forth, producing sheet after sheet from the late afternoon until two in the morning. During what amounted to nine hours of nonstop work, we managed to polish off what represented her meager supply of wine: three bottles of chardonnay. We conked out right where we were sitting.

Dead to the world and disheveled was how Nina discovered us when she arrived home, at whatever hour she came through the door. The only evidence that Nina had bothered to come home was the heels left thoughtfully by the doorway; Gabby breathed a sigh of relief when discovering them in the morning. "Usually, Nina leaves them just outside her bedroom door," Gabby told me. "It's her way of letting me know she made it home safely; that way, she doesn't have to disturb me in the middle of the night, nor need I disturb her beauty sleep come morning. Mitch," she deemed it necessary to add, "she is, after all, my younger sister by three years, and I still feel it's my job to look after her."

"Of course," I acknowledged. I did not deem it necessary to add further—Nina's rank in the Norwich matriarchy aside—that her uniqueness and complexities alone make her someone worthy of looking after.

Once again, it was off to Ebenezer's Café for dark roast coffee and scones. The coffee took care of any lingering cobwebs in our heads put there from nine hours of nonstop writing and wine sipping; the scones filled the hole in our tummies. Next, it was off to Camden Lock Market with our notepads and pencils. Combing our way through the marketplace kept the story more than fresh but alive; it also provided the initiative with a remarkable sense of authenticity: *This was where the killer struck, this was who he killed, and this was where baffled, frustrated detectives crouched around a victim.* Gabby immersed herself in the killer's mind; I took on the persona of Detective Tovey. Before long, we expanded our roles: Gabby played both Jane and Melissa Tovey; I played the chain-smoking Detective Hellickson and the gruff Lieutenant Van Pelt. Granville Tovey, Joe—the craggy detective's coffee-pouring confidant—Jane and Melissa Tovey, Detective Hellickson, and Lieutenant Van Pelt: I had confidence in the core characters' strength and the story's vitality. I also came up with Blane Stewart, the pesky reporter who was always snooping about and whose mere appearance would cause the craggy senior detective to grumble and wheeze. Only one detail remained: how to catch the killer or how the killer would make the fatal misstep that would lead to his apprehending. However, a third option remained: the murders would simply stop, and The Camden Lock Killer would go on to enjoy similar phantom-like infamy that had "The Ripper" himself. Gabby and I both thought the notion was irresistible but, ultimately, decided that current times require us to deliver a modern ending, which means the killer must get caught; the reader must not be forced to suffer an unsatisfying ending.

Again, we lunched at Lord John Russell Pub, then it was back to the grindstone, aided with chardonnay we purchased for the occasion and plenty of enthusiasm for the task. On the following morning, I woke before Gabby and penned a letter to Molly:

Dear cousin,

In the event you've wasted any worry, allow me to assure you thus far, I have been enjoying a most delightful stay in London. My take on the city is as follows: What's not to like? And here's the best part: I'm already knee-deep into my next novel; I call it The Case of the Camden Lock Killer, and I'm confident it will be my best effort yet! Since the story takes place here in London, for the sake of authenticity, I have decided to remain overseas much longer than anticipated. Luckily for me, those lovely Norwich sisters have agreed to put me up for the summer and are allowing me to use their domicile as a workplace. Awfully considerate, wouldn't you agree? So, as it shall come to pass, I'm afraid I won't return to the States until mid-August. Meanwhile, I shall keep you enlightened concerning how this latest effort is progressing. I wish you the loveliest of summers, my dearest cousin, and, make no mistake, Molly, you are my dearest.

Love, Mitch

How was that for performative bullshit? Impressive, if I don't say so myself. And I could well imagine Molly's reaction: *She's a real vixen that Gabby Norwich; like a black widow spider, she spins her web, and you moronic Morningstar men simply cannot help yourselves from getting caught.* Afterward, she'll grumble that this time she means it when she claims to be through trying to talk sense into people, then crumple up my letter and deposit it into a handy receptacle. Poor Molly.

Save for two Sundays spent driving out to the charming towns that make up the Cotswolds (the English Countryside), Gabby and I spent all our days working; we were on the mother of all rolls and didn't want anything to derail our momentum. Though one Friday night in mid-July, having grown cross-eyed, weary, and admittedly oversaturated, I told Gabby that I needed to cut away and used the time to escape to Doc Watson's for a drink and to sit in on Nina's first set. She noticed me in the crowd and winked my way when singing the bluesy and somewhat mysterious *Mr. Guder.* Then, like before, she stole up on me from behind when her set had finished. I set aside my drink for the sake of an embrace, and while in my arms, Nina used the time to whisper, "I appreciate what you and Gabby are doing, Mitch; really, I do. You have created this alternative universe where, from sunup to sundown, the two of you joyfully exist while holding at bay anything that might complicate matters. But, Mitch, dear, it's already the middle of July; are you really going to get on that plane come mid-August, not having fucked my sister? I understand you have a life waiting for you back in the States and that Gabby feels a responsibility to look after me, but I'm a big girl, Mitch, and you shouldn't worry about starting up anything for fear next month it must end because it simply is not the case." Nina tightened her embrace, then devoured me with a kiss. "It's time you complicated matters, Mitch Morningstar."

And so off I went, with the taste of Nina lingering in my mouth, well-motivated and inspired to complicate matters. Nina's biography aside, I was growing keen on the notion that she wanted me for Gabby so I would remain in her orbit. Her vixenlike motives notwithstanding, I entered Gabby's bedroom as stealthily as Nina had entered mine. Gently, I kissed Gabby from a peaceful slumber to an amorous reality. Her bedroom was where I would spend the remainder of my London nights. Come the morning, when the sun broke through the window, I noticed Gabby's sketchpad was resting on her nightstand. Without disturbing her, I reached across her still restful form and took hold of it. The pad was open to the place where she had been working. The illustration, as best I could tell, appeared complete. I sat up to better examine it and saw a most thoughtful and disturbed Granville Tovey down on one knee. Across from him, also on a knee, was an equally pensive, disturbed, chain-smoking Detective Hellickson. They were flanking the corpse of the recently slain Harold Halsbury minutes after his body got fished from the canal. Impressions of onlookers stood clustered nearby; some were positioned on a stone footbridge that spanned the canal.

"The word on the street is the killer struck again," Joe muttered as he poured out a cup of coffee.

"Late last night," came the low rumbling voice of the weary senior detective. "Got the call at one in the morning: a young man, all of twenty-three, was found stabbed to death under the Camden Lock overpass. Two swift and decisive blows did the trick—about the time it takes to light a cigarette—and the poor bastard was dead before he could make a sound. I never came across anything like it; he materializes from out of nowhere then disappears without a trace."

"That makes it eight," said Joe.

"Eight, and he's getting more proficient with each kill. His first victim, you might remember, was a massacre—thirteen stab wounds in all. We imagined he was a psychopathic butcher with two left hands; nine of the wounds—the medical examiner ruled—were unnecessary and precisely why his first victim was declared a crime of passion. It wasn't until a third body was found within a particular boundary that we were certain of dealing with a serial. And *my*, how our man has evolved! Thirteen plunges of a blade down to two, and I have a suspicion that I'm about to find out that the second wound was only for good measure. But I have a theory, Joe, that our thrill killer may have a goal after all."

Tovey strolled into the precinct and laid out for Hellickson and Van Pelt all that he had collected on the case file of H.H. Holmes.

"So, you think our man could be a medical student?" Van Pelt did not seem all too convinced of this possibility.

"Not necessarily," said Tovey.

"Then what?" Hellickson displayed a lack of patience, which the senior detective chose to ignore.

From the throat of Granville Tovey rumbled a noise typical of a large-chested man of a certain age. "Regarding our man's intelligence, I believe him to be exceptional. What's more, it's also possible he has a specific talent and once had a lofty goal. Was his ambition to become a surgeon? Perhaps. But, on the other hand, it's just as likely he's a violinist whose lifetime dream was to play for the philharmonic. The point is that somewhere along the way, a door slammed in his face, and all he had left in this world was a broken dream. Still, we're looking at a man with a very high opinion of himself—a man who believes he's more intelligent than ninety-nine percent of the population and resents deeply that so great a portion of that percentile manages to lead lives richer and happier than his. Indeed, gentleman, our man is filled with resentment—unparalleled resentment. Worse, he doesn't look in the mirror and see failure but a man the world has betrayed, and it drives him to kill all those he deems undeserving."

"Ninety-nine percent is quite a lofty ambition," remarked Hellickson. "A might size loftier than a chair at the philharmonic if one may consider killing an ambition."

"Our man isn't thinking in terms of exact numbers—his goal isn't *that* specific. Instead, I believe what we have here is a string of impulse killings. For example, the killer spots a man who's unable to finish a thought without the benefit of profanity, then notices that he's wearing a pair of shoes that, for the killer, costs a week's wages. Another example would be a man found to be ill-mannered emerging from an automobile that, for the killer, costs a year's wages. How is it that such uncultured people possess such privilege? That, I believe, is a burning question that triggers his suffering and is the alleged albatross of his life. He reconciles these dilemmas through killing, and with each killing comes the satisfaction that the world is closer to whatever he may deem an acceptable balance."

"It's a good profile, Gran," said Van Pelt. "Fascinating, I'd say. Better yet, we finally have something to build on. But why Camden Lock Market?"

The Bohemian

"Could be a matter of simple geography," Hellickson theorized. "The killer may live nearby and knows the area like the back of his hand. So it would stand to reason that if you're someone aiming to commit murder numerous times, you'd wanna do it in a familiar place, within boundaries where you're comfortable."

Hellickson and Van Pelt each turned their attention to Granville Tovey. They could tell from the demeanor of the craggy senior detective that he had an addendum to the theory he wished to share. "I believe our man has a deep-seated hatred of capitalism; in some misguided way, he may even fault it for his shortcomings. I imagine he sees Camden Lock Market as a human carnival, a place where a wide range of people, who have spurned the lofty and the intellectual, be it literature or other highbrow art forms, mindlessly attempt to consume their way to happiness, and he blames this practice for keeping him and his dreams exiled."

"So, those who peddle junk or junk *food* have no right to a living? Then why not kill *them*?" wondered Van Pelt. "Why not eradicate the mindless lower end of consumerism by killing the suppliers instead of the buyers; that way, we'll all be forced to exist in his so-called world of 'loftiness and intellectual elitism.'"

"Eradication may not be what he's after," said Tovey. "I'm guessing that with each kill, he's imparting us with wisdom and that one day, sooner than later, we'll see the error of our ways."

"So, he has a God complex, our killer," Hellickson remarked.

Granville Tovey smirked somewhat ironically. "Don't all serials?"

"Okay, let's get this straight," said Van Pelt. "We're looking for a socialist, or full-blown commy—with talent but was denied access to using it as a means to a living—who, with any sorta luck, resides within reasonable proximity of his killing grounds. Let us hope, for our sakes, he has known socialist or communist ties. More and more, these types are getting bolder in beating their chests over what they see as the ever-corruptible West."

"Nowadays, it seems almost everyone in the world of academia has socialist and communist tendencies, if not actual ties. Either way," said Hellickson. "Thanks to Gran, the proverbial needle in the haystack just became a spike."

CHAPTER SEVEN
DON'T CALL ME ROBBY

The year was 1969. London Bridge got sold to an American named Robert P. McCulloch, who had the famous structure, which spanned the Thames and years ago had replaced a 600-year-old bridge of the same name, dismantled and transported to the United States by way of the Panama Canal, where it was reassembled, in Lake Havasu City, Arizona. A not quite school-aged Gabby Norwich was taught by her father to sing:

London Bridge has fallen down, fallen down, fallen down.
Into the Thames, it just came down and was sold to America.
Ship it out across the sea, across the sea, across the sea.
Brick by brick, how can it be? It's now in America.

Regardless in which country the famous bridge had stood, in 1969, the United States and England each saw their share of anti-Vietnam War demonstrations turn violent. Students and the youth of both nations staged rebellions against the war, establishments, authority, and anything else that appeared to hold some measure of dominion over their lives. It was in this volatile climate that Robert William Norwich was born.

Gabby was the apple of William Norwich's eye: and not to suggest that either Norwich parent neglected to dote over their newest arrival, whom they affectionately took to calling Robby, but doting became unnecessary, for Gabby made it her business to do enough for all three of them.

"I half-expected her to be jealous," said Evie Norwich. "They usually are, you know."

"Must mean that she's well-adjusted," said William. Naturally, both mother and father were quick to attribute Gabby's well-adjusted character to successful parenting. Had Gabby displayed any inclination to reject their newest arrival, the fault would have been hers alone. So, it goes.

And so, the newest arrival grew, walked, spoke, ran, played, and learned many things, including William Norwich's version of *London Bridge*. He was happy and well-adjusted in childhood, then arrived the day when toddlerhood passed into boyhood. "Happy" and "well-adjusted" were no longer terms used to describe Robby Norwich; "vague" and "distant" became the prevailing themes of the day, and also the words that William and Evie Norwich would use when describing a five-year-old boy who, when frailty and beauty were the measures, showed himself exceptional.

"He certainly isn't anything like our Gabby," William often remarked. "She's always smiling and a ruddy young girl to boot."

Evie had little appreciation for William's use of the word "our" when doting over Gabby. It seemed to imply that Robby was a minor part of their family—an afterthought. "He isn't a library book, William," she hissed. "You can't simply return him because he isn't what you hoped for. And why should he smile all the time like Gabby; Robby is his own person—quiet and thoughtful."

"Vague and distant, quiet and thoughtful; those are nothing more than polite ways of acknowledging that a person is a bit on the peculiar side." Gabby, who had been standing in the hallway and heard her father's words, crept back to her bedroom.

As Robby grew and evolved, so continued the constant challenges to William Norwich's perception of normal. So striking was Robby, concerning frailty and beauty; he made those around him feel uncertain of his essence and strangely uncertain of themselves. By age twelve, despite her affections never waning, the eccentricities that formed this person called Robby became more difficult for Evie Norwich to defend.

Late one night, twelve-year-old Robby Norwich went creeping into the bedroom of his fifteen-year-old sister. "Gabby," he called softly, once nestled alongside her. Gabby woke with a start and went reaching for the lamp on her nightstand. In the light, she saw that Robby had been crying, despite stopping minutes ago and steadying his composure before venturing across the hall.

"Robby," came Gabby's gentle return. Robby was lying on his side and facing Gabby. After mirroring his position, Gabby placed a tender, reassuring hand on his cheek. "Can't you sleep?" No sooner had Gabby asked than it became clear that difficulty sleeping was not what prompted Robby to come to her during the night.

"Gabby," he began, his voice quaking. "Is it possible for God to make a mistake?"

Gabby was wise to believe that a sober, thoughtful, and honest answer was required, or else Robby might unravel. Also, Gabby's tender hand resting on Robby's face slid to the back of his head; it was a deft maneuver to draw him to her womanlike bosom. "My dear, sweet baby brother," she cried, "with all my heart, I love you; do you understand? And no, God does not make mistakes; He is perfect, as are you. You're my gift, Robby—you've always been my most special love in the whole world; don't dare ever think your creation is anything less than perfect, and to hell with those incapable of understanding."

Gabby rained kisses all over Robby's beautiful face and again pressed his delicacy to her bosom. Finally, he burst into tears, but his cries got muffled by Gabby's womanliness. She held onto him as if owning the viable fear that should she relinquish her grip, Robby would tumble through the vastness of the universe and be lost to her forever.

"May I stay with you tonight, Gabby?" It was a desperate entreaty and one that Gabby answered with a cluster of kisses before drawing Robby closer yet to her bosom. For the remainder of the night, Robby Norwich would lay in the arms of his adoring sister. How loved and protected he felt in the arms of Gabby, a sister who, come what may, swore herself a refuge—a haven—and behind that protective cloak, he would not merely exist but rejoice in the truth of his essence.

Come morning, Gabby sat up in bed and tousled Robby's hair. "Wake up, you sleepyhead!" It was a playful command, though no sooner came her words than her playfulness vanished, usurped by her momentary captivation of the radiant glow of Robby's restful face.

"I would be the most popular girl at school if only I had *that*," she said.

"What, Gabby?" Robby sleepily chirped. "What would make you the most popular? Can I give it to you?"

"I'm afraid not, Robby," she said. "Unfortunately, I'm stuck with this round, freckled, and quite ordinary-looking face."

"But you're beautiful, Gabby!" Robby cried. "The *most* beautiful; I've worshipped you ever since I could remember having thoughts."

"I'm honored, Robby… to be your sister and that we are part of one another." Robby followed Gabby's words with downcast eyes and the confession: "This face has taken its share of hits lately."

With alarming force, Gabby flung herself from a lying position to her haunches; like a predator about to spring, she had settled atop her bed. She took hold of Robby's face. "Show me these bullies, Robby! You show them to me, and I'll make sure their balls end up on a stick! I swear it!"

Gabby did not take away any trophies as it would come to pass, but with a swift and decisive right foot, she managed to mash a set of testicles. And while the juvenile bully was busy tending to his condition, Gabby found enough daylight in his fetal pose to crack a rib, then finished the job by coming dangerously close to twisting off his ear. She followed the thrashing by holding the head of a second bully under the fountain water of Russell Square until she nearly drowned him.

When making his way home, it was customary for Robby to cut through Russell Square; thus, it was where Gabby awaited his tormentors. Three boys were chasing after him. She tripped the one in the lead. After he tumbled to the ground, she gave his testicles, ribs, and ear a good working over. The second boy was so stunned by the assault he had not the capacity to react and thus ended up with his head submerged. A third boy had enough sense to make himself scarce. After Gabby was through with her drowning and thrashing, she pointed a threatening finger at the two battered boys—they stood before her open-mouthed and motionless—and warned: "Any of you ever again lay a finger on my brother, I'll kill *you*, your parents for not having the good sense to grasp the concept of abortion, your dog, cat, goldfish, and then I'll burn down your fucking house! Are we clear?"

After that day, no one ever again laid a hand on Robby Norwich, especially in a hurtful manner. Moreover, now a high school sophomore, Gabby cemented herself as a legend amongst Robby's seventh-grade peers. Whenever anyone felt threatened, regardless of how unfounded, they would alertly boast of having a friendship or alliance with the ever-dreaded Gabby Norwich. "She'll thrash you until every drop of life is gone from your body" was one of several claims that would make everyone stop and think twice about what they were doing. "And if she suspects you're still alive, she'll come and burn down your house in the middle of the night."

The frail, beautiful boy walked away from Russell Square that day, clutching the arm of his heroic big sister. But there would be more bullies on the horizon—the sort upon whom physical force could not be applied, less could they get tricked into believing that Gabby Norwich was the Grim Reaper or avenging angel. Robby hadn't much time to enjoy his new status at school before he was whisked away to a barbershop and brought home, only to find a wardrobe comprised of the most rugged and masculine kind awaiting him.

"Congratulations, Father," sneered Gabby, "my dear, sweet brother is now a delicate lamb in wolves' clothing. I hope you're satisfied."

"Robby is a son, Gabby." William Norwich flared with disdain. "And as long as he lives in this house, I'm going to see to it that he looks like one. And while we're at it, you should bear in mind, it wasn't all that long ago, in this country, people like *him* were against the law."

"People like *'him?'* You mean sweet, gentle, loving people who do no harm but have plenty done to them? Would you like to ring the police, Father? Or perhaps you would prefer to have him committed? And, incidentally, *'him'* has a name!" Gabby matched William's disdain, then looked to Evie for support; however, support was in short supply, and what little there was, was halfhearted and feeble.

"Thank you very much, Mother," Gabby hissed before storming off. Meanwhile, Robby, who was thought to have retired to his room but was standing in the hallway, heard the entire exchange. From there, he crept into Gabby's bedroom. "Gabby, it's not his fault," he cried once Gabby joined him. "What father would want *me* for a son?"

"For starters, one who isn't a homophobic brute." Still in the throes of her agitation, Gabby was sneering as she spoke. Also, she was prepared to take Robby, who appeared resigned to the whole affair, into her arms when she snapped, "Go back to your room this very instant and change out of those ridiculous clothes!" Then she stormed back into the kitchen to have another go-around with William. "How very fortunate for you, Father, you're 'normal,' or whatever your perception of normal happens to be, and not a square peg some 'moron'

100

keeps trying to jam into a round hole: I would imagine someone as strong-willed as yourself might have a great deal of difficulty being tampered with; but here's the matter, in a nutshell, Father, so that you may better understand it: A cripple isn't suddenly going to rise and challenge Sabastian Coe to a race simply because someone has bought them a pair of running shoes, nor is Sabastian Coe going to become a cripple because someone took his shoes away; we are who we are, and no set of clothes or coat of paint can change it, so if the men at your club have difficulty with Robby, tell them to come and see me! I promise to set them straight!" Gabby ended her diatribe with a tight-lipped smile and snapping nod. She gave William a moment to respond, but he was set too far back on his heels to make an offer. By the time he recovered, Gabby had gone storming off again, this time to Robby's bedroom. "That's better," she said when she saw that Robby had shed his new clothes in favor of the old ones. "Now, all we need for matters to return to 'normal' is for all your beautiful hair to grow back."

Most sons or daughters seek approval and praise from their parents; however, Gabby, asserting herself on Robby's behalf as she had, presented a new dilemma: Robby wished to please his father, as any son might, but also craved the approval of Gabby, his heroine. So Robby did what he believed to be fair-minded; he mismatched his old clothes, which were not nearly so gender-specific, with the newer rugged and masculine ones chosen for him, and grew his hair back, but only to a point. He managed to find ground where he could be somewhat true to his essence, which delighted Gabby without causing William to rise and take issue. The following two years, Robby walked an imaginary tightrope, and the teetering effort placed squarely on his shoulders kept a tenuous peace within the walls of the Norwich home. But a person can deny their true essence for only so long. Since Robby could not openly celebrate his femininity, he immersed himself in Gabby's. The two would spend their Saturdays barricaded in Gabby's bedroom with Robby pampering his big sister, in a variety of ways. Robby would style Gabby's hair, give her facials and skincare treatments, expertly apply her makeup, and spend hours meticulously beautifying her hands and feet; however, regardless of their roles, Gabby saw Robby as the beautiful one and herself as plain and ordinary. Thus, it was often difficult, on those Saturdays, to reconcile looking down at this lovely, delicate creature of rare beauty who, with delight, slaved away at the tips of her fingers and toes: in Gabby's judgment, Robby's beauty was far worthier of such attention and adoration, and, if ever awarded the privilege, would produce far more impressive results. Once, when Gabby intimated as much, Robby rejected the notion with vehement disfavor, citing: not only was Gabby beautiful and "worthy of a handmaiden," but someone worthy of worship, and he would see to it that worship was doled out to her routinely and copiously.

When Gabby was through being primped and fastidiously assembled, she and Robby would venture out from their enclave for a romp about town. Often, they would pretend not to hear the snickering behind their backs. "Look, there go the Norwich sisters," was one example. Occasionally, Gabby would turn toward Robby and remark loud enough for a giber to hear: "You see, Robby, there truly is a moron on every corner." Most often, Gabby would dismiss such nonsense as harmless taunting. The only time she flared with any real agitation was when overhearing a young man accusing her and Robby of having entered into an incestuous relationship. For Gabby, such an accusation hurled their way, aloud and in public, surpassed harmless taunting and, in her judgment, "crossed a line." She turned a menacing glare upon the young man in question; it would have given anyone the impression she intended to levy an unforgettable reprisal. Perhaps the young man was disbelieving concerning what transpired two years ago in Russel Square, that Gabby Norwich's reputation was all smoke and no fire. Gabby ripped her hand free from Robby's grip and launched a threatening and resolute march in the young man's direction. Robby, and the others cluttering the sidewalk, watched the young man freeze with fear, then wilt. When Gabby closed the gap thus that the young man could sense her presence in force, he began treading backward. When at a range close enough to where she could pounce, he turned tail and ran off.

"Crazy fucking bitch," the boy hollered out. Gabby started after him but managed only a few strides when realizing she had well made her point. When turning toward the gathering, first, she grinned victoriously. Then, once upon them, she reestablished her menacing glare and threatened, "If I ever hear talk like that again, I don't care which one of you morons utters the words, one by one, I'll hunt each of you down, and cut your fucking tongues out!" Then she purposely sought out the young man among them who, in her judgment, appeared to be the most physically imposing. Waving a finger in his face, she posed the compound question, "Are we clear on the matter, or does it need repeating?"

Despite towering over Gabby, Robby could sense the young man's heart was sinking in his ample chest. The young man was unclear whether he should nod *yes*, that the matter required no clarification or *no*, and that Gabby need not repeat herself. Finally, following a moment of indecision that proved cumbersome, never mind fretful, the poor chap decided it was prudent to address the latter portion of the question.

"Gabby, what would you have done had that boy not run off?" Robby wondered.

"I suppose I would have run the risk of ruining my manicure; because, make no mistake, Robby, I would have wrung the fucker's neck."

"How I wish I had your balls, Gabby."

"My balls?" she intoned. "And here, all along, I thought it was my vagina that you coveted."

"Oh, but I *do*," Robby chirped before the two of them erupted into a chorus of laughter over what was a silly irony.

Gabby went on to the local university in Bloomsbury, where she majored in English Literature and minored in art. Robby, meanwhile, sang in the high school choir. When on his own, he sang the songs of his favorite singers: Dusty Springfield, Joni Mitchell, and Karen Carpenter, and would emulate their styles. Often, he would experiment by applying one vocalist's technique to another's signature song; though, Karen Carpenter, Robby's favorite and, like Robby, a contralto, became a source of frustration, as there were elements to her vocal prowess he was unable to duplicate. Finally, it was decided that the cooler tones of Joni Mitchell's voice were more suitable. The prevailing style would be Dusty Springfield's, particularly the bluesy melancholy style she applied when crooning *The Look of Love*. Robby combined elements of all three female singers: Joni Mitchell's tone, Dusty Springfield's style, and Karen Carpenter's unique ability to sing as though she was sitting next to you and only for you. Ultimately, a style all his own and one compelling attention emerged. Come his senior year of high school, Robby became much more known for his vocal art than as an androgynous figure more suited to pique curiosity over inspiring friendship—otherwise, a scenario that earlier on kept him apart from his contemporaries. He even won over those who used to target his pretty face and push him to the ground.

But come one Sunday in early May, life would change for Gabby and Robby Norwich, and the change would be swift. It was not the sort of change one can plan for, less could they see it coming. In one moment, their young lives carried on as such; then, in the time it takes to blink, the world became something else entirely for two young people hitting their stride.

Robby was all day at a Sunday dress rehearsal. The year's spring musical at the high school was Pippin, and it was only natural that Robby should play the lead—the decision went unchallenged. The son of Charlemagne and heir to the throne, Pippin returns from the university, thirsting for something in life to fulfill him. Meanwhile, there are forces afoot that work to manipulate him. So young, determined, and hopeful is Pippin, though still a troubled teenager. "Gabby, I don't have to *play* Pippin; I *am* Pippen," Robby had gushed upon learning he had landed the part. Only two others were bold enough to deem themselves a worthy Pippin, but after watching Robby shine in his audition, they backed away; for shine, he did. Weeks later, during that Sunday dress rehearsal, he emptied his whole heart onto the stage when singing *With You* and *Morning Glow*. The cast, musicians, music director, and stage crew beamed in anticipation of opening night.

Meanwhile, Gabby was with a group of friends from the university, gathered at Lord John Russell Pub. It was late in the afternoon, nearly evening; a soccer match between Liverpool and Chelsea had ended. Liverpool scored the lone goal to earn a 1— 0 victory. Gabby had no rooting interest in the game but would glance at the television whenever a collective roar rang through the pub. When the game ended, the news aired. Gabby was paying little, if any, attention to it, but her peripheral gaze took in Dana Kelsey, an on-the-scene reporter, standing on the shoulder of a road alongside a steep embankment.

Although they tend to border on the ethereal, feelings known as premonitions can turn out to be palpable and, at times, sobering. A greater sense of foreboding Gabby Norwich had never experienced: She sprang up from her seat and demanded the barkeeper raise the volume of the television.

Earlier, there were brief patchy showers throughout the city in the late morning and early afternoon, but nothing to spoil the day.

But a hundred-plus miles to the northeast of town, the rain came down in torrents, making visibility for those embarking on road trips to the Cotswolds a challenge.

The driver either lost control of his burgundy Jaguar or never saw the bend in the road. As a result, the car, driver, and three passengers tumbled down an embankment. Cameron and Emma Lang, the couple in the back seat, were taken to nearby North Cotswold Hospital; the extent of their injuries has yet to be determined. Unfortunately, the driver and his wife, identified as William and Evie Norwich, were not so fortunate...

Dana Kelsey's voice slowed such that it fell upon Gabby's ears in an indecipherable garble. Also, it resounded in a lower register—it was akin to sound traveling through water—and the distortion swelled in volume, its crescendo applying unbearable pressure to Gabby's head; tighter and tighter, like a vise, it squeezed. Gabby put her hands to her head for fear it might burst. Finally, the crescendo reached a new threshold; thus, the garbling quickened; all at once, the buzz of countless insects assaulted her ears, and as many lights blinded her eyes; she turned away, but there was no escaping the harshness of the sound and glare. The pressure mounted; her head grew feverishly hot. Then came an eruption and, with it, a release in pressure: Gabby's skin cooled; she grew pale and cold. She glanced up at the television. The garbling and buzzing were gone, replaced by a lucid voice shouting: "Your parents are dead, Gabby! Dead; do you hear? You and Robby are all alone in the world, orphans!"

Gabby began to back away from the bar. "Gabby, wait," a voice called out to her. "You're in no condition to be alone," came a call from another.

"I must go to Robby," was her impassive return. "I must go to him at once."

In a perfunctory manner, Gabby twisted and weaved her way through the pub; it was not until her unsteady feet found the sidewalk and the coolness of the air kissed her face that her mind and body appeared unified in urgency. She went running off in the direction of the high school; it was imperative she got to Robby before anyone informed him of the news or Robby learned of it on his own. She walked into the auditorium midway through the finale. Hundreds of empty chairs—chairs that, come Thursday night, would be occupied—stood between Gabby and the stage; otherwise, a domain that for Robby Norwich represented a universe, one of pretending that took place in a vacuum amid the madness of a madding world, and Robby was its shining star. So beautiful was his face and how it glowed when on stage. *My dear, sweet baby brother: how I wish you could remain on stage, a province where your unparalleled brilliance generously illuminates the world around you, and you never again are forced to know the meaning of suffering and torment.*

"Hey, Gabs, Mother and I, along with the Langs, are taking a drive into the country," said William. "Stow-on-the-Wold is our destination. There's room for one more if you're interested. It should make for a lovely day, I would imagine."

"It *does* sound lovely, Father, but I already promised to meet some friends from the university this afternoon."

"Maybe next time," said William.

Gabby went tumbling through an auditorium exit and into a hallway. "Sure thing, Father," she cried. "Next time." What followed her words was laughter—acerbic, hideous, and ironic laughter before uncontrollable sobs sent her careening along a wall, then wilting to the floor. The rehearsal ended. Gabby heard the stampede of feet coming down from the pretend universe and spilling into the real one. She would wait until Robby had separated from his peers to explain how their lives altered and why: then, together, they would sob, tremble, and know fear like never before. It would paralyze them, a bustling city would narrow all around them and choke off their air, yet they would manage the journey home to their empty abode. It was unimaginable that William and Evie Norwich would never walk through the door again.

If life is a possession, then, like any possession, it can get stolen. Gabby spent many moments in the throes of such ponderous reflection. "I'm having difficulty arranging my thoughts," she told Robby. "Everything is flying at me; it's like being trapped in a hailstorm."

Gabby likened the tragedy to a barely conscious soldier brought to a trauma hospital who woke days later to discover he was made a double amputee and forced to relearn matters that were once second nature. On their first night in the half-empty house, the Norwich siblings went to Gabby's bed, where, all through the night, they wept intermittently and held one another's trembling bodies. But the show must go on, and by Thursday night, Robby had shed every tear he would ever need to for the ill-fated William and Evie Norwich. He delivered a performance that, under ordinary conditions, would have been judged remarkable. But nothing about the circumstances was ordinary, nor was Robby's performance: exhilarating, spellbinding, and heroic were some of the superlatives hurled throughout the auditorium, and when it came time for Robby's curtain call, the eruption of applause was deafening, and nary a dry eye accompanied the joyful lauding. The boy who was once thought an oddity, a curiosity, and was forced to run from bullies, had won the hearts and minds of everyone.

Again, on Friday and Saturday night, Robby poured out his whole heart for the benefit of a packed auditorium that, in turn, showered praise and applause like April rain. But just as the show must go on, so, too, must it end. Weeks later, as the school year was dwindling, the adulation began to wane until all that remained was a lonely soul teetering upon a threshold separating male and female whose parents got struck by the same bolt of lightning. The woman within, who so desperately longed to begin her reign, was surging toward the surface. How she longed to assert herself, to move about freely and breathe the same air as the rest of humanity, but William's voice was always in Robby's head reminding him: *You failed to honor me while I lived, at least do so in my death*. Once, he heard the voice and felt what he believed was William's hand on his shoulder. The phantom touch caused Robby to send his fist through the bathroom vanity mirror. He gathered the many shards that came crashing down into the sink into his hands. Tightly, he clenched his fists until he saw scarlet moistness seep between his fingers. Finally, he put his blood-stained hands to his head and shouted, "You no longer have a hold on me!"

Later that same night, Gabby arrived home and was alarmed to discover Robby sitting naked at her vanity with his face, neck, and hands stained with blood. He appeared distant and uncommunicative; his vacant stare was pointing toward the mirror, but Gabby sensed he didn't see himself. Before Gabby could launch into a fit of hysteria, Robby became alert to her presence and assured her, "It isn't what you think, Gabby."

"Then what?" she cried.

"I'm free, Gabby," he said softly. Robby's words resonated with pathos; his bearing was symbolic of one whose fight for freedom, although successful, proved too strenuous. At first, when juxtaposed to his condition, Gabby found Robby's composed manner anomalous, but when peering into the mirror, she saw tears trailing down his face and mingling with his blood. When next he spoke, his words were tremulous—his timbre wavering. "I'm free, and now I want to be like you. Do you understand?"

"Yes, Robby, I *do* understand."

"Will you love me, Gabby? Will you love me and care for me as your sister?"

Gabby took Robby by the hand and led him into the bathroom. Next, she drew him a bath, washed his blood-stained skin, and went to work on the mirror's bits embedded in his hands.

"I'll always love you, Robby," she said. "And, of course, I'll take care of you: as a brother or sister, it doesn't matter; it never did. Father may have despised what was locked inside you and begging to get out, and Mother was ambiguous, but I found it dazzling. I *find* it dazzling. Although, I have one minor request: The next time you decide to achieve a new paradigm of consciousness, please do so in a room where there isn't any glass."

Next, Gabby led Robby back to her vanity and began running her fingers through hair that had not seen scissors since late winter and was flowing beautifully down past his shoulders. She gazed at his reflection in the mirror and, as might an artist, assessed his finer points and determined: *there are so many! His beauty is so striking; never has so much exquisiteness come together in one person!*

"Make me beautiful like you, Gabby." It was an inspired entreaty that Robby made. Gabby stooped down to view her and Robby side-by-side in the mirror. *What is it that he sees?* Gabby knew better than to ask, for whenever she decried herself, Robby reacted forcefully. Then something occurred to Gabby: her strength translated to beauty in Robby's mind. Robby may have coveted Gabby's womanhood, but it was her strength he worshiped.

Gabby took her hairdryer and brush and went to work, and when she was all through, Robby's hair hung in a luxurious gleaming wave to one side, where it covered the corner of an eye, thus loaning an appearance brimming with seduction and mystery. Next, she applied makeup. When she stepped back and assessed her work, she concluded that all she managed was to find a suitable frame for a work of art that did not require proper lighting, less a trained eye to understand its beauty. Robby searched the mirror for Gabby's eyes, and once their gazes locked, he pleaded, "Call me Bobbie."

As it would come to pass, Bobbie's performance in *Pippin* opened a few eyes and earned her a spot in the West End revival of the musical *Me and My Girl*. The opportunity further led to her understudying for the role of Sally Smith, which she played for thirty-five performances over the space of a year to glowing reviews. And that became Bobbie Norwich's life: performing on stage, taking dance classes, voice lessons, and hobnobbing about London's West End. One night, upon arriving home, she went to look in on Gabby and kissed her goodnight, as became the custom.

"Were you wonderful, yet again, my beautiful sister?" Gabby asked.

"I tried to be," said Bobbie. "I hope I was." Bobbie seemed more interested in the book sitting atop Gabby's nightstand than speculating over her performance and grabbed hold of it.

"You *must* read it, Bobbie! It's fascinating. *Infinitely* fascinating. We could spend days discussing it, you and me."

"Mitch Morningstar? I never heard of him."

"He's a newbie and an American," said Gabby, "but he's brilliant!"

"Some Americans are, you know," was Bobbie's cheeky reply.

Despite the flippancy with which Bobbie alluded to Americans, she retired to her room with *Funhouse* tucked under her arm. Days later, she would find it somewhat disturbing that Gabby did not deem it necessary to forewarn her that Davey Coyle's parents perished in an automobile accident. Was it an oversight, she wondered, or a case of Gabby not wanting to spoil a poignant moment in a novel? Given their history and symmetry, she thought it unimaginable that a fatal car crash could have slipped her sister's mind. However, it was days before she could approach Gabby concerning her frailty disregarded for the sake of a novel.

"Frailty?" Gabby flared indignantly over what Bobbie had implied and her reason for doing so. "To have survived the overbearingness and harrying that routinely marred your childhood and become who you are today: I should think you're far more fibrous than frail, if not the most resilient person I have ever known. But here's the reality, dear sister; people perish in car crashes every day—whisked off the planet, just like that." Gabby snapped her fingers to indicate the promptness with which some leave the world. "I promised to love you and take care of you. Am I not doing a satisfactory job?"

Bobbie had spent hours pondering what she alleged was her sister's thoughtlessness before daring to approach Gabby on the subject. Her efforts awarded her the experience of getting torn to shreds in a matter of seconds, then she took a seat and hung her head as one might when feeling ashamed and pitiful. "I'm nothing without you, Gabby," she sobbed. Later that night, during what marked a dark but clarifying moment, Bobbie gazed at her reflection for an undetermined period. The image alone filled her with delight but came with a price: Guilt. She had, at last, arrived at the understanding that her being and potential in the domain they were currently flourishing sprang forth from a tragedy. Just as Joey Coyle's feet got set upon a path that spawned a deranged killer, for a like reason, Bobbie Norwich, with a bit of help from her big sister—her champion and advocate—was free to evolve into the woman she was forced to suppress; and, although she did not compel William Norwich to drive through a storm or push his Jaguar down an embankment, the result of this ill-fated succession was an instant death and subsequent birth: Bobbie Norwich. She tried to fool herself into believing that "Bobbie" would have risen and flourished no matter what, when, in reality, if not for that fateful Sunday, "she" might have been years yet on the horizon. But it was her life to live, and she would not waste it in penance, never mind that Gabby would never permit such behavior. Forging ahead, all she could hope was that William and Evie were resting in peace because, for better or worse, Bobbie Norwich was here to stay.

Not long after *Me and My Girl* closed, Bobbie had a chance encounter with Carlton Clemens, a bass player who played for a jazz band that was weeks searching for a lead vocalist. Upon arriving at Doc Watson's for an audition, she requested to sing *The Look of Love*; the band gladly accommodated her. Once she was through crooning the first verse, the musicians laid to rest their instruments. Bobbie continued to sing, assuming the band wished to hear an acapella version. Poised, she obliged. Next, Bobby noticed that Carlton Clemens was smiling and that his smile was contagious, but when those contagious smiles turned to laughter, Bobbie filled with dread, sensing she had flubbed the audition and was getting laughed off the stage. She stopped singing, dropped the microphone right where she stood—it made a jarring and echoing thud as it met the floor—and, like an unwanted wretch, stepped down from the stage. That's when Carlton Clemens went lunging for her.

"We're not laughing *at* you," he told her. "We're laughing because our search is finally over!"

Bobbie's sultry, haunting contralto was precisely the kind of vocals the band, who called themselves Monty's Meld, needed to accompany the cool texture of their sound. In his raspy voice, Monty Pearson, the band's saxophonist, told Bobbie, "Look here, girly. Bobbie Norwich works fine if you're an English gal pouring tea at a ceramics class, but if folks around this neck of the woods hear 'Bobbie' right away, they're gonna think bobby socks, bobby pins, Goodie Two-Shoes, and Little Red Riding Hood. You understand what I'm sayin', don't you? If you're gonna be a lead vocalist for a jazz band, you're gonna need you a stage name."

As if the name had been resting on her lips, Bobbie blurted out, "How does Nina Linette sound?" Her answer came in the form of a collection of satisfied grins. Then Monty Pearson beamed, "Nina Linette sure sounds like a jazz singer to me! Anyone feel different?"

No one uttered a word in opposition, and so born was the dual personae, Bobbie by day and Nina by night. When first learned that Monty's Meld was to accommodate a young female vocalist, many assumed that Nina, judging from her photograph, would prove little more than an ornament set in front of a capable jazz band; however, it would not take long—stunning heels and revealing dress featuring a slit and low-cut back notwithstanding—for her to dispel the hasty assumption: The result was Monty's Meld catapulting their status from a jazz band of some note to a headliner act that never failed to pack the club the nights they played.

Gabby played her role of the caretaking big sister admirably. It was a role she accepted and performed graciously, and it served to help cultivate the Bobbie-by-day version of her sister. But, then, time passed: the true essence of Bobbie Norwich was on full display and free to flourish; her wings had spread and were poised to soar, and the venue it became most evident was on stage; her seductive power when behind a microphone was, in a word, compelling. But the more Bobbie flourished and Nina shined, the more the luster seemed to wear from Gabby. From the day the bullies chased Robby through

Russell Square, Gabby became her brother's keeper: and whether it was for the sake of Robby, Bobbie, or Nina—a brother or sister— Gabby knew no other role or life, and the more her transformed sibling flexed her dynamism, the more into the background Gabby faded; she had become "plain old Gabby Norwich," guardian to a femme fatale younger sister.

Moreover, aside from looking out for Bobbie, Gabby assumed the responsibility of managing their affairs. And despite the Norwich sisters inheriting advantages upon William and Evie's death, Gabby, alone, had the daunting task of dealing with lawyers, bankers, and other matters concerning the estate; it was Gabby who, tirelessly, oversaw their situation; thus, her passage into adulthood was more than swift; it was instantaneous: one moment, she was a daughter, student, and older sister; in the next, gone were two of the three, thus into her lap fell the demanding roles of parent and executor. Admittedly, her swift indoctrination into adulthood, aside from tragic and unwelcomed, became wearing and the source of her looking and behaving older than her years. Then, one day, an American airman strolled into Lord John Russell Pub, and the sparkle returned to her eyes.

"There's a handsome man in uniform sneaking peeks at you, Gabby," Bobbie giddily told her sister.

Gabby dismissed the notion, stating, "If anyone is sneaking peeks in our direction, it must be you who has snapped up their attention: I bet if I allowed my eyes to rove the pub, I'd find fifty men whose shifty eyes are paying you a tribute. Hell, Bobbie, you're my sister, and *I'm* having difficulty taking my eyes off you!"

"You can hem, haw, and deny it if that's what you prefer, dear sister, but that handsome devil in that sharp uniform is looking only at you. Trust me; if there's one thing I've learned to spot over these past few years, it's the lecherous eyes of men. So now, next time he looks our way, meet his gaze and give him an inviting smile. Then, a moment later, I'll make my exit."

"Bobbie, don't you dare leave me!"

"Stop your protesting, Gabby. You've been my keeper for far too long; it's time for you to get that luscious vagina of yours out of mothballs so it can give and receive pleasure. Now turn and smile."

It was not until Airman Morningstar stood before Gabby that she realized how set aside she allowed herself to become. She had been a caretaker, nurturer, protector, and peace broker—rarely had she considered her own needs, and she was only in her mid-twenties. But now, there stood before her a young man whose journey began on the east coast United States, with stops in Texas, Ohio, and Kenya, and he fancied her above all others. Gabby Norwich was alive and well.

CHAPTER EIGHT
THE MAKING OF A MONSTER

I would leave London in mid-August—as became my altered plan—never imagining a departure that would include a half-written manuscript of what would materialize as my third novel and several pages of a detailed outline of a biography, one I would work on intermittently and would not see its completion for many years.

"That ought to keep you busy, Mitch," Nina told me. "And remember, although it's a biography, treat it as you would a novel; take plenty of latitudes. In other words, feel free to spice it up. You never know; one day, it may boost both our careers."

At times, Nina would make utterances, sometimes in passing, leading me to the eerie notion that she was a rare soul capable of peeking into the future. And although she played the part of a femme fatale or seductress, especially when behind a microphone, behind her eyes, if one was to look deeply, there resided a person of uncommon depth and insight. Doubtless, it must have been all the conflict—both internal and external—that overwhelmed her earlier years that contributed to her evolving into a person of exceptional perception. Thus, she was correct when theorizing: a tell-all novel involving the life of a singer whose talent was destined to take her beyond the walls of Doc Watson's written by a novelist—hopefully, by then, I'll be a writer of note—who knew her personally, would be just the recipe to generate a spark.

With clouds dominating the periphery and ocean below, I spent hours plowing through what remained of *The World According to Garp*. It left me with nothing but admiration for Mr. Irving; like no other, he had a remarkable facility to breathe both joy and pathos into quirkiness and dysfunction. It also left me wondering what someone with Mr. Irving's literary prowess would make of my summer vacation.

The Bohemian

The plane touched down; I was back on American soil. I went scrambling for my bags, then hailed a cab. It was still early in the day—five in the evening—when I arrived home. I left my bags on the curb and went racing for my front door. What happened next came unexpectedly: Upon unlocking the door and stepping inside, intolerably thick and still was the only way I could think to describe the air within my domicile; thus, as might a sloth marked the fashion with which I moved through what I perceived a dense, lifeless space. When I reached the center of the room, I felt my heart plummet; it dropped precipitously, then I heard a sickening thud. What seized me was the realization that I missed nothing about my life; moreover, I could have broken down and cried out loud to an empty room over how desperately I missed Gabby and Nina. Had they, by some miracle, made themselves present upon my opening the front door, I would have instantly brightened and rushed to embrace them or fallen to my knees and exalted the heavens. In two short months, the Norwich sisters became my life. Without them, I felt utterly and dismally alone. I would not see them again until winter break. Meanwhile, I would teach literature, ride my ten-speed bike, and delve into my manuscript; but the time would not pass quickly enough. But before I could begin resuming my life, I had an unenviable task to perform.

I retrieved my bag from the curb, thoughtlessly tossed it in the foyer, dashed to my car, threw myself behind the wheel, and headed straightaway for Queen Village—a tiny but charming section near downtown Philadelphia. The reason for the trip: to see dear cousin Molly. Yessiree, I was off to Queen Village, where I was sure to receive bitter-tasting medicine administered by the hand of a batshit crazy moralist who once subscribed to the theory that Nietzsche's prime motivations were dismantling Christianity and the West. Days ago, I considered avoiding Molly. Then, just this morning, I decided that if a mild confrontation concerning Gabby and the "real reason" I trekked to England was to occur—its occurrence had a likelihood similar to death and taxes—it was best to get it over with sooner than later. Besides, given how my heart ached for the sight of Gabby and Nina, a mild confrontation might help snap me out of my gloom. I could hear Molly's tone brimming superciliously: *So, how was the book talk, Mitch? I imagine your mouth ran dry after two months.* During what would evolve as a one-sided conversation, she would eventually add: *Gabby Norwich spins her little web, and you moronic Morningstar men can't help yourselves; you can't wait to play the role of the unsuspecting fly,* or something to that effect.

I checked my watch: it was 5:50; Molly would come strolling up to her apartment by six, six-fifteen at the latest. So I decided to make myself conspicuous. My rationale? It would be best for Molly to discover me, to spot me from a half-block away, looking like the ever-loyal dog who waited all day for her mistress on the doorstep. Moreover, the half-block would give her more than enough time to consider how thoughtful it was that I made seeing her my first order of business upon my return to the States. Had I, as they say, hid in the bushes—there are no bushes in Queen Village—and knocked after Molly entered, I may have startled her. Moreover, upon recovering, she would have uttered somewhat snidely, for example: *How fortunate for us bourgeois Americans, Mitch Morningstar is back in town,* or something to that effect.

Molly was fifty yards away when she spotted me. I noticed a warm smile form on her face. She was glad to see me, to discover me waiting for her at the end of her day; I could not have asked for a better start. Then the better start got better yet: As Molly approached, her gait was lilting as though she might begin skipping like a school-girl! Standing before me, she referred to me as "Dearest cousin, Mitch," and then threw her arms around me. It was more affection than expected. What followed came even more unexpectedly: Molly usually kissed me on the cheek—it was her "cousinly" custom. To-night, she kissed me full on the mouth, and there was an unmistakable sizzle in her lips. Mmm. I did not bother alluding to this curious break from protocol but told Molly I missed her and was happy to see her. When we broke our embrace, she could detect that something was weighing on my mind.

"I came to tell you something, cousin," I conciliatorily began.

"Say no more, Mitch: You delivered a most riveting book talk, fell head over heels in love with Gabby Norwich, engaged in the sort of summer romance people can only read about, departed England with the knowledge you can't live without her and have arranged to return for winter break, after which you'll bring her back to the States and marry her."

My jaw dropped to the curb. Under the circumstances, I cannot imagine a mouth that would have failed to fall open. I reached for my head with the notion that attached to it was a sign flashing my thoughts. Then I narrowed my eyes and, with both caginess and admiration, intoned, "Oh, to have a vagina," a sentiment to which Molly casually countered, "It has its advantages: A crystal ball is all well and good, but nothing can top female intuition."

"So, you're okay with it?" Naturally, I was referring to what her superior intuition had her rattle off, not the inscrutable capacities of the human vagina. I cringed, anticipating all that awful-tasting medicine I dreaded was still yet to come, but Molly seemed wholly unconcerned with what transpired in London.

"Come upstairs, Mitch," she urged. "I have so much to tell you."

It had to be good: I could not hazard a guess why, but an inspired Molly was intriguing; thus, I readily trailed after her.

"Mitch, since you are a writer, I shall defer to you," she began once we stood facing one another in her living room. "Is it lame to suggest that I experienced an epiphany?"

"No," I lied. But what was I supposed to say to someone about to reveal something that could prove poignant, if not the depths of a revelation?

"It wasn't until after I dropped you at the airport back in June that I came to realize just how much I admire you." My first inclination was to say, *well, it's about time,* but I thought better of it when noticing the thoughtful demeanor that came over Molly. "You were not about to sit back and allow life to occur all around you and hope that things would break in your favor if you proved yourself a good person; you dove headlong into the world and seized control of matters; you traveled clear across an ocean! As for me: I'm educated, attractive, and have a career, but what does any of it mean? What was I doing with my life? From the moment I dropped you off until later in the evening when I arrived home, all I thought about was your life versus mine. So I ordered a pizza, and while waiting for it to arrive at my door, I paced this very room, making every effort to work up my courage. Once my courage was in order, I prayed that the delivery person would be male and a reasonably attractive one."

"Molly, you didn't!" I interjected.

"I most certainly did." Her reply frothed with confidence; she appeared taller than I remembered.

"You fucked the pizza delivery man?"

"No, Mitch, I fucked the pizza delivery *boy.* He was all of seventeen—a kid with a summer job putt-putting about town in mummy's Ford Escort. I thought he had a worthy penis, but what did I know? I had never had one of those things shoved inside me. Anyway, I threw the little bastard to the floor and mounted him. It was an enlightening experience; I had no idea sex could be so damn exciting and couldn't wait to have it again."

"You ordered another pizza?"

"Don't be silly, though my young pizza stud is surely deserving of props." Then, casually, Molly added, "No, Mitch, I've since moved on to bonafide adult men: For starters, I fucked my next-door neighbor, my upstairs neighbor, and my upstairs neighbor's father. The poor man is going through a divorce and has dinner with his son three nights a week. His cocksmanship and stamina leave much to be desired, though I wouldn't dare intimate as much; that's not the sort of shortcoming men take kindly to hearing. Still, he's a sensitive and generous lover and has often made me climax with a wickedly skilled tongue."

"This is far and away the most stunning turn of events that I have ever come to learn! Here I am, a novelist, at an utter loss for words. I'm fairly confident it's never happened. Flabbergasted is the only word that comes to mind, and it's nowhere near sufficient. Molly, my dear cousin, you've gone and become a genuine monster, and all because I flew to England to see Gabby Norwich?"

"It wasn't because of what you did specifically, Mitch, that I became a monster; it was more a case of your initiative that was the key. I had denied myself for so long—me and all my structure and virtue—and now I ... I want to fuck everyone. So, what do you say, cousin?"

"What do you mean by, 'what do you say, *cousin?*'" In the air hovered an impending sense of dread. Had I heard right? Was I just propositioned?

"Now, don't you go getting all virtuous on me, Mitch Morningstar," Molly jeered. "And may I remind you: it was *you* when we were teenagers who practically had your nose up *my* skirt. Do you no longer find me attractive?"

"That's beside the point," I protested. "We are, in the event it has slipped your mind, cousins!"

"For Heaven's sake, I'm not suggesting we make out in the schoolyard like two hormonal teenagers. But make no mistake, Mitch, you're not walking through that door until I've had your prick inside me."

No sooner had Molly uttered those final and decisive words that resonated like a command; she enthusiastically shed her clothes. At first, I looked on with mild amusement, wondering how far she intended to take what I hoped was a charade. But when she had finished and stood before me, naked and wonderfully erect, I was quite swollen with admiration. Molly was remarkably statuesque—a sculptor's dream, I would go so far as to say, surpassing all that I had ever imagined, and I have no qualms admitting that during those days prior to losing my virginity (to a nonrelative), Molly, time and again, had crept into my adolescent head and guided me to the promised land. But now that my boyhood fantasy was about to come true, what once seemed a land of milk and honey transformed into a minefield, and all I could think was: Heaven help me; I'm about to bed my cousin! Although, by all accounts, it would seem that Molly was about to manhandle yours truly.

I followed Molly into her bedroom and, while doing so, marveled at her back view: her broad well-postured shoulders, how she gathered at the waist, her heart-shaped bottom, those sturdy but magnificently shaped legs; in my head, I could hear my father's voice saying what he usually said whenever he spotted a woman with a physique similar to Molly's: *Christ, she's built like a brick shithouse!* As a youngster, I failed to understand the correlation between women with splendid physiques and buildings where one goes to void their intestines; though, at age fourteen, I remember thinking it was an amusing idiom. By age eighteen, I thought it was obnoxious. Today, it was spot on! If a tornado swept through town, the only structures left standing would be brick shithouses—assuming any are still in existence—and Molly. My next thought was far less than amusing; it was disconcerting: I had embarked upon England with Molly, a virgin—a woman of unwavering virtue—only to return to someone who currently possessed a facility to cause me anxiety. What if I failed to perform to her set standards and expectations, assuming I would even survive the encounter?

Following what proved a shillyshally effort to make myself properly naked, Molly took hold of my wrists, pulled me on top of her, then guided me inside; I was getting handled and manipulated by someone who treats sex similarly to how a born-again Christian treats religion. *Cousin, would you care for some fanaticism to go with your screwing?*

119

And did I ever sense Molly's power! It was especially evident when she wrapped her legs around me and locked her ankles. I could not overstate enough that there was no escape; I was akin to prey for a great white shark, python, or some other creature whose prevailing feature was physical supremacy; and beyond Molly's palpable physicality, her vagina possessed the characteristics of a vortex—it drew me further and further inside—thus impressing upon me the preposterous notion, had Molly wished to, she had the power, like a black hole to a star, to engulf the totality of my being. Thus, I had no choice but to assert myself, to meet Molly's strength with rapid and forceful thrusts. Then I considered the consequence of premature ejaculation. For example, the upstairs neighbor's father—Mr. Substandard Cocksmanship—numerous times, had to finish Molly off with what she described as his *wickedly skilled tongue*. I, too, am a generous lover—I have yet to learn otherwise—and since I was already penetrating Molly, I had no sober reason to think tasting her would lie any further afoul from the lines of acceptable behavior. But that was how I judged it and imagined Gabby would as well were we to confess our insanity. With that in mind, I settled myself to a slower and more even pace; I prayed it would prove enough to accommodate both Molly and my fear. I watched as her eyes went all aflutter. Her reaction inspired me to bring our lips together. Then, upon hearing her purr with delight, I kissed her again, though more deeply.

"Mitch," she whispered, surprised by my affection.

"It'll be more memorable if we don't treat it simply as a 'roll in the hay,'" was my whispered return.

"Mitch," she sighed, "you're a romantic!" This time when her eyes went all aflutter, her ankles unlocked, and the vise grip that was her legs fell at ease. Molly surrendered control and allowed me to make love to her as I wished.

"So, how was it, Mitch?" Molly was eager for a reply; her eyes possessed the hopefulness that often accompanies uncertainty. Before I could satisfy her curiosity, she added, "Isn't sex wonderful!"

"Dear cousin, you truly are a specimen with unparalleled mechanics," I said, alluding to the former. "It wouldn't surprise me, in the least, to learn that your Kegel muscles could produce a full glass of juice from a single orange."

"Not exactly the warmest compliment I ever received from a lover, dear cousin, but I'll take it." Next, Molly launched the protest,

"Reaching for our clothes, are we? Where do you think you're running off to?"

"Molly, we're cousins—not that you require any reminding—we're not permitted to bask in the afterglow. Now get dressed, and I'll take you for coffee."

"Spoilsport," she hissed. "I'm telling mummy you fucked me."

Ringing in my ears with the dissonance of someone beating a trash can lid was how I imagined Aunt Belinda confronting me concerning my latest perversion. But, on second thought, it was best not to allow my mind to travel to such places.

And so we went for coffee, and the entire time we sat together sipping and chatting, one prevailing thought had plagued me: Had Molly already laid with Nicholas? I was in love with Gabby and, despite her one fatal flaw, smitten by Nina. So the thought of Nicholas—he was stationed nearby at McGuire Airforce Base, thus had access—permitted to bite the proverbial apple before I was granted an opportunity should not rank as a matter of consequence. So be it if my cousins had an illicit encounter while I was overseas. But goddammit, it did matter! The question was, why? Exactly how flawed a human was I? Or was it more a case of sex—even for coherent people clinging to rational emotions—having the facility to alter matters, including ones that rank as ill-advised encounters likely to occur only once? Funny how one prevailing thought can turn into several with complex variables.

Before our little coffee date ended, I faltered. I would like to claim not having proved myself undisciplined, but that was not the case: I needed to know if Nicholas had Gabby and Molly before me. Though no sooner had I formulated a way to pose the question that would not deem me petty and pathetic, Molly peered at me from across our petite café table and resolutely stated, "No, Mitch, I have *not* made a victim of our dear young cousin."

Afterward, she fell against the back of her chair and grinned victoriously. "You know, Mitch," she added paradoxically, "the best part of the evening could have been witnessing your arousal when I stood before you fully naked. Another likely candidate could have been how you made me climax. But, as it has come to pass, the best part was watching you stew with jealousy over the notion that Nicholas might have struck pay dirt before you. In all my life, I've never been so flattered—flattered by your jealousy and that there's still a part of you just as in love with me as when we were young teenagers. And to answer your next question: no, I have no intention of screwing Nicholas; the 'family plan,' dear cousin, begins and ends with you.

"Incidentally, aside from making up for nearly three decades of celibacy, I took the time this summer to read *Somnambula*. It's brilliant, Mitch! Positively brilliant! In a tragically maniacal sense, one would be hard-pressed to find a more compelling character than your Ted Truman."

We spent the time walking back to Molly's apartment discussing the complexities of Ted Truman. I was thrilled to learn Molly enjoyed *Somnambula* as much as she had, but what thrilled me more was the knowledge that she had no intention of making Nicholas part of her summer experiment. There was no sober explanation—none forthcoming—why this affirmation came as a delight. Although later that night, when having returned to my empty, lifeless domicile, something occurred to me: Molly and Nicholas were cousins. Molly and I were cousins. But Molly and I also enjoyed a relationship that traveled well beyond the norms of family dynamics. In other words, we were friends—real friends—and her and Nicholas having had a go-around, on some level, could have diminished our friendship. In that respect, perhaps the twisted jealousy plaguing me was not so complicated after all.

The following day began my re-acclimation of life in the States: taking bike rides, preparing for another school year, and delving into a manuscript. In other words, typical Mitch stuff. I tried not to dwell on the reality that Gabby and I were an ocean apart and that our only means of communication would be odd-hour telephone calls and written letters for the next sixteen weeks. *The good old days.* The other subjects I tried to keep from crowding my thoughts were Nina's second 3:00 a.m. visitation and Molly's absurd autodidactic indoctrination (the "pizza boy" episode) into a life that would not merely include sex; it would prevail as the crux of her existence. Unfortunately, I failed on all three counts: not only did I occupy my mind with thoughts and images of Gabby, Nina, and Molly, I did so obsessively.

I allowed a whole week to pass before calling on Molly. "I'll meet you in town for dinner," was my hopeful offer. "How about Bookbinder's?" *A downtown restaurant within walking distance from Molly's house.* I approached her in what I would describe as *good ol' cousin Mitch* fashion. It was not unusual for Molly and me to arrange dinner dates. "Let's catch up over chow and drinks" was how our eating engagements usually were proposed, but since we were together a week ago, the need for "catching up" would not justify a dinner reservation. I sensed hesitation on the other end of the phone: perhaps Molly was detecting that I required perspective concerning what transpired a week ago, and an evening devoted to "searching for perspective" was not something she favored. I sighed with relief when she hissed, "Bookbinders? Mitch, that's where all the tourists go."

So it was not the company nor any suspected motivation that triggered her hesitation; it was the restaurant selection. That was a relief. After her moment of disinclination passed, she said, "Why don't we go slumming around Headhouse Square and South Street and eat outside amid all the noise and fumes with the rest of the city's bohemians?" I readily agreed. I did not particularly care what or where we ate; I was more interested in Molly's company and, more specifically, curious to learn whether she and I could return to being friends and cousins in the wake of an encounter that surpassed our expectations.

There was no awkwardness in our hellos; our greeting consisted of our usual cousinly kiss and embrace. Moreover, no surge of wantonness emanated from Molly, and I was confident nothing aside from benignity beamed from my aura. And best of all, not a moment that could qualify as an uncomfortable silence had hovered. While glancing over a menu, Molly proved her usual chatty self as I quietly obsessed over whether she had informed anyone of our elicit encounter. Had she, doubtless, such a juicy tidbit would pinball through polite society like a chain letter until the day some moronic colleague of mine gives me the ol' *atta boy* pat on the back. It was killing me. I could not wait until Thanksgiving to find out, only to have Uncle Lambert, Aunt Belinda, Uncle Peter, and Grandpa Alexander, among others, sneer at me, assuming I would earn a spot at the table. *Dear Mitch, Molly was still wearing her training wheels; you should have known better. P.S. You're out of the family!*

"You didn't tell your mother about us, did you?" I didn't suspect that Molly ran straightaway and told Aunt Belinda, as she had playfully threatened, but she may have confided in a friend, who told another friend, who bumped into Aunt Belinda and was bursting to intone, "Guess what?" Anyway, it seemed an innocuous manner to broach a subject that was anything but innocent.

"Mitch, don't be silly; it would never occur to me to do such a thing." Molly's words were trending toward dismissive. She returned to her menu, but only momentarily. Then, slowly, she peered above it and intoned: "But you already knew that, didn't you? And that can only mean one thing: you were looking for a way to rehash last Thursday night. And *that*, Mr. Morningstar, can only mean one of two things: either you've decided that our encounter was regrettable, or you've gone and fallen in love with me."

I gazed at the fullness of Molly's mouth, which I had kissed and kissed deeply: it reminded me that what transpired was not as simple as a thoughtless impulse; there was nothing simple about two people committing an act, even the most immoral among us would allege a sin. Though Molly was wrong: there was a third reason for my wanting to rehash last Thursday night—I had difficulty admitting it to myself—and it was far more illicit than the two she had proposed. If I may be perfectly frank, I wanted another bite of the apple. Exactly why I did was not easy to explain. Of one matter, though, I *was* sure. My shamelessness had more to do with the depravity my mind manages to conjure than any illicitness on Molly's part. But then a theory, however warped, was beginning to manifest: Another encounter might help me better understand myself, my place in the world, the extent of my flaws, the ambit of my character, the degree to which my soul was corrupted or corrupti*ble*, and a dozen other matters whirling around in my head that on a good day would require a confessor with a fondness for paradoxical repartee. Anyway, all that psychobabble sounded far more justifiable than admitting the hots I once had for my cousin as a teenager were rekindling with a vengeance.

"We'll finish our drinks, then go." Molly's tenor was authoritative and arousing. We were sipping chardonnays and snacking on goat cheese. "We'll come back and have dinner."

Molly's apartment in Queen Village was a golf shot from second and South, where we attempted to eat before being overcome with dubious inspiration. Instead of swelling with the sort of misgivings or qualms that should burden two people about to commit a forbidden act, our march toward Molly's abode was purposeful and resolute. Moreover, we gazed at one another with stirring avarice that our relationship had veered so far off course. We could not get through the front door fast enough; it was madness; no other word was suitable. Were we aware of it? Who knows what one is aware of when trapped in a state of psychopathy and a slave to their worst impulses? We went spinning and twisting our way through the living room with a recklessness akin to cars careening out of control on an icy highway; our mouths came together with the maddening fury of ravenous carnivores celebrating the end of deprivation. Somehow, we managed to shed our clothes and were fully naked when we reached the hallway. We slammed into a wall—our recklessness caused the entire apartment to rattle; I could only imagine what the folks living below were thinking—then dragged one another to the floor. Biting, scratching, and thrusting, we shimmied along until we reached Molly's bed. She threw herself atop and urged me to follow.

"Fuck me, Mitch!" she ordered. Her hunger was rapacious, her glare predatory, and the ether in the room swirled to form a cloud raining every sort of perverseness. "Fuck me until it hurts, until I can't move!"

I dove on top of Molly: I was wild, crazed, a flesh-deprived predator going at his prey with force akin to a raging storm surging, swelling, bending trees, and pounding a defenseless landscape. From where was all this madness deriving, I wondered? Was it some deep-rooted synthesized matter bound up in bone and subcutaneous tissue that, like a virus, occasionally emerges? Or perhaps the more simplistic explanation, I have been a deviant in denial, applied? But wait, there is a third explanation; there usually is: Molly represents my last great fling before settling down for good with Gabby. *Gabby?* Could a case be made that faithfulness remained unbreeched, for Molly, in a traditional sense, was not *another woman?* But just as laying with Molly was sheer madness, so, too, was any justification. "Not in a traditional sense," notwithstanding: to a love interest, lying with your cousin would not be construed as harmless flirting or a session of masturbation triggered by a "dark side fantasy" imagined with a stranger. I watched Molly's eyes go aflutter, then felt her teeth pierce my shoulder; I knew she had drawn blood.

Afterward, as we collected our clothes, Molly whined, "I get it; we're cousins; God forbid we bask in a moment of afterglow."

"I appreciate your allowing me to set the ground rules," I said. "Now, let's go and see whether or not our table is still available."

Thursday is not a big night in town. We managed the same restaurant, table, and waitress; it was all quite comical. What was particularly amusing: watching our poor waitress—not more than a half-

hour ago, she served us chardonnay and goat cheese—notice our
rug-burned elbows and wrists, the blood seeping through my shirt,
and correctly theorizing the reason for our battered condition while
making every effort not to snicker at the absurdity of it all. Then
Molly saw it fit to explain, "We've been trying for months, and I felt
myself ovulating." Our waitress let out a little chortle and was off
with our orders. My eyes followed her. I reset my gaze on Molly and
asked, "How many?"

"How many *what?*" Her tone was defensive.

"Don't go getting all standoffish and make me spell it out for
you," I said. "You know very well what I'm asking."

"Three since our first time together," she said. "The usual suspects: next door, upstairs, and upstairs' father."

"Kinda prolific, aren't we, cousin?"

"Mitch, don't look at me as would a jealous lover, or worse,
that you disapprove."

I readily tendered an apology. I had no right to judge Molly,
and I sure as hell had no right—barring her screwing Nicholas—to
act jealous. "Next door, upstairs, and upstairs' father; do these lovers
of yours have actual names?"

"Bill and Russ," she replied.

"That's only two names."

"Next door and upstairs both are named Bill. Upstairs-Bill's
father is named Russ."

"Do you simply refer to them in the third person as 'next door'
Bill and 'upstairs' Bill, or actually address them by those names?"

"If you really must know, I prefer my Dr. Seuss parody 'Bill
One and Bill Two,' if not 'Prick *One* and Prick Two;' it tends to rein-
force it's *me* who maintains firm ownership over *them*. And make no
mistake, Mitch, my ownership is never in question. As for Russ, or
Daddy Russ as I sometimes like to call him: he is a gentle and sensitive
lover. As I had stated earlier, his cocksmanship and stamina, at times,
are in short supply, but he makes up for it in other ways: Unlike most
men, he's not your typical brutish tits and ass monger; he understands
how to love and pay homage to every inch of a woman; I've felt his
mouth on the bends of my knees, the small of my back, the arches of
my feet, even under my arms. An experienced lover like Russ can teach
a novice like me all sorts of things about her body. So, what do you
say, Mitch: until you and Gabby are joined together in matrimony,

would you like to be *owned?* I can pencil you in for a Thursday night stand-in. I must admit, cousin, you are fiendishly superb in the sack."

Molly's grin smacked of wickedness—the most wicked I had ever seen. My cousin, the devil! And the devil's offer, as ol' Beelzebub proposals tend to be, was quite tempting, but order, as I was beginning to reconcile, had to get restored, which meant it was time for the madness to end. "I love you, Molly," was how I began. "But I want to go back to loving you as a dear cousin and best friend. I'm afraid if we continue, I'll begin to see you as Turkish Delight or a drug that has gotten under my skin and haven't the strength to live without and to say that you're the best lay I ever had would be an understatement, but if this 'thing' we started were to go too far—and who's to say when that might happen—matters could become complicated if not destructive. In other words, the situation is liable to escalate to where I could no longer trust myself."

A contemplative look came over Molly. She was buying my reasoning; our return to a relationship based strictly upon friendship and cousinhood would not require even a moment's discourse. However, while walking her home, I could not resist lustful downward glances at her sandaled feet and shapely ankles striding past the hem of her skirt. Molly and I were the same height, and the nearer we got to her place, the closer together we walked until I could feel our shoulders rubbing and our hands mingling. We were weakening. Upon arriving at her front door, not only did we firmly and resolutely shake hands, but we also executed a pinky swear that this "next time," for sure, would be our last. We behaved no differently than alcoholics, drug addicts, and smokers who unequivocally, incontestably, and beyond all shadows of any known doubt vow that the drink, hit, snort, or drag they were about to take would represent the grand finale. I have no data to back this absurd claim, but I am going on record and stating that Molly and I were the only two, related or otherwise, to pinky-swear a final fuck—a carnal encore.

Upon entering Molly's apartment, I could sense a shift in her demeanor—her fervor which was visibly frothing over when we turned onto her street, was waning right before my eyes. And given how she began her sex life—in hyperdrive by launching the dissolute undertaking of wanting to fornicate with every member of the male species, including her cousin—I found it a peculiar turn of events. Indeed, her deportment had altered; it was softer. Her eyes fell upon me

and intimated that our final encounter should not resemble our frenzied pre-dinner interlude but something much closer to 'Daddy Russ-
like' lovemaking. In other words, she wanted to be worshipped and
adored, to have every part of her beautifully sculpted form paid homage. And why should she not, this possessor of such a glorious ensemble?

I obliged. At first, I did so with my eyes closed and imagined
I was diving into the softness of Gabby—my round-faced, sparkle-
eyed angel; where are you? —instead of a woman whose length and
tone personified a figure descending from atop Mount Olympus. Oh,
how I obliged! Then I opened my eyes only to discover no need to
pretend or imagine: I wanted to celebrate my wantonness and rapa-
ciously gorged myself on every delightful inch of Molly's superb
form. What expression other than sheer madness could I apply to
how I rejoiced in all of Molly's womanly splendor? But was I, indeed,
rejoicing, or was this performance, our finale, more a case of me
competing with Daddy Russ and wanting to usurp him as Molly's
most capable and thoughtful lover? Whatever the case: who would
ever come to learn of my motives or the events of what was a sinfully
wicked evening? Who would ever come to know of our deviance?
Grandpa Alexander used to say, "If no one sees you hitting the ice
cream carton, the calories don't count." We shall see.

I returned to my lonely domicile and contemplated the value
of a pinky swear and whether or not moving on from Molly as a lover
would require locking myself away until having shaken through with-
drawal. Luckily, I had *The Case of the Camden Lock Killer* upon which to
obsess.

****

It was late Saturday morning, close to noon; it had been raining
most of the morning hours; the marketplace was unusually sparse.
Scattered rays of incandescent sunlight pierced the ether in places
where nimbus clouds began to separate. Aside from being brilliant in
effect, those scattered beams seemed a reliable indication that the afternoon could prove promising. Contemplatively, Detective Tovey
spent most of the rainy morning strolling the marketplace while attempting to look at the world through the eyes of a deranged killer.
What did the killer see? What were his judgments of the world, his
indictments of man? The rain, which persisted for most of the morning, had ceased; the craggy, veteran detective drew in his umbrella. He

found himself in the precise spot where he stood last Saturday: on the high ground overlooking the canal, approximately twenty meters from the overpass and steps leading to the narrow path shadowing the waterway. He was unaware his knuckles had turned white as he gripped the rail far tighter than he realized. How many times had he stared down into the murky waters of the same narrow canal, hoping that somehow it might spit out an answer? Nine months, nine bodies, and all he had thus far was a profile. He had spent the past six weeks well immersed in London's world of the performing arts and came away with not a single pursuable lead—not one embittered self-claimed virtuoso on the outside looking in. Throughout the morning gloom, what preyed on his mind was a sense that he had reached that proverbial place known as the end of one's rope. He was tired, frustrated, and feeling much older than his years. Before he knew it, the usual midday volume had descended upon the marketplace.

"Here," he heard a nearby voice utter. A single word amid a bustling marketplace, yet he had a keen sense the utterance was for his benefit. He glanced over his right shoulder, down his nose, and saw a hand offering him a cigarette; it was already protruding from the pack and awaiting his attention. Detective Tovey suspected that the chain-smoking Hellickson, whom he last saw last night when walking away from several glasses containing the remains of melted ice, guessed his whereabouts and had stolen up beside him. It surprised him to learn the offer had come from a stranger.

"I don't know whether you indulge, but a man with so much on his mind is likely in need of a smoke, I should think," the stranger affably maintained.

"Was I that obvious?" the detective intoned.

"Only to someone like me—*or* yourself," the stranger replied.

"So, we are alike, are we?" The craggy detective seemed mildly vexed that a perfect stranger made such a leap to assume a shared character trait, despite the stranger being well-dressed, well-groomed, and having what one might describe as an intelligent-looking face and insightful eyes.

"Surely you don't believe that you're the only man who, when immersed within a multitude, feels detached from the crowd and even more alone than when he's alone? There are plenty of us, you know. We may not make up a large sector of the population, but are nonetheless around, we thoughtful souls who walk the world over, hoping a meaningful encounter will get thrown in our direction—that circumstances or events might provide the gateway."

"So, you offer me a cigarette, and, in return, you now get to wield seven minutes of psychology; is that the game?"

"I assure you, it's no game, sir." The stranger turned his gaze from the detective to a multitude beyond the canal, shuffling in every direction. "Look at them all," he said. "They woke, trekked here, and during the course of the day, they'll satisfy a few meaningless impulses, then return to wherever it was they came; and were you to ask any of them, 'What does it mean, and are you happier as a result?' there's little likelihood any among them could form an intelligible answer."

"So, you're an existentialist?" the detective theorized.

"Ask me tomorrow, and I'm liable to tell you I'm a proud theist. Yesterday, I might have confessed to being an atheist."

"Are you toying with me, sir?" Granville Tovey raised a disagreeable eyebrow.

"Hardly," said the stranger. "The mysteries of the universe and human existence are well-immersed in both science *and* theology; only a fool would try and extract ideas from one while wholly ignoring the other: To acknowledge only one universal principle is otherwise known as an intellectual cul-de-sac, which must not only count as a tragedy but, with regards to human potential, a colossal failure. Incidentally, the name's Albert. Dr. Albert Stahl."

"Granville Tovey." Following the detective's introduction of himself, he tipped his hat and then remarked, "So you *are* a psychologist."

"*Had* a practice, for some years, I did, but nowadays I would describe myself, if I may, as a renaissance man: woodworking, painting, the violin, along with working on a novel based on my anthropological theories. So I suppose that suggesting I'm a renaissance man wouldn't be *too* far of a reach?"

"And what *are* your anthropological theories, if you don't mind my asking?"

"For starters, insanity by definition, so said Albert Einstein—although Mark Twain or Benjamin Franklin may have said it first—is doing the same thing repeatedly and expecting a different result. Bear in mind, it's not the mindless repetition but the expectation that qualifies insanity; otherwise, a man mowing his lawn could be judged a lunatic. Whether right here on Earth or in the far reaches of our galaxy,

130

nature has been repeating itself for millions of years, and to varying degrees, it achieves the same results. That being the case, if we were, indeed, spawned by nature—that wondrous, cyclical, and repetitive force—would it not stand to reason that we are a species doomed to mimic its creator? How often in our life and times have we given a loved one or dear friend every opportunity to prove we misjudged them, only to see them once again come up short? One could easily attest that punishing ourselves is a genetic predisposition, which would beg the question: is eternal optimism a function of nature or insanity?"

It was Dr. Albert Stahl's last two remarks, in particular, that resonated with the craggy, senior detective: He thought of Jane, Melissa, and the numerous times, come morning, each or both had discovered him in a chair beside an empty bottle, and all the prayers that went unanswered; decades of empty bottles; decades of unanswered prayers.

Dr. Albert Stahl continued: "The theist believes, if somehow, we could rewind time to the very beginning and started over, everything—from wars to earthquakes, from dynasties to floods—would happen just as it had the first time. Why? The divine plan; it cannot be altered, or so it is written. To the theist, the concept of preordinance is paramount."

"Is that what you believe?" the detective asked the psychologist.

"Ask a man what he believes at sixty, and he'll tell you something altogether different from what he might have told you thirty years earlier; our experiences tend to shape our philosophies. As for the atheist: He is forever fascinated by all that could change had we the ability to rewind civilization and begin again. Of course, nothing so arbitrary as ten-year-old Adolph Hitler given ice cream instead of stale potato chips for a bedtime snack would have spared six million Jews. But, conversely, a decision of any consequence, even as far back as two millenniums ago, were it made differently, much of human history—Jesus Christ, the Roman, British, and Ottoman Empires, along with Soviet Russia and Nazi Germany—might have developed differently as a result."

"Doubtless, the random world of atheism provides infinite possibilities, and those possibilities lend an infinite amount of fodder for the intellectual. But, the all-important question," added the craggy, senior detective, "isn't whether the atheist, with his evolutionary theories steeped in reason, is right or wrong? The real question is: does he

131

extract answers from science hoping to validate his atheism, or is his true quest to find God?"

"I take it you favor the theory of a universe with an ideological component?" There was a slight tenor of accusation in the tenor of the former psychologist.

"Guilty," said Granville Tovey. "And in the event that you're a natural devil's advocate or contrarian about to bury me with the full breadth of epistemology or claim Socrates's method of reasoning was humanity's true beacon and Christ its madman, allow me to state: it is my belief the human cell is the finest and most complex piece of architecture in the universe, as far as we know it, and such an intricate piece of architecture would require a great architect. Now whether or not the architect is a spiritual deity, we could debate until you have run out of cigarettes; but what I won't subscribe to is Darwin's theory that we evolved, more or less, from pond scum."

"I knew I would like you the minute I saw you," said Dr. Stahl. "What a pity I have to be on my way." As the doctor turned to leave, Granville Tovey called out, "Dr. Stahl, do you think *you're* insane?"

"Quite," the former psychologist unhesitatingly replied. He went on to add, "Many years ago, I had a Hungarian colleague who worshipped Bartok. So far as I was concerned, Bartok's compositions were brutal and savage-like, but my colleague maintained, cleverly immersed within all that brutality and savagery were folk songs. I listened but failed to hear them. I listened again, and the result was the same. He had a particular affinity for the string quartets, my colleague; I found them the least approachable of all Bartok's compositions. I attempted to make sense of them on my violin—I'm somewhat proficient—but to no avail. That was twenty years ago. I'm still trying, repeatedly doing the same thing, and hoping for a different result. The sad part is should Bartok become as crystal clear to me as, let's say, Vivaldi or Mozart, I won't be able to share the revelation with my colleague, for he has recently passed. Good day, Detective."

That night, Granville Tovey went to his bed, contemplating his sanity. He had been doing the same thing for nine months with the same result: failure. Then he heard a voice in his head—a jarring voice belonging to Dr. Albert Stahl, who concluded their encounter by uttering the words, "Good day, Detective." With a start, the detective launched himself into a sitting position, then began to replay the entire encounter in his head, giving special attention to his contributions. He was sure of it; he had not identified himself as a detective. He hurled himself from his bed and went racing downstairs to the parlor, where Jane Tovey sat well-engrossed in Somerset Maugham's *The Razor's Edge*.

"I've got him, Jane!" he cried. "I've got him! I know the killer! I know the goddamn killer!"

Jane Tovey marked her page and settled her book onto her lap. Then she gazed curiously at a man who, hours ago, vowed only to himself—the detective did not wish to run the risk of making another false promise—never to take another drink, acting wildly animated but surprisingly sober.

"Did he come to you in a dream, Gran?" A palpable note of irony resonated in Jane Tovey's tenor.

"No, Jane; of course not!" the detective bellowed. "I met him; it was around noontime today; we had a somewhat lengthy and philosophical exchange."

Detective Tovey rang Hellickson's telephone. The two met Lieutenant Van Pelt, who, in turn, arranged for a sketch artist; it was 1:00 a.m. when all four converged upon the precinct. In just a few hours, the manhunt would begin for Dr. Albert Stahl, a killer who succeeded in terrorizing one of the world's greatest cities.

****

It was 2:00 a.m. on the east coast of the United States when I rang Gabby's telephone. I read to her for an hour as she sipped coffee while delighting over how well our brainchild was developing.

CHAPTER NINE
TRUTH OR DARE

And so, I filled my days and nights teaching, cycling, writing, and once a week would venture into town to have dinner with Molly. She kept Thursday nights open, and during those Thursday nights, I discovered tiptoeing through the lion's den awarded me a sense of exhilaration; any encounter where success and failure hang in the balance is bound to deliver excitement. We got through the first Thursday without faltering, although our illicit affair remained the prevailing theme of our dinnertime conversation. The following Thursday, again, we managed temptations and spoke less of our illicitness; by the third Thursday, we had moved past it entirely; the phenomenon of our blazing affair was over. I sat and listened to how Molly had and continued to use sex to liberate herself from what she alleged was pointless structure, needless virtue, and the stranglehold of middle-class morality. I argued, "How is that liberating? Surely you are no one's sex slave, but haven't you, in essence, become a slave to sex itself, if only in the abstract?"

"Mitch, you wouldn't dare say such a thing if I were a man." After her brief bout of huffiness, Molly went on to assert, "Don't you get it, cousin? I'm a predator! I hunt, I eat, then leave the remains for the vultures. In other words, I take what I want and dispose of the rest. Better yet, try thinking of me as crack cocaine and not the addict." With a sigh, she added, "Perhaps one day I'll fall in love—it's bound to happen—but until then, why should I sit home in my lonely living room and masturbate in front of the television when there're plenty of strong, healthy young men to service my needs?"

Although flawless, her logic made it no less inconceivable that I would advocate for virtue and morality because Molly, in the space of a season, became what many would perceive as the antithesis of those traits.

134

The Bohemian

On the first day of winter, bright and early, Molly was at my front door, preparing to taxi me to the airport. "Are you going to tell her?" Her tenor registered more concern than curiosity.

I was not yet buckled in my seat when Molly posed the question, and despite the earliness of the hour and my lack of alertness, I knew full well what Molly was asking; thus, I did not bother to feign ignorance. "I truly don't know," I told her. "And it isn't as if I hadn't thought about it three or four thousand times because I have, yet I haven't the faintest idea what I'm going to do; it may not occur to me until our eyes meet. But, come the New Year, if I arrive back in the States empty-handed, you'll know I revealed an unbearable truth. On the other hand, if Gabby is with me and smiling, you could well assume either she's uniquely understanding or that yours truly was too chickenshit."

"If it ends up the latter—and I'd ante up my tits and ass, that'll end up the case—and you're plagued with guilt: together, we'll simply explain to Gabby that her absence in your life created an unbearable void that brought you to the depths of despair, and in my effort to rescue you from an abyss, I suffered a moment of madness which led to me taking full advantage of your weakened condition."

"Gee, cousin, could you make me out to be any more pathetic," I somewhat sourly replied.

"What's life but a series of tradeoffs? If someone pulls your ass out of the fire, but bruises your ego, consider yourself ahead of the game. Besides, with what you've told me of Gabby, I hardly think she will turnabout and hop the next plane back to England. No, I'm guessing she'll be so excited about life with you here in America that the news, like a summer breeze, will float painlessly past her ears."

As it would come to pass, Molly's words would ring true. Also, upon arriving in London, I was thrilled to learn that Monte's Meld, twice, had the opportunity to play larger venues by opening for well-known bands and, in both instances, played to glowing reviews. But the best news of all: Songs were explicitly written for Nina to sing. Instrumentally, Monte's Meld may have been a worthy band, but the voice of Nina Linette sparked much of the attention.

Before Gabby and I departed from England for the States, we, along with Nina, real-life Harold and Jane, and other members from the book club, rang in the New Year at Lord John Russell Pub. There were happy goodbyes, sad goodbyes, goodbye-for-now goodbyes, and goodbye-forever goodbyes. The next day, at the airport, Nina was firm in her not wishing to shed or see any tears. "We will all be together again," she said. It was peculiar, even eerie, how her words resonated. Of course, we would be together again, Gabby and I understood. There would be winter breaks, spring breaks, and summer vacations. But Nina's vow that we would reunite in the future rang with the insightfulness of prophecy; it was as though she was aware of matters Gabby and I were not yet ready to know or saw what no one else could see.

When Gabby and I arrived in the States, I behaved like a zealous tour guide concerning how I advocated for my hometown; my enthusiasm bordered on the absurd. It was not until we met Molly for dinner at an English restaurant in Headhouse Square, aptly named The Dickins Inn, that I was informed by my dear cousin I was "overdoing it." "Philadelphia is a fascinating city with many fine features, Mitch, but London, England, she isn't. Besides, Gabby didn't come to our fine city for its bricks and stones. And now, Miss Norwich, I must confess to you: following the 'Nicholas debacle,' which led to the ensnarement of our dear Mitch, I regarded you as public enemy number one, but now that I've met you and have experienced your charms, I can see plainly why the Morningstar men have thrown caution to the wind on your behalf. It was a real pleasure meeting you, and I'll be looking forward to many more evenings like this one."

"You're leaving us already?" I sulked. "No dessert?"

"I don't want Daddy Russ to think I've forgotten him; he's such a sensitive soul. I'll bet he and Upstairs-Bill finished their dinner an hour ago, and now the poor man must be fretting terribly; no doubt he's camped out on my doorstep moping like a lost pup."

"Daddy Russ? Upstairs-Bill?" Gabby was keen for an explanation once Molly excused herself and was on her way.

"Don't ask," I said, though I did manage to illustrate that Molly was a shining example of what can happen when a woman is too long suffocating primal urges.

Gabby became well acclimated to her new environs; she even developed an appreciation for what Molly meagerly referred to as "bricks and stones." In other words, from Old City to Rittenhouse Square to the Ben Franklin Parkway, Gabby found her new surroundings quite pleasing. She became especially fond of strolling the pathway that coursed between the East River Drive and Schuylkill River and made sketches of the many stone sculptures and bronze statues that dotted the way and was no less captivated by the bridle path of Wissahickon Valley. She never failed to point out the arch deck stone bridges that spanned the river and creeks and the many rock formations that lined the river drive and were also present in the valley. I found it quite clever that she described both areas as "tectonic wonderlands." Yours truly had long since gone blind to the many aspects she found fascinating, and it left me with the impression: If you wish to tour your city, bring along a foreigner, they are bound to point out all the good stuff you spent years overlooking.

****

Life went on. Gabby taught art, I taught literature, and come the evenings, we delved deeply into *The Case of the Camden Lock Killer*. The lives of Detective Granville Tovey and Dr. Albert Stahl became a universe within a universe. Most evenings, the respective lives of what were merely fictional creations supplied much of our dinnertime conversation, for we allowed them to flourish and breathe until they became as palpable and atmospherically perceptible as the love we would make afterward.

We married in June: Nina and real-life Harold and Jane flew in for the occasion; unfortunately, my place was barely big enough to accommodate Gabby and me. Initially, we planned to push things around to make room for Nina at our dwelling and have Molly accommodate real-life Harold and Jane. Thankfully, we arrived at our senses, realizing that Molly would likely present a terrifying proposition for an asexual couple. *Gimme a week with these two; I'll straighten out their program.*

"We already killed off poor Harold in the novel," Gabby reminded me. "It would be a sin to kill him off, dare I say, in *real life*."

"It would," I agreed. "But should we reverse the accommodations and somehow Molly was to discover Nina as she would not wish to get discovered, it would be anyone's guess what sort of kerfuffle such a happenstance could cause." No sooner were those words out of my mouth than we decided that two hotel rooms in town would be just the thing to avoid any bizarre sexual odyssey or indoctrinations.

My apartment was a one-bedroom efficiency; in other words, a writer's pad. Gabby never complained; consequently, I wrongly assumed it was adequate all these months. It was not until we considered accommodating guests that I realized how unsuitable our living conditions were. Gabby traded away a luxurious three-bedroom/two-bath flat in a ritzy section of a cosmopolitan metropolis for what was essentially a bachelor's pad with meager amenities in a town many alleged has seen better days. It was time for improvements.

We abandoned our brainchild and went full speed ahead, searching for real estate. Unfortunately, we were two people who put more of a premium on what we did rather than where we did it and thus behaved impetuously throughout a process that requires diligence. Luckily—we owe our success to a capable agent—we were placed in a lovely three-bedroom cottage in a charming suburb just west of the city. We moved in September. It was then that Ursula and Warren entered our lives.

CHAPTER TEN
THE BIG WHITE HOUSE

Gabby and I arrived at our new abode from our respective days at the same time and discovered that waiting for us, neatly wrapped, was a plate of chocolate brownies. Attached was a note that read: *Welcome to the neighborhood. Ursula and Warren.* However, there was no address, which left us guessing which next-door neighbor provided the thoughtful offering. The house to our right was the same model as ours, built sometime in the early 1950s; even the landscape was similar; doubtless, the original landscaper owned a particular fondness for laurels and boxwoods.

The house to our left, however, was altogether different. For starters, it was double the size of ours. Moreover, what was in plain view—which was not much—was coated with white paint, and the one window I managed to spy was trimmed with red shutters; French tiles blanketed the roof. Also, the landscape was much denser, though "overgrown" might be a more fitting term to describe it, if not "unkempt," which led me to theorize: Whoever lived there was attempting to achieve some measure of privacy from the outside world and had grossly overcompensated. Gabby, who was always ready to assert her well-inspired imagination, concluded: "Possibly, whoever lives there is a recluse and has died, perhaps years ago; I'll bet their bones are still upright in a chair, a leather-bound classic still held by skeletal fingers, and the result is this awful tangle of trees and shrubbery. Or, better yet, the person is a complete psychopath or a deranged serial killer, and they want their house to appear wholly unapproachable if not downright scary."

"Might we finish the novel we're presently working on before concocting another?" Gabby ignored my supercilious tenor, adding: "Maybe he has a strange fetish or neurosis that compels him to enshroud himself in foliage and, in his twisted mind, he has decided that the most expedient way for this to happen is murdering people and using their shredded decomposed remains as fertilizer."

"And maybe his gardener had a heart attack, and he has had difficulty hiring another. It's usually the simplest explanations that end up being the case."

"You mean the most boring," Gabby retorted.

Five houses in a row lead to the big white house, then a driveway followed by two more homes. It was told to us by the realtor: Once upon a time, the big white house, constructed in 1870 or thereabout, was all that stood, and all the acreage around it was farmland. Yet, despite a landscape that was suffering from neglect, the old place, in an odd way, had charm. Ivy climbed the walls, vines covered trellises, there were brick walkways and stone benches, and the placement of the shrubbery was such that it created a winding pathway— it was an elaborate design that in palmier days might have enticed curious explorers and, with a great deal of effort, could again. It struck me as the sort of place children from a fairy tale wander up to at dusk after being lost all day in a forest. Hungry, exhausted, and wary, they wind their way through the winding landscape until reaching the front door in hopes of encountering a kind face.

"Mitch, you have got to taste one of these," said Gabby, as her mouth made smacking sounds loud enough to shatter my sensibility concerning the big white and nearly camouflaged house.

I suppose there was never any doubt about who supplied the brownies. We promptly devoured them inside, then went next door to pay Ursula and Warren our first visit and let them know how much we appreciated and enjoyed their neighborly gesture. It was Ursula who answered the door. Gabby and I reacted similarly to Ursula making herself visible. Moreover, it was unnecessary to look at one another to ensure that our reactions were similar. In that lingering moment, our thoughts were as follows: A rare few walk the earth with beauty so utterly arresting that they can make you forget where you are standing, who you are with, and why you are there in the first place. Unwittingly, and sometimes otherwise, those creatures of such rarity challenge our sanity while the world around them either consciously or reflexively yields. I first encountered beauty of this nature at Doc Watson's when setting eyes upon Nina. Ursula was not quite the pinnacle of perfection that Nina was—the lure of Nina's tragic eyes was unparalleled—but if you saw them together from the vantage point of even a modest distance, one could easily mistake one for the other.

Ursula invited us in for cold tea and what likely would evolve into a safe, routine getting-to-know-you chat, to which we readily showed ourselves receptive. We followed Ursula into the dining room. Along the way, I was captivated by the elegance of her footfalls; they beautifully suited her lengthy, sinuous form. Ursula oozed culture and refinement, striking me as the sort who, right away, if someone mentioned Byron, would think of the poet, not Byron Nelson, the golfer. I pegged her as a liberal arts major. Through the east window of the dining room was a full view of a well-manicured landscape; it rambled on for several yards, stopping at a Privet Hedge. Jarring to what otherwise would have been a peaceful suburban scene was a man wearing sunglasses, an undershirt that permitted the viewing of far too much hair and skin, a do-rag, and he was also sporting a five-day-old beard while zipping about on a tractor. *Workmanlike determination* was how I would describe his expression. The tractor traveled in neat lines and made hairpin turns with precision. Occasionally, I noticed him glance backward; doubtless, he was making sure every blade of grass was not only cut but cut to the set specifications.

"Oh, that's Warren," Ursula told me, as my preoccupation had not gone unnoticed.

My first impression of Warren was as follows: a man who mows his lawn with an attitude and takes himself too seriously. Again, I began to fixate on Warren. It made no sense, I thought. It would not matter how well Warren cleans up; there was no way he could stand beside Ursula and have the pairing make sense. He was door number three—an unfortunate choice one must learn to live with, else go home emptyhanded—if not the result of an ill-advised dare taken too far. I began leaping to all sorts of conclusions, starting with Ursula, once a prostitute Warren rescued, and ending with Ursula losing a wager: the consequence was her having to marry the goon on the tractor.

"It was sweet of Ursula to invite us over for drinks and hors d'oeuvres this Friday night," Gabby said once we were back and snug in our new abode.

"I beg your pardon; she did? Friday night?" I could not conceal my astonishment over what had transpired without my knowledge.

"Were you not paying attention at all?" Gabby could appear quite lovely when using her scolding tone.

"I paid *some* attention," I lied. "Did we accept?"

"Mitch, you're impossible!" Gabby cried.

I followed her into the kitchen. "What about that Biff charac-ter?" I asked. I was already beginning to imagine the tedium of endur-ing an evening of drinks, hors d'oeuvres, and what would doubtlessly prove emptyheaded conversations with Tractorman: Monster trucks, wet t-shirt contests, and competitive eating, and that was assuming he brings his A-game.

"Biff?" The lovely roundness of Gabby's face narrowed and twisted with vexation. "His name, as you were told, is Warren."

"I don't care what Ursula told me; there's no chance his name isn't Biff."

"For Heaven's sake, Mitch, do *not* keep telling yourself that! Come Friday night, I would prefer not to suffer any embarrassment in front of Ursula. Incidentally, she's a psychiatrist."

"Really," I crooned. And there went my liberal arts college theory, shot to hell. So much for my perceptibility. "When did you learn that?" I wondered.

"When you were busy staring out of the window, like an im-becile, at *Biff*," was Gabby's sharp retort.

Finally, I settled on the notion that drinks, hors d'oeuvres, and conversation of any sort would not prove too awful and could be worth suffering through, assuming Ursula and Warren gained in-sight and knowledge concerning the big white house, those who dwell in it, and were willing to share with the newbies on the block.

Gabby was mildly annoyed with me. I suppose she had every right to be; I had behaved idiotically in front of Ursula—or, at the very least, not as one should have when in the company of a new acquaint-ance, especially in the home of that new acquaintance. Having made for some other area in the house, Gabby left me standing somewhat slumped in the kitchen. So I decided to wander onto our back patio; it was redbrick and stretched beyond an awning that shaded it more than halfway. Beyond the redbrick were the remains of what was, and would again be, a lovely garden—its flowers, as I would later learn, from Ursula, were bountiful groupings of daisies, coneflowers, and rudbeckia. Beyond them was a grassy slope that eventually leveled off and continued until it reached a border of laurel shrubs. Lining the sides, as I would get told, also by Ursula—she seemed to know a great deal about horticulture—were olive hedges. I felt the itch to investigate and spread apart the tight scaffolding lining the left border to better peer into the yard behind the big white house. The first thing that grabbed my attention was a large patio of well-weathered flagstone; it traveled for several feet off the back of the house and ran nearly its entire width. Enclosing it was a white concrete balustrade spindled railing. Its centerpiece was a grand three-tiered Mediterranean-style water fountain; it was inactive, tarnished, and, like the flagstone, well-weathered. Scattered around it were pieces of ornate wrought iron furniture once painted white but now mainly rust-colored. I permitted myself time to gaze and wonder and, in doing so, imagined luxurious garden parties of yesteryear, perhaps long ago as the nineteen-twenties and thirties. I saw people of society finely attired; some were holding cocktails and regaling in the scent of a summer evening; others were dancing under the moonlight to the whimsical strains of a Haydn string quartet. How lovely it all must have been; it made me long for a past I never knew. When my reverie ended, my eyes came to rest on the many bird feeders situated around the patio. Busy at each one was a variety of finches, indicating the presence of feed and the reasonable deduction that someone must have placed feed in them. And so there went Gabby's theory of a recluse presently decomposing upright in a chair, its skeletal fingers holding a leather-bound classic; however, her alternative theory of an outlandish psychosis to explain the state of the landscape was still very much in play.

I went inside and scampered up the stairs to share my discovery with Gabby. Unfortunately, she was not nearly as impressed as she should have been, or I had hoped.

"*Birds* are your evidence that someone is still living next door?"

"Well, *someone* had to place feed in those feeders," I theorized.

"It's more likely those birds were pecking away at bugs and insects feasting on a thick film of micro-organisms that have accumulated on the feeders the past decade … or two."

"Well, now, aren't *we* the scientist!" I hissed. My snippiness was not over Gabby's sudden lack of curiosity; it was because, in all likelihood, she was correct. There was no big mystery surrounding the big white house. Concerning Gabby's absence of interest: it had far more to do with how I behaved in front of Ursula than any pragmatic-based scientific theory.

"Instead of sulking, Mitch," Gabby suggested, "why not just go next door and knock? *Hi, I'm Mitch Morningstar, your new neighbor. I just thought I'd come by and introduce myself.* One way or another, you'll be sure to solve the mystery if, indeed, one exists."

"Perhaps tomorrow," I said, looking out our bedroom window, over the olive hedge, and down onto the large flagstone patio. When below, I had not the proper angle to notice the amount of moss that had grown between the stones where chunks of mortar had gone missing. Beyond the patio was a tangle of trees and shrubbery equal to the mess out front. The following day, I did not venture next door as I said I would, or go the day after (Wednesday) or Thursday. Moreover, I was unable to explain my timidity on the subject. I waited until Friday, hoping that Ursula and Warren might shed some light on the mystery of the big white house.

"We've never seen anyone venture out from the house," Ursula told us. "But we're sure someone lives there. Three times, now, in the year plus that we lived here, we've spotted a young girl—I've placed her at age fourteen—get dropped off in front of the house. In each instance, she arrives by way of a limousine: A driver drops her at the curb and drives off once the girl unlatches the gate. Then, in making a beeline for the front door, she disappears in the denseness of all that tangled foliage. Not that it matters, but I find it strange that the driver never bothers to help the girl with the door or gets out of the car to see her safely inside; he ignores all limousine protocol. What's more, he can't drive away fast enough, or so it seems. And the strangeness doesn't end there: We've noticed—as too has Mr. McGruder, who, incidentally, is your across-the-street neighbor and owner of Paper Mill Tavern on Paper Mill Road—the girl always arrives wearing the most lavish dresses. One would swear she's attending a prom or a ball for debutants."

Gabby's head may as well have been transparent for how easily I could see her wheels turning, though it was unclear whether she had multiple theories forming or a *real doozie.*

"In the beginning," Ursula continued, "we theorized that the girl, who, incidentally, is a beauty, was sent every so often to look after an aging relative. But then why the dresses? It wouldn't make sense for a caregiver to dress so lavishly. However, Mr. McGruder has an alternative theory: The girl comes from people with a lifestyle requiring her to dress in a certain fashion. And in the old house, there dwells a reclusive old grandmother or great aunt who once was a capable seamstress and performs alterations for a granddaughter or great-niece."

144

The Bohemian

"That's all well and good," said Warren, who seemed anxious to move past the mysterious girl and her wardrobe, "but now tell them the story about the dog."

"Ah, yes, the dog," Ursula began. "It happened months before we moved in, Mr. McGruder told us. Ray and Laura Salisbury, who live two doors down from us, had a little white dog named Rocky, who habitually ran away. No matter what Ray did to fortify the yard, somehow, Rocky managed to foil his efforts. He would never venture too far, 'the rascally runt'—that's what Mr. McGruder calls the pup—but one day, he took off up the road and slipped through the wrought iron gate to the big white house. Everyone began searching for poor little Rocky: Mr. McGruder, the Salisburys, the Westons—the Westons are the couple that used to live in your house—they searched for hours and hours, past midnight, with flashlights, and again the next day, but Rocky was nowhere to be found. The Westons suspected Rocky might have ventured further than the big white house, and his boldness resulted in him being eaten by Mr. Finnegan's ferocious-looking Akita. The Westons were wise not to share that awful theory with the Salisburys, who remained convinced whoever lived in the big white house had something to do with their pup's disappearance. But how does one go about proving such a thing? Ray Salisbury considered calling the police, but what could he say to them: get a warrant to search the big white house because I suspect whoever lives there stole my dog—a dog who runs away on an average of twice a week? Anyway, the Salisburys had all but given up on poor Rocky when one day, months later, there he was, scratching away at their front door. Mr. McGruder theorized: whoever lives in the big white house noticed Rocky outback, thought owning a dog was a novel idea, and eventually decided the novelty was too much trouble and turned him loose. Even after months of captivity, the little pup knew just where to go."

"Does Mr. McGruder know who lives in the big white house?" Gabby wondered. I could see Gabby swelling with the hope that perhaps Mr. McGruder could provide a gateway to the novel *The Mystery of the Big White House* brewing in her head; it would feature a family who, for years, kept hidden a deranged killer in its midst. Nothing could put the sparkle in Gabby's eyes more readily than a murderous psychopath.

"He doesn't know who presently resides in the house, if anyone, but does have a theory, aside from knowing the house's history."

I interrupted Ursula to interject, "If no one currently resides in the house, what can explain the girl who comes to visit?"

"There are some who believe—the Westons, it was told to us, were among them—that the house came to relatives who have yet to decide whether or not they wish to live there but have a daughter who comes all dressed up in gowns, plays pretend, and acts out harmless fantasies."

I could not imagine a more charming scenario: A young girl born into great wealth, sheltered from the ills of the world by oppressive parents, convinces the sympathetic limousine driver instructed to take her to the library to, instead, drive her to the big white house, where, at last, she is free to unleash her true essence, act capricious, unlock the mysteries of her womanhood, and—as it is a common trait among girls coming of age—imagine that she is in love. Often, the house is her stage: she dances, leaps, twirls, and curtsies, as would a delicate ballerina to a chorus of imagined applause. Sometimes, she sits regally, as would a queen in a high-backed chair of finely-carved walnut and brocade material, and commands the world of make-believe she has created. After all, she is limited only by her imagination. Then her young lover comes along—the very young man for whom she was warned to be wary, if not forbidden to see. He has stealthily made his way through the woods leading to the backyard and patio, then unseen slips through the back door. At last, in each other's arms, alone in a haven shielding them from a world that seeks to tear them apart, they act out tragic love stories: Tristan and Isolde, Eugene Onegin and Tatyana Larina, Anna Karenina and Count Vronsky, and Romeo and Juliet; they pour their hearts into the façade of literary lovers, then ponder whether their love runs deep enough to endure a forbidding world.

"Do tell us of Mr. McGruder's theory and the house's history," Gabby begged Ursula. Before Ursula could begin, Gabby explained that I was a novelist and that an old house with a peculiar past might greatly interest me.

"So, you're a writer," Warren remarked. It had been nearly twenty minutes since Warren contributed anything to the conversation. I detected a note of accusation in his tenor; he had labeled me a "thinker," not a "doer," and that I merely "imagined," not "executed." Perhaps that was the impression I gave, though I cannot imagine anyone reaching such a conclusion based only upon what thus far had transpired. Anyway, my initial inclination was to tell Tractorboy Biff to go fuck himself, but I did a good job keeping myself restrained.

"I'm a novelist," I respectfully explained to Warren. "I concoct stories, in particular, ones about serial killers. Writers, meanwhile, whip out features, articles, and columns and have the constant burden and pressure of deadlines. Honestly, I can't imagine how they do it; but I suppose we all have our strengths.

"I also teach English Literature for a living wage, so it matters not whether I complete a novel in a year or two or four." An English Lit teacher and novelist: where a hairy hulking tractor rider is concerned, I'm a fairy with a wand.

"Good, Mitch, now, can we finally get to Mr. McGruder's theory and the house's history?" Gabby implored.

"I'll begin with the history," Ursula decided. "There seems to be a discrepancy over which year the house was built; some say it was before the Civil War, others maintain 1870, when the first known owner, Daniel Montague, inhabited the old place. Montague wasn't a farmer, but all the land on which our homes currently sit was once farmland, and it all belonged to him. It's also known that he was a descendant of Francis Daniel Pastorius, a German Quaker from the Rhineland. Like others, Pastorius came to the new world seeking land and religious freedom; he acted as an agent on behalf of a land purchasing company from Frankfurt and bargained with William Penn himself to acquire a tract of land that afterward became known as Germantown. That was sometime in the early 1680s. Soon after the news reached Pastorius's homeland, The Concord, a ship carrying thirteen families from Germany, arrived in Philadelphia with plans to settle in their new home: Germantown. They were agricultural people—peaceful, industrious, and typically pious. It was said of Pastorius that inscribed on his front door were the words: *No words of welcome to the godless and profane.* One can only imagine what those early German settlers would think of the moral decay of America in the late 1990s and where it seems to be heading."

Ursula paused. I assumed it was to allow her moment of digression to sink in. "Although," she continued, "I'm hardly one to advocate for morality."

Now that's what I call a remark meant to give one pause! Had Ursula just admitted to, of all things, illicit behavior? Her eyes did not shift in Warren's direction when delivering her self-recrimination.

Moreover, missing was any note of apology; Ursula simply issued a statement that failed to faze Warren in the least. My mind leaped to my *rescued prostitute* theory that Ursula's illicit behavior occurred before any romantic involvement with Tractorboy Biff. But what was the likelihood that a woman capable of acquiring Ursula's position and possessing her manner and intellect ever needed any rescuing, never mind once prostituting herself? So I formed a second theory: Ursula and Warren were polyamorous or had the sort of marriage that allowed for peculiar quirks; thus, neither was an advocate for morality.

Ursula continued: "A great deal of history came to pass between the day Francis Daniel Pastorius arrived in America, and Daniel Montague, who Mr. McGruder learned was Pastorius's great, great, great nephew, moved into the big white house. Montague, who also owned a townhouse in Old City Philadelphia, was known to be a socialite, playboy, a formidable acquaintance, and who, at age forty, took a child bride of seventeen. The young lady's name was Eloise, and the poor thing miscarried four times before a fifth child, a daughter, was born. Tragically, the infant did not survive but a month. So it was not until age thirty-seven—1900—that Eloise brought a very healthy Daniel Montague II into the world."

"Daniel Montague I and his child bride died some years before Mr. McGruder's family settled in the area, but Mr. McGruder became well-acquainted with Daniel Montague II. He was thirty years Mr. McGruder's senior, so they were not what you would call "chums," Mr. McGruder told me. He also told me he had numerous conversations, many in passing, and during these exchanges, Mr. McGruder learned quite a bit of the Montague family history. At an early age, Daniel Montague II, with no siblings and deceased parents, settled into the role of "Lord of the Manor." So it was only natural that he became quite the eligible bachelor and a desirable one at that. But now, here's where the story gets interesting: Daniel meets and marries Giselle Davis Parker, a well-connected socialite from Boston, and he brings her here to live in the big white house. They threw the most lavish parties; their home was where the who's-who of Philadelphia society would gather; limousines would line the length of the pike. But it all came to a crushing end when Giselle, who became pregnant, died in childbirth. Days later, a midwife was seen leaving the house in tears and was never heard from again. No one knew whether the child was a boy or girl

The Bohemian

and whether or not he or she had survived, for a child never was seen. But there were rumors; everyone had a theory.

"Daniel's public life was over; he kept mainly to himself and seldom was seen about town; he was usually spotted walking the quiet streets in the early morning or late evening. Occasionally, women came to visit but would stay only a few hours or a day; they were assumed to have been Parker women coming down from Boston to check on a grandson or granddaughter—a niece or nephew. Eventually, no one came to visit the big white house. Mr. McGruder was fifteen when he first met Daniel, who was age forty-five. He, too, had heard the rumors of a child who had survived but, for whatever reason, was never permitted to make a public appearance. Mr. McGruder was infinitely curious, for the child would have been his age but was forbidden to ask. The prevailing rumor was that the child was a daughter and that Daniel, despondent after Giselle's death to the extent of madness, groomed his daughter to become his child bride. Whether or not the awful rumor was true, as Mr. McGruder has told me, 'It was all based on the assumption that there was ever a child in the first place.'"

I managed to chime in: "The existence of a child aside, is it possible that Daniel is still living and that it is *he* whom the young woman visits every so often, all dressed up in evening gowns? In a warped way, it might make sense for a man of influence who used to throw lavish parties for others of influence, as Daniel had, to want to recapture his glory days and does so by summoning an obliging great-great niece or second cousin two generations removed to his home to reenact his past. And if that happens to be the case, it would also stand to reason that the girl is showing up at the big white house all dressed in evening gowns once worn by Giselle herself!"

"I can certainly see why you're a novelist, Mitch," said Ursula. Her tone was complimentary. "It's a fantastic theory, and one that's as believable as it is fascinating; unfortunately, one minor detail spoils it: Daniel Montague II died sometime in the early 1970s. His death was no less mysterious than his life, and I was told his funeral was a private affair. Years passed without the house having a single visitor or activity; then, out of the blue, a girl dressed up in evening gowns began making periodic appearances. The way Mr. McGruder sees it, there are two possibilities: The girl is the daughter of those to whom the house was passed and is an eccentric with an overactive imagination. Or she comes to visit the son or daughter of Daniel and Giselle

Montague—a son or daughter who would be Mr. McGruder's age, sixty-two, and has yet to see the light of day."

So there went my theory of a young woman dressing up in Giselle's old gowns to the delight of a delusional old widower. I've noticed that lately, my theories are getting scrapped no sooner than I indulge them. Nevertheless, as Ursula illustrated, it was a fantastic theory, both fascinating and believable, and well worthy of inserting somewhere in the novel that Gabby had been secretly concocting in her mind these past four days.

"Well, that was certainly one of the more enlightening evenings I've had since coming to the States," Gabby said once we were back and nestled in our abode.

"*Enlightening* is just the word *I* would be inclined to use," I said. "And did you notice that when Ursula spoke, which was a great deal of the time, she looked only at you? The only time she looked my way was to compliment me on my theory concerning the young girl, which turned out to be an impossibility, and even then, it was a fleeting glance."

"With how you behaved earlier in the week, it was a wonder that you got invited, never mind having had any attention paid to you."

"I admit it; I behaved badly, but my keen novelist's sense tells me there's more to the story. And what's more, the whole time that Ursula seemed to be doing her best to avoid engaging too much with me, Tractorboy Biff's eyes were burning a hole in my head. I wasn't sure whether I was getting graded, though on what I couldn't hazard a guess. Perhaps he was daring me to ogle his wife."

"Mitch, I thought that we agreed you would no longer refer to Warren as 'Biff' if for no other reason than you'll likely slip up at an inopportune moment." Gabby frothed with irony when issuing her reminder and further suggested I was acting paranoid, if not trending toward the characteristics of a paranoid schizophrenic. Far be it from me to submit I am not without my share of quirks—who would, nowadays? —but I am somewhat intuitive, and I know what I saw, and what I saw led me to surmise there was more to our new neighbors, who, ostensibly seemed our contemporaries, than meets the eye.

We did not catch a glimpse or hear a peep out of Ursula and Warren all day Saturday. "Must have gone on a road trip," I had guessed. It was a good day for an adventure, and later we learned that

The Bohemian

our new neighbors had gone kayaking on the Lehigh River up near a charming village named after an elite athlete from yesteryear, Jim Thorpe. However, the very next day, we saw what I would describe as *plenty* of our new neighbors when peering over the olive hedge bordering on the right and down into their backyard. Specifically, it was Ursula who became the source of my fixation and engendered my open-mouthed gaze. Save for her accessories, which included stylish sunglasses, fully naked on a chaise lounge was how I found her posed. Gabby came strolling into our bedroom midday and witnessed me sitting in a chair, staring dumbly out the window.

At first, she likened me to an overmedicated mental patient captivated by some meaningless banality; however, upon further review, she noticed that I was wide-eyed with fascination and came to suspect something was triggering my arousal. She stole from behind me and rested her chin on my shoulder; we shared a view. Ursula had her hair gathered in a ponytail; the lower frame of her sunglasses was resting on cheekbones made especially lovely by her face in repose. Another feature worth honoring was her throat: the well-defined protrusions of bone at the point where her throat meets her chest were inspirational; those below, made by her hips and pelvis, which accentuated where she was most curvaceous, roused me to where I became envious of the sun and air.

"We didn't pay nearly enough for this house," I remarked. I expected to feel a playful slap connecting with the back of my head. But, instead, Gabby replied, "She truly is an eyeful. Ursula, from her pretty head to her slender lovely toes, is positively scrumptious looking."

I thought "scrumptious" was a peculiar term for one woman to describe another; it seemed to trend less toward admiration and more toward desire. Nevertheless, I let it pass, holding to the notion that "scrumptious" was present-day British hyperbole for beautiful. Naturally, yours truly had a theory of his own for why Ursula was taking such delightful advantage of the dwindling rays of the summer sun. I had myself convinced it must be a voyeuristic ritual, and one which saw Ursula sunbathe in the nude while Warren remained hidden away inside, peeping from a window, a deviant furiously masturbating while fixed on the loveliness of Ursula's well-toned figure. Another suspicion occurred to me: Was this all that Ursula allowed? Instead of witnessing a form of foreplay, however bizarre, that would lead to an afternoon of splendor, did Ursula find Warren unworthy? Or, perhaps it was Warren who deemed himself undeserving? Gabby maintained that the paranoid schizophrenic tendencies she accused me of possessing Friday night were still very much in play. At first, I took exception to what I alleged was a groundless accusation. Then I began musing over the possibility myself. And going for my binoculars, not to better view Ursula—my vantage point was sufficient—but to spy into the bedroom windows across the way, for I had suspected a captive audience, only served to legitimize Gabby's charge and my self-doubt.

"*So?*" Gabby seemed to intone that the possibility someone else could be spending their midday Sunday, as was I, was remote at best. But I was happy to report that there was more than one peeping Tom within the township—that Ursula had inspired plenty of spectatorship. Shortly following my discovery, I set aside my binoculars and rose from my chair as though overcome by a sense of urgency.

"Lost interest already, have you?" Gabby seemed both surprised and disappointed. The latter, I found peculiar.

"*The Case of the Camden Lock Killer!*" I told her excitedly. "I know how it ends!"

"*Really?*" she intoned.

Again, my behavior surprised Gabby. "Did the inspiration arise from Ursula's nakedness or peeping into the bedroom windows across the way? Never mind," she was quick to add, "I'm not sure I want to know the answer."

"It's a good thing because I'm not sure myself," I told her, which was the truth. "The inspiration, if that's what it was, came upon me just like that." I snapped my fingers to illustrate the thin air from which the motivation materialized, then excused myself. Gabby and I had unwritten rules concerning my writing: when struck by inspiration, she would leave me alone to capture what was pinballing around my head; otherwise, she was free to become part of the process; the same rules applied when she was sketching. So I disappeared, leaving Gabby at the window, where she continued to gaze at Ursula.

****

It was early Friday evening, warm and balmy; the square was settling down from the constant parading of feet on what had been a typical London day. Like any big city, London was a fireworks display whose first impressive boom came Monday morning, followed by an unrelenting buzz until the Friday afternoon finale. The night

revealed its earliest signs of dusk; the climax subsided to a low murmur reluctant to dissipate, though those who remained in the square
could achieve a sense of insulation from a city stubborn to wind
down fully. Strolling a sixteen-month-old boy named Jackson
through the court was an aging detective and a woman who years ago
forgave him.

What hasn't a sixty-two-year-old detective seen? The answer:
Not much. And yet, Granville Tovey has turned his back on all vices
deemed destructive. Nowadays, the only accusations the veteran detective might face was being too attentive of a husband, father, and
grandfather; still, he entertains two obsessions: The case file of Jack
the Ripper and one Dr. Albert Stahl. Of these dual obsessions, only
the latter causes the craggy, old detective to sleep fitfully. Over and
over, Granville Tovey had replayed the conversation he and Dr. Albert
Stahl had engaged in while overlooking the canal that runs through
Camden Lock Market. Nearly word-for-word, he wrote down the
lengthy exchange and, as a ritual, read it morning and night. In each
instance, he came away asking the same question: Why did this former
psychologist choose his inability to understand the strains of Bartok
to illustrate Einstein's theory of insanity? It was a perplexing question,
one that led the detective to theorize, with concern for the music of
Bela Bartok: Dr. Albert Stahl may have experienced a profound moment of clarity; thus, encrypted in one of the great Hungarian composer's opuses—as the doctor would come to interpret it—was the
mystery of what turned a former psychologist into a deranged killer.

Granville Tovey knew nothing of Bartok but managed to
gather every available opus, among them: piano concertos, violin concertos, string quartets, *The Miraculous Mandarin*, Hungarian folk music,
and the renowned *Concerto for Orchestra*; he listened to what he described
to Lieutenant Van Pelt, Detective Hellickson, Jane, Melissa, and Joe
over coffee, as screeching and howling accompanied by savage percus-
sions. It took months of listening before anything that could qualify as
a line of melody became even somewhat discernable.

"My virgin ears!" he kept crying. Still, he continued listening,
but to no avail, uncovering no hidden codes, messages, or meanings—
nothing to put him further inside the killer's mind or help better understand the killer beyond the initial profile he created. Instead, he
pondered the possibility that Dr. Albert Stahl, rather cunningly, set the
detective upon what he hoped would be a subliminal pathway leading

to insanity. Twice, Detective Tovey attended concerts of the London Philharmonic: first to listen to Isaac Stern play *Bartok's First Violin Concerto*, with Pierre Boulez at the baton; later to hear the great Hungarian composer's *Concerto for Orchestra*, with Bernard Haitink at the podium; it was far less for a musical experience and more for the hope of spotting among the crowd, disguised or otherwise, the former psychologist turned serial killer who compelled him to endure Bartok.

Still in the glow of excitement brought about by discovery, as best he could, with Lieutenant Van Pelt agitatedly pacing about and Detective Hellickson blowing cloud after cloud of smoke into the air, Detective Granville Tovey described Dr. Albert Stahl, if indeed that was his real name, to a sketch artist. A lieutenant, and two detectives, who only an hour ago were bleary-eyed from exhaustion and failure, were as alert and energized as they had been in months.

"I'd say he was in his late fifties, perhaps early sixties, six feet tall, tipping the scales at 190 pounds," Detective Tovey began, addressing the sketch artist and his colleagues. "His eyes weren't set too far apart nor too close; they were normal and seemed to possess a great deal of knowledge he enjoyed passing off as wisdom." Van Pelt, growing more anxious by the minute, shot his senior detective a look. *Forget the intangibles; stay on point with the physical description,* was what the detective read in the lieutenant's eyes. "His eyes had a smile all their own... like, like a twinkle, and all his facial features seemed more relaxed when he spoke; he seemed most happy when talking." Again, there came a look from Van Pelt, who was failing to see any relevance in the demeanor of Dr. Albert Stahl. "His eyebrows were bushy like he was weeks overdue for his barber; also, his hair was graying and over his collar; and even though he was wearing a Tam, I could tell he had a full head of hair."

"Let's get back to the face, Gran, shall we," the lieutenant urged. "Anything outstanding other than twinkling eyes and bushy eyebrows?"

"Yes!" said the senior detective, as though struck by an unexpected notion. "I didn't realize it until just now, but Stahl had red cheeks, not the kind you get from too much boozing; they were blotchy, like a skin condition. He also had a straight across mustache, not Hitler-like, much wider; it gave him a grandfatherly appearance."

"That's just dandy, Gran," said Lieutenant Van Pelt once the artist revealed the sketch, "you just described Bert Lancaster!"

The Bohemian

"Widen the nose a drop and make the chin slightly rounder," said the detective. "Perfect!" he exclaimed. "That's our man!"

Early the following day began a manhunt for a deranged killer who called himself Dr. Albert Stahl. "We know who he is, Joe," Detective Tovey told his friend after he signaled for Joe to lean over the counter so that he may reveal the news in whispers. "It's just a matter of finding him before he kills again." But Dr. Albert Stahl never did kill again, nor did he make another attempt. His career was over—a career which he, of his own accord, decided to bring to a conclusion. When Stahl had said to Granville Tovey, "Good day, detective," it was not a misspeak, but purposeful words Stahl was confident would not register until gone from the detective's sight, if not much later. Then the doctor went underground, becoming more or less a nonperson. Moreover, some theorized Stahl went on to lead a life that ran contrary to Dick Whittington's, for he took along only two possessions—his violin and cat named Pavlov—thus going from riches to rags.

It turns out that there was a Doctor Albert Stahl, who was a product of privilege and attended St. George's University of London years ago before going on for his Ph.D. at Edinburgh in Scotland. He was born and raised in Hounslow and set up a private practice in Camden in 1967, where he worked until 1982. His last known address was in Islington. Then, just like that, he disappears, drops out of society, seemingly without leaving a trace: no address, current banking records, forwarding information, ties to former patients, friends, or family relations; it was as if he had foreseen what he would one day become, and thus followed through with the procedure of cutting all known ties. Now, on the other side of what marked a thorough self-reinvention, he has taken to existing in places some call "the cracks of society," becoming a pseudo vagabond living on the fringe but with hidden assets at his disposal. That was one theory, which happened to belong to Granville Tovey. "I'm guessing he stays in a different hotel every night under an assumed name; he manages to escape suspicion using disguises and poses himself as a road-weary traveler. But no need to worry; he'll slip up. He's a man who can't help himself from engaging, from sharing his knowledge with the notion he's imparting others with his worldliness and wisdom. Everyone has his picture and profile. It will only be a matter of time; we need only remain methodical."

Hellickson was not entirely sold on Tovey's theory; his own was that a man of Stahl's intellect and inherited and accumulated wealth would have long since made arrangements to flee, and tracking him would make for a difficult task. "If not in Europe, he's probably taken up a life of meditation in India and aspires to become a Hindu. It pains me to say it: our best chance is that he has entered a cooling-off period but will return to England and begin killing again."

"He won't do that," grumbled Lieutenant Van Pelt. "He's perfectly aware that we know who he is. In other words, he's already gained recognition—his brilliance has been realized and duly accredited. So if he fled the country, there's no goddamn good reason for him to return. It also means we're stuck relying on our friends abroad, which is the polite way of saying we got schooled and screwed by a man who could've been a public intellectual but opted for public enemy number one!"

"He's not a madman for nothing," added Hellickson.

The manhunt continued for weeks. Unfortunately, a nation cannot allow a single assailant to hijack its entire roster of law enforcement. Following the due course, each precinct could only commit so many men to the cause. As the months wore on, the committed manpower had dwindled; the trail became colder. To Van Pelt, Tovey, and Hellickson's dismay, a serial killer may have slipped through their fingers, but after nine quiet months following a nine-month killing spree, the city of London felt less threatened, if not breathing easy.

"Nine goddamn months," grumbled Van Pelt, "and the best we have to offer that collection of vultures we call a press is that we only *may* have pressured a deranged killer into retirement."

A year had passed since Stahl's last kill. Granville Tovey delved into researching serials that had taken unusually long hiatuses between what had been their standard killing interval and ones caught long after they had stopped killing. Indeed, it was a shortlist; its applicability, at best, was sketchy.

Another year passed. The Toveys were spotted strolling their first grandchild, a girl named Jessica, or Jesse as she was fondly called, through the square. Not too long ago, there was a time when the likelihood of such an occurrence could not have been entertained, not even as a passing thought. Moreover, it was hard for the Toveys to look at their granddaughter, whom in unity they cherished, and their rescued marriage, for which they were both grateful and not think of a man who terrorized all of London by taking away nine of its citizens. Doubtless, it was a source of disconcertion, this curious irony that occurred to both Granville and Jane Tovey, and it was an irony that neither dared to intimate aloud. After all, the cause and effect of one Dr. Albert Stahl were much less profound and impactful for the Toveys than it was for the families of his nine victims. In other words, it simply was not necessary to lend credibility to the notion: If not for the actions of Stahl, Harold Halsbury would still be alive, and a certain craggy aging detective would still be drinking.

A third year passed. For many, Dr. Albert Stahl was no longer a top priority. His picture and profile were still handy—and he remained on the A-list of everyone in law enforcement—but the network of investigators once committed to the Stahl murders had shrunk considerably. Occasionally, Detective Tovey would stroll the bustling grounds of Camden Lock Market, holding to the notion that should he prove capable of adopting a particular perspective, he too might judge humanity as once had a deranged killer owning a skewed philosophy. Moreover, it might shed some light on where Stahl may have fled, assuming that Hellickson's theory was correct. There was a time, not all that long ago, when Grandville Tovey saw the world through suspicious eyes and shared, albeit for different reasons, Stahl's contempt for humanity. But nowadays, as a man with many miles on his odometer awarded a second chance at life and a granddaughter, viewing humankind through the eyes of Dr. Albert Stahl would not come easy. With baby Jesse lingering never far from his thoughts—most days, she was his prevailing thought—a world he once held in contempt had become a place filled with hope and endless possibilities.

In year six, Dr. Albert Stahl was still at large when Lieutenant Van Pelt retired, Detective Tovey got promoted to lieutenant, and Hellickson became the senior detective. It was also the year Hellickson quit smoking. "Cold turkey," he repeatedly reminded everyone. "He went from miserable to proud to piously outspoken against the ills of tobacco," Lieutenant Tovey told Jane. "Some folks are more palatable when they're busy killing themselves."

It was also the year the Toveys welcomed into the world their second grandchild, a girl named Melissa, for her mother; the family took to calling her Mel. It also marked the year the new lieutenant entertained the possibility that Stahl had died versus the new senior detective's latest theory that he was living out his days as a gardener at some poor centuries-old monastery somewhere abroad.

"He made his point," Hellickson maintained. "He was a killer with a goal, a philosophy—or, as you've stated numerous times, 'a lunatic who saw humanity going astray'—and now he intends to live out the rest of his days peacefully, prattling away with tomato stakes and fertilizer. Just because it's never been thought of until now, who's to say that deranged killers don't understand the concept of sunsets?"

"Lately, Hellickson talks of Stahl as though he were a man whose brilliance is worthy of scholarship," the new lieutenant complained to Jane Tovey. "He was a privileged young man who, as an adult, failed as a psychologist, then rode off into the sunset a successful killer. Perhaps it's me who's blind, but I fail to see the brilliance!" Despite his rebuke of Hellickson's opinion, the new lieutenant, all along, suspected that Stahl was not a failure as a psychologist but electively walked away from one career because he found another more rewarding.

"You were never meant to catch them all, Gran," Jane Tovey consolingly told the craggy old lieutenant. "In your line of work, perfection is not an attainable goal; it's in the stars for some to escape the law. And I know what you are thinking: it would be worth trading away ten of your successes to bring Stahl to justice; unfortunately, not everything in this world may be bargained for or traded, and regardless of how you may feel, failing to bring Stahl to justice in no way tarnishes your career."

Jane Tovey's logic and wisdom were easy enough to follow, especially for a forty-year law enforcement veteran. Still, her words provided little satisfaction for the craggy lieutenant, who continued to experience fitful nights of sleep over a conversation with a killer once in his mitts. He was sure Stahl had come to the marketplace that morning because he suspected the detective, whose habits Stahl had been tracking, would be available to seek out and engage. That much was clear. How many times, Grandville Tovey strenuously pondered, had Stahl lurked nearby, immersing himself in a crowd, or was spying from the vantage point of a café while sipping coffee as he and Hellickson were leaning over the body of a victim found under an overpass or fished from the canal? In those moments, and one's similar,

Hellickson would hand the senior detective a cigarette without him needing to ask. For years, Tovey remained convinced that somewhere encrypted within the lines of a conversation currently six-years-old—one he reconciled was a scripted affair, thus, making him a victim of manipulation—there were clues that Dr. Albert Stahl was through killing, what his plans were following his reign of terror, and where those plans were to take place.

Four years later, when the Toveys were strolling sixteen-month-old Jackson, their third grandchild, through the square, the craggy old lieutenant had an eye pointed toward *his* sunset. He had been sleeping better of late, and as was the case with the Jack the Ripper file, Dr. Albert Stahl had become, more or less, a pastime. Moreover, he had since developed a deportment indicative of a man in the twilight of his career; in other words, somewhat absent was the obsessiveness and bulldog determination for which he was once well-known.

"Jackson loves the way you can get the pigeons to eat right out of your hand," Jane Tovey brightly chirped. The little lad clapped whenever a pigeon would pick a morsel from his grandfather's fingertips.

"I was once a pigeon myself, you know," the old lieutenant told his grandson. "That's why I can communicate with them, you see. It's true. For years, I flew all over London; I knew every bridge, building, and square; I called all these wonderful places way up high my home. Then, luckily, one day, I landed on your grandmother's windowsill. Well, she dashed as quickly as possible, threw open the sash, patted me on my beak, and presto, I turned into a real live person!"

"Your grandfather omitted part of the story," Jane Tovey told Jackson. "At first, when I threw open the sash, I tried to shoo him away, but, like all Tovey men, he was stubborn, your grandfather, and refused to fly away. It wasn't until he flapped his wings and looked at me with his sad pigeon eyes that I petted his beak. So, you might say your grandfather and I are very much like the story of The Frog and the Princess."

Folks paraded through the square, seemingly anxious for their destinations; on their faces, they wore expressions indicative of the time and day; nevertheless, many took a moment to acknowledge an alert young boy receptive to all interactions. However, many failed to notice or, more accurately, pretended not to see the wretched soul sitting cross-legged out by the perimeter of the square, positioned with his back to all the eager-for-the-weekend alacrity. He had a tattered old cloak draped partly over a shoulder; the rest spilled onto the ground: That it covered but a small portion of his person was a warning to others of his undisputed ownership. Given the balmy conditions, a cloak of any sort seemed incongruous. Still, the likelier scenario concerning an article of which he was the original owner or harvested from someone less fortunate: he had no place to store it, thus was forced to drag it about until arrived the days ahead when it would serve him well. On the ground beside the cloak, he kept a basket. Moreover, he was sitting what he alleged a respectable distance from those whom the square accommodated. Possibly, he did not wish to bear witness to the effect his wretchedness had upon others—or, as Jane Tovey had theorized, was too proud to face passersby kind enough to toss their spare change into his modest receptacle.

"The poor fellow doesn't believe he's entitled to the very space upon which he's sitting," she moaned to the lieutenant. Granville Tovey rose from the bench where he sat doting over Jackson and made his way toward the wretched soul. Along the way, he took a bill from his fold, discreetly placed it in the basket, and turned to walk away. Only a few paces had the lieutenant tread when what settled in his ears was the bowing of a violin. He stopped and began to gyrate—his figure saw the completion of a slow and somewhat unsteady pirouette—and during this maneuver, his eyes surveyed the square in search of a musician; his ears had greedily gathered in the notes hanging buoyantly in the balmy air. The music: had he not heard it before? This eerie, swerving, meandering strain, seemingly striving to arrange itself into a discernable phrase: was it not familiar? Had he not heard it ten times, one hundred times, perhaps a thousand? A grin formed on his face; it was caustic, ironical, and indicative of self-deprecation over a discovery that took far too long to realize.

All along, well-concealed by the man's tattered cloak and the rumpled brim of a planter's hat was a violin which, despite the modest accumulation in his basket, he elected to keep silent until Lieutenant Granville Tovey displayed his generosity. Then, in a pianissimo manner, he bowed when he felt the weight of the lieutenant's gaze at his back. Then he uttered, unmistakably for Granville Tovey's benefit, though without the slightest turn of his head to pass for an acknowledgment: "I believe I'm finally beginning to understand the madness of this Hungarian. What about you, Detective? I beg your pardon: Lieutenant. Nowadays, it *is* Lieutenant, am I correct? Have you, too, begun to understand?" Softer and slower, the violinist continued to play what the lieutenant recognized as the *non-troppo lento* movement of *Bartok's String Quartet No. 4.* He dropped to a knee beside the musician.

"Congratulations," he began, "it took you nearly half a lifetime to disprove Einstein's definition of insanity."

"And you, my friend, have disproved it in far less time than I, although, in the spirit of fairness, you'll need to award me credit for an assist. But enough talk of insanity as it may apply to music and law enforcement. I see matters have continued quite swimmingly since last we spoke: you've patched up your marriage, haven't touched a drop of alcohol, your former partner gave up his fiendish tobacco habit, Van Pelt's retirement led to your elevation in the company, and I see you have quite an extended family in whose lives you routinely participate."

"In your spare time, you've managed to keep accurate tabs on me, I see; who could've imagined I'd become a person of interest?" Despite not fearing Stahl and suspecting that Stahl admired him, the lieutenant sneered as one might when owning profound disdain concerning an alleged notion.

"Between my travels, yes, I have kept tabs on a great many things, but of you, especially. Incidentally, I've visited India, seen The Parthenon, hiked the Black Forest, sailed the Danube, and written quite a detailed journal of all my travels, but I always return to my native England. Why, might you ask? And please, Lieutenant, do me the honor of confessing your curiosity."

"Go on." The lieutenant would have preferred his words to sound gruff and burdensome. Had they, Stahl could no more have resisted enlightening the lieutenant had they not. Nevertheless, the lieutenant's curiosity would not allow any ill temper or exhaustion to resonate.

Since Granville Tovey had shown himself obliging, Stahl spared him any supercilious preamble. "To see if, in any way, my efforts have served to influence our society, of course. And just as important, particularly where you are concerned, Lieutenant, to see whether or not eliminating poor Mr. Halsbury has proved a worthwhile endeavor. Congratulations, Lieutenant; it seems that only the latter has shown me a man of steep accomplishment. You have my gratitude, and I do not say this with irony."

"You are quite correct, Doctor; if not for you, I'd still be a solitary man who every night finds his way to the bottom of a bottle—a man who would have lost his wife for good to someone who, at the time, was far more deserving—a man who today, would not be involved in the lives of his three grandchildren. But…"

"…But," Dr. Albert Stahl interjected, "your role in society is not one of an existentialist; you are a guardian of public trust limited by empiricism and therefore duty-bound to arrest me."

"Doctor," said Lieutenant Tovey, "I could not have said it better myself."

****

Ignoring Gabby and attempting, with only marginal success, to place Ursula's nakedness far from my thoughts, I barricaded myself in my writing room for thirteen hours. The result? I delivered what I believed thus far stood as the best chapter of my career. I limped out of the room at 2:00 a.m. to discover that Gabby was sound asleep. I placed the final pages on her nightstand and attached a note that read: *finito*. Having had the benefit of a whole night's sleep, Gabby rose early, and with a mug of coffee and the final chapter of our manuscript in hand, she nestled herself in the parlor. I crept partway down the stairs. Without Gabby noticing my presence, I watched as she read the final six pages. She had a hand to her mouth; I could see her eyes shifting back and forth, devouring every word. She was even more captivated than I could have hoped. I went creeping back to our bed, hoping to steal another hour or two, but it was not long afterward that I heard Gabby stampeding up the stairs. Assuming I was still asleep, she threw open the door, raced to the bed, and took a flying leap; the maneuver saw her land squarely on top of me. "Mitch!" she cried out. "It's brilliant! Not in a million years could I have concocted such an ending!" Then she added, with the very devil sparkling in her eyes: "How are the winters here in Philadelphia, Mitch? Would it be too much to ask Ursula to lie naked year-round?"

That same evening, come the nine o'clock hour, my eyes drooped shut, which was how they would remain. However, I felt Gabby's lips press against my forehead before she reached for her sketchpad and made for her chair in the parlor. Come morning, I found a drawing of Dr. Albert Stahl on my nightstand, just as I had imagined him to have appeared in the final scene. He is sitting cross-legged on the ground toward the outskirts of the square; long un-kempt hair hangs below a tam, a tattered cloak is partly draped over a shoulder, and his bow is resting. Behind him, slightly off to the side, stands Lieutenant Tovey. The lieutenant's juxtaposition allows for the viewing of Stahl's profile. Stahl's head is posed at a slight downward tilt; a shifting eye appears to regard something unseen over his shoulder. His countenance is not apparent to the lieutenant. Tovey is only seen from the waist down—a dangling hand is visible—but there is a clear sense that astonishment has triggered his rigid posture. The doctor's expression is one of complexity: evident is the satisfaction that Lieutenant Tovey has familiarized himself with the many opuses of Bela Bartok; also, the resignation that a story, which began several years ago and was made personal by the slaying of Harold Halsbury, has, at last, ended—its conclusion written by the doctor, himself, a man whose life was one of many phases and journeys. If the final chapter of *The Case of the Camden Lock Killer* was my finest work to date, the same could get said of its artistic representation. It was Gabby's most poignant work; the subtleties she captured in her sketch may have surpassed the very words themselves.

CHAPTER ELEVEN
MISS HAVISHAM

Lucky me, Gabby and Ursula struck up a fast friendship, which came as no surprise, particularly on Gabby's part, coming from overseas and having no ties, save for those to whom I had introduced her. Gravitating toward someone of Ursula's beauty and intellect, given the proximity, was a predictable scenario, but it came with one glaring drawback: Gabby had gushed to Ursula her enthusiasm over *The Case of the Camden Lock Killer* when, one Saturday afternoon, they were sunbathing together (not in the raw; they were wearing swimsuits) and sipping mint juleps. It was not so much Gabby divulging aspects of our brainchild to Ursula that became the drawback. The downside was Warren. Instead of inside, near a window, and masturbating, he invented what seemed a plausible reason to occupy the yard near our bathing beauties (he was spreading mulch) and overheard Gabby, in her adorable British accent, crowing over my literary prowess. This seemingly innocuous scenario would yield an unfortunate result: Warren would launch himself into hyperdrive to prove that he was the one "true man" on the block. *I'll show the book boy what a real man does!* The following day (Sunday), hoping for peace on my back patio—for the first time in many months, I allowed myself to become immersed in writing that was not mine; Somerset Maugham's *The Moon and Sixpence* was the choice: a novel based on the life of the artist, Paul Gauguin—I became familiarized with every motorized gas-guzzling piece of equipment Warren owned; anything that required cycle one or two engine oil, whether necessary or not, was started, revved, and run: a tractor, edger, trimmer, leaf blower, chainsaw, pressure washer, even a goddamn rototill were all applied with unparalleled zeal. Warren invented reasons to run them all; thus, I received the whole gamut, the complete contents of what a "real man" houses in a "real man's" shed. The result was a glorious afternoon featuring armpits, biceps, sweat, pull cords, blaring engines, plus an overabundance of back hair—otherwise, an afternoon that came dangerously close to negating the thrill of viewing Ursula's nakedness. Upon the day's completion—although I would not qualify it as a compliment—I upgraded Warren from Tractorboy Biff to The Canadian Elk Hunter.

"I'll eat my shoes if I ever learn that Warren hasn't killed and eaten an elk, if not a grizzly bear," I said to Gabby.

"You're just bothered because you're unable to make sense of him and Ursula together," was Gabby's retort. "Not everything in the world needs making sense of; some matters should be allowed to carry on, deprived of scrutiny, or a novelist trying to figure out how a given matter fits into the grand scheme of his worldview. After all, Mitch, what sense was there in Nina having been born a sweet little English boy—or, for that matter, *someone* fornicating with their cousin? If you spent less time trying to figure out Warren and more time trying to get to know him—more traditionally—you might, to your surprise, discover that he owns qualities that even 'the great Mitch Morningstar' finds palatable."

Although forcefully eloquent and potentiated with irony, *that*, unmistakably and unequivocally, is what is known as getting called an ass. And perhaps Gabby was right. I had not given The Canadian Elk Hunter a fair chance; also, I had failed to see the extent of my quirks which, as Gabby scathingly illustrated, have been known, a time or two, to run afoul. So, the constant issuing of physical challenges notwithstanding, for Gabby's benefit, I accepted Warren as a friend and managed it without sardonically posing as an intellectual elitist. The result? The subsequent years involved white water kayaking and rafting the Lehigh River, hiking and canoeing the Adirondacks, and mountain biking rigorous stretches of the Appalachian Trail. Not long after taking up this lifestyle I fittingly dubbed an *odyssey of adventures*—for which Gabby had developed a measure of enthusiasm—I learned that Warren was little more than an empty-headed lumberjack from Canada, that these activities the four of us would routinely partake in belonged to Ursula. As a novelist, I should have known better than to judge a book by its cover. Ursula, a northern Pennsylvanian, who had not an opportunity to navigate a cityscape until attending Temple University—our time there, in our vastly different pursuits, had overlapped by four semesters: Ursula had arrived first—spent much of her formidable years negotiating rivers, lakes, trails, and mountains. These new activities that I had taken on, at first with reluctance, when learning that they were an extension of Ursula, somehow made them more palatable than they might have been otherwise. And so that was the basis for my friendship with Warren: I aimed to please Gabby—happy wife, happy life, I believe goes the idiom—and, perhaps to a greater degree, *covet thy neighbor's goods.*

The summer following our initial year of adventurous rigors, Ursula was no longer sunbathing alone in the nude; alongside her, posed on a matching chaise lounge, was Gabby's shorter, curvier form—and both would sip mint juleps. I would spy the bathing beauties from the bedroom window, as it provided me the necessary trajectory to see over the olive hedge and into the yard. Strange, but viewing Gabby's nakedness out of doors while well-positioned beside Ursula gave me a surge of vitality and titillation that came wholly unexpected; it was as if I were seeing her for the first time—or, better yet, through another's eyes. Perhaps those eyes belonged to Warren: doubtless, The Canadian Elk Hunter had hidden away inside and was masturbating, at first regarding Ursula, then it was the newness of Gabby inspiring him. Then, lastly, and with fury, it was the sinuousness of one and curvaceousness of the other and how they might come together to form a most delightful tangle that inspired a state of idyllic and transcendental thrall. It was madness, utter madness! But to whom did the lunacy belong; who was its rightful owner? Were my assumptions of Warren shaped by my predilection for deviance? Was it, dare I admit, *my* twisted sense of reality at play? Perhaps Warren was never camped out near a window, peeping as might a pathetic wanton? Maybe, in every instance, he was in his parlor watching monster trucks on some remote cable network while yours truly—Mitch Morningstar, creator of deranged killers and otherwise inexhaustible cousin-fucker and libertine extraordinaire—remained with his face pressed to a windowpane transfixed on two glorious subjects and engaging in furious onanism that was both delightful and wicked? I forced myself to rise from my chair and walk away from the window. When doing so, a most inane thought crept into my head: What if Warren and I were lying alongside one another on chaise lounges fully exposed, sipping not mint juleps but bottles of suds? Would Gabby and Ursula—with each unbeknownst to the other—find themselves pressed to a windowpane, sharing in the delight? Of course, they wouldn't! Instead, they would

The Bohemian

wave and wish us a nice day. They would refer to us as "you boys" in a lighthearted tsk-tsk-tsk sort of manner, then head straightaway to the local mall. They might even let loose a giggle or two over a state of affairs they would designate as "impossibly frivolous." Oh, the cruelty and unfairness of feminine charm—from the Garden of Eden to the decadence of Western modernity—how delightfully cruel and unfair.

****

The Case of the Camden Lock Killer hit shelves in the States and England eighteen months following the day of submission. The endorsements of *The London Times, Philadelphia Inquirer,* and *Boston Sunday Globe* were solid. The same could get said of minor newspapers and magazine publications that bothered with a review. Noticeably missing, however, were even bitty little blips from *The New York Times, Newsweek,* and *Vanity Fair*; I suppose those behemoths don't take the time to dabble in serial killers or reserve their endorsements for the more well-known novelists, genre notwithstanding. Gabby maintained I sounded like sour grapes and should feel fortunate—given my genre and irrespective of how well-wrought—for any endorsements. She was right: solid reviews, regardless of where they come from or who was missing, were not a cause to complain; my purpose, after all, is to entertain; I'm not producing the sort of output that gets the attention of those who award Pulitzers and Bookers. Hell, even Erskine Hatch—currently writing for *Rolling Stone*—who, in the past, had accused me of wasting too much time "humanizing" my killers, failed to find fault with Dr. Albert Stahl, thus praised the "flawed" Granville Tovey as a "compelling central figure worthy of examination." There was cause for celebration, so we flew the novel's dedicatees, real-life Harold and Jane, to the States. Gabby was thrilled; it had been a spell since she said goodbye to her dear friends the day after exchanging our nuptials.

Real-life Harold and Jane could not have been more easy-going houseguests as it would come to pass. Insofar as their quirkiness and peculiarities were concerned, when we sat, four couples in all, on my back patio celebrating Gabby's and my achievement (I gave Gabby her due credit) over a catered feast accompanied with plenty of wine, the dedicatees seemed to fit right in. And, it should get noted we were quite the menagerie. Who could imagine a couple more ill-suited than Ursula and Warren? And there I sat, a man who coveted and eventually married his first cousin's ex-wife, had a

167

bizarre encounter with said wife's stunner-of-a-sister who was not quite a sister and engaged in a two-week fuck-fest with his dearest relative. And speaking of that dearest relative, there she sat, not having brought next-door or upstairs-Bill but upstairs-Bill's father, Russ, or Daddy Russ as she often referred to him.

Molly had moved on from, or, as she put it, "relinquished ownership" of next-door and upstairs-Bill, but continued to "reserve" her "rights" to Daddy Russ. Molly had a habit of discussing sex as though she were negotiating with a labor union intermediary. Concerning Daddy Russ, she told me: "He's kind, gentle, and has impeccable manners, and it's reassuring to have someone like that on your arm in public and, in particular, when in mixed company." Also, Daddy Russ, from his knees, worshipping every inch of Molly's bounty of physical beauty while maintaining no misgivings that she occasionally sought men half his age to pound savagely into a mattress might have attributed to the success of a relationship that came with its share of quirks. And so there we sat, four couples, long on uniqueness, and arguably the most suitable and sane among us were real-life Harold and Jane. Notably missing among us, though, to Gabby's and my disappointment, was Nina.

On average, Gabby and Nina would speak once per week, and Gabby was always the accommodating one with concern about the time difference. I also would talk to Nina: our conversations were far less frequent and usually covered aspects of her life and times concerning her biography; sometimes, we would exchange letters. However, it had been weeks since Gabby and I heard a peep from Nina. Moreover, learning that real-life Harold and Jane, in the weeks leading up to their trip to the States, also had not seen or heard from her was weighing on our minds. The last Nina *had* spoken to Gabby, she hinted that she would be busy in the upcoming weeks but was vague when asked to explain the reason. A month passed, then two, with no letters or phone calls. The holidays came and went, and the result was the same. It was not until spring that a letter came sailing in from across the pond and was addressed, specifically, to yours truly.

Dearest Mitch,

Consider this a letter of apology. The reason I chose the written word: were I to call Gabby, doubtless, I would receive quite an earful, as you could well imagine, and though well deserved, I am not prepared to listen. The reason? I'm exhausted! Regarding busyness, bees have nothing on your sister-in-law. We just finished a tour of Europe—which began in Barcelona and ended in Berlin—and to be perfectly frank, although, at times, exciting, the travel was a grind. Years ago, you and I talked about how exhausting it can be to pound a square peg into a round hole. I'm afraid Monte's Meld fits this theme; we're not a rock band with a typical rock band persona or outreach and are far better suited for more intimate settings—two-thousand-seat facilities instead of stadiums and arenas. That's how I see it; so does Carlton Clemens, our bass player. Monte, however, has been gushing over the notion that we've been able to "successfully invade" a world in which we may not belong but nevertheless have fixed ourselves a place at the table. The other members of the Meld, meanwhile, are on the fence. Anyway, concerning the art and logistics of the matter: it has become a discussion that routinely evolves into one of us going off on a tirade that, in turn, escalates into ill-tempered feelings all around, and I'm afraid all the discord will lead to our undoing. I miss the days of playing at good-old Doc Watson's; then, only the music mattered. It's exhausting to learn that the dream you thought you wanted has all the makings of a nightmare; nowadays, everything seems so hollow, synthetic, and the hollower and more synthetic, the better some like it. In other words, there's far too much microwave popcorn and not enough entrée for those who long to wet their beaks with worthwhile music. How fortunate for you, Mitch, that the world of literacy, for the most part, remains one of merit. And speaking of literacy, I spent every night this past week immersing myself in The Case of the Camden Lock Killer. What an achievement! The strength of the story, the characters, and the delivery; it's your best work yet! I'm proud of you, Mitch—proud to know you, proud that you are my brother-in-law, and I'm especially proud that you are my biographer.

And speaking of my biography: I'm also writing to present you with brand new material for the project, juicy material, you'll no doubt agree. Mitch, darling, yours truly has arrived at a decision. It may not come as a big surprise to you, and certainly not Gabby, but it will end up the most important of my life, and one that will require a dedicated chapter, if not an entire section of the book, though I shall leave it entirely to your judgment. Mitch, I have decided, at long last, to divorce my penis. It's about time, wouldn't you agree? And despite that it will be an uncontested divorce with nothing to settle and nary a legal issue; it will be a messy one, nevertheless. Although, you know what they say concerning this matter of great complexity: it's much easier to dig a hole than build a pole. Still, I'm nervous. I never even had a mole removed, never mind surgery, and I still have my wisdom teeth, which may account for that sexy little overbite doubtless you imagined when I took you to the promised land many moons ago: A fond memory. Anyway, holes and poles aside, it will prove a procedure nowhere near as simple as strolling into Harrods, only to leave feeling like a million bucks over purchasing a new outfit meant to inspire all sorts of wickedness among your gender. Unfortunately, it's far more complicated, and, what's more, nowadays, it's no longer referred to as a "sex change operation" but "gender reassignment surgery." Incidentally, upon my initial visit, it took me darn near having to perform a striptease to convince the doctor that I desired to become a full-fledged female and not the other way around. "Seriously, you truly are not a woman?" he kept persisting. It was clear that my offer of a striptease got him all in a tizzy, not to mention quite aroused. He may even have suspected me of being a crazy woman looking to expose herself for the sake of a jolly. Either way, he could not imagine I was not a woman in every basic sense. I suppose being blessed with an Adam's Apple virtually undetectable was what threw the poor devil. At least, in some respects, God was kind.

I have a long road ahead of me, Mitch; it won't be a process that will see its completion in weeks or months; more likely, it will be years. I can understand how Pinocchio felt; all the poor devil wanted was to become a real boy. I've been running about without strings or training wheels for years and was ready for the knife yesterday; unfortunately, it isn't that simple: To see my dream to its conclusion, I must follow procedure, no matter how painstakingly grueling. Next month, I'll be undergoing a psych evaluation to determine whether or not my motives are genuine. Then I'll be turned over to a behavioral science professional, otherwise known as a shrink, for who knows how long, and they will require me to live both in private and public as a female. You would think all that should be required of me is strolling into the office long enough to say, "Hey, Doc, I think we got it covered." Unfortunately, the clock doesn't begin ticking until I come under their care and advisement. And the game doesn't end there: enter the endocrinologist, otherwise, the specialist whose job is to determine whether or not I'm physically fit or viscerally and gland-wise suited for such surgery. So, as I have said, it will be a process, but I will be sure to keep you and Gabby abreast throughout. And please, Mitch, be a dear and smooth over matters with my sister concerning all the months of silence. Tell her that I love her with all my heart, my admiration for her has never waned, but that I needed to prove to myself that I could handle my personal and professional affairs on my own.

With all my love,
Nina

The Bohemian

When I retrieved the mail and noticed a letter stamped overseas and addressed only to me, I deemed it prudent only to show Gabby once having examined its contents. So I crept alongside the house on my way to the back patio.

Even when at her happiest, acting ironically or frightening alluring, if one cared to look beyond Nina's physical beauty, however stirring, and discovered her true essence, painfully evident was a vein of sadness. Often, I imagined the life Nina might have led or the heights to which she might have ascended had she been born as she should have. Every aspect of Nina screamed female; she was quintessentially a woman—one whose beauty was unparalleled, except where it mattered most: but what marked a cruel trick of nature, sometime in the future, would see its rectification.

I refolded the letter and returned it to its envelope when I heard a door pushed open. I realized, at once, that this activity was not coming from my back door. I was well familiar with the sound my door made when pushed open, and the sound that reached my ears was altogether different; it reminded me of an old screen door featuring a tightly wound spring that long ago required oil. I rose from my chair and stood perfectly still. Filtering out the chattering of birds, humming of insects, and the rustling of foliage created by a gentle breeze, I attempted to recreate the sound in my head to determine the direction from which it came. It was a futile exercise, I realized; thus, I was no less sure from where the unpleasant sound had come. It must be the young girl, I theorized, preparing to receive her forbidden lover, who any minute would come sneaking through the woods that led to the once-grand patio; although, by now, she was no longer a girl but a woman nearing age eighteen.

Nevertheless, I heard a door pushed open, but not one pulled close or permitted to slam shut. I went tiptoeing over to the olive hedge. Once there, I parted its tight scaffolding to better peer into a setting I once imagined, in palmier days, served as a magnificent venue for parties. As I suspected, the door was still in an open position, held in place by a hand that was dainty and unmistakably feminine. At the wrist was a frilly finish to a white sleeve of satin and lace. *A wedding gown* was my first thought. I was half expecting to see emerging from the woods a fine-looking young man clad in a tuxedo and that two young lovers, who were years forbidden to one another, in secret, would spend the afternoon performing a mock wedding ceremony. *That must be it!* I was swollen with hope and could feel my soul flourishing with the sort of excitement and desperation that can only accompany love that has been forbidden and arranged a stolen moment. What happened next dashed my hopes and caused my flourishing soul to plummet. There would be no dashing young prince emerging from the woods to claim his princess, even if it was for just an hour. There would be no ceremony or ritual suitable for forbidden lovers who seek a lofty province known to poets and romantics as "eternity." But all was not lost, as I got introduced to a brand-new feeling: intrigue; it was zipping through me as might the most sensational of all sensations; but was I hallucinating, seeing ghosts, or was it possible that I was setting eyes upon someone who, in all these years, no one else had ever glimpsed—someone whose very existence had remained in doubt? The child of Daniel and Gisselle Montague, if indeed one existed and had not, like her mother, died during childbirth, was thought to be a myth, a legend, or a spook story. Others held to the awful rumor of what might have transpired between Daniel Montague and a daughter. All that I knew with any certainty, assuming I was unable to see apparitions or given to hallucinating, was that Daniel and Giselle Montague indeed had a daughter because I was looking straight at her!

She was all dressed in white, clad in a gown becoming to her figure. It was not quite showy enough for a bride, nor was she of an age when a bride would dare consider wearing white, but it was far too frilly to be worn as a housedress. On her feet were what appeared to be ballerina slippers. All that was missing from the scene was a parasol in her hand, a French artist positioned somewhere on the patio, busy at his easel, but it was no time to digress: The white specter, whom I assumed was the daughter of Daniel and Giselle Montague, moved about the patio most peculiarly; she put me in mind of an old cartoon woman—the one who played the tender of Tweety Bird—in that, instead of ambulating by taking steps, she appeared to hover and that something unseen was transporting her from station to station. The stations were birdfeeders, and she filled the feeders with seed by way of a small hand trowel kept in a bowl so large it required the support of both her outstretched arms when carrying it. When she was through filling the feeders, she moved to a rain barrel, where she drew water into her bowl, then topped off a birdbath partially encrusted in a film of algae or micro-organisms. After completing these simple tasks, she made for the door, but something stopped her—something unseen or unknown to me prevented her from venturing another step. Then I heard her call out, "You there!" Her words resounded well above the collaborative din of chirping birds, buzzing insects, the rustling of leaves in the trees, and the distant whooshing of motorists on the pike: they sustained an unmistakable note of command.

"Are you spying on me?" came her lofty accusation. My heart sank; I went numb the way one might when caught doing something one never expected to get caught doing. She followed my stunned silence by adding, "Don't pretend that you are unaware that it is *you* to whom I am speaking." Next, she ordered, "Now come around to the other side of the hedge at once, so I can better look at you: you're hardly visible through that sea of twigs."

I had an eerie sensation that my car had just broken down on Sunset Boulevard, and I was about to become Joe Gillis to a strange woman's Norma Desmond. However, the daughter of Daniel and Giselle Montague put me much more in mind of Miss Havisham, despite my being far too old to assume the role of Pip. *Get a hold of yourself*, Mitch, I pleaded. *You're facing a moment that could prove the opportunity of a lifetime—to unlock a mystery that has persisted for some sixty-four years, never mind how it might set into a novel!* Despite the numerous possibilities that could blossom from such an encounter, it was with more than mild trepidation that I crept along the olive hedge, which traveled both the length of my breezeway and driveway and stopped at the curb. From there, I made my way to the Montague gate. Once on the other side, I was forced to navigate through a tangled and long-neglected thicket of shrubbery until I found myself at the steps of the patio. There, I stood quite still and erect, giving full advantage to a pair of curious eyes keen to make an examination.

"Well, just don't stand there, Mitch; come join me." She had abandoned her authoritative tone; her invitation for me to step up to the patio had an air of casual urgency. Was it possible that I was dreaming or had slipped into an alternative universe? This woman—this alleged daughter of Daniel and Giselle Montague—who no one had ever laid eyes upon and whose very existence was a matter of speculation somehow knew my name! She gestured for me to sit beside her on what was a part white and mainly rusted wrought iron café ensemble for two. I obliged, though my reluctance, I well imagined, was painfully ostensible.

"I promise not to bite," she said. Her deeming it necessary to assure me of as much left me mildly embarrassed.

Despite the sun impeding my vision when advancing toward her, I could see she was well-preserved for someone sixty-four years of age, assuming Mr. McGruder's math was correct. She had not a single strand of hair out of place, and her coiffure was sculpted such that it was not merely dated but belonged to a bygone era. On her face was the application of more makeup than was necessary, though I guessed it was more to offset the paleness of her complexion, not to cover up any evidence of aging skin. She also seemed overly conscious of her posture, presiding over her mannerisms as carefully as one might when belonging to a family of nobility or century-old oligarchy—a time women of a particular station, particularly in public, were expected to display impeccable decorum.

"I'm not a ghost, Mitch," she said. "I assure you that I am quite real."

I was not about to ask anything so foolish as *are you a ghost?* nor openly doubt the cogency of what marked an unforeseen development, but the disbelief that so plainly registered on my face must have been more glaring than any words I might have chosen to express. "B-but I don't understand," I stammered. "No one has ever seen you, and many have doubted your existence, and yet here I am, a stranger invited over for a chat."

"Whatever do you mean, no one has ever seen me?" She seemed genuinely offended by words I hoped would fail to resonate as an accusation. "Why I'm known to plenty of people, and some quite influential; although no one would ever accuse me of being a socialite, I do admit to leading somewhat of a private life."

"So, you do, at times, venture away from your home?" I made sure my words rang such that they carried a palpable note of apology.

"Naturally," came her airy reply; it was as though she deemed the question a frivolous one. She then added, somewhat whimsically: "Why, just this morning, as is the case every Saturday morning, my driver arrived, promptly as always, at 7:00 to take me to my hair appointment. Justine does my hair and has now for better than thirty years. She keeps me abreast of all the town gossip. For example, this very morning, she told me that Claire Smith, the woman who, for years, has owned the dress boutique on Fitzwatertown Road, finally worked up the nerve to ask her husband, who hasn't worked a single day this decade, to leave. Though I'm afraid Justine, in her excitement, applied coarser language. Justine heard that the indolent fool came stumbling home from Paper Mill Tavern—that's Mr. McGruder's place, in case you are not aware—only to find that Claire had packed up all his belongings and set them at the curb. Now, Abby, the girl who does my nails when I'm under the dryer: she talks only of her boyfriend—on and on, she moans about his many shortcomings. But does she ever consider leaving him? She wouldn't dream of it!" She sighed before stating, "Nowadays, folks are strange, Mitch. I'm afraid we're living in strange times, and matters are bound to worsen before we're due to see any improvement. I sit under the dryer and watch women pour into the salon, all in tatters, looking as if they're still in their nightclothes. Heaven forbid! And they *dare* to look upon me as though *I* was the queer one? It's frightening what's happening to the world. The decorum of yesteryear, I'm afraid, is doomed to remain in the past and relegated to points of nostalgia for folks like me."

"You know my name," it finally occurred to ask now that I got over the notion I was speaking to a ghost. I didn't necessarily care that the ghost already knew my name or what else she may know about me, but I was curious to learn how it came to be.

"A woman of my age, living alone, can't be too careful," she said. "When through the grapevine I heard I would be getting new neighbors—strangers—I made it my business to learn all I could about them. Nowadays, I believe a person has a right to know a thing or two about those who live within a certain proximity. I don't believe it makes one a busybody, just prudent. After all, had I—and please pardon the expression—not seen all that's under your fingernails, I wouldn't have known to send my driver to the bookstore to dig up all he could on Mitch Morningstar. You've kept me a busy woman, Mitch. Serial killers: infinitely fascinating creatures, I should say, and Dr. Albert Stahl was among the most fascinating that I ever had the pleasure of encountering... in the world of literature, naturally."

Her eyes sparkled with the brightness and clarity of a child's when delving into the aspects of *The Case of the Camden Lock Killer*. Then, all at once, she appeared fretful, her eyes shifty; it was as if something was lurking about and, whatever it was, had triggered a deportment of distrust. "I can't begin to imagine all that has been said of me over the years. Thanks to the ever-alert ears of Justine, what little bit I've learned was ghastly enough and would make anyone's skin crawl." Then she uttered with dismay: "Rumors! They're troubling enough in a suburb such as this one, but it makes it all the worse when you're a defenseless woman." She faltered. Several moments of uncertainty hung in the air; I couldn't hazard a guess where next the conversation was heading, assuming it had yet to reach its conclusion. Then, all at once, her vigor returned. "My sincerest apologies, Mitch. I seem to have misplaced my manners. I hear this sort of thing can happen when a woman of a certain age finds herself in the company of a young, handsome man; she becomes so distracted that she forgets to introduce herself. I'm Elizabeth. Elizabeth Montague. Now would you like to come inside and join me for tea?"

Inside for tea? How could I resist? It was the mother of all invitations fallen right into my lap! I was about to enter a domain where no one in town had ever set foot. The question was: would anyone believe it? Perhaps more relevant was the question: why would they?

Elizabeth led me through the house to a sitting room that featured a doorway to a grand parlor, and since we entered from the rear, it was to the right of an atrium. Also, by way of sliding doors of dark walnut, this comfortable nook of a room was obscure from the hall. Along the way, I walked under a classically ornate chandelier, ambled past rich wood panels that traveled halfway up twelve-foot walls, many Tiffany glass fixtures, and furniture featuring rich fabrics. Not to be outdone was bric-a-brac collected from all four corners of the globe: some, as I was able to ascertain, were from the early part of the twentieth century, while other pieces began their journey at the dawn of The Enlightenment. Yet, as I was winding my way through the house, one matter was unmistakable: whether by her own dutiful hands or those belonging to an employee no one, including the vigilant Mr. McGruder, had yet to spy, there was overwhelming evidence that Elizabeth Montague had quite the compulsion for housekeeping. Given the tangle permitted to thrive throughout the landscape, I found the state of the house a delightful anomaly. Upon entering, I had imagined closed-off rooms, covered furniture, and a home that had fallen into utter neglect and disrepair, not to mention the expectation of breathing in more dust than air. Instead, I found myself marveling at the impeccability of a home whose furnishings and care could rival any museum.

The Bohemian

On two of the sitting room's walls were floor-to-ceiling built-in bookshelves filled with old volumes of classic literature: some American, some British, others European; many were first-edition copies. Save for the later efforts of Steinbeck and Hemingway, signed copies of Ray Bradbury's *Fahrenheit 451*, Kurt Vonnegut's *Slaughterhouse-Five*, novels that were part of my curriculum, Ayn Rand's *Atlas Shrugged*, which I had yet to penetrate, and a smattering of opuses of lesser note, not only did every volume predate Elizabeth Montague's birth, so too did most editions that filled the shelves. Little, if anything, was collected in the past sixty-four years. I also noticed that many volumes and editions predated the births of Daniel and Giselle Montague; thus, the collection was representative of the efforts of Daniel Montague I and his wife, Eloise. Among this extensive collection were rare first-edition copies of Mark Twain's *A Connecticut Yankee in King Arthur's Court*, Horatio Alger's *Ragged Dick*, and *The Autocrat of the Breakfast Table* by Oliver Wendell Holmes. Along with William Cullen Bryant, Henry Wadsworth Longfellow, James Russell Lowell, and John Greenleaf Whittier, Oliver Wendell Holmes was a "fireside poet." Also, he fathered a future Supreme Court Justice.

So there I stood in this plush chamber, gently clutching to volumes and turning pages that predated the Civil War. Giddiness had overcome me that I had access to what quite possibly was the country's finest private collection of classic literature. Lock me in and occasionally slip food under the door. I could spend a year in this room!

"It is quite a room for a novelist to find himself, I should think," said Elizabeth. I was too enraptured to hear her footfalls nearing the room, and her tone, which was sharp to begin with, had startled me. It was tea time.

"My apologies," I begged as I got caught handling treasures without first seeking permission.

"They're not delicate artifacts, Mitch; books are meant to be handled—to be read."

"And how many of them have you read?" I wasn't challenging Elizabeth; I was curious.

"Quite a few," she replied. It was not a boast, but I did detect a note of pride. "Although," she added, "I haven't penetrated this magnificent collection in any particular order, nor do I think I shall live long enough to finish. You might have noticed that a double-u is missing, for a copy of *A Picture of Dorian Gray* is presently on my nightstand. But you disappoint me, Mitch."

"How so?" I wondered. I was far more curious than I was offended. I saw Elizabeth's eyes shift to the only wall not covered with books or windows. The wall featured five paintings. It was the one positioned in the center—a work called *No lo Despiertes (acuarela)* by Spanish impressionist Joaquin Sorolla, to which Elizabeth was trying to draw my eyes. The subjects were a man and a woman watching over a cradle-lain infant. The woman was wearing a simple flowery-printed frock. The man, who was stooped lower than the woman—perhaps he wished to feel the child's breath on his face—was wearing a bandana and vest. They were common laborers, I could tell. On their faces were hopes and dreams for the future, not ones bound for riches and nobility but ones of happiness born out of the strength of their love. I suppose Elizabeth found it curious that I delved into a collection of books without first noticing or giving any honor to what was a small but worthy gallery. I was angling toward the Sorolla. As I stood before it, Elizabeth said, "This house is home to many works of art, but the Sorolla is my favorite. Imagine that you are fully enveloped by trustworthiness before you can appreciate the most rudimentary form of its essence. I submit this is unimaginable, for only during one's earliest days can such a feeling be known, though it cannot be known consciously; hence, it begs the question: can such a matter as blind trust that is unwitting transcend the cradle? And if it can, however subliminal, how deep into our lives can it penetrate?"

Of course, the Sorolla was Elizabeth's favorite. Never experiencing a mother's love and inheriting a father who was broken and possibly struggled with resentment early on, it was only natural that the Sorolla would lure her. Perhaps in the ensuing years of childhood, beyond, and even today, Elizabeth imagined that *she* was the cradled infant watched over by the vigilant eyes of a loving mother and father.

"Not very far, if at all," I replied. "It's likely our infancy is wiped clean from our memory, and we're set off into the world to skin our elbows and knees, which is as it should be." I did not look at Elizabeth when I spoke but kept my eyes pinned on the painting. When I did shift my eyes in her direction, her face formed a smile filled with irony and skepticism. I pretended not to notice, but the mixed expression faded as quickly as it came. In its stead, vulnerability prevailed: the sight of her unguarded facade made her seem altogether more youthful, more attractive, more affecting—that somewhere within lived a child that longed to move, breathe, *and*, perhaps most importantly, be known to someone at some meaningful level of intimacy.

Elizabeth placed a handled tray accommodating a sterling silver tea set comprised of two cups, a gracefully spouted urn, a bowl for sugar cubes, a creamer, two delicate spoons, and a tiny tray holding thinly sliced lemon atop a coffee table. I abandoned my admiration of the Sorolla and went to sit beside her. I was "all in," as they say: the infancy that passed while a shattered father grieved; the sheltered child who was never seen and had the spoils of the world brought to her home by a father whose guardianship developed into an obsession; the unseemliness alleged to have transpired between Daniel and Elizabeth upon her transition from girlhood to womanhood; the lifestyle that ensued following Daniel's death; and lastly the person who has been desperately trying to escape a past comprised of being programmed by a grief-stricken man gone mad, which led to Elizabeth futilely striving for an identity she could call her own. Right before my eyes, the life of Elizabeth Montague became an open book I could leaf through at will, and I was fascinated—infinitely fascinated! Who wouldn't be?

The child Elizabeth Montague had no playmates, but she had plenty of dolls and books to amuse herself. Once she outgrew the books, many got donated to an orphanage. As for her dolls: it was a magnificent collection—some were vintage, others were rare, none were easily come by unless you were a person of some means—and Elizabeth brightened when she told me they were all still on display in her bedroom. They served, at first, as her playmates, then later as her captive audience when she danced ballet and played modified pieces of classical music on her very own console piano—its size and finish were well suited to the bedroom of a girl in youth. Daniel had a piano instructor from Philadelphia brought to the house once a week. Ms. Kenny was her name, and Elizabeth looked forward to her weekly appearances with great eagerness. As for her rudimentary ballet skills: their acquisition came when attending a performance of Tchaikovsky's *Swan Lake*. It was rare that father and daughter went on an outing. For the occasion, Daniel had Elizabeth dressed as a fairy princess and had them chauffeured to and from The Academy of Music in downtown Philadelphia. The following day, a young girl taught that enchantment existed beyond fairytales in books woke to a tutu and ballet slippers placed on her nightstand. That day, an inspired Elizabeth Montague alternated between the roles of Odette and Odilia as she danced for her dolls.

"Father never cared for me to venture out of doors, especially alone; he always found the conditions unsuitable. Either it was too hot, too cold, too damp, too windy, or raining. Afterward, he would remind me how each condition would affect my health adversely. It wasn't until my second birthday that I met my father. It was a modest and quiet celebration: women I learned were my aunts, and great aunts came from afar. Lydia, my nanny, was the only person I recognized. Lydia, I had always known.

"In my early years, Father spent a great deal of time away from the house. Lydia told me that he was a man of great importance and had to be in many places. Still, come the nighttime, when all was quiet and still, and I was about to drift off to sleep, I had the sensation someone was watching me—be it a person, phantom, or an angel—it felt quite real, and every bit as palpable as this cup to my lips and tea trickling down my throat. Despite being a mere toddler, I was sure this extraordinary sensibility was not the byproduct of a fairytale Lydia read to me in the afternoon. One day, though, I would come to learn the truth.

"Father and I were never in the same room on the day of my birthday party, though he remained nearby, always in an adjoining room and spying on me while half-hidden behind a doorway, archway, or from the balcony when I was in the hall. At times, I would catch him spying and delighting over having been caught, for whenever my alert eyes met his spying ones, a broad grin would form on his face. Somehow, I knew this strikingly handsome man, whose smile that day and every day after would win me over, was my father—the man of whom Lydia often spoke. From the day forward, Father and I were inseparable."

And so it was: Daniel and Elizabeth were indeed inseparable—the wealthy dandy and his sidekick princess who, as her aunts and great aunts maintained, was developing into a tintype of her mother, Giselle. Then Elizabeth turned age eight. Daniel was convinced, first by Lydia (Lydia adored Elizabeth but recognized it was time to let go: her reasoning was predicated on the notion that, when a girl reaches a certain age, alleged delicacy aside, the secondhand accounts of others would no longer do and they must venture into the world and gain their own experiences) then from Giselle's family from the north, that Elizabeth thus far had been smothered, and, for better or worse, should be permitted to spread her little wings to see how far she could fly, if at all.

And thus, a decision got made: young Elizabeth would attend Mary Craft's School for Girls, a boarding school nestled in a sleepy little borough in upstate New York. "If ever an issue arises, we're but an hour's drive away," Aunt Pricilla had assured my father. "Aunt Pricilla was a stern and authoritative woman; at least, she seemed so to an eight-year-old. Whenever she spoke, everyone would stiffen and zip up their lips; you wouldn't dare want to miss a word of instruction for fear of the consequence."

Elizabeth, typical of an eight-year-old thrust into newness or the unfamiliar, was as excited as she was nervous, wide-eyed but with her tummy all in a jumble. When Daniel drove onto the grounds of Mary Craft's School for Girls, this sheltered young girl, who thus far was home-tutored, first brightened, then shrank in the shadow of sudden novelty and the precariousness of the unknown. It didn't take her but a few short hours to decide she hated Mary Craft's School for Girls; the absence of Daniel and Lydia was unbearable, and there were no vintage dolls for whom she could dance and play the piano. The next day, Elizabeth discovered the school was equipped with a piano—a Lester upright bigger and richer-sounding than the console in her bedroom—and could play it far more proficiently than the girls her age and better than most older girls. Naturally, it gave Elizabeth a burst of confidence but failed to preclude her from writing to Daniel daily to complain she was lonely, sad, and miserable and that he ought to rush to come and rescue her.

"'Rescue me, Father,' I would write. One might imagine I was unjustly sentenced to prison or a labor camp. But Father was unwavering in the matter and always responded to each of my silly letters with the assurance that there was no better place for me than Mary Craft's School for Girls, and sooner than later, I would reach this conclusion on my own. He would always end his letters with a love poem, and it was because of those poems that I cherished his letters and kept them."

A dreamy look came over Elizabeth. Then she recited:

"What could inspire me more than the appearance of the sun following a
storm?
Or enchant me as might a faun in the woods?
Or intoxicate me like the scent of roses in the summertime?
Why nothing other than the loveliness of my darling Elizabeth!"

The letters became an every-other-day affair, then once a week until they ceased altogether. The turning point came when a girl named April Cassidy befriended Elizabeth.

"You could not find two girls more dissimilar than April and me in the whole school. I was an introvert and spent a great deal of time reading and playing the piano. April cared nothing for books. As for music, it would never occur to her to make it a study, and even if she showed any inclination, good luck getting her to sit still long enough to engage effectively in such a pursuit. Putting it plainly: April had the agility of a mongoose and competed ferociously in all games and activities, especially ones that required a measure of agility; April ran like the wind and had a bottomless pit of energy. We admired one another because we excelled in opposite ways. That was the basis of our friendship, which lasted five years. Unfortunately, April didn't return for her last year at Mary Craft's School for Girls. Come early September, when I arrived, she wasn't there. It was not unusual for a girl to return a touch on the tardy side since some came from great distances or were returning from summers spent abroad, but, come the end of the day, there was still no sign of my dear friend. I thought perhaps she was sick with one of those dreadful summer colds and would be along in a day or so, but then a whole week had passed! When I went to inquire, they told me April would not be returning and were not at liberty to disclose why. So here I sit, fifty-one years later, still wondering what became of my once dear friend. I think of her often."

When Elizabeth returned from Mary Craft's School for Girls after her final year, she and Daniel took up what one might describe as a "cosmopolitan" lifestyle. They would spend whole seasons away from home: be it in France, where they stayed mainly in Paris and adopted Parisian customs—occasionally, they would journey to the Burgundy region and save a weekend for the French Riviera—or in Italy, where Venice was the favored destination. It gave Elizabeth joy to find herself within the confines of the cavernous and architecturally grand and pigeon-occupied Saint Mark's Square. A short walk from the square and the Bridge of Sighs was another of Elizabeth's favorite places: The Church of the Pieta, otherwise, the place where the great Italian composer and violinist Antonio Vivaldi composed music for orphaned girls. That she was a musician herself, and bearing in mind her unorthodox upbringing, perhaps it was only natural for Elizabeth to find the Pieta and its history a source of fascination.

"When I was first sent away to Mary Craft's School for Girls, I felt let go of, forsaken, perhaps similarly to how an orphan might feel; though with my father loving and attentive as he was, and tried to be, I should dare not pretend to know the plight of an orphan. Anyway, playing the piano gave me a sense of worth during those early days. I can well imagine how those orphaned girls must have felt, what the gift of music and the attention of a great composer meant to their self-worth, and how far into their lives the experience traveled. For that reason, mainly, I've always adored the music of Vivaldi; the second I hear a strain, instantly, I'm able to recognize it as belonging to the great Venetian composer, and it never fails to transport me back to Venice and The Church of the Pieta. It's funny how you can feel a connection to a faraway place that's not, in any way, tied to your lineage, but I imagine everyone has a similar story in that regard."

I was inclined to interject: *few have had the privilege to live entire seasons, many times over, in faraway places.* Instead, I said, "You had a great deal of affection for your father, I can tell, and glow whenever you mention him directly or, in any way, allude to him." I managed this comment without a hint of insinuation and thus opened a door. To what end? I could not fathom any more than I knew what had compelled me.

"He was a complicated man, my father," Elizabeth began. "He would take me under his wing for weeks, sometimes months, and during those periods, I would feel my spirit soar; there were times it seemed that everything in the wide world existed for my sake alone. Then Father would disappear, taking trips alone without telling Lydia and me where he was going. Other times, he would disappear for spells without leaving the house. Those were especially bleak times; he would vanish to his room for many days, sometimes weeks, and wouldn't see nor speak to me. Reduced to a stray animal, lingering about, owning only the strength to starve for his affections, was how I would feel.

And he was not unaware of how utterly barren I was inside; still, he ignored my existence. If I saw Lydia fixing Father a food tray, I would beg to take it to him, but he would disregard my knock and plea for attention. I would sit crouched at his door beside the tray, whimpering like a child, but it wasn't until he was sure I had gone that he would obey his hunger. Many times, I had cried to Lydia, 'Why? Why does he reject me so?' Her answer was always the same, and I never understood or knew what to make of it: 'It's because he loves you so deeply, so steadfastly,' was what Lydia told me. During those bleak times, I often would hear Lydia leaving Father's bedroom in the middle of the night; I could always recognize Lydia's footsteps."

Elizabeth sighed over what she came to appreciate and perhaps still views as illicit behavior, though insofar as I could tell, Daniel and Lydia's middle-of-the-night trysts long ago were reconciled. She brightened by adding, "As I have stated, Father was a complicated man. When we were in France, he embraced the virtues of syndicalism and developed theories on how it could work worldwide and peacefully. And as you may have already guessed, there was no greater lover of culture than Father—some he had a greater fondness for than others but embraced them all. More importantly, Father understood the uniqueness of cultural expressions as a product of people, not political doctrines or theocracies; he struggled with the concept of quantitative experiences making up our collective consciousness only to get captured and framed by religion and politics. Eventually, he advocated for an anarchy-driven utopia. I suppose describing Father as a Trotskyist is not altogether unfair."

I was not indifferent to the notion of Daniel Montague as a Trotskyist, nor did I lack interest in what might have engendered a man to adopt the philosophies of Leon Trotsky and the core principles behind radical socialism. Any man who succeeded using methods made available by a democratic republic embracing free market capitalism and benefited from generations before him utilizing the same system only to shun it would rank as a source of fascination. But I was far more interested in what kept a man, once known as a socialite, hidden away in his room, though I was already beginning to formulate a theory similar to what others had suspected of Daniel Montague, had he a daughter. So I asked Elizabeth whether any clarity ever got reached concerning Lydia's stock reply to her long-ago plea, "Why? Why does he reject me so?" I received a polite spurn, and my spurning came in the form of Elizabeth repositioning herself in her seat, pouring more tea, and, with the slightest tenor of huffiness, decided it was time to delve into *my* affairs. Was her sudden shift an admission of guilt that illicitness had indeed transpired between Daniel and Elizabeth? Had Lydia, once Elizabeth came of age, offered herself to Daniel, only to see unspeakable urges prevail? I had little doubt and thus saw no need to press Elizabeth any further on the matter.

Our second cup of tea got whittled away by me regaling for Elizabeth how *The Case of the Camden Lock Killer* became a project and telling how Gabby and I came to be as a couple. She was enthralled by the former and genuinely charmed by the latter. The latter, though, prompted her to wonder, "And what of Ursula?"

She was amused—or, more accurately, quite pleased with herself over how flustered her accusation caused me to appear. Then she added, paradoxically: "You should have been made aware, Mitch, the olive hedge, although it may appear as innocuous as any other shrub on our conjoined lots, has keen eyesight and acute hearing. But it's quite all right, Mitch; you're hardly the first man to covet thy neighbor's wife, and you certainly won't be the last. And, may I say, it's plain to any bystander—current company included—that you're still very much in love with Gabby. But the matter does beg the million-dollar question: do you truly covet Ursula, or is it more a case that you find Warren dreadfully inadequate?"

It was more like a one-hundred-million-dollar question the spying and remarkably intuitive Elizabeth Montague put to me. And it set my wheels in motion to search for something of which I did not possess: a clear and sober answer. Did I truly covet Ursula, or was it a case of me seeing her as Nina with a vagina or Molly minus the incest? And then there was the Warren factor: despite he and I warming to one another and becoming, for lack of a better term, friends, I *had* judged him unworthy of Ursula and imagined, if ever awarded an opportunity, I could show her the true meaning of worthiness. So there I sat, sifting through a menagerie of absurd notions sipping tea with a woman whose very existence has been the subject of debate while becoming enlightened to the unfortunate possibility: not only might I be a man of narcissistic psychopathy, but one whose worthiness, when juxtaposed to Gabby's, was glaringly suspect.

It never occurred to me that an unknown spectator lurked during our many backyard soirees, which never failed to include Ursula and Warren, Molly and Daddy Russ, and sometimes others. And I was learning, as our tête-à-tête developed, this she-fantom was quite adept at assessing the character of others. My eyes roamed the room until they rested upon a clock atop a gate-leg table. According to the clock, I had taken up quite a bit of Elizabeth's time, and Gabby, not to suggest that she makes a habit of fretting over my whereabouts, must be wondering where I had disappeared. Nevertheless, there was one remaining issue into which I wanted to delve, for Lord knows if or when a future encounter would come to pass.

"Please, Elizabeth," I began, "tell me about the young girl—I beg your pardon; nowadays, she's a young woman—who occasionally comes to visit. And why does she come to you dressed so lavishly?"

"Ahh, that would be my great-niece," was the answer Elizabeth Montague unhesitatingly supplied; she seemed quite pleased to have an opportunity to mention her great-niece. "And a glorious creature she is; I would challenge anyone to point out a lovelier-looking young woman." I joined Elizabeth in her lofty praise of her great-niece; however, not as a girl or a young woman had my eyes come to rest upon her. Conversely, Mr. McGruder, Ursula, Warren, Gabby, and others who live on the block, have not only attested to seeing a girl in a gown but are all in accord with their admiration of her beauty. It has become a subject that has left me suspecting they are gaslighting me, and their weapon of choice is a novelist's curiosity. It was comforting to learn otherwise.

"I'm old-fashioned with concern to how a woman should present, Mitch. And I believe that when a woman is endowed with great beauty, it ought to be honored. And to be perfectly frank: I'm appalled at how women of the nineties carry themselves. Of course, I said the same of women of the mid-ninety-sixties through the seventies. The trend seemed to turn in the eighties, thank goodness, because the period spanning Kennedy and Reagan was bleak, both in women's fashion and deportment. I thought President Clinton, who acquits himself as quite the charmer, would inspire more of the same; unfortunately, he seems to have proven himself inspirational in other ways. But I digress. Back to my darling little Jenny: you might say, concerning virtue, womanhood, and interest in young men, I have assigned myself her proxy; whenever a young man fancies her, or she, him, I have them over for a chaperoned date, during which time I shall decide whether or not he is worthy of my dear great-niece."

My friends and neighbors have gone out of their way to mention the periodic appearances of a "beautiful young maiden" but never the young man whose arm she was on. Perhaps that part of the equation was a delusion on Elizabeth's part. Nevertheless, I decided to play along. "And what happens once it's been established that a poor fellow has failed to make the grade?"

"Why, he's killed, naturally, usually by means of poison, then dragged to the cellar. There must be a half-dozen or so young men decomposing below us as we speak. Oh, Mitch, dear," Elizabeth intoned after pausing long enough for her words to register fully, "take that silly look of astonishment off your face; don't you see that I have just given you a plotline for your next novel! 'Deranged older woman kills would-be suitors of beautiful great-niece;' it would make a titillating serial killer spoof if such a genre exists. It's bound to be a best-seller!"

And that marked the end of my first-ever encounter with one Ms. Elizabeth Montague.

CHAPTER TWELVE
THE BOHEMIANS

And so, there I sat, slumped at the end of a picnic table bench on my back patio, my hand still clutching the envelope housing Nina's letter. Hazy would most accurately describe my current state. And all this cloudy pondering had me doubting whether or not my encounter with Elizabeth Montague had occurred and whether there even *was* an Elizabeth Montague. Had I, when peering through the olive hedge, slipped through a portal to another dimension because everything that followed seemed too fantastic, even for a novelist? My haziness dissipated when I heard Warren operating a piece of manly equipment. I gave him a halfhearted wave, then raced inside to confront Gabby.

"How long was I missing?" I huffed.

Narrowing her eyes, Gabby peered at me with scrutiny akin to one who suspected another has gone mad. "Apparently, not long enough," came her retort.

"Gabby, dear, I need you to be serious," I implored. "How long was I missing? Did you happen to notice me outside, and if so, was I suddenly not there?"

Before uttering a word, Gabby took a step back as one might when accosted by a situation that was ostensibly mundane but owned the potential to become unpleasant. "Yes, Mitch, I did notice you outside, well-engrossed in what I presumed was a letter from my delinquent sister, and yes, you were suddenly gone. First, I assumed your keen eyes must've spied Ursula through a convenient gap in the olive hedge and that you were masturbating behind the cherry laurel. But Ursula wasn't sunbathing, which led to my next assumption: you were roped into a conversation with Warren and positioned in an area where I hadn't a vantage point. Can there be more mystery to your disappearing act than that?"

The Bohemian

I collapsed in a chair and breathed a sigh of relief. Gabby found this reaction—under normal circumstances, why wouldn't she? —unwarranted if not peculiar. "Gabby, you'll never believe where I've been these past two hours: Our next-door neighbors!"

Gabby's eyes swelled with astonishment, then, with equal incredulity, uttered, "You mean our next-door neighbors, as in the big-white-house next-door neighbors?"

"Precisely!" My reply was triumphant. Indeed, everyone else may be familiar with the beauty of Jenny, but yours truly knows Elizabeth!

"Well, don't just sit there gloating, Mitch; get on with it. Do we live next to a reclusive old coot or looney old bat?"

In matters of suspense, Gabby was all child, and no child deserves torture; thus, I readily recalled for her, in every detail, my encounter with Elizabeth Montague.

"A real Miss Havisham sort, she seems," Gabby posited. It is not infrequent that Gabby and I think alike and end up with similar impressions.

"Indeed," I added. "And, what was more, she pitched me an idea for a novel." Gabby scoffed at the concept of a serial killer spoof. I went on to further add, not yet having reacted to Gabby's disapproval: "As I was making my departure, she said, 'Goodbye Mitch Morningstar; I wish you a good life.'"

"Peculiar parting words," Gabby acknowledged.

Perhaps they were peculiar parting words, yet, my initial impression of Elizabeth pitching me an idea for a novel was that it would open the door for a friendship to blossom, albeit a strange one, both in premise and development. A week came and went. I saw no sign of Elizabeth. Her lack of availability was hardly a phenomenon, especially given the years that passed before I—the only one on the block who could lay claim to engaging this phantom of a woman—caught my first glimpse of Elizabeth. Nevertheless, the luster of novelty stroked my desire to see her.

A month passed. Still, there was no sign of Elizabeth. It led me to theorize that Elizabeth placed little merit upon what I believed, touted to others, especially Warren, was a fascinating encounter. Then another month got crossed off the calendar: I decided it was time to take action; no longer would I spy out of windows or part the tight scaffolding of a hedge. Instead, I shall, as Gabby rather bluntly and scathingly put it: "Take matters into your own hands and boldly do what no other man or woman in town has ever done. Go and knock on Elizabeth Montague's front door, for crying out loud!" Gabby was busy with other matters and flailing about thus the area in the room seemed terribly unaccommodating. Then, backhandedly, she added, "Now there's a novel idea, I should say. Instead of spying or hoping to get discovered *while* spying, locate those delicate orbs you call nuts and approach the matter as might a civilized human being."

"A civilized human being?"

"Yes, remove your hands from your pockets and use one of them to bang it on the woman's door!" As I slinked away, I heard Gabby mutter, "If men weren't so busy trying to connive their way into women's drawers, they wouldn't get tripped up over mundane matters like doorbells and telephones."

When linking Gabby's sentiment to the notion that I'm a novelist in a genre given to hyperbole and complicating matters, it can equal me behaving rather imbecilically concerning my approach to the mundane. Nevertheless, I convinced myself it would be best if armed with a credible reason before knocking on Elizabeth's front door. Saturday, I puttered away in the front yard awaiting the mail-man's arrival; Wayne is his name. Wayne is on a first-name basis with Gabby but knows me only as Gabby's thoughtless husband who, most days, offers but a halfhearted wave. Today, I approached Wayne like we were drinking buddies whose habit was lamenting the failures of the Eagles. It was a mistake and one that instigated a sneer from Wayne. How was I supposed to know that Randall Cunningham no longer played for the Eagles when years ago, my family's worship of Nicholas's football exploits was so unbearably fervent it all but killed my interest in the sport? Still, I added brightly, "Ms. Montague will be away for a spell and asked if I wouldn't mind taking in her mail." Wayne regarded me with suspicion, then spotted Gabby in the window when I gestured toward the house. It was not until Gabby gave him the "okay" nod that Wayne handed over Elizabeth's stack of mail. Admittedly, it was humbling that my bride had to vouch for my honor. Doubtless, somewhere in that exchange, there was a lesson to be learned.

Aside from the usual volume of junk mail, there were not one but two envelopes from Merrill Lynch. "Don't you dare, Mitch Morningstar," Gabby warned. I was curious to know just how well-

The Bohemian

off Mr. Daniel Montague had left his daughter. Old money, aside from historical, can supply intrigue, and the content of those envelopes could open new doors for someone with a healthy imagination. But Gabby was right: deceiving Wayne was one thing; opening Elizabeth Montague's mail was another. Later that afternoon, I went strolling over to the big white house to inform Elizabeth her mail got delivered to the wrong address. First, I rapped on the door, followed by the window, then rang the bell. I waited for a spell, then repeated my efforts in the same order. The result was the same: either Elizabeth was away, thus giving my deceitfulness a dash of honesty, or had chosen to ignore what a recluse would likely rule a midday intrusion. Neither was a reason enough to give up on this new and peculiar acquaintanceship, not yet. Hope would come in the form of our end-of-season backyard soiree, which would not just include Gabby and me, the anomalous Ursula and Warren, and Molly and Daddy Russ; Nina, too, would be joining us, or so she promised, and would be bringing real-life Harold and Jane. The temptation would prove too much: Elizabeth would not only spy on us but would lurk within earshot, and afterward, be it a day, a week at best, will make herself visible for my discovery, and once we engaged, with enthusiasm, she will dive into all the saucy details concerning the lives of our eccentric group. But should it matter? Should any of this madness matter? And what, exactly, was driving my fascination for a reclusive woman now pushing seventy? True, the life of Elizabeth Montague, past and present, marked one of intrigue, providing that you were not the one forced to have lived it. But another aspect piqued my thrall: her idea for a serial killer spoof proved more titillating than I was willing to admit to Gabby. But why should the life and times of Elizabeth Montague, and her whimsical concept for a novel, push me to the point of obsession? The answer was simple. I was unconvinced this serial killer spoof—whose premise would see a great-aunt dispose of her great-niece's unsuitable suitors—originated from the whimsy of a reclusive older woman's imagination, that, quite possibly, it was a concept spawned from Elizabeth Montague's reality. I had to get to the truth, not just of Elizabeth Montague herself, but the young woman she calls "My darling little Jenny."

To suggest that I was suffering from preoccupation was an understatement, and Gabby, by way of several severe glares, served notice that she was alert to my condition. I managed to detect her

displeasure during the few moments my probing eyes were not attempting to penetrate the tight scaffolding of the olive hedge or spy a
spy at a second or third-story window of the big white house. Everyone was behaving as expected with yours-truly being the lone exception: Warren, per usual, was manning the grill as though it was a battle
station during the height of conflict whose outcome was hanging in
the balance. He, along with his muscle tone and hairiness—aspects of
his manliness made far too available by the skimpiness of his shirt—
was a self-proclaimed grill master. Often one might hear someone assert: "It ain't rocket science." Some prefer the term "Brain surgery"
when diminishing the aspects of a specific endeavor. According to
Warren, grilling food was on the same lofty plane as the abovementioned, and only he was fit for the task. Meanwhile, real-life Harold and
Jane were jabbering about what they called "a delicious scandal," taking
up far too much space in the headlines that entailed a young White
House intern "polishing the presidential knob."

"However, on our side of the pond," Harold needlessly explained, "it's often referred to as 'the royal knob.' And I'm afraid your
poor Ms. Lewinsky, despite that she is far more attractive than our
Ms. Parker-Bowles and polishing a far worthier knob—although I
wouldn't know firsthand—isn't likely to enjoy a good fate. In Britain,
you see, scandal can mold one into a celebrity, whereas here in the
infantilized States, it's bound to get you scrapped if not banished."

"Good point," Molly added. "Look what became of Gary
Hart; no one sees hide or hair of the poor bastard."

While Molly took the liberty of refreshing our memories
concerning the former presidential hopeful undone by a sex scandal,
real-life Harold and Jane were celebrating their agreement that, between Bill Clinton and Prince Charles, it was the American president
who possessed the worthier knob. At first, I found it curious that
real-life Harold and Jane were making such a fuss over Bubba and
Monica and with nary a thought aimed at politics. But nothing sells
like sex, especially when it is scandalous and the buyers are a species
unable to control the impulses produced by their hypothalamus. Our
asexual friends were no less intrigued by the goings-on within the big
white house on Pennsylvania Avenue than the rest of us.

Daddy Russ alerted everyone to the prospect of Ms. Lewinsky
approached by a second-rate writer hungry for a book deal: doubtless,
one of those juicy tell-all efforts comprised of enough liberties to

make it read like fiction and sure to inspire a repudiation effort from a second-rate writer known to the Clinton camp. Although likely, I'm having difficulty imagining a stained dress and a little cigar hanky-panky stretched beyond a hundred pages. However, were Bill to pledge undying affections to Monica and divorce Hillary—the result would see the former unseat the latter as first lady—we would have in our midst "The scandal of the century," one with which the Brits could not compete: hence, a thousand-pager would fly off shelves; they could not print copies fast enough; entire forests would be stripped bare! However, a scandal of such magnitude was not unlikely; it was unrealistic. Moreover, it would shred our bourgeois American sensibilities and leave us little choice but to turn, God forbid, to the Bible belt to readjust our collective moral compass. As it currently stands, all we have is a soiled dress and a cigar with curious DNA. However, I could be underestimating America's thirst for junk news and moral decay; a cigar and dress might be all that is required to produce a national number one!

All this talk of knobs, whether royal or presidential, caused poor Nina to wince. Total liberation was yet on the horizon, and I could see the investment was making her restless. How she longed for a day when she could spread her wings as wide as they could go and soar to the heights she had always dreamed. Beyond her wincing and restlessness, I could tell Nina was mildly annoyed that I had yet to shower her with the attention she was accustomed to receiving. Later, I shall explain to Nina the Elizabeth Montague/Miss Havisham phenomenon; I'm confident she will understand. Meanwhile, I grew weary of what quickly evolved into excessive and inane chatter about knobs and scandals. So, once again, my eyes searched for my latest obsession.

The conversation shifted not a minute too soon, though I failed to realize it until I heard Molly somewhat whimsically proclaim, "It was from as early as his mid-teens that Mitch began his pursuit of a Bohemian lifestyle."

Given that we were an assortment comprised of four Brits, four Americans, and one Canadian, owning sexual appetites ranging from insatiable to non-existent, the subject of our respective upbringings and experiences that shaped us should prove far more interesting than what thus far marked the prevailing theme.

"Our parents were Philistines," Molly went on to add. "Their idea of culture was work—and the harder, the better—followed by beer and football. Mitch, to his credit—for he was not the oldest—was the first among us cousins to become an independent thinker. Must have been all that Kurt Vonnegut you devoured, ay cousin?"

"We all must have our influences," real-life Harold brightly intoned. "How could we not," chirped real-life Jane. Next came the predictable celebration that they had agreed.

"Must we?" I challenged. "Are we not of independent mind, the human race? Can it be that *all* our success is due to external influences?" I was not attacking real-life Harold; I simply could never abide by the concept that no one is "truly" original; it suggests we are all part of an ever-widening lineage, if not advocations for creationism.

"That would about sum it up," said Daddy Russ. We no longer viewed Daddy Russ as Molly's sensitive and seasoned lover who got dragged to our backyard soirees; he was one of us. Meanwhile, Molly, to a large extent, tapered her predatory ways. Aside from rare and bizarre encounters with pizza delivery boys in their late teens or UPS drivers in their mid-twenties, which Daddy Russ dismissed as "playtime" and went so far as to encourage—Daddy Russ would not have Molly purge all her impulses, which included sex so strenuous it would ravage a non-athlete—Molly and Daddy Russ were essentially exclusive. "And there's no greater external influence than our folks," Daddy Russ continued. "They could be as clueless as sawdust when guiding us but pure geniuses when setting examples of what we *didn't* want. I loved and respected my father, but it didn't take me longer than uttering the words, 'I don't want to be a meatpacker,' to figure out that I didn't want anything to do with packing meat. Still, you can't escape your genes."

"So, in one way or another, we're all destined to become our fathers?" Indeed, I was challenging Daddy Russ, the son of a meatpacker who went on to manage pension funds.

"We don't take after strangers, Mitch," came Daddy Russ's retort. "Your father embraced hard work, beer, and football. Translated: that's effort, vice, and passion. I'd be willing to wager that you have all three bases covered. I know I covered *my* bases, however many there were. But, in most cases, I find there's simply no avoiding the "gifts" that get handed down to us."

The Bohemian

I was anxious to learn the correlation between Daddy Russ's and his father's respective livings, but Daddy Russ chose another example to explain his "inheritance."

"If it was eight o'clock in the morning and my mother hadn't reached her tenth complaint, it was time to check if she was still breathing." Daddy Russ's tenor matched the anecdote. "Whenever I looked at my father, if he wasn't pinching his brow or rubbing his forehead, he stared down at his shoes. Anyway, one summer, when vacationing in Niagara Falls, we had yet to open our lunch menus at Simon's when my father excused himself to the restroom. Minutes later, this man appeared: all three of our mouths fell agape—my mother's, my sister Beth's, and mine—and we stared, incredulously, at someone who, in many ways, resembled my father: He had the same posture, same gait, and emerged from the restroom wearing the same clothes, but beyond that, he was unrecognizable. Moreover, his face was vacant with eyes that seemed to rest on a horizon only he could see. When he walked by our table, he did so without a glance or flicker of recognition. It marked the first time I was rendered incapable of uttering a word. It was also uncharted water for my mother, who never understood that conversation required a participant. Anyway, I managed to gather myself in time to confront my father in the parking lot. I hollered, 'Dad,' but he didn't turn or break stride. Finally, I caught up to him and grabbed hold of his elbow. When he turned and faced me, I asked, 'Are you all right?'

"I turned sixteen that summer and was nearly as tall as my father. We had a good relationship in those days, and I sensed, with his mundane job and nagging wife both clinging to him like an albatross, that I represented one of his few saving graces, but not in all my sixteen years had he exposed to me, or anyone else, his bald head. I asked, 'What happened in that bathroom?' The silliest grin formed on his face; I can still see it today. He told me there was no toilet paper in the stall. It was unimaginable that this man who, for years, was so guarded about his baldness had unsoiled himself using his toupee: but as I gazed at the fringe of hair on the sides of his head, the whiteness of a scalp never exposed to the sun in my lifetime, and the grin that persisted, I realized that I was witnessing the most liberating moment in a man's life. And as I would learn, with his very next breath, his liberation would not begin and end with the disposal of an ill-used toupee. 'Russ,' he told me.' He reached for my shoulders;

his grip was firm. 'Whatever you do, never lay with a Bible belt conservative. But if, for some reason, you can't help yourself, make goddamn sure you're prepared; never take her at her word; and, if you can help it, make doubly sure you're head-over-heels in love; anything less, you're booking a one-way ticket to misery.' He walked away, leaving us stranded in Niagara Falls. Six years would pass before I saw him again... at my wedding!

"College campuses weren't nearly as diverse then as they are nowadays. But at Penn State, there were plenty of lapsed Catholics, atheist intellectuals, Zionists, and free-thinking Jews who thought being Jewish meant listening to Lenny Bruce, and the political spectrum ranged from moderate to radical; nevertheless, yours-truly couldn't see himself satisfied with such a robust breadth of lonely hormonal humanity—couldn't wet my beak with all that was available. So, senior year, I went and found myself a staunch pro-life Christian conservative who, upon my 'sobering up,' —that's a euphemism for 'I already planted my seed,' —I discovered nagged like a champ. The only difference between my father and me: I had a touch more stamina; my marriage lasted twenty years."

Silence followed Daddy Russ's soliloquy—silence, agape mouths, and furrowed foreheads surrounded the table. Perhaps we sat as speechless as Daddy Russ, Beth, and their mother were all those years ago at Simon's in Niagara Falls. Despite diverting my eyes, hoping to glimpse Elizabeth Montague because I sensed a story was about to evolve into a *history repeating itself by way of genetics moralistic*, I remained just as stuck as everyone else on the notion that a beaten-down man pushed too far by a harridan emerged from a restroom imbued with a different spirit after taking a mop of synthetic hair to his hindquarters. One might exhaust every known superlative to describe what quite possibly was a never-before-gone-to height of absurdity and still not do justice to the method Daddy Russ's father chose as a pathway to liberation. But there remained one pressing question: How did a sixteen-year-old, along with Beth, who we learned was twelve, and their nagging mother wind their way from the Canadian side of Niagara Falls back to Philadelphia after being stranded without much in the form of resources?

"Mom called Uncle Bill collect," Daddy Russ told us. "He took the call and was good enough to reverse the charges, then wired enough money through Western Union for us to get home. We took

The Bohemian

a bus from Niagara to New York City; a train took us back to Philly from Grand Central Station. Uncle Bill was waiting for us at the 13th Street concourse to drive us home. He was a helluva good guy, my Uncle Bill."

"You wouldn't have named your son after your uncle had he been otherwise," Molly thought to add.

"And just how is Upstairs-Bill fairing nowadays?" My whimsical tenor seemed reason enough to trigger laughter. Once, when asked how they met, Molly and Daddy Russ revealed the whole next-door/upstairs scenario. "What are backyard soirees for, if not to expose ourselves using our most absurd anecdotes," Gabby had stated. "Nothing could be more liberating."

"He's been and remains a good son," said Daddy Russ, to which Molly added: "Who, despite his feelings and without raising too much of a fuss, respectfully yielded to his father."

We finished devouring the main course the Canadian Elk Hunter expertly grilled, and side dishes supplied by Gabby, Ursula, and Molly. Finally, we arrived at wine time—or, as we had become accustomed to saying, and had borrowed from a segment on a local radio station: *Time out for fine wine*—which provided Warren further opportunity to revel. Warren is quite a connoisseur of wines and boasts an extensive collection. Over the years, he and Ursula have traveled to many vineyards; the result was acquiring enough knowledge of wine that the painfully overused term "connoisseur" was applicable. However, Gabby has maintained: while Warren has developed a great fondness for wine, it was Ursula— "A true doyenne of many subjects," as Gabby describes her—who was the acquirer of knowledge and true architect behind their boast-worthy collection.

"Perhaps a Pinot Noir from an Oregon vineyard," Ursula proposed as Warren was about to make for next door and their cellar. How Ursula offered her suggestion concealed any possibility she might have provided instruction. "I have a hunch it will blend beautifully with the coolness of the early October air; do you agree?"

Before Warren could offer any concurrence, Nina, who had been especially quiet, brightly chirped, "I would love to see your collection." Nina was hardly uneducated concerning the virtues of wine. I also detected an anxiousness to be away from the table, and Warren gave her an excuse. She sprang to her feet before Warren could agree to her company, though once Nina was fully erect, The Canadian Elk

197

Hunter seemed especially eager to have her along. I found it all quite curious. Did Nina genuinely desire to examine a worthy collection of wine, or was it possible, dare I even think it, she fancied Warren? I had never known Nina to be attracted to brutish-looking men. Not that I would go so far as to label Warren a brute, but one might arrive at such an assessment given only the benefit of a glance. But that was not the real issue plaguing me: Why I was covetous that Nina was walking off with Warren marked the "real issue" and became a prevailing point of emphasis curdling in my viscera. I could go further, and I had: Nina walked off with Warren because she intuited that doing so would spark jealousy.

Moreover, why did I find what any sane person would perceive as an innocuous and irreproachable act so confounding? I was married to the one woman with whom matrimony would always persist as unremittingly agreeable. And poor Gabby: real-life Jane aside, when in present company, she saw herself as "the ugly duckling." Molly was a hardbody, long and athletic, able to break anyone; Warren included: it was a wonder Daddy Russ—even with Molly at her most accommodating and acquiring an affinity for gentleness and finesse—had thus far survived. As for Nina and Ursula: it was not a matter of opinion or up for debate: Not only were they exquisite but alike in their exquisiteness.

"This ought to be interesting," said Ursula, specifically to me, as Warren and Nina disappeared from view. It marked an example when "interesting" resonated as a curious choice of words. Moreover, Ursula seemed somewhat reticent, even unconcerned, despite what her chosen word implied. With a glance, I managed to capture Gabby's attention. She was seated beside real-life Harold, whose mind was still stuck in Niagara Falls and thus remained well engaged with Daddy Russ. Meanwhile, real-life Jane and Molly were droning on that, based on a similar degree of unattractiveness, Prince Charles and Camilla Parker-Bowles were made for one another. Also, how unfortunate it was that Diana's untimely death robbed her of any chance of happiness with the swarthy Dodi Fayed had become a point of emphasis. Molly and real-life Jane made no bones that Diana was far more deserving of happiness relating to a couple that managed more headlines than all the living and ill-fated Kennedys combined. "It's always the good ones who die young," I heard real-life Jane lament. Meanwhile, Gabby offered me a shrug of the shoulders and a roll of the eyes. The gestures were indicative of someone trapped between confusion and apology. Finally, my eyes shifted back to Ursula, who remained reticent and unconcerned, or so she appeared. "Interesting?" I uttered. My intonation made it clear I needed Ursula to elaborate.

"Mitch, dear," she began, though not without deeming it necessary to reach across the table and seize hold of my hand. It was all too reminiscent of how one might treat a bourgeois American owning a sensibility so delicate they find any degree of social evolution too shocking: The notion that I required coddling was unbearable. "You spend so much time with your serial killers that you miss all the juicy stuff happening right under your nose." Gabby shot me a glance as if to say: *I told you so.* "As for Warren," Ursula added, "Nina would be a tasty treat either way."

So Gabby confided in Ursula that Nina was transitioning; I suppose that was no great surprise. But the prospect that Nina would be a treat either way... for Warren? Could it be? It was unimaginable! On the other hand, it made all the sense in the world. I had always sensed an air of peculiarity between Ursula and Warren but never suspected they were anything other than a mismatched heterosexual couple. That they were two-way treats who gave one another free range to explore did explain a lot, but when such enlightenment gets thrust upon one in a sudden burst and at an inopportune moment, it can give one pause. I did my best to appear unfazed; in other words, I did not react as would the typical bourgeois American but the "bohemian" to which I had always aspired. Did I succeed? If I did, it was because my mind fast-forwarded past Ursula and Warren to where it became burdened with obsessing over Nina: lust, jealousy, greed, envy, and about a half-dozen other unworthy emotions stewed in my viscera and became the cause of me pissing all over the moral code of human behavior, which doubtless includes coveting your wife's sister. It was maddening! But more important: why was Nina able to lead me down this forsaken road to the edge of an illicit precipice? If only, somehow, I could untangle the mess known as the road map of my heart as it pertains to the complexities of Nina's unique sexual potency. If only it could be as simple as the most elementary equation. Unfortunately, when numbers are scarce, and the only entity available to lend perspective is the brain's limbic system, which, in weak men, tends to run roughshod over the prefrontal cortex, adding together one and one can make for a messy proposition.

Moreover, because, like most males, I was visually masochistic: I envisioned the sinuousness of Nina slithering over the hardness and hair of The Canadian Elk Hunter until her knees met the floor and, to his delight, welcomed him into her mouth, just as she had once welcomed me. How pathetic was I, a man barren of any facility to envision Nina enthralled over what I knew to be a worthy collection of wine? So many years ago was that maddeningly splendorous night in Bloomsbury, and still, I am struggling to regain my equilibrium. It may be a struggle that will always persist.

Real-life Harold and Daddy Russ; real-life Jane and Molly; Gabby and Ursula: three simultaneous conversations mingled in a sonic crossfire that produced what my ears construed as cacophonous and irritating gibberish. I felt out-of-place, unneeded, devoid of any desire to contribute; to not feel jettisoned, my eyes searched for Elizabeth Montague. She must be watching or nearby listening; Elizabeth would not have wanted to miss out on the goings-on of this eclectic assemble of odds and ends. Our soirees, although a routine, seldom included Nina and real-life Harold and Jane. Though I began to ponder a possibility: had the ever-perceptive and intuitive Elizabeth already figured out Ursula and Warren, the uniqueness behind the façade of Nina's unparalleled beauty, and that real-life Harold and Jane, in their own right, were every bit as fortunate as Ursula and Warren in that one of them reached into a haystack and managed to produce the proverbial needle? Her capacities aside, Elizabeth must be about, watching, lurking, and listening: before long, she would prove herself powerless to resist seeking me out to enlighten me of all she managed to acquire by way of her acuity, and I, Mitch Morningstar, shall anticipate such an engagement with eagerness. Indeed, I was confident of another go-around with one Miss Elizabeth Montague/Miss Havisham. But goddammit, how fucking long does it take to select a bottle of wine!

No sooner had I finished fretting than Nina and The Canadian Elk Hunter emerged from the cellar. Ursula looked on with approval. Each had entrusted in their mitts what was requested—a Pinot Noir from an Oregon vineyard.

"Domaine Drouhin," Warren proudly announced. For a Canadian, his French was cumbersome at best.

The Bohemian

"Perfect," Ursula intoned, then had Warren pass the bottles around the table so everyone could read the labels. "The Pinot Noir grape earned Burgundy its reputation," she told us. "First, what will strike you is its red fruit aromas and flavors; next, your noses and palates will enjoy a subtle array of characteristics such as earth, smoke, violet, and truffle."

"It must be considered rare," Daddy Russ theorized, "for a grape to reach its potential in such different regions as Burgundy, France, and the Pacific Northwest. I suspect it's a versatile little piece of fruit, the Pinot grape."

"Temperamental and high-maintenance is more like it," Ursula added. "But with hard work and perseverance, it can do far more than adapt; it can go on to achieve remarkable results. Much of Oregon is affected by conditions emanating from the Pacific Ocean, which often means mild winters and wet summers; in other words, conditions not ideal for ripening grapes. But some maintain—and in a few moments, you're likely to agree—that the harder a grape has to struggle, the more complex it's likely to become."

"Here's to struggling to adapt," said Nina, who, more than anyone seated, could identify with the struggles that beset the type of grape we were about to enjoy. Everyone raised their glass. Before anyone managed a sip, Molly added, "And here's to us: a collection of postmodern bohemians proudly blazing their own path and in their own unique way."

CHAPTER THIRTEEN
WHAT REALLY HAPPENED

Along with Nina, real-life Harold and Jane stayed with us for a spell before returning to England. When Gabby and I were busy teaching, our darling asexual friends kept themselves occupied hiking our rambling, hilly suburb.

"We were happy to learn, Mitch," Harold began upon my return, "that our dearest old friend and favorite novelist has stayed put since our last visit. It truly is a charming hamlet."

"Quite charming," Jane could not help adding.

We were all last together to celebrate *The Case of the Camden Lock Killer*—my third successful novel among four efforts: The fourth, a novella called *Requiem for a Madman*, featured a clergyman whose twisted sexuality compels him to kill, failed to make much of a dent; Gabby's sketches were far more impressive. I should have known better: a priest with a warped predilection that took him down a murderous path was low-hanging fruit, a plot any moron could have developed, and damn if Warren didn't let me know it.

"Anyway," Harold continued, "we were winding our way about town when we discovered a pub, The Paper Mill Tavern. The second we stepped inside, we could tell the tavern made its bones serving regulars the usual. I wouldn't go so far as to say they were unfriendly, but we had the impression that they could do quite nicely without us. In other words, we didn't receive, as they say, service with a smile."

"No service with a smile," Jane parroted.

"And the beer was weak," Harold moaned. "They must water it down!"

"Must be," Jane eagerly agreed. "There could be no other reason for beer to taste so weak."

"Anyway," Harold continued, "I mentioned to the chap that poured what passed for beer that we were in town for a spell and guests of Mitch Morningstar. *Well*, with the mere mention of your name, his whole demeanor shifted; his eyes grew to the size of saucers!"

"Saucers!" Jane parroted.

"Right away, I assumed he was a fan," said Harold. "And what better hook into a friendly chat than novels? But I quickly learned he has yet to read a single word you've written."

"Not one word," added Jane, somewhat gravely, as though the snubbing of my opuses was an unpardonable offense.

"Was he slight of build with graying hair that you could place near seventy or thereabout?" I asked.

"That's what he looked like, precisely," was Jane's spirited reply. "And about how old he was, too."

"Yes, precisely," added Harold. "And he began asking us about the big white house next door. He told us for decades, who resides in the house had been a mystery, and all sorts of spook stories and legends have circulated throughout town. He refers to it as 'a real head-scratcher' that you—the last to move onto the block—came to solve the mystery. He sounded more than doubtful. In fact, I'd say he's downright sour over the matter."

"I don't doubt it," I said. "Mr. McGruder is his name—you were speaking with the proprietor of The Paper Mill Tavern—and he has had a long preoccupation with the big white house and counted on being the one to uncover whatever mysteries were thought to surround it."

Regarding Elizabeth Montague and the mystery of the big white house, I told Gabby, who straightaway with giddiness ran to tell Ursula, who shared the news with Warren, who was delighted to forward it to Ray and Laura Salisbury—the couple whose dog went missing and was thought to have been held captive in the big white house but eventually returned—that beyond all the wrought iron and awful tangle of branches resided a real live person. On the news traveled; it reached the end of the block where resides Mr. Finnigan and his fearsome-looking Akita, then up the other side until it fell on the ears of the disgruntled Mr. McGruder, who sourly complained to Somerset Beasley, the proprietor of the auto repair shop at the end of the pike, "Is the dang woman's name, Elizabeth Montague or Miss Havisham? She can't have two names. And if it's Havisham, why would a daughter of Daniel Montague invent another surname?"

It was forgivable that Mr. McGruder was not a fan of Charles Dickens or read *Great Expectation,* never mind was unfamiliar with the Miss Havisham character. But what made the matter especially irksome where I was concerned: by the time the news reached Mr. McGruder, the poor man—instead of learning that Elizabeth Montague, because of her white dress and great-niece, *"reminded"* me of Miss Havisham—was given an either/or proposition; thus, I felt it was my unenviable duty to go and tender a satisfactory explanation. Mr. McGruder, although he seemed pleased with the clarification, was later heard accusing me of "fakery" and of having "gone off the reservation" and that the mystery of the big white house "was likely to turn up in one of Mitch's kooky novels." And here, I thought that my across-the-street-tavern-owning neighbor liked me. I suppose, like everyone else, he fancies Gabby, whereas me, he tolerates.

As for our other guest: Nina spent most of her stay cooped up in her room resting, reading, and giving herself beauty treatments. Sometimes she made an appearance at dinner; other times, she passed, and Gabby would leave a tray with a bedtime snack by her door. If Nina bothered helping herself to breakfast or lunch, she left no trace. Real-life Harold and Jane, Gabby, and I all had our theories: Nina had grown despondent that her transformation was not going swiftly enough to suit her, was one; she was exhausted and needed a break from her career, marked another. Despite never failing to make themselves available with unwavering friendship when across the pond, real-life Harold and Jane purported that Nina missed a place known as *the bosom of her family*—a place where she could let go and fall apart—or, putting it in simpler terms: Gabby. As I would discover upon taking the initiative of entering Nina's room on the Friday following our Sunday soiree, all three theories were in play.

"Deep reading, I should say." I stood, posing in the doorway. Nina marked her page, closed a copy of *Ayn Rand's Atlas Shrugged,* and placed it beside an empty wine glass on a nightstand. Upon further examination, I knew, without doubt, it was the very copy I saw on a shelf in Elizabeth Montague's library. "How did you come by this?" I asked. In my next breath, I apologized for my demanding tone. "I discovered it on the picnic table," she said. "I don't remember how we got on the subject, but Sunday, Daddy Russ described it as one of the more important novels of the twentieth century and promised him I'd give it a go one day. I assumed he was kind enough to drive it across

The Bohemian

town because it came with a note." The note read: *A little something while you convalesce.* Nina refilled the glass with the remains of a bottle left for her by Warren: A Grand Estates Chardonnay, a recent vintage.

"You're a terrific writer, Mitch; you truly are," Nina began. A vestige of loss and regret lingered in the ether. "But do you ever long to write *the* book—not a timeless literary classic, but a fictional piece based on your metaphysical and philosophical analysis of the twentieth century—an important book bound to keep you on shelves long after we're gone?"

I went and sat on the edge of the bed. Taking firm hold of the Rand opus, I said, "There's that which titillates my intellectual curiosity and what I can draw from my novel imagination, and never the twain shall meet. In other words: just as the world needs Schubert, it also needs rock `n` roll." Nina frowned. "I'm sorry if my answer disappoints you, but even as a young idealist, it was never my ambition to write allegory on the news, less a stringent rebuke based on a flawed system run by corrupt power brokers that long ago allowed it to get captured by markets, assuming either subject was liable to remain relevant for a century and beyond and keep me, as you have said, 'On shelves long after we're gone.'" I placed the weighty volume back on the nightstand and added, "The mere thought of diving into objectivism or poststructuralism as a thesis for a novel gives me a headache. Although, maybe I could write a futuristic thriller based on the 'wag the dog' principles currently gobbling up the West. I could have the extremes of our corrupt duopoly—neo-conservatives and radical progressives—growing rabid with hate and killing one another in their effort to seize control of the tail, and while busily engaged in street warfare of epic proportion, our multi-national corporations will have unified and raised an army mighty enough to overthrow what by then would have become an inept and archaic central government, erecting in its stead a system based on unchecked market anarchism. I think I shall call the novel *Atlas Sagged: A 21st Century Guide to Cannibalism!*"

"Oh, Mitch, you're making fun of me."

Nina frowned, then put the rim of her glass to my lips. I sipped. A comfortable silence followed, during which time we gazed at one another. Finally, I asked, "Was it a mistake for Gabby and me to leave England? Was I selfish to take her away from you, and did I place you in a position where you couldn't express your feelings on the matter?"

Nina's reply, *"No, no, and no!"* was quite emphatic. She added, "I was attempting to launch a career; I could hardly have expected you and Gabby to remain on standby had matters gone south, or some bully in the industry hurt 'poor Nina's' delicate feelings. I'm tougher than I look, Mitch."

"Then what?" I asked. It was clear that some matter or another was troubling her. She appeared to be looking off in the distance, the way one might when contemplating aspects of the past or an uncertain future. I knew Nina's history. Thoughtfully and with sensitivity, I had filled page after page with it; I had immersed myself in her earlier days such that I felt every bit as attached to them as Gabby, who had experienced them firsthand. Was there more? Was not every aspect, painful or otherwise, disclosed to her biographer? Was there a memory she unwittingly suppressed that she was just now remembering?

"Back in the days when everybody knew me as Robby Norwich—a boy too frail to be a boy—I would crawl into bed with Gabby; she would hold me and, in a whisper-soft voice, sing childhood songs in my ear. I remember each one; she would sing them until I fell asleep. Sometimes, come the morning, when I had awakened, I would still find myself safe and snug in her arms. But you already know that Mitch, just as you know how often I spent weeping with my head in Gabby's lap while she stroked my hair and tried to reassure me when the world was proving unbearable for someone like me that kindness and benevolence were on the horizon. Also, you know of the many months I followed Gabby around like a loyal puppy, knelt at her feet, and watched, with fascination, her transformation from girlhood to womanhood. Indeed, Mitch, you know all that and more. But here's what you don't know, nor does anyone else: There are some needs that I have never outgrown, and in many ways, I'm still a child—a delicate flower that needs the protection of her big sister. And it isn't that I lack strength, Mitch; I never imagined, after all these years—decades—I'd be so utterly and dismally alone and condemned to purgatory. And I won't settle for the love of a gay man. I'm a woman, Mitch! A real woman. At least I will be soon enough, and I want the love of a man— a man's man—the sort who can make a woman feel protected."

What began as a heartfelt soliloquy evolved into a diatribe of passion, and the result saw me holding Nina, who had enjoyed too much chardonnay, flush to my chest. When she finished crying, she asked, trying to sound whimsical, "So, how's the biography coming?"

"It's coming," I assured her. "I have every confidence you'll be pleased."

"I know I shall be, Mitch," she said. "You're a terrific writer. I haven't a single doubt my story will get told as thoughtfully as possible and in a way that's sure to make me proud. And although I told you numerous times in the past how honored I am that you've taken on this project, I promise the best has yet to come."

From the depth of a naked soul to a sense of balance and ending with a smirk—that signature and sexually galvanized smirk that always had me doubting myself. Indeed, my ever-generous sister-in-law never failed to captivate me with her breadth, otherwise the many aspects of a multifaceted persona known as Nina Linette.

"Incidentally, Mitch, I didn't betray you," she told me when she saw my hand reaching for the doorknob and about to take my leave.

"Betray me?" came my quizzical reply—a reply that saw Nina frown, for she knew I was feigning ignorance concerning what she had implied.

"To put it more plainly," she added with an edge, for she was not inclined to spell the matter out *plainly*, "I didn't betray you in any manner you torturously imagined. So that terrible distraction you suffered last Sunday, which lingered for days afterward, was all for nothing."

There was no point in trying to forge a casual façade concerning what transpired between Nina and Warren; the effort would have proved futile. So I went and sat back down on the edge of the bed. "I truly am fascinated by wine collections," she continued. "And no, Mitch, I'm not a fool; it was quite clear to me that Ursula was the true connoisseur and that Warren, as they say, was along for the ride, but such a benign fact made my being privy to their collection no less fascinating. However, I would soon discover that Warren was as fascinated with me as I was with so many bottles that came from so many regions of the world. He kissed me. My first inclination was to recoil, but I didn't, so he kissed me again. I can't explain what came over me, but whatever anxiety I kept bound up came seeping out. I stood there with eyes closed, my body limp—I had transformed myself into an empty canvas upon which he could play, and, in doing so, I allowed him to discover me. Strange, but I wasn't the slightest bit wary of causing the sort of revulsion that could trigger a robust heterosexual man to strike me. On the contrary, when I afforded myself a downward glance, not only was there no evidence of disgust, I witnessed a flicker of delight. It was then that I realized Gabby must have confided in Ursula, who, in turn, informed Warren that she had a sister who, as far as sisters were concerned, was atypical. Imagine my surprise when I discovered that Warren came with his own peculiarities. What was especially strange was watching him, with unquenchable lust, devour the one part of my person for which I harbor disdain. My goodness, we are a marvelously queer species."

Nina lurched forward from her lolled position and kissed me faintly on the mouth. It was a gesture devoid of any invitation or implication; I could sense a vestige of benignity. Then she fell back against her pillow and sighed. Next came the promise that, sometime tonight, she would grace us with an appearance.

CHAPTER FOURTEEN
THE LETTER IN THE HEDGE

The next evening, Saturday, we met Daddy Russ and Molly in town at Headhouse Square. They booked a table for nine at The Dickens Inn, an old English-style restaurant and pub, to celebrate real-life Harold and Jane's and Nina's last night in America.

"At the very least, we can have every confidence in the suds," I said while winding my way through the city to the center of town. "We can always count on the English for good beer."

"All those months spent in Bloomsbury, and you mean to tell us, Mitch, you didn't acquire any love for bubble and squeak or blood pudding, only our beer?" It was Harold who feigned indignance from the back seat.

"Unfortunately, 'English' and 'cuisine' are two words rarely heard together," Nina admitted. "English 'food,' English 'grub,' but never English 'cuisine.'"

"I'm afraid you're right about that," added Harold. "I suppose you could attribute the shortcoming to all those centuries spent conquering foreign lands when we should have been devoting more time and attention to the gastronomical arts."

"You're so right, dear," said Jane. "And besides, save for a handful of islands, all our territories have gone on to gain their independence. Meanwhile, we're stuck with blood pudding and bubble and squeak."

"Bubble and squeak," Harold repeated with a sigh.

"Don't fret," said Gabby, "it'll be the Americanized version of bubble and squeak and blood pudding. Trust me; folks don't grow to become such sizes as they do in the States from nothing."

"But the beer, I promise, will be noteworthy," I added.

And so there we sat, nine in all, around a table: an asexual couple, bisexual couple, heterosexual couple, a couple comprised of a sensitive older lover and his much more youthful and, at times, predatorial lady friend, and then there was Nina, who we hoped sooner than later would come equipped with the facility to make our eclectic consortium an even ten. Indeed, we were a marvelous menagerie of human diversity preparing to break bread. Nina and Ursula hoarded the lion's share of attention; their incomparable beauty drew oglers of every gender and age. Where Ursula was concerned, the attention received was strictly for her beauty, whereas how Nina carried herself gave folks the impression that she was a celebrity making an effort not to create a stir. Molly was also worth noticing but more often enjoyed projecting what she called her *"Are you looking at me? ala Robert De Niro"* reaction to an ogler. With Molly, you never knew. She was just as likely to frighten a fellow into wetting his britches as she was dragging the poor bastard home to fuck him until he wished he *had* wet his britches before running for his life. Doubtless, Nina was on to something when she dubbed us humans a queer species. But as far as the nine people who clanked together nine mugs filled with English beer were concerned, when lumped together, we felt no less typical than nine innings of baseball or a road trip in a Chevrolet.

Bright and early the following day, we saw real-life Harold and Jane off at the airport. Nina remained. I'm not sure when the decision got made, but neither Gabby nor I were informed of it until within minutes of arriving at Philadelphia International. We said our goodbyes to Harold and Jane, who were sad but supportive concerning Nina's need to remain behind. "I need a break," she said but did not bother to share with us from *whom* or from *what* a period of disassociation was required, nor did we pester her to elaborate; the fatigue in her eyes was glaringly apparent, and no one need imagine why: Performing, traveling, recording, the constant dealings with an agent, manager, and musicians, never mind an attending physician, psychiatrist, and psychologist; in totality, it added up to more than she could bear, and a week of lounging while plowing through Ayn Rand would not prove sufficient in regaining her sea legs. A place where she could drop out of society for an undetermined period would prove the essential medicine.

We returned home to make all the necessary phone calls to inform all the essential people that Nina, in all likelihood, wouldn't be setting foot on British soil until sometime after the New Year. Her associates in the music industry seemed to understand. However, her medical team proved less understanding; I could hear their frowns of displeasure on the other end of the telephone. I responded in kind by informing them: here, in America, we have psychiatrists, psychologists, surgeons, and general practitioners glad to oversee such processes should Nina's hiatus become too much of an inconvenience and that these American doctors would be perfectly willing to see it through until the end and cost was no object. I did not speak rudely or bully; I simply stated the case as a matter of fact, and each of them saw the upside of cooperation when it got spelled out.

In the first two weeks following real-life Harold and Jane's departure, we saw very little of Nina; she more or less kept herself hidden away in her room and gave us every indication that she would prefer not to be disturbed. From what Gabby and I could gather: she read, rested, and soul-searched. Meanwhile, Gabby and I behaved like imbeciles. We removed our shoes so the stairs would not creak or our heels knocked on the floor. At breakfast and dinner, we spoke only in whispers. Then, come the evenings, we dared not turn on the television; instead, I more or less kept to my writing while Gabby sketched and sometimes read. It was not until November that Nina began to make appearances a routine, and when they started, Gabby and I handled her as if she were a priceless knickknack in someone else's home. Perhaps, in a way, we both felt guilty over her weary condition—that if we lived in London, we could have done something to prevent it. But a week later, she was going outside for walks in the fresh autumn air, and before we knew it, was back to her old self, though not in any particular hurry to return to her life or career. "Will I be a burden, Mitch, if I stay on a bit longer?"

"What can I say," I told her, "I'm a sucker for beautiful women."

The three of us had managed a lovely state of contentment and coziness when real-life Harold and Jane—after first working themselves into a tizzy—called to inform us of what the tabloid journalists in England were writing about Nina. *Singer Nina Linette carries on steamy affair with American novelist and brother-in-law Mitch Morningstar*, claimed one. *Nina Linette missing; not seen in weeks. Feared kidnapped*, claimed another. One rag went so far as to claim that Nina, without citing specifics, had denigrated the Prophet Muhammad and, as a result, was forced to hide out in America much in the way that Salmon Rushdie had to in England. Poor real-life Harold and Jane; they were livid that such claptrap got strewn about without Nina in a position

211

to defend herself. It took some doing, but Gabby did manage to calm our dear friends by citing: "Nina won't be any worse off from all the drivel written about her. If anything, it's likely to further her celebrity. By the time she's back on English soil, she'll have gone from a well-respected vocalist of some note to a bonafide star!" Gabby was rarely without perspective, and in this instance, it served to calm our dear, annoyingly sweet, strangely loveable, and quirky friends.

"Accused of an affair, the victim of a crime, forced into hiding: I'm exhausted just thinking about how busy I'm supposed to have been." With a sigh, Nina retired to the quietude of her room.

****

It is now mid-November, that time of year when the days have become dreadfully short. I woke early Sunday morning, ventured out into my kingdom, or backyard, stretched, deeply inhaled the crispness of the autumn air, and reached for my rake. Unlike most household chores, which I would describe as drudgery and perform under protest, I own a genuine fondness for raking leaves. Call it a queer sensibility, but romance and the wistful elegance of a Chopin Nocturne come to mind when my nostrils fill with the subtle smell of spent foliage in November. When raking it into piles—as is often the case when pedaling my ten-speed miles on country lanes or through the streets of the town—my mind slips into an alternate universe otherwise known as *a work in progress,* and *I* begin to think as would my protagonist or some other core character I have created. I can never be sure if what occurred was the craft of art subliminally inspired by exercise or exercise overwhelming all perspectives of reality, thus making creativity possible. Either way and however incidental, it has proven reliable and led me to ponder whether laborers enjoy better mental health than those who have found a more sophisticated pathway to a dollar.

Conversely, Warren lacks sensibility and perspective concerning the fall cleanup. While the process, as I tend to it, may take me days, and I hope it does, Warren goes about the task like a ravenous wolverine whose snout is pointed toward a scent ripe for conquest. Warren's motivation is to finish before one o'clock; otherwise, kickoff time. Despite being a native Canadian, Warren is quite passionate about all that takes place on the gridiron, especially as it pertains to the NFL; he's not so keen on the college game. Gabby finds it nonsensical that a sport that sees little contact between the ball and the foot and is based strictly on collision should be called football. "If anything," she has often pointed out to Warren, "it should be called 'war' if not 'armored savagery.' What we do in England: *that*, my friend, is football!"

And speaking of the devil—not Gabby, The Canadian Elk Hunter—he just came bursting from his garage bearing no horns and a pitchfork but lugging a piece of manly lawn equipment to attack his leaves. He appears focused and determined, does Warren, thus manages but a halfhearted wave upon noticing me and my shillyshally pace of raking. A moment later, he disappears behind the olive hedge. Next came the roar of an engine propelling a machine capable of vacuuming everything in its path and grinding it into dust. If it requires yanking a cord to start, gasoline to run, and the facility to disturb the peace, you may rest assured such a machine has a place in Warren's shed. Countless leaves and twigs vacuumed into his contraption are ground into pulp and fed into a large bag clamped on the side, then used as mulch. Before long, I lost interest in Warren and returned to my alternate universe where, intermittently, I went from being immersed in a new work of fiction to being reminded of the nostalgic elegance of Chopin. In that universe, I floated about, dreamy and contented with whatever reverie it provided, when my eye managed to catch an envelope; either by the wind or a hand placing it there, it had taken up lodging in the olive hedge. Whichever, I decided it was worth investigating. The envelope was not rumpled or weathered; it appeared recently placed, perhaps as early as this morning, but well after the morning dew would see it spoiled.

Moreover, it was sealed. I took the liberty of unsealing it, for, on its face, there was no indication of a destination, less a name. I removed the content and unfolded it; I should not have been surprised, but I was—surprised *and* delighted.

Dear Mitch,

Have you given any thought to my idea for a serial killer spoof? If so, I would so much enjoy an opportunity to discuss the matter further, as well as a matter of a much more, shall we say, "Machiavellian" nature. I've made tea and delightful sandwich wedges if you care to join me.

Fondly,
Elizabeth

I folded the note and returned it to its envelope, which I promptly stuffed in my pocket. I felt a twinge of resentment that my relationship with Elizabeth Montague—assuming that the term relationship was applicable—was wholly on her terms. After being left standing on her doorstep and ignored after several attempts to gain her attention, suddenly, after a year-plus of no communication of any kind, I'm expected to drop what I'm doing for the sake of tea and "delightful" sandwich wedges. Well, la-di-goddamn-da!

My twinge of resentment would not endure but for a fleeting moment as it would come to pass. The reason? Elizabeth was not only a woman but one older than my mother, and on those fronts, I suppose she was due some respect. Besides, I suspected all along that were I to engage in any relationship with this enigmatic woman, it would be *primarily* on her terms, if not *entirely*. With that in mind, I laid down my rake beside the pile of leaves I worked to gather and headed straight away for the front door of the big white house. Upon reaching the porch, I noticed the door was left ajar. First, a note, then an open door; thus, it finally occurred to me: Elizabeth had no tolerance for being summoned. Knocks, bells, or rings were not appreciated; Elizabeth was not one to snap to attention as might a dog at the sound of a ringing doorbell or telephone, assuming she owned the latter; moreover, she resented anyone attempting to garner attention through such abrupt or what Elizabeth likely perceived as "crude" means, but if you were someone whom she was expecting, a rite of passage was readily provided. With only a moment's hesitation, I took advantage of my golden opportunity and entered the big white house.

At first, I called out Elizabeth's name with wariness, for she was not in plain sight, then louder but was careful to use a chirpy timbre.

"Mitch," she called back; her tenor rang out with enthusiasm. "And here I thought you would whittle away the entire day with that silly rake in your hands and daydreaming; although, who could manage a daydream living next to Warren? Poor Ursula!" A moment later, Elizabeth emerged carrying a tray upon which she was transporting the promised tea and sandwich wedges—a sign that she had every confidence I would show. But far more fascinating was that Elizabeth was attired as she had been the day of our first encounter; she was not clad *similarly* but was wearing the same white dress, and the same ballet-style slippers were on her feet. "How about we make ourselves comfy in the sitting room, shall we," she said with an aristocratic air. "I remembered how you favored that room with all its art and literature; you're a man after my own heart, Mitch Morningstar."

The Bohemian

I should not have, for there was no intent on Elizabeth's part, but I found being reminded of why I favored the sitting room pretentious and condescending. I am perfectly aware of my likes, and it was irksome to hear them used to lure me as might a cookie entices a child. I realize I felt overly sensitive concerning a matter where oversensitivity should not have been a factor. Call it a character flaw—one of the many I seem to be collecting—but whenever someone says to me, "Mitch, you're gonna love it," I immediately begin looking for reasons to rain on their parade. Could it be that I'm a natural contrarian or stubborn prick who takes offense whenever someone assumes the liberty of knowing my mind? I could not say: but in this particular instance, I managed to resist revealing palpable signs of my idiotic flaw, and like an obedient boy skipping after a cookie-wielding adult, I followed Elizabeth to where I was enveloped by fine art and classic literature. We sat as we did during our first encounter. Her eyes were alive, effervescent—it was as if, all at once, numerous ideas were swimming in her ever-widening pupils, causing her to seem much younger than her years. I would learn, in due course, that during our prolonged dry spell, Elizabeth had two birthdays but did not reveal her age.

"So, tell me, Mitch, and please, *do* be honest," she begged while frothing over with anticipation, "have you given any thought to my idea for a serial killer spoof?"

I admitted to Elizabeth that the concept of a serial killer spoof was not only intriguing but also one I had given due consideration to, despite the opposition I received from Gabby, who had no difficulty expressing disfavor in my spending time reinventing my genre. However, I told Elizabeth I would need another year, perhaps two, before my calendar was clear enough to begin the project. I also told her I had two stipulations: I wanted to meet her phantom great-niece Jenny—whom everyone on the block has managed to glimpse but me—and I wanted a tour of the cellar.

"Why, Mitch, of course, you can meet my darling Jenny," Elizabeth intoned. "And she, I'm quite sure, would be delighted to meet her Great-auntie Elizabeth's favorite living novelist. But, Mitch, a tour of the cellar? Is it possible you believe there's a chance you'll find the corpses of murdered teenage boys once deemed unsuitable for my great-niece?" Elizabeth sighed, then added, "But, as you wish.

Stipulations should be honored. But first, let us enjoy this modest little spread I was careful to prepare."

"A lovely idea. And meanwhile, tell me a bit about Jenny." It was clear this great-niece of Elizabeth's was a preferred subject; thus, her eyes widened upon readily honoring my request.

"I'd say she's quite typical of a young woman born into too much privilege in that she has developed an appetite for rebellion, particularly in matters of love. It seems she only favors the 'bad boys,' otherwise, young men her parents are sure to disapprove of, though my intuition tells me it's typical of most young women nowadays, not just the ones born into privilege. I remember from my youth the phases some girls went through at Mary Craft's School for Girls."

With her last thought, Elizabeth's voice trailed away: she lapsed into a momentary reverie, her mind had flung to the distant past; doubtless, she was reminiscing the impetuous April Cassidy, a girl she never stopped wondering about—a girl who had captured her heart. In some ways, Elizabeth's emotional maturity never advanced beyond the point of being told that her friend was not coming back to school. "Anyway," her sharpness of tone had fully returned. "When Jenny was fourteen, I took her under my wing, so to speak, and what blossomed was a relationship that saw me develop quite an affection for her, and she, in turn, learned to have absolute faith in my judgment. I was entrusted to be an independent and unbiased arbiter with concern for love interests—and there have been many, and you shall understand why when you meet her. I never spoke harshly of any young man I had the opportunity to meet. And believe me, there were at least two instances, I can recall, when I could have easily said, 'discard that one; he's bad news and always shall be.' I make every effort to avoid, presently, as I have in the past, rushes to judgment. We sit down over tea, Jenny and I, and discuss a particular young man's character composedly and thoughtfully. From our discussions, we attempt to arrive at a unified decision concerning his suitability. Over the years, if I have learned anything, it wasn't all about rebellion with Jenny; to her credit—and this is true of many women, and it has produced disastrous results—my dear great-niece is a nurturing soul with a nurturing heart and uses these benevolent traits to reform wayward young men. However, she's no longer a young woman; she's an adult, as are the potential suitors she attracts or selects. Luckily—and this is a sign of maturity drawn from learned

216

experience—she realizes that not everyone in this chaotic world is redeemable.

"Now, regarding the cellar: Might I put to you a hypothetical question? After all, are not hypotheticals the most interesting of all questions? What would you do, or how would you react if such-and-such were the case? It's so delightfully gray, abstract, and often circumspect while leaving plenty of room for doubt and debate. But I'm preaching to the choir: who but a novelist would understand better the importance of heterodox thinking? So here goes it, Mitch: What would you do were you to discover bodies in the cellar, perhaps hung by their scruffs from hooks protruding from cement walls? Would you continue to conduct interviews until ample material was gathered to fill a novel or run straightaway to notify the authorities? It could be quite disconcerting to ponder the depths of depravity to which man has turned a blind eye or sank for the sake of his art. On second thought: dwelling upon such matters could become a terrific source of amusement."

As Elizabeth spoke, her eyes swelled with anticipation, for she assumed her question would present a challenge—one that would leave me grappling between art and morality, their respective boundaries, and where they might overlap. It was for reasons of gratuity that I hesitated—I did not wish to disappoint Elizabeth, who believed that she had presented a genuine dilemma—then I told her: "However fascinating delving into the consciousness of a woman capable of committing murderous acts would prove, I would resist the inclination and notify the authorities."

"A satisfactory answer, Mitch," she intoned.

"Really?" I was unable to conceal my surprise. "And here, I was willing to wager that my answer would prove *dis*satisfying."

"Quite the contrary, Mitch: Your answer proves that you are a citizen of the world first and an artist second, which is as it should be. Those foremost artists tend to be far too enamored with their intellect and insights, and, as a result, they hold the world in contempt. So I much prefer you, Mitch. And incidentally, that you are foremost a citizen of the world does not make you any less an artist, nor does it make you, Heaven forbid, down-to-earth. However, it does make it difficult to explain your dilemma."

"My dilemma?" My curiosity triggered an imp-like smirk to form on Elizabeth's face: It was the sort when someone, far more intuitive than first assumed, has learned something about you that even you had yet to learn.

"Yes, Mitch, dear; a dilemma. You see—and I'm quite sure that I've alerted you in the past—the old olive hedge has been blessed with keen eyesight and acute hearing and has gotten into the habit of reporting what it hears and sees directly to yours truly."

"And, what exactly has the 'old olive hedge' seen and heard?" I decided to play along. After all, what had I to lose? Meanwhile, I would provide an older woman with some amusement at my expense.

"It seems to me, Mitch (Elizabeth began to reveal her hypothesis in an *I hate to be the bearer of bad tidings, but...* fashion), you do quite well when in the company of Ursula and just as well in the company of Nina. When you're in the presence of both stunning women, however, you seem out-of-sorts. If I didn't know better, Mitch, dear, I'd swear that you're so conscious of giving each equal attention and fearful you might fail that you end up doing your darndest not to look at either woman. When addressing Nina, you gaze at your hands, shoes, an imaginary person in the window, birds that aren't in the sky, and always with an eye in reserve for Gabby. It's no different with Ursula, except Warren is the beneficiary of a diverted eye. But you never gaze directly at either beautiful creature when they are together. Indeed, Mitch, I would say that qualifies as a dilemma, albeit quite a curious one."

It can be somewhat alarming when someone points out a matter you never suspected was obvious. Was I perfectly aware of my pet obsessions and the desire not to favor Nina over Ursula, or vice-versa being a recent acquisition? Indeed, but not to the lengths I had gone: Imaginary figures in windows and birds absent from the sky? Now aware of how apparent my efforts led me to ponder whether Daddy Russ and Molly and real-life Harold and Jane had also noticed, and if so, why was I not pulled aside and told: *Mitch, you're acting a bloody fool; you've got to stop!* I'm especially disappointed in Molly and Gabby: rarely, if ever, does either let anything slide and are the first to point out when someone has behaved such that they proved themselves an ass.

"But there is one matter of which there is no doubt, Mitch: you're still very much in love with Gabby, and there are aspects to your marriage—if I may remind you—that are richly rewarding and can never be replicated with another."

"Is that what the olive hedge says?"

The Bohemian

"Indeed, it does, Mitch." Elizabeth raised her cup triumphantly, then sipped her tea. "It has also told me that Mitch Morningstar is not the sort of fellow who appreciates conquest less cheap thrills, so the matter begs the question: Why is it that Ursula and Nina possess the facility to drive you to distraction? I refuse to believe you're still stuck on the notion Ursula stirs you because you find Warren an unworthy brute. Mitch, dear," Elizabeth pleaded, "say it isn't so. And as for Nina: it's clear she's a different kind of creature altogether; aloof and complex are two words that come to mind. And suggesting there is more to her than meets the eye would be quite an understatement. In other words, who *wouldn't* find her stirring? But need I remind you, Mitch, Nina Linette is your sister-in-law, and although an encounter with her may not be ruled as incestuous by any known doctrine, it would be highly improper. Besides, you need not explore women other than Gabby to prove you're not a bourgeois American; there *are* other ways. I would submit your career alone qualifies you to the contrary. Now, shall we take to the cellar?"

Elizabeth's sudden eagerness for the cellar engendered a spell of trepidation I managed to conceal. Was I about to fall victim to this enigmatic older woman? It would seem unlikely that Elizabeth Montague, a woman nearing seventy and slight of build, had the facility to harm me fatally. Then again, who knows how many young men approached the matter by applying the same reasoning, and, as a result, their corpses are currently dangling from hooks. Either way, I regretted adding a cellar tour as a stipulation for a writing project. However, I was put at ease when Elizabeth suggested *I* follow *her*. I found it favorable to remain behind while keeping Elizabeth in my sights. First, she grabbed two very stout candles fixed into ornate pewter holders. "Here, Mitch," she said, handing over one of them, then lit both, "we'll need these." And there I went, venturing to the one area of the big white house made suspect by the most eccentric person I have ever known, who quite possibly was a murderess. I could have easily said: *Never mind, Elizabeth, I believe you, there's no need for a tour of the cellar*, but there is a reason curiosity killed the cat: it tends to overwhelm fear, and when you are someone who writes about deranged predators for a living, curiosity will win out every time.

"There's no electricity in the cellar?" I peeped while clutching my candle. I had raised a legitimate concern, for the house got built long before wiring houses with electricity became standard, and when added, perhaps the cellar remained without utility. It was a logical conclusion I had drawn but also a disquieting one.

"Oh, there's electricity, all right, but not one good lightbulb. You'll have to forgive me, Mitch; the older I get, the slower I am at getting around to matters."

I did not bother to ask Elizabeth for an interpretation of what she meant by "slower at getting around to matters;" I could well imagine it not being a case of weeks since the cellar had last seen artificial light but a year, if not several of them. I also assumed it was futile to wonder aloud about a modern invention known to many as the flashlight.

The cellar smelled as musty as one might expect a subterranean hollow, three-quarters underground and built nearly a century and a half ago, would smell, and the smell hit me no sooner had Elizabeth opened the door that led to it. Although musty old cellars are not devoid of charm and often promise the possibility of discovering buried treasures that have been ignored or forgotten for a century or beyond and the one under the big white house—a place with a known history and heyday—promised to be a doozie.

As I watched by candlelight Elizabeth descending the stairs—perhaps because she was peculiar in a way one might describe as "arcanely nefarious"—what struck me was the notion she was a viable woman. Not to suggest I fancied her, but it was well within reason that someone with a few more birthdays might. When she reached the landing of the stairs, seemingly concerned for my safety, she turned to face me. I beheld her face in the candlelight. Until that point, Elizabeth's attractiveness, which exceeded the description of "well-preserved," had not escaped me. Moreover, what occurred to me as I began to feel somewhat diminished in a dark and unfamiliar environment: if not for Elizabeth's outdated hairstyle and costume, which lent her the appearance of a docent in some historic venue, she was not merely viable for a man her age, but viable period. Conjoined with the mystery that seemed to enshroud her, this new perception was causing me to experience Elizabeth Montague in my loins. Thus, I could not definitively say that had Elizabeth displayed an inclination to perform for me as Warren had for Nina once I reached the landing, I would have objected.

"As you can see, Mitch, there are no corpses or skeletal remains of any kind. The only question is whether you find the realization a relief or disappointment." Again, Elizabeth turned toward me. Again, the loveliness of her face illuminated kindly in the candlelight. What followed was me smiling somewhat idiotically for forcing her to prove she was not a serial murderess of romantically ambitious young men. Next, I noticed the limited daylight breaking through small rectangular casements positioned high on the walls below the ceiling. It was enough to make out that many objects were covered with canvas drop cloths. Elizabeth seemed agreeable to my unveiling one but spoiled the surprise. It was a spinning wheel that, in days of childhood when displayed in a spare bedroom, once fed her vivid imagination.

"Lydia would set me upon it, and, together, we pretended to create a gown for a princess betrothed to a handsome prince, and they were to be married in a palace in a foreign land. I asked her if the spinning wheel had belonged to my mother. She told me she was unsure but later wished she said it had, for playing pretend with anything that once belonged to my mother added enchantment to my childhood. Later, I learned that the spinning wheel was an old relic of unknown origin."

I did not bother to ask Elizabeth who spoiled the fantasy. Who else would have but her father? But doubtless, when Daniel Montague got asked, his full attention was captured by another matter; perhaps an item in the newspaper was the cause of distraction. The result was him thoughtlessly spewing the simple truth of the spinning wheel.

I went reaching for another canvas drop. Before Elizabeth could issue the kind of protest that would have thwarted my effort, I had already unveiled the object: a portrait of Daniel and Elizabeth resting on an easel revealed in candlelight. Daniel was impeccably attired and strikingly handsome; the proudness of his protruding chin was a noteworthy feature, one giving the impression he was someone of noble lineage. Next, my eyes fell on Elizabeth: I could tell she was in her young teens, perhaps fourteen; otherwise, the spring of days considered youth—a time when a bud, although young at heart, begins to stretch into the makings of a lovely flower—but was fashioned to appear much older. And despite the grooming she had undergone, ingrained in her expression was a girl thrust into womanhood long before she was ready. Perhaps it was shortly before sitting for the portrait that Daniel Montague made Elizabeth a woman; that would well explain its demotion to the cellar. I saw no sense in asking Elizabeth where the portrait was once displayed. I assumed it sat in the sitting room among the other works of art and collection of classic literature. Also, it was needless to wonder aloud why such an effort featuring two compelling subjects had suffered banishment to a dark and musty old cellar. The answer was painfully clear; my morbid curiosity required no confirmation. Poor Elizabeth. Understanding the depths of her piteous life and who she might have become otherwise were themes worthy of contemplation, and the paradox of it all was embodied in how glowingly she spoke of her father. Somehow, Elizabeth developed a resource that allowed her to separate Daniel Montague the man, who was admired, from the father she despised. The portrait, doubtless, was a loathsome reminder of the latter and of the dark days when Elizabeth first was taken; thus, it was likely dragged to the cellar upon the internment of Daniel Montague, if not the very moment following his last breath.

I turned toward Elizabeth. She failed to sense the weight of my gaze. *Hers, meanwhile,* was fixed on the portrait, though it was apparent that capturing its essence was not her aim. Instead, buoyantly, she seemed to set herself adrift; perhaps she harkened back to that first summer of discovery and the foreign land she and Daniel had traveled to—a place and time before her tenderness and youth endured manipulation and reshaping until emerged a girl who resembled Daniel Montague's daughter but in her soul was unrecognizable.

I once heard it said that people, often unwittingly, return to their childhood to claim some if not all of what went missing: the love of a mother, the authority of a father, the right to play, the freedom to wander, the opportunity to know the world through a mistake. Was there any hope remaining for Elizabeth? Had she enough vigor left to close the vastness of those gaps, and if so, had she the desire? Nina crept into my thoughts: In so many ways, her childhood, too, had gone missing. Though for Nina, there was still time, decades, let us hope. Poor Elizabeth. I was moved by the desire to show her genuine and proper affection between a man and a woman. For a fleeting moment, I saw myself as the typical man—a faulty merger of heroism drenched in male arrogance—holding to the notion he could overwhelm all the wrongs done to a woman. Doubtless, such a rationale is a fool's paradise—a place which no man, including yours truly, could enjoy success.

The moment passed, thankfully not regrettably. Keeping company with Elizabeth would have to be enough; my friendship, if not a saving grace—to think of it as such was the height of arrogance—must prove sufficient.

"Mitch, dear," I heard Elizabeth call out weakly. "If it's all right with you, I would like to return to the sitting room."

"Of course," I softly replied. Then I fixed the canvas drop cloth over the easel. Afterward, I followed Elizabeth up the stairs. By the time we reached the sitting room, she had managed to shake off the ill effects of seeing herself in all her youthful splendor while wrapped in her father's arm and was restored to her usual engaging self. When I made my departure that afternoon, I did not do so empty-handed but with a gift-wrapped book, or rather, what felt like three books.

"Don't open it now, Mitch!" Elizabeth implored. "Wait until later, when you're in the company of Gabby. That way, you and I will be guaranteed a stimulating discussion when we next meet."

I was giddy like a child; I could hardly wait to unveil my new treasure. I was inclined to tear away at the wrapping once I was out of sight or had reached my back patio, but I dared not, for as Elizabeth had now twice warned me, the olive hedge has eyes! So I stepped inside, where I was sure to be safe, and set the package on the kitchen table. My knees buckled when I was through unwrapping, though I managed a chair before experiencing an abrupt meeting with the floor. It was not possible, I thought. Why would Elizabeth part with such a treasure? I went tearing up the stairs in search of Gabby. She was seated by the window—the same window and chair by which I often spied her and Ursula surrendering their naked bodies to the sun. Gabby was sketching. She kept her full attention on her sketch pad when wondering aloud why I was "stampeding through the house" and "all short of breath." She also informed me that she was sketching me earlier when toiling away with the leaves, but I "upped and disappeared." She wondered where I had gotten to, then rolled her eyes when adding, "Never mind; I could easily guess where you've been."

"Don't sit there pretending that you're not every bit as fascinated with Elizabeth Montague as I am," I scoffed. Gabby frowned as might a child, then admitted that she was suffering a "twinge of jealousy" that I was the only one to whom Elizabeth Montague had extended a hand in friendship. However, her eyes quickly brightened when I handed over what I was holding: From Chapman and Hall

Publishers in 1861, a first edition and first impression three-volume set of Dickens' *Great Expectations.*

"You mean to say she *gave* these to you?" Gabby swelled with incredulity while handling each volume as she might a newborn. She turned the pages as if there stood a chance they might shatter should she not handle them with the utmost care, and occasionally she brought a volume to her nose and inhaled the mustiness of one-hundred-and-forty-year-old paper. Then, inexplicably, an imp-like grin formed on her face. Finally, she gazed up at me as if having made a remarkable discovery—something of which only she was aware.

"Well, don't leave me standing here feeling every bit the fool. Out with it!" I implored.

"Mitch, dear," she began, "I'm afraid you've become the victim of a practical joke."

"A practical joke! How so?"

Gabby hesitated to allow me to make a plausible guess. But I was in no mood to play a guessing game, nor was I concealing that I found it irksome Gabby's enthusiasm over spoiling the joy brought about by Elizabeth's extraordinary kindness.

"Mitch, don't you get it?" Gabby intoned. There is nothing more annoying than that moment of hesitation that lingers before the enlightenment of one's denseness. I wanted to deliver a snappy retort to Gabby's "don't you get it?" but was steadfastly unappreciative to tender a guess why I was a dunderhead. Finally, Gabby added, "How many times these past months have we—although you much more than I—referred to Elizabeth Montague as 'Our neighbor, Miss Havisham?' And now here you are, the recipient of a first-edition copy of *Great Expectation.* A coincidence? I should think not. I'd say your new friend has extraordinary hearing and is now having a bit of fun at your expense."

Gabby was right. Elizabeth had several first-edition volumes; why part with *Great Expectations* if not for overhearing me refer to her as Miss Havisham? The answer? Elizabeth indeed heard me; I saw no viable reason for doubt; still, it was some practical joke! In time, Gabby and I would learn just how expensive a practical joke: this first-edition, first-impression copy of the great classic novel, now in our possession, was appraised at over eighty thousand pounds, which was the equivalent of nearly one-hundred-and-twenty-thousand U.S. greenbacks. Sheesh!

CHAPTER FIFTEEN
MIDNIGHT RAMBLERS

"So, you mean to say there were no dead bodies in the cellar, not a single cadaver or sign of foul play such as the redolence of multiple murders or that anything nefarious has ever taken place?"

"No, no, no, and *no*," was my emphatic reply to my disappointed bride one evening when taking a stroll through town in the brisk December air.

"So, Elizabeth Montague is nothing more than a wildly eccentric and reclusive older woman; is that the sum of it all?"

"Gabby, you say that as though you would *prefer* that Elizabeth was a deranged killer of young men. I submit it simply isn't possible; the poor woman is a hundred and five pounds soaking wet! She's no more capable of dragging the dead bodies of poisoned young men to the cellar than Mr. McGruder's terrier!" (A year ago, the owner of The Papermill Tavern added a pup to his household, and I am convinced, out of spite—for he had difficulty accepting my acquaintanceship with Elizabeth—he has trained it to bark incessantly.)

"For your information, Mitch, Mr. McGruder has a hound, not a terrier, and more specifically, a beagle. But if I may remain on point: maybe Elizabeth's great-niece is in on the deal. Have you given any thought to *that* scenario, Mr. Serial Killer Novelist?"

"But there were no bodies, no skeletal remains," I reminded Gabby.

"You said that she had several canvas drops covering who knows what, and all you managed to see was a spinning wheel and portrait. It was dark; was it not? And you had only the benefit of candlelight, am I right? Has it occurred to you, Mitch, that Elizabeth Montague may have her very own crematorium down that hundred-and-fifty-year-old cellar?"

225

I was unable to control myself and erupted with laughter. Perhaps it was because I had grown fond of Elizabeth or was sympathetic to her life, but I found the notion of her shoving victims into a crematorium utterly absurd. "Better yet," I added as one might when piling on to the already inane, "maybe Elizabeth and Jenny have buried the bodies in the woods behind the yard. I bet if we went back there at midnight with flashlights, we'd find a shallow grave or two."

"Mitch, you may be on to something!" I saw the sparkle in Gabby's eyes. She was frothing over with enthusiasm for a mission in which I had little interest. I should have known to keep my mouth shut. Come midnight, I had the honor of explaining to Nina why we were all dressed in black, including black knitted hats, and supplied with flashlights and a shovel should we need to unearth something or some*one*. "Good luck," she said and chortled amusingly on the way back to her bedroom.

Then off we went, Gabby and me, two prowlers, into the black of night. It felt nothing like the day years ago when we scoured every square inch of Camden Lock Market, where the only serial killer of any relevance was the one materializing in our heads. Tonight presented an altogether different sensation and, despite the remoteness of discovering nothing beyond what one would expect a forest floor to offer, that there was the slimmest possibility to the contrary, lent to our current effort a twinge of titillation. Not to suggest I was keen to discover that Elizabeth Montague was a deranged murderess. I desired to keep what I know of her, palpably speaking, intact: it being, she was an eccentric, kindly older woman with whom I occasionally sipped tea and enjoyed conversations, and discovering something unexpected in the woods would put the kibosh on what was developing into a uniquely arousing friendship. But why, I kept asking myself, despite her saying so in jest, did Elizabeth claim to murder her great-niece's unsuitable boyfriends? That Elizabeth's mind traveled so nimbly to such nefarious places could suggest *something*; at the very least, she was unbalanced. But a murderess? I was beginning to feel somewhat unstable myself. Then a thought occurred to me: Elizabeth—a lonely old recluse starving for attention, whose only interactions were with Jenny, a seldom-visiting great-niece, and her hairdresser, Justine—hinting at the possibility that she was a deranged killer to someone who makes a living writing about such creatures, catapulted her to instant relevance. It undoubtedly created a stimulating scenario for Elizabeth, though the stimulus was well-reciprocated. But, more importantly, how vital must it be, following years of suffocation by a twisted father who saw her less as a person and more as a cult object through which he could satisfy his deviance, to have acquired the stimulation of friendship? Poor Elizabeth.

Poor Elizabeth, indeed. My empathy notwithstanding, I suspected we were playing right into her hands; but who was I to deny a lonely old recluse her folly, much less Gabby her sense of adventure?

It was early December. All the season's spent foliage had settled on the ground, making it nearly impossible to walk as stealthily as we would have preferred. With that being the case, and despite Elizabeth's tangled landscape capable of cloaking anything in daylight and Gabby and I presenting as shadowy figures in the night, we decided it was prudent to access the woods behind the big white house by walking clear around the block to Arbor Road. At midnight, as expected, we encountered nary a soul on the streets of this sleepy bedroom community of Philadelphia, though twice I was forced to conceal the shovel behind my back for the sake of a passing car. Call it paranoia or a guilty conscience, but there was little to no likelihood that a man dressed in black carrying a shovel was up to any good at midnight. Moreover, I could not have appeared more suspicious when trying to conceal a shovel.

Despite the absurdity of it all, we arrived at our destination just north of midnight, two suburban ninja-wannabes, not having roused any suspicion, or so we chose to believe. Then came the downside to our covert operation: there was more terrain to cover than first suspected, which was fine as far as I was concerned, for I assumed Gabby would discourage quickly, and we would soon be snug in our bed where we belong; however, once again, I underestimated my bride. We were there to find evidence of foul play, and Gabby was as undaunted as I had ever seen her; no mention of nocturnal creatures gave her a moment's pause, not even a possible encounter with the ever-poisonous Southeastern Pennsylvania Night Viper, which does not exist, but I made sound plausible, gave her a case of the willies; thus, with locked arms, and venturing one deliberate step at a time, we scoured the floor of the woods with our flashlights. Not once but twice, we came upon a boulder thought ideal for topping off a shallow grave; however, the effort it would have taken to move such masses of solid earth disqualified Elizabeth and Jenny, individually or working in tandem. That was what I supposed. But not Gabby. No siree! We would not walk out of those woods with a stone unturned. One o'clock in the morning came and went. So, too, did 1:30. It was not until I shined my flashlight on my wristwatch, which read just seconds before 2:00 a.m., that Gabby spotted an area she maintained was worth investigating.

"Mitch," she whispered. I looked to where Gabby pointed her flashlight and adjusted my beam to join hers. The earth was as hard and packed down as the rest of the forest floor but appeared to have been tampered with; something was not quite right or natural-looking. "Look!" Gabby added. Her eyes swelled with a sense of discovery. "Terrain was dug up, set aside, put back into place, and topped with a rock. You can see that, can't you, Mitch?"

"Congratulations," I said. "You found the proverbial needle in the haystack." Indeed, we had covered about two acres of what we estimated was a four-acre wood, traveling one methodical step at a time until finally, we hit what Gabby hoped would prove the culmination of a worthwhile mission. But, conversely, it was the moment I prayed would not arrive—a moment that would see me forced to acknowledge the possibility of Elizabeth as a murderess: I did not want to face it; I wanted to go on sipping tea and nibbling sandwich wedges while engaged in conversations about art, literature, and the many peculiarities that added up to the life and times of Elizabeth Montague, all which could prove helpful if or when I decide to craft her serial killer spoof.

"Mitch, what are you waiting for?" Gabby urged. Weakness settled in my hands and knees. I could have blamed the condition on exhaustion or the lateness of the hour; either would have been plausible, however illegitimate.

"Are you sure you want to go through with it?" I positioned my flashlight so Gabby's face was well illuminated, albeit defused.

"Mitch, we came this far; why would we turn back now?"

"Granted, it makes little sense, but have you given any thought about what happens next should we unearth actual human remains?" I hoped that citing a valid cause for trepidation would resonate and that Gabby would take a moment to ponder the gravity of the situation before it escalated into a legitimate concern—one that could see us in over our collective depth.

The Bohemian

"Why we notify the authorities, of course." Gabby shrugged as though no scenario could be plainer. "Mitch, I realize that Elizabeth is a person of interest for you, but if she is, indeed, a murderer of young men—those who have most of their lives in front of them and a world of potential—then she needs to be stopped."

"Notify the authorities?" I glowered. "And what, pray-fucking-tell, would we say to 'the authorities' when they pose the question: 'And what exactly were the two of you doing in the woods with flashlights and a shovel at two o'clock in the morning?' Oh, I know: perhaps we could tell them we're geologists who occasionally sleepwalk—or, better yet, archeologists who get their days and nights mixed up. Let's go with the latter; then we could offer the punchline: we were digging for an earthed-over pair of Ben Franklin's specs because it's been rumored these woods were where he took his lady admirers for a dally."

"Why can't we just tell them the truth: we suspect our neighbor of foul play and leave it at that?"

"Perfect!" I superciliously intoned. "Why didn't I think of that? And what do you think will happen when the police knock on Elizabeth's door and find we accused a ninety-pound weakling of murdering adult-sized males before dragging them two hundred feet into the woods? I'll tell you what'll happen: Elizabeth will retire to her drawing room with tea and a smirk while you're left to scurry off and find a lawyer to defend your husband, who has taken up residency in a prison cell, eating gruel and weeping."

"All right," Gabby admitted, "maybe the situation requires more thought than I initially realized, but could we please push aside that rock and begin digging?" The rock was not nearly as large as the others we came across. In other words, it was not unimaginable that someone Elizabeth's size, alone or with help, could have moved it.

"Right away!" I snapped to attention and gave Gabby a mock salute. Her use of the word "we" got me all rankled, for it would be "yours truly" doing the digging. I stooped, then rose having cradled the rock, heaved it aside, then took to the task of jamming the blade of my shovel into the earth—one heap after another, Gabby's two-o'clock-in-the-morning minion had dutifully scooped dirt. My spade pierced ground not yet hardened by winter, and I was well-perspired despite the lingering chill. I was making satisfactory progress and had spent a great deal of exertion when the business end of my shovel hit a mass of matter it failed to pierce and met with a thud—a sickening thud! Moreover, the impediment seemed to offer resistance in the form of pliability; I could thrust the blade only so far before experiencing the sensation it was being pushed back at me.

"Mitch," Gabby cried before stooping to brush aside the loose soil covering the resistant mass. No sooner had she knelt alongside what she identified as a shallow grave than something we had not expected was about to materialize.

"Gabby!" My whispered shout possessed enough urgency that Gabby snapped to attention. "Look!" I pointed toward Arbor Road—the same road by which, two hours ago, we had entered the woods. I watched as the headlights of a car that came to a rolling stop illuminated the area. It was not until the car itself came into view and its markings and characteristics became recognizable, that I alerted Gabby. She promptly rose to her feet. Next, two men—their silhouettes were unmistakable—emerged from the car and came marching toward the woods; they wielded flashlights far more powerful than the ones Gabby and I had brought along. Someone with poor sleep habits must have noticed beams of light flickering through the trees and deemed it an occurrence worthy of investigation. Gabby nor I wasted a moment speculating who among our neighbors whose property lines butted up against the woods was so thoughtful as to place the 2:00a.m. phone call to our local men in blue. Instead, I tossed my shovel aside, and we scampered pell-mell through the woods. When we reached Elizabeth's property line, we shut off our flashlights and ran with more urgency while bent over to ensure we did not decapitate ourselves on one of the million or so neglected branches. And speaking of Elizabeth: if she happens to be at her windowsill and recognizes us, so be it. The prospect of concocting an explanation for her benefit as to why Gabby and I were prowling in the woods at such an hour seemed a far friendlier proposition than explaining ourselves while in the custody of law enforcement.

We went spilling through our front door, huffing and puffing; we made quite a racket. Not a moment later, Nina appeared at the landing of the stairs; she glared at us like we were misbehaved children in need of a reprimand. "Run into any middle-of-the-night apparitions, did we?" she haughtily intoned. "Or perhaps some killer at large is responsible for your frenzied state? On second thought: I'm betting it was *The Hound of the Baskervilles* that sent you both through the woods running wee-wee-wee all the way home. Now, if you two skedaddlers are all through with your middle-of-the-night folly, I'd like to resume my slumber."

Mimicking Nina's haughtiness once she returned to her room, Gabby said, "I guess *she* told *us*." Afterward, Gabby and I pondered what might lie ahead should those two policemen penetrate far enough into the woods to discover what we nearly had unearthed. By tomorrow afternoon, the entire township will be all abuzz if the blade of my shovel hit what Gabby suspected it had. And following the buzz will come the launching of an inquiry concerning the two figures seen fleeing the woods. My stomach was in knots that we were already too involved in the matter and with no control over the outcome, assuming it was beyond our character to lie to the police.

"Mitch," Gabby began, quite sober and ringing with concern. "I say it would be best if we don't wait until the police come around asking questions but, instead, go to them and explain why we were in the woods. Most people in town are aware of what you do; it won't seem too unreasonable that you acted on your suspicions, however wild. Besides, if it's someone's remains that get discovered and somehow our DNA is found at the scene, it won't bode well for us that we failed to come forward."

"DNA!" I shrieked. "Half the high school has gotten laid in those woods, never mind the samples left behind by all the beer-guzzling teens who have taken a piss and the dozen or so dog walkers that routinely find their way back there. Proof that *we* were in the woods is the least of our concerns."

So it was agreed upon that we would lay low and allow matters to materialize without going out of our way to influence them. *What's that you say, detective: two figures dressed as ninjas carrying flashlights and a shovel? Nope, never saw 'em.* But before I could become a denier owning any degree of conviction, I first needed to find out who knew what; so, despite a minimal amount of sleep, come eleven o'clock the following morning, I found myself perched on Elizabeth's doorstep, prepared to launch a probe. Elizabeth's aversion to being summoned notwithstanding, I rang the doorbell. Also, I called out her name and identified myself. My plausible excuse for disrupting her morning was to inform her of the stir her gift of a first-edition first-impression copy of Dickens' *Great Expectations* had made with our friends. *I'm the envy of everyone I know!* is what I shall tell her. But as was the case the first time I showed up at Elizabeth's front door soliciting, I made one fruitless attempt after another. Then I peeped in the window through the lace dressing but saw very little before canvassing the house and establishing no light was in use. Then I did the unthinkable: I began testing windows to see if any were available to climb through; although locked or not, I should have known that one-hundred-and-fifty-year-old sashes would not open readily, if at all. Next was plan B: When all else fails, try the obvious. I twisted the knob of the front door, and to my delight, I could push my way inside. Indeed, a trusting soul was my eccentric friend. Then came the suspect part of the operation: alerting Elizabeth of my audacity, but I am, after all, Mitch Morningstar, writer of serial killer novels; if there is one matter at which I am adept, it is thinking on my feet: *Elizabeth, I rang the doorbell, called out numerous times, and, before long, I became fearful that you were sick or had become incapacitated!* Could walking into a friend's abode uninvited because you fear a misfortune has befallen them be seen as a misdeed? I should hope not. Anyway, that was how I chose to see the matter and convinced myself that Elizabeth would see it that way as well.

I ventured beyond the vestibule to the grand staircase in what typically was a well-illuminated hall separating the parlor, Daniel Montague's old study, a billiard room to the right, and a cloakroom, library/gallery, and drawing room to the left. The hall was darkened; standing in it felt ominous, but what was even more portentous than the darkness itself and me in it: I could see my breath before my face. The house was freezing! I had spent hours in the big white house and had become familiar with much of it, but this morning everything about it felt foreign, and what came over me, in a rush, was a queer sense the old house had been abandoned for decades never mind suffering years of decay.

Why would Elizabeth turn off the heat? I kept wondering to myself. She must be frozen stiff wherever she happens to be in this big white mausoleum of a house. "Elizabeth?" I called out, hoping not to startle her. I checked all the rooms on the first floor. Each was the same: dark, cold, and showing no sign that Elizabeth had occupied them recently. Finally, I decided to venture to the next floor, though ascending the staircase made me feel less of a concerned friend and more of an intruder. "Elizabeth," I called out again once I reached the top of the stairs. There was no answer.

The hallway leading to the house's many bedrooms was darker yet. I advanced, but not without trepidation. Occasionally, I jerked my head to see if someone was sneaking up on me from behind. So many scenarios pinballed around in my head, including one that had Elizabeth spot Gabby and me last night and anticipate the boldness of her new friend and favorite living novelist, which, in turn, prompted her to stage the house in a manner sure to give anyone, including a writer of serial killer novels, a case of the willies. Indeed, the darkened rooms, the coldness of the air, a house that appeared years undisturbed: it all must be an elaborate ruse. Or must it? I could feel my heart sink, contemplating the notion I was trapped in a House of Horrors and that all I had come to learn of the life and times of Elizabeth Montague was but a tortuous sham meant to lure me to my death. If I had any sense, I would make a mad dash for the front door. *Get the hell out of there, Mitch,* I kept imploring myself, *before you end up in the woods, not as a midnight rambler but as a corpse!* Indeed, within an hour, I could have my feet up while sipping beer and watching football with the Canadian Elk Hunter. But I was Mitch Morningstar, writer of serial killer novels and husband to Gabby Norwich, a woman who tingles with delight whenever awarded an opportunity to investigate the unknown. So despite whatever danger the house or Elizabeth Montague herself might present, be it all in my head or otherwise, there would be no turning back.

I knocked on the first door I came to and called out Elizabeth's name. I received no reply. Next, I pushed open the door just enough to create a passage, then slipped inside the room. Right away, my eyes fixed on a white rocking chair; it sat beside a small white table with a circular top and beveled edge of Roman Ogee. A reading lamp and a copy of *1001 Arabian Nights* beside it rested atop the table. At first, I considered it a curious selection: the story of a king so distraught by his wife's infidelity, not only does he have her executed, but afterward, he marries a succession of virgins only to have them killed the following morning before they have an opportunity to dishonor him. Then it occurred to me: it was not Shahryar with whom Elizabeth identifies, but Scheherazade—who offers herself as the next bride—a woman whose ability to weave story after story, night after night, keeps her alive. At no juncture was Elizabeth's life in jeopardy: but who can know how many fabrications were invented and fantasized until a satisfactory one stood as the overarching creation, all for the sake of veiling what had evolved into the sordid reality of her and Daniel?

I took time to examine the book thoroughly. It would have been asking too much to have discovered the first-edition English language offering of 1706; I would have to settle for a copy as old as the house I had boldly invaded. Elizabeth's *Linnea in Monet's Garden* bookmark was placed approximately at the halfway point of the opus. I set it back atop the table when it occurred to me that I was standing in the very room of Elizabeth's childhood—a room that has remained unaltered and was likely used as a refuge since the day of her indoctrination into womanhood. There was a hand-painted rocking horse—the cheery-looking steed's body was all pearly white, and the mane, tail, saddle, and hooves were coated red. Another of the room's remarkable features was a dollhouse of the most intricate detail—perhaps Daniel had it custom-made and modeled after a home that he and Giselle had visited during their travels. There was also a tea set: although miniature in scale, its style and quality were fit for an English Duchess. In some meaningful order, a collection of fairies, elves, and vintage dolls was displayed throughout the room. Also present: a collection of picture books filled with beautiful princesses, knights in shining armor, children lost in the woods at the onset of nightfall, wicked witches casting all sorts of magic spells, and damsels hoping that fate will allow their rescue; it, too, had a meaningful arrangement. On the ceiling were white puffy clouds dominating the brilliant blue of an afternoon sky; the walls were a pale yellowish-tan from which bright green leaves and many colorful flowers sprang. I was standing in a room constructed wholly of fairy tales—a place that, even if endowed with a meager imagination, would force one to surrender fully to enchantment. For Elizabeth, it was a place where she could well immerse herself in a world of make-believe, and it was for that reason I viewed my curiosity as a contaminant and felt much more of an invader than a friend. Indeed, I had infringed upon space to which no one other than Elizabeth Montague had any right or privilege. Perhaps there will come a day when, properly, I will be shown this room and permitted to linger.

I made a swift departure in favor of the darkness and gloom awaiting me in the hallway, which led to five additional bedrooms awaiting my investigation. None, before my entering, echoed a reply to the somewhat apprehensive call: *Elizabeth?* Assuming Elizabeth provided me with an accurate account of the house's history, the first four bedrooms have been resting wholly undisturbed as had been the case for decades; there was even a sense that the air itself had not been jostled by a presence. Each lavishly decorated cloister smelled of age—the age of old material and decaying space—as absent was the lingering scent of a living person. All that was missing from these rooms were ropes to discourage one from penetrating any distance into them and a sign reading: *Do not touch.* It was apparent the bedroom that once belonged to Daniel and Giselle: the presence of the tragic mistress of the big white house still lingered, both in memoriam and with mystery. A walnut vanity stood opposite the foot of a sleigh bed; it featured a trifold mirror and lace panel; atop the latter were various types of bric-a-brac and a hairbrush with a gold handle and backing. And not since before Elizabeth's birth had someone seated themselves at the vanity's matching chair. Giselle was a vision; a romantic could easily imagine her busy at her vanity, primping herself to a ravishing outcome. Upon Giselle's death, Daniel moved to another room; the evidence was the suits still hanging in the closet. His new bedroom—where still tidally displayed were his personal effects—wholly lacked the bountiful frills of feminine charm so richly apparent in the room where he once celebrated his marriage.

I honored the room assumed to have belonged to Lydia with only a passing glance and did the same for one reserved for guests. One room remained, and I noticed the door was ajar when coming upon it. It was also the only room in the house—the cellar aside—I had yet to investigate, so with good reason, upon peering inside, I fully expected to find Elizabeth either in a deep slumber or too ill to have responded to my calls. In neither state did I discover her; Elizabeth was not there. Unless hiding, like a child, she was nowhere in the house. What I did find were dresses lain across a hurriedly made bed; beside the bed was a large suitcase standing next to a much smaller one; missing was the medium-sized one of the group. Elizabeth had gone. That was what I theorized. She had taken a trip, possibly a spontaneous whim encouraged by glimpsing familiar-looking silhouettes emerging from the woods and the fear that her burial ground was no longer a secret. These were little more than wild guesses and baseless assumptions on my part, but one thing *was* certain: Elizabeth Montague was nowhere within the confines of the cold, dark, big white house.

I returned home shortly after Gabby's impromptu visit with Ursula. Gabby's mission was the same: to apply all her cunning to uncover whether Ursula spotted two people who, despite dressed as ninjas, might have resembled us and were carrying flashlights and a shovel; although Gabby need not summon her ability to extract information through ambiguity or craftiness; not as I would have had Elizabeth been present; for I could well imagine Ursula, had she been awake and alert, intoning before Gabby could utter word one: *And what were you two doing prowling the neighborhood at midnight with flashlights and a shovel; looking for buried treasure, were we?* But Gabby was happy to report that neither Ursula nor The Canadian Elk Hunter spotted any suspicious behavior last evening. Conversely, and rather fretfully, I had to report that not only was Elizabeth not at home—which was an anomaly—there was every indication she had taken a trip. Gabby's reaction to this news was not what I would have predicted. I expected her to decisively conclude, as did I, that Elizabeth spotted us running from the woods, packed a bag, called for a ride to the airport, and jetted off to some faraway destination where she would remain hidden away for months if not years. What else would an enigmatic woman of superior wealth do when others suspect her of being a murderess? But, instead, Gabby offered the unimaginable: she told me that she was beginning to doubt whether Elizabeth Montague existed.

"Mitch, dear," she began, employing a polite but patronizing tenor, "ever since we moved in, we've had all sorts of wild theories concerning the big white house. Conjoin that with the fact you're a writer of serial killer novels and ... well ... no one could blame you for confusing fiction and reality or for having delusions."

"Delusions!" I shrieked with indignation.

"It's nothing you need be ashamed of, Mitch; I understand they're quite common."

"Is that so," I protested. "Then how do you explain *this?*" I made a mad dash to retrieve and, in an instant, returned with the copy of the first edition/first impression of Dickens' *Great Expectation.* "Does this resemble a delusion?"

"All that proves is that you were inside the house—be it by way of invitation, or somehow you managed to finagle your way inside—and then helped yourself to a novel for whom a collector would sell his wife."

At that point, I was too exasperated to speak, and had I tried; I'm confident my words would have been regrettable.

The Bohemian

"Mitch, all I'm suggesting is that you look at it from my perspective or the perspective of anyone objective. Elizabeth Montague, if she does indeed exist, has lived in that house for nearly seven decades, and no one can claim to have seen her but you. So surely you could understand why someone might have doubts."

"Then how do you explain Jenny, the young woman who every so often comes to visit and who, incidentally, unlike you, *I* have never seen? And then there's the hairstylist, Justine; she sees Elizabeth every Saturday morning."

"I'll grant you, Jenny, if indeed that is her name. If not meeting a forbidden lover, she's likely visiting *someone* in that house unless, of course, she's a loon. But then there's the alleged driver you claim Elizabeth has, who takes her here and there, but no one has ever seen. And as for Justine, the hairstylist, if there is such a person: I say we make an appointment with her and discuss our good neighbor, Miss Elizabeth Montague."

"Fine," I snapped. "We'll do just that. My barber will undoubtedly frown upon my disloyalty, but I agree it's a good idea."

We made Friday night appointments with Justine at the VIP Salon on Meetinghouse Lane. "We're the next-door neighbors of Elizabeth Montague," Gabby chirped to Justine once she had settled into the stylist's chair. By then, I was beginning to doubt myself: that perhaps the lines between fiction and reality had blurred, thus relegating the lengthy encounters I enjoyed with this person known to me as Elizabeth Montague to nothing more than hyper-romanticized fabrications run amok by a novelist able to adroitly, or perhaps regrettably, slip into an alternate universe. With that in mind, I cringed over the possibility that Justine would utter, in response to the innocuous icebreaker offered by her newest hair client, "Elizabeth, who?" Hearing those two words would cause me to slump in a heap of misery before growing despondent that my once sharp mind was fraying and in danger of coming undone. *Please, Justine, throw me a lifeline!*

A week of stored-up angst oozed soothingly from my pores when I noticed Justine brighten at the mention of our next-door neighbor. "I've been doing Elizabeth's hair for more years than I care to mention," she chirped. Naturally, Justine was not alluding to the effort it took to beautify Elizabeth Montague but that those inferred-to years were a tool to measure her age. Either way, I felt vindicated. "If you're Elizabeth's next-door neighbors...." Justine paused, and her eyes widened as they traveled from Gabby to me. "Then you must be Mitch Morningstar, her favorite novelist!"

Vindication *and* recognition; I don't care how badly my hair gets muffed. But, unfortunately, as I would learn before long: Elizabeth had recommended my novels, which Justine promptly devoured; thus, I got roped into discussing my *Funhouse* killer, Davey Coyle, the sleepwalking of Ted Truman, the cat and mouse affair between Detective Tovey and Dr. Albert Stahl, and the plotline of my fifth novel, *Raging Angel*: the story of Amy Blaylock—a girl raised by a heroin-addicted mother who enters into one abusive relationship after another.

From inner-city slums to trailer parks and back, Amy and her mother went, scavenging and scoring. When in periods of respite from the worst kind of men, Amy watches her mother perform sexual favors in alleyways in exchange for a fix and a few dollars so they can eat. At age twelve, Amy gets coerced into a threesome with her heroin-stoned mother and her mother's drunk, vulgar boyfriend. Later that evening, after passing out, not atop a bed but on a crude mattress carelessly flopped on the floor, Amy kills them both; she takes a knife to their throats. She stands over them, not in shock or exhibiting any measure of horror, but with a sense of bemusement and thrill, as mother and lover convulse and then bleed out. Amy wanders off into the night and a world filled with treachery. That she turns to prostitution is no anomaly, for she possesses no viable understanding of sin and redemption or honor and shame. Amy lives among the disenfranchised, those whose souls long ago joined an ever-growing scrapheap known as the dispossessed but whose knack for survival—day by day, hour by hour, minute by minute—becomes a well-developed instinct. To understand perseverance, *not* as it pertains to dreams buoyantly floating on a promising horizon, but for the right to breathe in the dank ether of decay, to move within its margins, and expose oneself to an unforgiving world, knowing the only certainty is the pain invariably levied upon the wretched, is a tragic human failing. Such bleakness crafts an existence both piteous and admirable; it walks a tenuous line dividing spiritual atrocity and awakening. But Amy knows no particular god; empiricism is her accepted wisdom. Thus, her life's elixir is her rage, otherwise the one aspect of her essence assertable in a world over which she claims no dominion. She drinks it in. Storms gather in Amy's viscera; she chooses not to deaden them with needles, like so many around her, but permits them to grow, to intensify. She is seventeen when she turns her rage that stemmed from an unendurable childhood upon those like her mother and the many here-today-gone-tomorrow types of men whose only contribution to humanity is to heap additional brutality upon the wretched.

"Elizabeth is your first appointment every Saturday morning, I was told," I managed to interject after veering off-topic for nearly the entirety of Gabby's appointment.

"Bright and early," Justine chirped. "Elizabeth has always insisted on being the first appointment. Every Saturday, she's all rolled up and under the dryer a half-hour before anyone else walks through the door, including Vincenzo, the owner. You see, Elizabeth isn't what you'd call a 'social butterfly;' she's the most private of my clients—no one but me knows her name—and when here, I'm the only one with whom she converses, aside from our manicurist. Admittedly, she's not without peculiarities. For instance, she wears the same white dress and ballet slipper-style shoes every week and seems to relish the role of the reclusive older woman or eccentric; however, if you ask me, at heart, she's a genuine busybody eager for any town dirt she can learn. Anyway, I've long since grown used to her ways."

"But does Elizabeth have an appointment with you tomorrow morning?" Gabby, quick to the draw, managed the question before me.

"Funny, you should ask." Justine set down her implements. Her thoughts seemed too distracting to allow for any work. "Elizabeth made an overseas collect phone call just last night to inform me I wouldn't be seeing her Saturday morning, but that, 'rest assured,' I would be her first phone call upon her return. It was the French Riviera from where she was calling. She hasn't taken many trips in recent years, but whenever she has, I've not known about them until she has already arrived at her destinations. But, as I've already told you, Elizabeth is not a woman short on peculiarities."

Gabby and I arrived home looking better than when we left but had much to grapple with. If Elizabeth was indeed a killer and of the serial variety, we thought it unlikely such a person, whose traits would include cunning and well-measured, would slip up by blurting out their whereabouts to a hairstylist by way of an overseas collect phone call. And then there was Jenny to consider: Might she be Elizabeth's willing accomplice, or was she a delusional young woman unwittingly supplying a deranged great-aunt with victims? If Jenny were a well-balanced girl, it would stand to reason she would ponder the fate of never-again-seen love interests deemed unsuitable by her great-aunt; if she was delusional, that makes for another scenario. Either way, there were too many *what-ifs* to consider. In other words, the more Gabby and I discussed a matter known as Elizabeth Montague, the more convoluted it became. But one concern was for sure: the blade of my shovel hit something that night, and it was not dirt or rock.

"Mitch, there must be a thousand dogs in our community," Gabby generously estimated. "Perhaps one of them died, and its owners decided to place the poor thing in a burlap sack and bury it in the woods."

"Suddenly, you're a pragmatist?" I scowled. "You might have conveyed to me your "dog theory" a week ago and saved us a mountain of angst."

"It was difficult to see through loose dirt in the dark, but I'm fairly sure that I saw rough, brown material, which would indicate a burlap sack, and if that was the case, it's more likely it was a dog inside the sack and not a person. Besides," Gabby further theorized, "even if an adult-sized male human could fit in a burlap sack, why would a killer go through the trouble; what would be the point? For the sake of a beloved pet, someone would go through the trouble of a decent burial, but for a murder victim? It's unlikely they would receive such consideration; a killer would simply want them in the ground, and the quicker and more efficient, the better."

"What if the victim wasn't placed inside the sack, just underneath it?" I countered.

I watched as the sparkle returned to Gabby's tired eyes. "There's only one way to find out," she said.

****

Out again went the half-baked adventurers, at midnight, dressed as ninjas and brandishing the same gear: flashlights and a shovel. This time, since Elizabeth was overseas, they thought it wise to access the woods not by way of the road but through Elizabeth's backyard. Not only did their new course minimize their chances of being spotted entering the woods, but it also eliminated the possibility entirely. Moreover, they had little difficulty locating the sought-after shallow grave because it was far closer to Elizabeth's property line than the road.

The Bohemian

We found quite the surprise standing in the precise spot we stood a week ago when two figures assumed policemen—called to investigate what doubtless got reported as "suspicious activity" — thwarted our mission. The hole we were forced to abandon was refilled, and the stone was set back into place. I moved the stone aside and took to the task of digging. One foot, two feet, three feet, I toiled but hit nothing. At Gabby's behest, I expanded the boundary of the hole. Save for hard clay-like soil, stones, and tree roots far too stout to sever with the blade of a shovel, the result was the same, and I could not have dug an inch deeper had I the inclination. And unless endowed with extraordinary strength, no one else could have either. If indeed someone reburied what a week ago we partially exhumed, it was all but a certainty they did not do it in the same spot. But for what purpose was the original hole refilled, tamped down, and marked with a rock? Even had the police traveled into the woods to where we currently stood, managed to locate the precise spot where I had just dug, and finished unearthing a partially exhumed *whatever*, why bother relandscaping the area? It made no sense.

Had a body, indeed, been exhumed, the expected buzz sure to follow such a gruesome discovery never materialized. In a community the size of our modest-sized Philadelphia suburb, it is not every day that remains are discovered in the woods. It led Gabby and me to theorize our local police force was proceeding with the utmost prudence to avoid the sort of hysteria sure to send suburbanites into a tizzy. But then Gabby conceded, "Maybe it was just a dog after all. In a suburb the size of ours, it wouldn't be too difficult to find out whose family canine wagged its tail for the last time. And, if for some reason there's an ordinance that states you can't bury a dog in the woods—and with the police alerted—the owners were forced to take the poor pup back home to bury him in their yard."

That was as good a theory as any; a bit too pragmatic for Gabby, but a good theory nonetheless. Still, I continued striving to make sense of a refilled hole and rock set back into place, only to submit it did not make sense; however, not every action—the countless efforts throughout the corpus of human history meant to explain a random world notwithstanding—has a purpose. Human beings, despite incorporated into what many have alleged is a synchronized universe, are not Fibonacci numbers less have the reliability of gravity, thus are not compelled to follow logic, obey orders, or act rationally;

such aspects of evolution are merely recommendations, not requirements. But one lingering theory was beginning to tickle that miserly endowment known as "the matter between my ears." It was the most confounding of all and one I hesitated to but eventually did share with Gabby. Perhaps I have been looking at it all wrong from the very beginning. What if Jenny was not the accomplice of a reclusive, eccentric, deranged great-aunt whose control and influence were so great that the poor girl had lost all capability to reason concerning the finality of murder, or to distinguish right from wrong? What if it was Jenny who was the monster?

Elizabeth saw us coming from the woods and quickly placed a call to her great-niece. Bright and early, with Elizabeth already on her way to France, Jenny arrives, takes a shovel into the woods, finishes unearthing a body the police never ventured far enough to discover, drags it further into the woods, digs a grave, and before leaving fills not one but two holes. Indeed, this new theory of mine made sense; so much damn sense, it was scary.

CHAPTER SIXTEEN
ANGEL AT THE TABLE

Gabby and I decided the best plan was to lay low for the present. In other words, we would discontinue our careers as armchair detectives and amateur investigators and lead, as Gabby put it, "humdrum lives."

What would constitute a humdrum life? We shared Christmas Day with my family at the home of Uncle Pete and Aunt Belinda, Molly's folks. It marked the first time Nina had to endure my family; it was also Daddy Russ's first go-around with my kin. Because of her career and typical stunning appearance, Nina received the lion's share of attention, but Daddy Russ—because of his age, to Molly's—came under the most scrutiny. But, before long, Daddy Russ's engaging and relaxed manner put everyone at ease. As some seemed inclined, all that remained was to wonder how this composed man of a certain age, not especially endowed physically, would survive a woman capable of making a porn star plead for an extra week's vacation?

Adding to the inanity: cousin Nicholas was there with his wife, Janet, and their small army of hyper-active ruffians they inflicted upon the world who repeatedly received reprimands for touching all the items they were instructed not to touch. I could read Molly's thoughts from across the table; it was as though she was screaming them inside my head: *How dreadfully ordinary is our young cousin once believed destined for greatness? How dreadfully familiar and predictable is this scene representing our Christmas Day celebration?* Ordinary and predictable tend to occupy the same domain. For example, Grandpa Alexander was droning on and on, as he has been since the 1970s, about his short-term memory loss, to which Uncle Lambert replies: "It's because it's been years since you've done anything worth remembering." But I suppose that is how it is in most families; everyone reads from a script written a generation ago—recycled thoughts mixed in with a few current events, then dessert.

"I can well remember what your grandmother wore on our first date," Grandpa Alexander maintained for the twenty-fifth consecutive year as his aging eyes scanned the room, "but I can't remember what the hell I had for breakfast this morning." Before Grandpa Alexander becomes a memory, I should explain to him: *It would stand to reason—due to first-date anxiety and the youthful erection that heightened your senses—that Grandma's outfit would persist as a more impactful memory than the tasteless bowl of oatmeal you chase with a putrid glass of Metamucil every goddamn morning to ensure your ossifying bowels still function.* Maybe next year.

Then there's my dear mother: since the fall of Soviet Communism, she has been bitching about her carpal tunnel syndrome. "I miss carving the turkey, but I can't do it anymore because of my carpal tunnel syndrome," she once again reminded everyone in her customary complaining tone. It led me to ponder: Who was the knucklehead that decided a bum wrist was worthy of being dubbed "a syndrome?" Whoever it was could not have imagined my mother, who never stated her condition simply as "carpal tunnel" —regardless of whether or not anyone asked—the word "syndrome," with a capital S, was always emphasized. *I used to be a person, but now I have a syndrome!*

And poor Aunt Joy, Nicholas's mother, who never could live up to her name. Aunt Joy went from, as she would often lament, "the underappreciated chore of raising children," straight to menopause before being racked with the aches and pains that can accompany aging, and, according to her, this thankless progression reached its completion without an interval long enough for peace and happiness to flourish. A strenuously typical *if-it-isn't-one-thing-it's-another* type of moaner would best describe Aunt Joy. When asked, *how are you doing?* she would reply, "Who wants to hear me complain?" Then, without hesitation, she would transform into an avalanche consisting of the most inconsequential bullshit ever uttered. Any time Aunt Joy moaned the phrases "who wants to hear me complain" or "don't ask," it was time to skedaddle.

And now for Uncle Pete: Ever since Uncle Pete learned the terms "global economy" and "globalization," he has had us all downsized, outsourced, and age-discriminated out of our respective jobs, and America becoming a banana republic featuring a wealth gap analogous to a foreign principality, but in his next breath would offer the contradictory theory: anyone who qualified for a colonoscopy before the advent of the internet, with a gun pointed at their backs, should be marched toward a volcano and forced to jump. "We'll kill two birds with one stone," he would gleefully maintain. "Everyone coming out of college will be guaranteed employment, talk of social security going bankrupt will cease as a national conversation, and the digital age, which is coming faster than we realize, will be run by those who actually understand it; and the best part of all: no one will ever get stuck listening to some old cocker droning on about the good old days, like when ice cubes came in trays. What the hell was so wonderful about ice cube trays?" *I should point out to Uncle Pete that his proverbial stone killed three birds.*

It was no wonder why, at holiday dinners, I made a point of seating myself beside Aunt Belinda, the one member of the Morningstar clan—no matter the circumstances—never without optimism and a woman to whom a young girl could aspire. Pretty and energetic are two words that come to mind whenever I think of Aunt Belinda. These attributes once captivated a twelve-year-old boy. And this captivation coincided with Molly launching *said boy* toward the awakening of early pubescence days and the joys of their possibilities. At holiday dinners, Molly always sat directly opposite Aunt Belinda. Thus, in a liminal sense, I was awarded the privilege of gazing at the object of my youthful desire while sensing the loveliness that created it, and this dubious honor led to my ruminating on the abstract principle: anything fortunate enough to have traversed Aunt Belinda's birth canal, it stood to reason, would grow into something that looked like Molly. What seemed particularly odd to me, even in those days: despite that Aunt Belinda was an aunt through marriage, thus rendering my fascination for her (however inappropriate) less incestuous than my fancying of Molly, it somehow *seemed* more inappropriate. Anyway, a year passed, then another. Molly returned to being a cousin with whom I became friends. But Aunt Belinda, my acquisition of girlfriends who were permissible notwithstanding, continued to fascinate me.

Aunt Belinda aside, Christmas Day, as it had evolved, was a mishmash of humdrum, and it made me long for backyard summer soirees with Gabby, Nina, Daddy Russ, Molly, Ursula, Warren, and real-life Harold and Jane. Indeed, the usual stirring traverse from dialectical materialism to cultural relativism with a band of postmodern bohemians over well-chosen wine while enveloped with warmth and the mild scent of a floral profusion under a fading sun was so yearned for that I nearly wept—I wept for this day of captivity and what loomed on the immediate horizon: a long, frosty northeast winter. But there was yet more agony to endure: Over dessert, which featured a mediocre pumpkin pie (why anyone would choose to produce a dessert made out of squash was beyond me), I had to endure an around-the-table critique of *Raging Angel*. I learned what I might have guessed: among the Morningstar clan, the aspects of a typical serial killer novel were appreciated; dark realism was not. Molly was the first to defend what I believed was, thus far, my best and most affecting work.

"I like the way the story holds its shape—the way it tends to linger no matter how painful and raw. *Raging Angel* refuses to let the reader off the hook; it forces us to confront the uncomfortable truths of a world much closer than most care to imagine. And why shouldn't it? Why should a novelist always channel the sordid side of humanity through a heroic protagonist? Some stories are more effective without a kind light."

Atta girl, cousin; you tell 'em.

"But it was so bleak," Aunt Joy complained. Her eyes had fallen on Grandpa Alexander as though our patriarch could wield some authority concerning the matter. Turning toward me, she added, "Your other novels: although they were serious and gruesome at times, also present was a sense of fascination. In other words, the reader could remain at a safe range. But that's not the case with *Raging Angel*; it crosses a line."

Poor Aunt Joy. She needs her fiction to be unmistakably fictional.

"It's a novel meant to infringe on your space, your soul, and do so in a way that forces you to feel uncomfortable," Gabby reminded everyone.

"*I'll* say it was meant to," added Aunt Belinda. "I never read anything so grim and disturbing as the childhood of Amy Blaylock. The heroin-addicted mother, the awful men, the things that girl saw and was made to do. I can't tell you how many times I had to put down the book over how angry, frustrated, and helpless it made me feel; it was worse than when they show those commercials for abused dogs."

Aunt Belinda reads my novels because Molly insists; otherwise, she would keep to the romance section.

"But you have to appreciate how Amy offs her mother and that lousy prick, Melvin," Nicholas managed to chime in. "Darlene and that scumbag pass out and leave Amy awake and alone to contemplate who they are in their essence and the sorts of deeds they do. The power, the rage; you could sense something snapping in her mind. And the retribution: it was surreal. I felt like I had the knife in *my* hand, *and* I don't mind admitting, it wasn't a bad feeling."

"Sure, it wasn't a bad feeling," added Uncle Pete. "You had a few minutes of satisfaction when Darlene and Melvin got what was coming to them; who wouldn't feel a sense of satisfaction? That was the whole point. But then Amy—still a child, never mind her cumulative experiences—wanders off into the world, alone, and goes from bad to worse to irredeemable."

I could not find fault with Uncle Pete's assessment other than to ask: Have you ever known a Darlene or a Melvin-type to end well? Do the Amy Blaylocks of the world go on to live happily ever after? Uncle Pete grasped the novel's essence, especially its more disturbing aspects, but had no genuine appreciation for dark realism; it seemed to rattle his sensibility.

Whether or not appreciated or valued, everyone put forth, as intelligibly as their respective facilities allowed, what passed for their honest opinions, unlike yours truly, who informed Aunt Joy she "hit a home run" with her pumpkin pie. There were those at the table, I could tell, who wished that I kept my mouth shut. *Screw 'em!* Anyway, those who critique writing for a living wage gave *Raging Angel* a thumbs up, and the novel hit newsstands with no shortage of endorsements. Admittedly, from the perspective of a well-wrought and meticulously constructed plotline bearing complex variables, *Raging Angel* would not remind anyone of *The Case of the Camden Lock Killer*. In the latter, the reader mainly exists in the mind of a seasoned detective strung along by someone with a fierce intellect gone off the rails. In the former, the reader is given a front-row seat to the life of a woman gone so far afoul her child, who passes for the novel's only sympathetic figure, evolves into something utterly monstrous. The path upon which Amy Blaylock gets set is so dark and portentous that an escape, regardless of a reader's optimism, is beyond anyone's imagination. Amy's visual world is dark and narrow; the creatures who live within these pitiless margins are godless; the ether within this forsaken dominion is always rank.

Gabby brought her sketchbook to show Molly and Daddy Russ her work on *Raging Angel*. As usual, Gabby has displayed the uncanny ability to extract from my mind visuals precisely as imagined and, in some instances, depicts them with more affecting poignancy. One sketch sees Amy standing at the foot of the mattress upon which lay Darlene and Melvin. Her figure, seen from the back, looms ominously and all but eclipses the ill-fated pair. A bare shoulder and arm belonging to Melvin are visible on the left; a partially clad arm belonging to Darlene is visible on the right. Amy's head tilts ever so slightly; her tattered hair stops at her shoulders; her bare back sways gracefully to what has developed into a womanly bottom in recent days. Only a portion of Amy's bottom half is revealed in Gabby's sketch. Her left arm is dangling loosely; her hand is open. Her right arm is also at her side; its slimness is made rigid by a hand clenched tightly into a fist, obscuring the hilt of a knife. One could well establish from Amy's slight head tilt and closed fist that she is standing at a precipice and, with grim determination, in the final stage of contemplating an act of vengeance. The following sketch is a narrowing scene: it sees Amy—her front fully revealed—positioned at the foot of the mattress with her head tilting in a manner indicative of curiosity; a corner of her mouth is turned upward, thus forming an implacable smirk. Her right arm is hanging loosely, and in her right hand is an object from which she appears strangely disassociated. Her eyes—no longer do they resemble a child's—behold a mixture of terror and astonishment frozen on the lifeless faces of those on the mattress. Amy has killed. So brilliantly poignant is Gabby's sketched depiction that there need not have been a knife in plain sight to conclude that Amy Blaylock had crossed a line and that you were gazing into the eyes of a killer.

A third sketch is of an alleyway seen through watchful eyes belonging to a more youthful Amy Blaylock. Scattered about are the necks of bottles peeking out from brown paper bags; shards of broken glass are also present, as are liberal patches of weeds growing through numerous cracks in the cement, partially obscuring a mass of discarded material. The alley represents a vagrant's paradise—an inner-city black hole for those overpowered by what they use and discard. In the narrow distance, the legs of a man are visible; he appears to be walking away. Nearer and crouched on the ground, her back pressed to a well-stained brick wall missing chunks of mortar, is Darlene, the scene's central figure. Her neck is tilted such that her eyes point skyward; perhaps they are searching the night sky for

Heaven. On her face is a mixture of relief and euphoria. Resting in her open palm is a spent vial. In the foreground, off to the side, is a shadow—a partial figure in silhouette only. It is through the eyes of Amy Blaylock that solemnity and pathos wear so unbearably in this bleakest of depictions.

A fourth sketch sees seventeen-year-old Amy, her clothes in tatters, kneeling on a hideously unfit bathroom floor. Her head is hovering over a toilet; her hair, which has fallen forward, partially obscures the anguish on her face. Behind her, water runs in a mold-laden shower stall missing its door. Soon, Amy will get to her feet and attempt to scrub from her being the stench of human foulness. The following day, after darkness falls, she will hunt down and kill her rapist.

The *Raging Angel* sketches were among Gabby's most affecting. Dark realism seemed to bring forth new heights and unlock the untapped potential of her already astounding ability. So disturbing were her sketches; some prompted me to rewrite scenes, making *Raging Angel* a truly collaborative effort.

CHAPTER SEVENTEEN
LETTERS FROM NEAR AND AFAR

The New Year came and went, and a well-rested Nina jetted back to England to resume her career and reconnect with her battery of doctors. I was between novels—I had yet to begin, nor would I outline the promised serial killer spoof for some time—thus free to spend much of the winter gloom working earnestly on Nina's biography. As the gloom of winter relented to the hopefulness of spring, I made a genuine effort, at Gabby's behest, to become more receptive and friendlier toward The Canadian Elk Hunter. Gabby theorized that if I recruited a riding buddy, it might help me overcome my pet obsession: Elizabeth Montague. Warren was agreeable to the idea of a weekly ride and, without delay, purchased a 10-speed road bike comparable to mine. Admittedly, we were an unlikely pair strenuously cobbled together by two women whose growing affection for one another became the prevailing factor. However, it became natural before long—Warren and me as a riding tandem—and we looked forward to our outings. Besides, how many can claim the acquisition of a Neanderthal bisexual as a riding buddy? I should be honored; Warren was rarer than a unicorn! Fun aside, whether for the sake of our wives or the dynamic of our bohemian clique, we far exceeded tolerance to the point where we could refer to one another as "my friend," though we still had our moments of contention.

Molly got wind of our activity and wanted in. "Hey cousin," she began in grievance, "I was good enough to screw a few years back, but not your first choice when recruiting a riding buddy?"

I did not bother reminding Molly that our deviant behavior resulted from *her* coercion hastened by an awakening for the ages; instead, I told her where Warren and I had been riding and invited her to join us—Daddy Russ, too, if he was so inclined. On Saturdays, Warren and I would trek from our tiny suburban hollow to meet Molly—

she rode over from Queen Village—at the famous Philadelphia landmark Boat House Row. From there, we would pedal along a path dividing the scenic East River Drive and Schuylkill River; it would take us past statues and sculptures representing the immigrant, philosopher, scientist, poet, statesman, and soldier. Also, multi-figured works portraying freedom, pioneering, discovery, and the birth of a nation marked part of the array. Then, with stunning rock formations to our right, the sparkling Schuylkill River to our left, and arch deck viaducts overhead, we would pedal our way to the Falls Bridge. Next, we would cross over to West River Drive and pedal toward the Philadelphia Art Museum, thus circling back to our starting point. In all, it was a twelve-mile loop. We would complete it twice, though we would diverge partway through our second run, taking a spur to a brewpub in Manayunk. Daddy Russ would be there waiting for us on an outside deck at a table for four, sipping a local Lambic-style craft beer he favored dubbed "Schuylkill Punch." A river running through a city is a charming feature, and the Schuylkill did not lack charm. Moreover, it was home to a steady stream of kayakers and canoers; occasionally, it saw Dragonboat races. But yours truly did not fancy a city river as a source for beer, though had the brewpub used the river, no one, to the best of my knowledge, has died from its consumption. When first I made a face, Daddy Russ said, "What's a few microbes floating around your entrails? Drink up!"

That was our Saturdays: not a bad lead-in to our Sunday soirees, which Gabby and Ursula took the liberty of arranging concerning theme, cuisine, and vintage. But then came the arrival of early June and the discovery of another letter planted in the tight scaffolding of the olive hedge. By then, I *had* stopped obsessing over Elizabeth, not to the extent of out-of-sight-out-of-mind, but no longer did she occupy my every thought. For months, I had been living my life unburdened by plots, theories, or harebrained intrigue. Then it all came back in a tempest-like rush, and I was unsure of its welcome.

Dear Mitch,

It has been much too long; you must join me this very evening. And since it will be the evening when you arrive, we shall skip tea in favor of a cordial. I have one I'm sure will meet your approval. I shall look forward to seeing you and what I'm sure will be a pleasant chat.

Most fondly,

Elizabeth

I *must* run off and *join* Elizabeth? *This* very evening?" The woman acts as though it was *my* fault we have had no communication in several months, yet it is *I* who must join *her*, and not *tomorrow* night, but *tonight*. I could submit that Elizabeth was the sort who may be oblivious to Gabby owning wifely privileges and thus saw no viable reason why I should fail to jump at her whim. But, wifely benefits notwithstanding, Elizabeth, as she had in the past, was banking on her unconventional methods and quirky charms stirring me; hence, I would not think twice about opting out of a night of blissful matrimony. She did not miscalculate.

"Mitch dear, I won't ask whether or not you began our serial killer spoof, as I have honored only one of your two stipulations. As is the case with a man, I believe a woman should also be held to her word, and I promised you would meet my darling great-niece, Jenny. Well, as luck would have it, her parents whisked her away to Europe no sooner than her semester ended. I hear they'll be gone the entire summer. What a pity. Well, hopefully, you'll get your chance this up-coming fall."

It was uncanny Elizabeth's ability to ramble on as though we were old friends resuming a conversation that took place yesterday that had suffered an unexpected interruption. What was stranger yet: she never bothered mentioning her trip to the French Riviera. Worse, I could not risk asking. Why? For the simple reason, Elizabeth never confided in me that she was taking a trip, never mind offering a destination. I was right back where I was many months ago, running from the woods in a ninja costume, perhaps spotted by Elizabeth, who fled the country for fear of what Gabby and I may have unearthed.

Of course, I could have made up a story explaining my knowledge of her whereabouts; I do that sort of thing from time to time. For example, my barber croaked, and I made an appointment with Justine, who, perchance mentioned your impromptu trip. However plausible, I was afraid such a tale might reek of suspicion. Moreover, getting at the truth, I realized—assuming a sordid truth did exist—would require more than the implementation of anecdotal bullshit. Learning the whole truth about Elizabeth Montague could require gaining a plateau of trust that she may not be willing to surrender.

The Bohemian

Elizabeth rambled on, intelligibly, from subject to subject until arriving at the chief reason for my summoning: *Raging Angel.* "Mitch, dear, we must discuss *Raging Angel*," she began, but not before deciding that the discussion would be aided better by another glass of well-aged B&B—Benedictine and Brandy—a cordial I had yet to taste before tonight but found agreeable. The time had arrived for Elizabeth's critique. Although well-written and an effectively wrought journey into the darker reaches of society, she found *Raging Angel* "too disturbing." In other words, "for what it was," she found it remarkable, or as she put it, "a true achievement," but she did not care for "what it was." She compared Amy Blaylock to Davey Coyle but submitted that the latter's "derangement" was more palatable than the former's "vengefulness." In Elizabeth's estimation, Davey Coyle's killing spree was triggered by "a terribly flawed psychology" rooted in a random event that left a child parentless, whereas she perceived Amy Blaylock as more of a primal killer. Neither fascinated her nearly as much as the sleepwalking Ted Truman. Still, for Elizabeth, nothing could rival Dr. Albert Stahl.

"What could be more intriguing than a murderous ideologue—a principled killer able to twist matters to where one begins to doubt their rationale." Elizabeth's eyes went all aflutter when reminiscing about the Camden Lock killer. "Murder is a tough business, Mitch," she added. "But in *The Case of the Camden Lock Killer*, you made it an art form. And, as for what you call "dark realism," doubtless there is a market, and the critics may praise it, but an older woman looking to curl up with a book come the evening needs a bit of mystery to go with her murder. You understand, don't you, Mitch?"

I understood fully. My muse was unamused; thus, I was to run home to abandon a career in dark realism as it pertained to serial killing and immediately work on a novel that would put the "mystery" back in murder. After all, Elizabeth was my number one fan, and *we* surely would not want to disappoint *her*. My flippancy notwithstanding, she did have a point. It might not be in my best interest to follow up dark realism with a heaping helping of more dark realism; too many ruined children, hallucinating addicts, desperate low-end criminals selling their souls, and not enough inscrutable intrigue could cause my readership to suffer a falloff. So I began to concoct a novel where I chiefly recreated Dr. Albert Stahl but placed him not in London but upon Vienna's winding and cobbled streets and

alleyways circa 1870. The story evokes images of a phantom-like figure well-caped, all in black, who leaves his dwelling late in the evening
and exists wholly in the shadows of an old-world city. It took a year
of sketching and outlining before I began attacking the opus with any
measure of earnestness; perhaps the notion that I was ripping off
"The Ripper" had caused me to drag my feet. Eventually, I got
caught up in the spirit of the project. For what could be more titillating than a phantom asserting himself in an old-world city, especially
one so well cultured and steeped in the arts as Vienna?

Ernst Kromer became my literary successor to Granville
Tovey. He is not an alcoholic but, like Hellickson, has a fiendlike predilection for nicotine and is never without a well-supplied snuff box.
Ernst Kromer is one of a select few who have an open invitation to
the home of Caroline Trakoshtyan, a recent widow who has become
somewhat reclusive but manages to remain well-connected and is a
patron of the arts. As Detective Kromer had learned through his
friendship with Caroline's late husband, Kristof, the widow—whose
dowry was principally responsible for her and Kristof's lofty station—has far-reaching eyes and ears which, in the past, have proven
an asset to the detective.

Anslo Breuner is the literary successor to Dr. Albert Stahl.
Breuner—as would come to light in the novel's later development—is
the grandson of Count Anslo von Breuner. The Count served under
Leopold II, the last of fifteen successive Holy Roman Emperors from
the House of Habsburg, and then under Franz II. For a period, Franz
II was the sixteenth in the line but resigned and went on to start his
own empire, though not as a Holy Roman Emperor but as Habsburg
Emperor of Austria under the name Franz I of Austria. Anslo
Breuner, the murderous phantom: aside from being endowed with a
well-respected and worthy ancestry, was also a close acquaintance of
the Archbishop of Salzburg, Maximilian Joseph von Tarnóczy, who
just so happened to be known to the widow Carolina Trakoshtyan.

Anslo Breuner did not inherit a title. His grandfather—who
gained the title of Count through service recognized by a high-ranking crony who tendered a strong recommendation to Leopold II—
failed to produce a male heir, thus bestowed the title of Coun-
tess, *not* upon Anslo's mother, as she had died in childbirth, but to
the second of his three daughters, who would go on to bear the first
male grandchild, Garth, born, just days before Anslo. Garth would

stand to inherit the title of Count and would have, if not murdered. The first cousin of Anslo Breuner would be the first of six murder victims in 1870, accredited to the shadowy Viennese phantom, and all because they were deemed, by Anslo himself, the recipient of un-deserved privilege.

When Anslo Breuner became Ernst Kromer's prime suspect, terror became intrigue, and the church and the region's elites came under scrutiny. Understanding that Detective Ernst Kromer, at times, could be a blunt man, Caroline Trakoshtyan wrote to the Archbishop of Salzburg with the notion of brokering a meeting she anticipated would take place between her friends, the archbishop and detective— a meeting that potentially could develop into a contentious affair. Caroline proceeded with the idea that in forewarning the archbishop of what he was to expect, he would avoid taking the position of a man warding off an attack. She had assumed or perhaps knew, if ambushed by a blunt detective, a defensive archbishop would leave Ernst Kromer with the impression the church was covering up a crime and, in turn, would lead to two men—one of law and order; the other, sin and redemption—to dig in their heels to protect their respective moral high-ground. Unfortunately, the church ended up right in the line of fire despite Caroline's efforts: Guilt by association.

"A man as learned as your friend, the archbishop, should make it his business to know who his friends are," Detective Kromer stated rather frankly to Caroline Trakoshtyan one evening over a cordial.

"The church and scandal; perhaps there'll come a day when they *don't* go hand-in-hand," Caroline uttered with a plaintive sigh.

"Scandal aside, I have as healthy a respect for the church as the next man," Ernst Kromer said. "And I'm sure your friend, the arch-bishop, is well worthy of his title and position, but I have a truth to get at, and until that truth gets realized, I cannot treat the archbishop any different than I would a pawnbroker. Just as *he* believes we are all equal in the eyes of God, *I* believe we are all equal under the law."

Word leaked to Anslo Breuner that he was the prime suspect in six related murders. The commonality was as follows: all six murders occurred at night; the times were between ten and eleven; each murder got committed with a knife; the victims were of a high station and privilege. Moreover, Breuner was rumored to have disappeared from the cityscape of Vienna; thus, a concentrated manhunt had convened. Also, the certainty of Breuner's guilt hastened the discrediting of the

Breuner name by those in possession to wield such power: Hence came the verdict that Count Anslo von Breuner, who had served at the pleasure of Leopold II and to whom he was fiercely loyal, secretly despised Franz I and, accordingly, by all devised accounts, did all he could to undermine the transition from the Holy Roman Emperors from the House of Habsburg to the Habsburg Emperors of Austria. The idea was to portray an old Count, no longer around to defend his honor, as a man of treacherous deeds and to ensure that the name Breuner remained tied only to the old line and stricken from the new.

Breuner first fled to Budapest, where he remained out of sight for a period but became alerted that local officials were cooperating with Viennese officials. Then it was off to Romania and its winding, hilly countryside. He tramped along until settling in Bucharest, where he would remain for seven years; however, the passage of time can do strange things, not the least of which was the distorting of reality. One morning, Anslo Breuner awakened not with the notion that he was a fiendlike murderer who terrorized a city and, in doing so, became an enemy of the state but as a man who missed the sights, sounds, smells, and culture of Austria and wished to return. It was near a decade that passed since he last stood upon Austrian soil. Somehow, he managed to embrace the rationale that his killing spree, which endured for eight months and doubtless would have continued if not for becoming a prime suspect, represented a small sampling of an otherwise exemplary life, and his faulty reasoning led to him assuming because he found a pathway leading to self-forgiveness, others had also taken the journey. The prism through which Anslo Breuner viewed himself and his juxtaposition to the world was pure deception—a distortion of reality.

Breuner, clad in a hooded robe, turned up on the doorstep of his old friend, the archbishop of Salzburg. After displaying what the archbishop alleged was earnest regret, contrition, and a renewed love for humankind, the high-ranking clergyman—despite his bequeaths being unearned—granted absolution; then he placed Breuner at a country abbey, where he was to live out his days humbly, meditatively, as a groundskeeper. It worked for a while; for two years, Anslo Breuner led a simple, quiet life, filling his days with meditation and duty, but a man who believed himself destined for greatness could keep silent only so long. When Breuner broached the subject concerning what he alleged was his entitlement, some within the abbey and not far beyond its gates began to speculate. A local tavern owner was the first to recall an old Count that posthumously went down in disgrace. Then came the whispers concerning the phantom who terrorized Vienna more than a decade ago and that, although never apprehended, the killings had ceased. In late September 1883, Anslo Breuner was pruning an olive hedge lining the abbey's southern boundary when he discovered an envelope stuck in the hedge's scaffolding. He reached for it. To his surprise, he saw the written words: *for the groundskeeper*. It was highly irregular, Anslo thought, for any of the abbots, especially Prior Benjamin, with whom he had become quite friendly, to plant letters to assign additional duty. Upon opening the envelope and reading its contents, Anslo stiffened; he appeared a man struck by something unforeseen, be it a long-suppressed memory, the reality of an unkind future, or something capable of binding the two. Next, he sagged. And had anyone been standing between him and the olive hedge, they would have seen a man whose mien had twisted in resignation and irony. The once phantom, who for the better part of a year caused the citizens of Vienna to live in terror, need not have turned about to know that Ernst Kromer, a dogged man now wearing the satisfaction of someone who at long last had reached the end of a chase, was standing behind him.

Well done, Mitch! Elizabeth wrote to me in a letter that came floating in from overseas. *Now that's the Mitch Morningstar I've come to know and appreciate!* From the initial outline to the newsstand came the passing of two-and-a-half years. Elizabeth had two overseas stints during this period, each equaling six months; in both instances, I had to find out from Justine that my muse, friend, and next-door neighbor, or potential serial killer, had fled the country. In all that time—thirty months—I had seen Elizabeth only once, but she was exceedingly liberal in praising *The Shadow of Vienna* in her letter. She thought two aspects in particular—the relationship between Ernst Kromer and the somewhat reclusive widow, Caroline Trakoshtyan, and the letter in the olive hedge—were "nice touches;" it gave her joy that a part of "her" or "us" found its way into a novel. In *The Shadow of Vienna*, an opus not quite as beefy as *The Case of the Camden Lock Killer*, Anslo Breuner perpetrates a brand of terror similar to Dr. Albert Stahl's. But, how Breuner diverges: his killings are not as gruesome as Stahl's, nor are his motives, ideologically, in any way dialectical. Ernst Kromer's life is not as messy as Granville Tovey's, but he gets portrayed as "quite human" and thus adequately flawed. Also, there is no palpable psychology binding the hunter and the criminal. What's more, much of the intrigue—its textures and tones—can be attributed to the charm and ether of an old-world city, the placement of time (1871 to 83), and that the concept of "serial killing," as these murderous sprees would come to be known, was a somewhat novel phenomenon.

Predictably, my first and only sign that Elizabeth had returned from overseas was a letter strategically placed in the olive hedge. Tomorrow afternoon, I was to arrive next door "promptly" at two for tea, sandwich wedges, and my first-ever meeting with Elizabeth's great-niece, Jenny. It would mark a turn of events, owning one prevailing consequence. Once tomorrow was behind me, I would have no more handy excuses to push before a long-ago-promised serial killer spoof.

****

Jenny was as lovely as my mind all these years had allowed me to imagine. In other words, she was a terrific treat for the eye. However, something anomalous seemed afoot. Jenny was not dolled-up as one would expect a young woman to be when invited to a ball or formal engagement. One theory: Elizabeth's demand for such regalia was set aside for opportunities to judge one of her great-niece's would-be suitors. Another: Jenny was a woman, now well into her twenties, who no longer sought less required a proxy concerning her love life, womanhood, and their protocols. Whichever the case, she was dressed such that well displayed were her many assets but in a fashion most would consider smart and tasteful. If Elizabeth had shown any disapproval or objected to what Jenny chose to wear, it occurred before I arrived; though, from what I could tell, there was every indication they were getting along famously.

Elizabeth greeted me in typical Elizabeth Montague fashion, creating an ether that seemed to suggest we were resuming a conversation that had suffered an interruption only a day ago. But there was a departure from a past encounter, aside from the presence of Jenny, that would make this one different: When Elizabeth wrote to sing the praises of *The Shadow of Vienna,* the envelope had an overseas stamp, thus opening an opportunity for me to inquire about her trip, what prompted it, in what activities did she partake, with whom did she spend time—a question that, although innocuous, judging by her visage, she deemed accusatory—and was the weather favorable? However, in typical Elizabeth fashion, Elizabeth glossed over the typical questions put to one who returned from a trip with replies too vague to bother mentioning. I had always known Elizabeth as a woman of many quirks. Among them: either she offered far more information than I solicited or showed herself ambiguous to the extent of being aloof. But because she has endured as an ongoing source of fascination—in the past and today—I respect her age and womanly prerogatives. In other words, I grant her, for the sake of friendship, her many peculiarities.

It was Jenny—after Elizabeth told me she visited Paris and Venice, where she took "quiet strolls in the evenings" and enjoyed weather she described as "balmy" before sneering at the insinuation of a clandestine rendezvous—who rather brightly chirped, "Auntie Elizabeth favors European culture. She admits to being much more at home in old-world cities."

Old-world cities proved a natural segue for the three of us delving into the aspects of *The Shadow of Vienna*. However, following an exchange that was briefer than what Elizabeth would have preferred, Jenny, whose comportment made it painfully evident she was the recipient of a liberal arts education few could afford, decided to remain on the continent where many of the world's old-world cities exist. The result? I was enlightened to the virtues of social democracy versus the ills of a market-driven economy. Next, Jenny haughtily intoned: "Because American arrogance is edging toward an all-time high due to hawkish neocons holding us hostage and greedy corporatists draining our goodwill, we're no longer the leaders in areas deemed, in a global sense, the most vital."

Last I checked, Americans were not booking one-way flights to Sweden and Denmark, and I'm reasonably sure the cold temperatures are not the prevailing deterrent. It was with subtlety that I made this point: I did not wish to fracture Jenny's worldview, despite it being based on the progressivism of homogenized nations that rely on American hegemony should Russia decide to misbehave, among other matters.

It was all too predictable, as it was occurring more frequently: advantaged kids sent away to fortune-seeking institutions to be intellectually bullied by philosophers, spewing pet political theories based on failed systems that would thrive if only implemented in America. But was it ever a secret that academia, particularly at its loftiest levels, despises capitalism and, for the benefit of impressionable minds eager for new concepts, portrays it as a villainous entity reeking of corruption in the ever-decaying morally bankrupt West? Then again, why should the world of academia trouble itself to raise an army of empiricists when indoctrination requires so little effort? Anyway, it became no surprise when I heard the principles of dialectical materialism liberally spewed: Originally a Hegelian doctrine and later a Marx-adopted philosophy, dialectical materialism became the foundation for the political and economic theories behind Marxism; it also marked a pet subject raised at our backyard soirees, and despite "playing footsie" with the concept, as might any band of postmodern bohemians, it was merely fodder for discussion or abstract challenges; none of us seriously believed that a nation driven mainly by commerce and innovation would readily scrap the bourgeois capitalist in favor of the proletarian worker. But today, I was not in my backyard surrounded by friends; I was in the ring with someone who would have given Leon Trotsky a boner. So, for the sake of a challenge, I decided it would be fun to play the role of a worthy devil's advocate.

When she spoke, Jenny had a way of crossing her legs and arching her back that was suggestive of someone wielding command no one would dare challenge. Moreover, she had arms and hands one might imagine belonged to a concert pianist. They swished through the air, these pendulous assets, thus they drew my eyes to her perky breasts, which danced ever so prettily in time to her discourse and, for better or worse, and likely worse, became a distraction. Elizabeth inched closer to the edge of her chair. She looked on admiringly at me and proudly at her great-niece—who she hoped had not chewed up a chunk of the family fortune to become a social worker or bat-shit crazy activist—as we managed to maintain a provocative and meaningful volley. It seemed a natural leap that our current topic should segue into a tete-a-tete based on cultural relativism. I led by theorizing: quantifying human behavior based upon a system upholding moral fluctuation was ludicrous and that culture—geography and the notion of ethos seen as a social currency aside—tends to get gummed up in theism, which is strictly reliant upon revealed wisdom, a substratum owning a totalitarian tilt, and runs contrary to philosophy, reason, and independent intelligence. In other words, it is never a "cultural commandment" that women are relegated to second-class citizens in some regions while empowering others to castrate them; it's religion. Thus, culture remains unblemished while God and the rubrics of faith get scapegoated. How convenient! Meanwhile, *Jenny* hammered away at the concept that beliefs, values, and practices are byproducts of disparate beginnings producing disparate outcomes created by a lack of wealth distribution. In other words, more wealth would equal more civility and universality concerning ethics.

Invalidity notwithstanding—who could imagine, evenly distributed wealth or not, that tribes of different continental origins would evolve at the same rate, in the same way, and share a collective conscience? —Jenny articulated her points eloquently and confidently. And those goddamn tits of hers were another story altogether! Then something occurred to me: Was I being drilled or put through a test, which I could only assume, based on what appeared to be Elizabeth's approval, I was passing and doing so with flying colors? Then something else occurred to me, and it was far more disconcerting: What if I was failing to make the grade and not showing myself a worthy debater; would I be killed and, come nightfall, dragged off into the woods? Our discussion was no longer surging; it was in the winding-down stage. I was grateful because what started as stimulating discourse had begun to wear. Still, I had to be careful; there was time yet for me to slip up. I grew nervous and became hesitant; my convictions lacked an authoritative verve. Alas, I saw what appeared to be a look of disappointment flash in Elizabeth's eyes. I was faltering, and she knew it. Thankfully, Jenny shifted the conversation. Perhaps she sensed we were matching wits but with no effort to build a bridge even a mountain goat would dare cross.

"Men my age are dreadfully tedious." Jenny's pretentious tenor led me to conclude that she had developed a recent pet peeve, likely deriving from a circle of friends who collectively decided older men were fashionable. Not to suggest that Jenny's mild vexation was wholly disingenuous, just recent. "I much prefer older men," she predictably added. "Say, for instance, your age, Mitch." I flattered myself with the notion it was not merely my age or intellect that Jenny found attractive. Though not yet a moment later, I experienced a tremor of terror. Was I purposely being led astray or manipulated? Had I stumbled into a prearranged conversation orchestrated by Elizabeth, and worse, should I fail to exhibit what she deemed a proper inclination toward Jenny or showed myself too eager, would it lead to my demise? I must remain ambiguous.

"But my parents would never approve of a man your age," Jenny continued. "I'm not sure my dearest Auntie Elizabeth would, either."

Although Jenny's tone was far more ironical than conciliatory, it pointed toward concession. So, concerning the matter, I cared not how revealing my gratitude was or if my sigh mimicked a punctured balloon. However, no sooner had I enjoyed my moment of comfort than Jenny asked, "What are your thoughts, Mitch? After all, you're a novelist, and novelists are likely to be more insightful than the average person: Should a woman be forced to look for love only through a prism that society deems permissible? Can she not walk the world over with an audacity equal to men, embracing come what may and taking what she desires?"

I was back on the proverbial hot seat with only two choices: Either I could appease Jenny, thus annoy Elizabeth, or vice-versa. I know what Molly would say to the former: *Hell no*! To address the latter, she'd say: *Fucking right, she can!* But even if I were to use measured and tempered language, I risked upsetting Elizabeth. I felt the weight of Elizabeth's gaze, Jenny's too. My mouth turned dry; my tongue grew heavy; both women became imposing figures closing in on me, anticipating a reply. Worse, the punctured balloon that moments ago represented a release of anxiety managed to reinflate and place what I feared was visible stress upon what I imagined was my expanding viscera. But it was no time for excuses; I needed to supply an answer and fast.

"I don't believe it's sensible for a woman to look for love." The sound of my voice came as a surprise. "Instead, she should thrust herself into this wondrous abyss called life armed with passions she is forever cultivating. But first, she must abandon the search for context and meaning or anything else that tends to quell inspiration and embrace what it means to be alive among a multitude exercising free will in a free society, no matter how random and chaotic. It's an approach that has the potential to yield two favorable outcomes: it can heighten her sensibility for wanderlust and proffer a less cloudy horizon on the road to happiness, wherever it may lead."

I did it! I tendered a reply that set well with both women and, just as important, made my departure with my whole person intact. No woodland burial for Mitch Morningstar, at least not tonight! More to the point, I demonstrated that between the margins of hypercriticism and blissful ignorance, an expanse exists with ample room for happiness to flourish.

Admittedly, Jenny did pose a challenge, intellectually and otherwise; especially otherwise; for despite her beauty, imposing wit, declaring herself a "fan" of my novels, and voicing her appreciation that I befriended her great-aunt without Elizabeth feeling patronized or indulged, somewhere—not glaringly apparent but perceptible—in her bearing lies a young woman whose facility for threatening men is, to say the least, unique. I could attest that meeting Jenny was well worth the wait, but I was not eager for a second go-around. So be it that she caused beads of moisture to form on my forehead; I was not too keen upon seeking redemption.

****

Gabby was waiting for me when I arrived home. And resting on her lips were the predictable and anticipatory words, "How'd it go?"

"It *went*," was my terse reply, which should have been enough to indicate to Gabby that I was well worn from the encounter. But pithiness, primarily where Elizabeth Montague was concerned, was unacceptable; thus, Gabby intoned, "Well, Mitch, did you get the impression they were killers or not?" After all this time, it was still unclear whether Gabby was rooting for the notion that Elizabeth and Jenny were deranged killers or preferred them as a pair of kooky eccentrics. Then again, I was uncertain which scenario I was rooting for myself.

"Incidentally, Mitch, a letter on the dining room table stamped overseas is awaiting your attention."

I assumed it was from Nina. Who else? Real-life Harold and Jane would have sent a letter to Gabby and me, or Gabby specifically. After treating Gabby somewhat dismissively concerning Elizabeth and Jenny, I tried to conceal that my mood brightened over a letter from Nina. "I'll tend to it in the morning," I told Gabby, though I made a beeline for the dining room no sooner had she turned in for the night.

Lately, no one could describe the communication channel between Nina and us as busy. That being the case, I was anxious to learn whatever news she had to tell. Over the past thirty months, Nina managed a single trip to the States and shortened her stay to a weekend. Real-life Harold and Jane, who arrived on the same flight, allowed for a two-week holiday. Nina's career was always the prevailing reason she seldom came to the States and discouraged us from making a trip to

London. Once, I wrote Nina to remind her: *It's a bit difficult to construct a biography with no supply of material; I can't guess your goings-on.* Her swift and succinct response was to plead for patience and assure me: *When the time is right, there'll be plenty to tell.* With that in mind, I tore open the envelope, hoping "the right time" was now and that her words would launch a new chapter.

Dearest Mitch,

Can you imagine Pinocchio's joy when he cried, "I'm a real boy!" and then danced about to show his strings were no longer necessary? Not only can I imagine his joy, but I can also experience it; my strings, at long last, have been cut away; I'm liberated. Mitch, darling, I have a vagina; I'm a real girl!

Gabby has a five-by-three-inch photograph displayed in the upper left corner of her vanity mirror: She is age seven, posing on a Bloomsbury sidewalk, eyes sparkling and flashing for the world her winning smile. Below her, sitting on the curb and looking quite the pathetic little lump, is a boy once known as Robby Norwich. There is no sparkle in Robby's eyes; one can plainly see him forcing a smile. From Robby to Bobbie to Nina to Nina with a vagina: they are the iterations that mark the progressions of a lonely, torturous, and pains-taking journey. It was apparent in the photograph that loneliness, tor-ture, and pain began far too early.

But now, Mr. Morningstar, dearest brother-in-law, and favorite novelist, I have a favor to ask: Now that I am complete, I shall need a volunteer, someone to take me out for a test drive, so to speak, to see how well I handle, how quickly I can accelerate from zero to sixty; perhaps even a crash test would be advisable. You wouldn't happen to know any devilishly handsome, witty, sexually viable men who won't run the risk of falling in love with me because they're already married to an English beauty, would you? We Norwich sisters are a fine breed, are we not? I hope you do because, Mitch, darling, I'm coming to America and aim to bring trouble!

With more joy in my heart than one could ever express with words,
Nina

P.S. Mitch, please be a dear and explain to Gabby my reason for crossing the Atlantic. As far as sisters are concerned, she has been the best and the most understanding. And now, I shall close with two questions: Do butterflies ever forget they were caterpillars? Can you forget, Mitch?

The Bohemian

Gabby was thrilled to learn that her sister was, in every sense, "a real girl." "Mitch, you can hear the joy in her words just as clearly as if she were standing in the room."

Indeed, there was cause to celebrate. But looming was another issue: Gabby seemed wholly unfazed, even cavalier, that I was chosen as consummator to what got mishandled decades ago, following conception, by a higher order, if applicable, and left to the skills of a surgeon. It was perplexing that Gabby proved such a pushover concerning what any sober person would view as a moral dilemma. Thus, I imagined four entities: Gabby, me, our marriage, and Nina, trapped in a room with only enough oxygen for three, and Gabby's and my marital bliss drawing the short straw and bludgeoned until rendered breathless would mark the method of sacrifice, or worse an object thoughtlessly cast adrift in the movie *Lifeboat* would become the symbolism of our marriage's forsakenness. Consequently, it lay, washed up on the shore, an awful shade of blue, half-eaten by piranhas, while Nina's celebrity skyrockets from a vocalist of note to a sex symbol.

"Mitch, as usual, you're overthinking the matter," Gabby argued. "Nothing is ever as complicated as you make it out to be, and Nina's request is a perfect example. Besides, if not you, then who?" Gabby paused to allow me a moment to reflect upon the matter. "Imagine how nervous Nina would feel, a woman her age, never having been penetrated by anything other than a practice toy, entering into a relationship with no real understanding of how it feels with a man. Only you can vanquish her fear and anxiety. Besides, it isn't as if we didn't know this day was coming."

It would seem silly to act put-upon or assume the "poor husband" role—a man taken for granted for what his wife deemed a worthy cause. But, before I could imply as much, Gabby huffed, "*All* men are test dummies, Mitch, but are too sopping wet with self-aggrandizement to realize it."

That was otherwise known as putting the exclamation point at the end of a debate. But, if truth be told, I cared not whether I was "put-upon," taken for granted, or used as a test dummy. The not-so-simple reality was as follows: I was nervous that I would fail to measure up to what Nina, for years, had been anticipating. And yes, I could disguise my worry by displaying a casual attitude concerning the affair. However, I would be risking Nina's unparalleled perceptiveness obliterating my façade, thus relegating me to the role of the fool, which would not serve as a mood-enhancer. That leaves only one option: just be myself. It sounds easy enough: when all else fails, just be yourself. But I would be myself wading in uncharted waters.

Real-life Harold and Jane, unbeknown to me, flew with Nina for "the event." Gabby made preparations for what she dubbed a *welcome to full-blown womanhood* inauguration: she got to play the role of mistress of ceremonies, while yours truly would avail himself as a test dummy for the ultimate femme fatale. By the time I arrived home from the airport—with three Brits in tow—Ursula, Warren, Daddy Russ, Molly, and Gabby were already assembled on the patio and eagerly awaiting to raise a goblet of wine to celebrate a new beginning. It was summertime and Sunday, but was it a *welcome-to-womanhood inauguration* or *pre-consummation soiree* into which I was about to stumble? These were my best friends gathered on my patio, so why did I feel like I was entering a lion's den? And how would Nina feel? Would she shrink, even wilt, from all the attention? In the past, Nina would strut where and when she felt safe and in control but resort to aloofness when danger or the threat of a genuine encounter lurked. So how would Nina—a woman who kept the world at a comfortable distance for so long—act tonight under the glare of attention? I spent my worry needlessly: Nina was still too immersed in the "overjoyed" stage of her new beginning, and her wings, which she kept pressed to her sides, had disregarded and dared not raise, were spread wide, as wide as they could go, in unparalleled splendor, and the sparkle I had always admired in Gabby's eyes was now present in Nina's. There would be no more watchful gazing or cool demeanor from an aloof head-turning beauty; the Nina that came to America—the one who "aimed to bring trouble" —was a wide-eyed child standing on the threshold of a promising tomorrow. In other words, the Norwich sisters were true sisters in every sense.

"You don't intend to film the event for posterity, do you?" I managed to whisper in Gabby's ear. Then, after we all clanked our goblets and the toast became a collective buzz, she replied while grinning as though the idea had crossed her mind: "Mitch, dear, we're a band of batty postmodern bohemians, not pornographers."

The truth was: filming the event, according to how my mind's eye conceived it, would not have rendered it any less natural. Moreover, what else could I attribute the failure to besides the absence of impulse; it prevailed as an overarching stumbling block and genuine source of distraction. How could Nina and I *not* end up an anticlimactic affair? The thrill that I may fancy myself the envy of more men than I have ever known should be enough to overwhelm how dreadfully manufactured an experience tonight will prove. And how ironic for all those men to have coveted a vagina that, until recently, did not exist. Inside, I implored that I cease thinking of myself and remember what was to take place was for Nina's benefit. Indeed, I should allow Ursula's well-chosen spirit to delight my palate, trickle down my throat, soothe my senses, then reconcile Gabby's point that all men are test dummies. And Gabby's point was undoubtedly one of merit. Among every pair of aspiring lovers, Romeo and Juliet aside, one has assumed either the role of the recipient or one administering the indoctrination. Still, it vexed me to think that tomorrow, I would receive "atta-boy" swats on the back from real-life Harold, Daddy Russ, and The Canadian Elk Hunter.

"Mitch, dear, you've been out-of-sorts since we arrived home from the airport." This concern of Nina's got expressed later that evening when we were alone in her room. "I never imagined us stealing away for a spell would prove difficult. I suppose of late, however valid the reason, I've been feeling too bold, and it's caused me to act thoughtlessly, even selfish. You'll have to forgive me."

Nina took a step toward me and placed her head on my shoulder. I could sense her womanhood, her frailty. "I don't understand happiness enough to know everyone need not jump for joy because *I'm* feeling joyful." She stepped back. I watched a frown form on her voluminous mouth; it passed for an apology. Then her eyes traveled to the floor when she added, "I suppose I failed to take into account the length of the learning curve beyond the act of lovemaking."

Upon me gushed an unexpected awareness that Nina was more tortured a soul than I had imagined. To not know happiness as an experience was one matter—one in which Nina had plenty of company: Not to comprehend it was another, and she turned to us, Gabby and me—those whom she loved most and trusted—to set her on a pathway to glimpse happiness and its potential so that she may grasp, with confidence, she was a viable woman with a facility to assert herself into the world as do other women possessing stirring beauty. Strange, but it never occurred to me that lovemaking could be similar to learning a language: the older one was, the more daunting the task.

Unsure of what I wanted to happen next, I took hold of Nina and pressed her to my chest. "Your joy is our joy," I whispered to her.

Was I caught up in a moment or creating one? All I knew with any certainty was the sincerity of my words. I swept aside tendrils of hair that had fallen onto Nina's face and tucked them behind her ear. This tender gesture sent forth from her form an unexpected quiver. As it registered, there stirred within me an air of consciousness that Nina and I were celestial bodies whose orbits long ago were fated to collide with neither owning a concern for the outcome. Be it love, regret, laughter, or ambiguity, a consequence would prevail—it must—the question was which, and there was no leaping beyond the moment; no way of knowing which among the cluster would introduce a new reality, how long it would endure, or how strenuously. Next, I uttered the word "Yes." Nina's twisted visage and the lovely manner in which she tilted her head revealed that she intuited my utterance as one of incongruity. Then I told her, "Butterflies *do* forget they were caterpillars. But you were never a caterpillar; not since I saw you all those years ago on stage, serenading me, have I thought of you as anything other than a woman and the most beautiful I have ever known."

Closer yet, I pressed Nina to me until our forms molded together. Next, like a delicate flower yearning for nourishment, I sensed her wilting in my arms. "The letter I wrote you, Mitch…." She paused and faltered before admitting, "It was a falsehood." It was a whispered confession—one that hastened a mingling of my curiosity and Nina's regret. "I tried to pave the way to this moment with humor, irony, anything to impress upon you that we could never be viable lovers. The effort was futile, for the truth is—and this is a confession, not an apology—I desperately wanted this night to be meaningful." Searching my eyes, Nina sensed I had absorbed favorably the notion our encounter should endure as a meaningful experience. Next came a feeble smirk, one that led to yet another confession: "In my mind's eye, I saw myself performing a striptease with you looking on with avaricious lust, but what I truly want, more than anything, is to be discovered—to submit to the hand of a gentle, thoughtful lover, and when revealed, see a flicker of delight in his eye that I am all he could ever desire."

And so that was how Nina and I made love that evening: like Adam and Eve in The Garden of Eden discovering earthly delights, thoughtfully honoring each glorious sensation, and dazzled by the thrill each discovery brought to bear. And what began as a gentle, thoughtful indoctrination evolved into a night of splendor; yet, amid its generosity, foreshadowing us was a wistful spirit that tonight would be our only night and that we were helpless to stop time and linger in a moment. But the night would prove a generous steward of lovers, after all. Thus, the cosmos would render itself still long enough to permit the capture of a transcendental gaze, one that saw my eyes fill with worship as Nina lay silent: her stillness, the loveliness of her skin, the grace of her form—every part of her, at rest or in motion, screamed beauty of an unparalleled nature.

Indeed, that was the essence of Nina tonight and the first time I gazed her. Her body, when in motion, seemed compelled by sound echoing from some rarified plane, and whether choreographed or allowing nature's gifts to unfold impulsively, capturing Nina's movements was akin to capturing poetry. When in repose, she was a work of art—a sculpture of a nymph come to life.

My gaze became weightier than I realized and inspired demureness in Nina, and in this decorous state, she apologized for what she described as her "pubescent breasts." I decided "youthful and perky" was more fitting, for that which she alleged a deficiency suited her willowy form. My words made her smile.

At last, we reached the point of exhaustion—a time and place when the body betrays whatever lofty ambitions it may have embraced; yet, we soared to a higher realm than imagined and, with a voracity owning properties both loving and wickedly carnal, greedily drew into our lungs the esotericism that hung in the ether. And although the words may have gone unspoken, the notion prevailed: if such a dominion was attainable, a return visit must be permissible.

CHAPTER EIGHTEEN
A KILLER OF A SPOOF

The following day, I spent a few leisurely summer hours seated at what I dubbed—thanks first to Ursula and later to both she and Gabby—my "observation chair" positioned by the picture window in my bedroom. It was a place I had spent many a sunrise, sunset, and entire afternoons sketching scenes, developing plotlines, characters, and, more important, just the right narrative voice to suit a particular story. Today, I was working on a draft. It began with trekking to the airport to fetch Nina and real-life Harold and Jane and ended with Nina and me when through with our interlude, approaching Gabby; the coalescence resulted in the three of us sharing a bed. We placed Gabby between us so that Nina and I could sense the depth of her love and generosity. If Nina kissed Gabby once, she kissed her a hundred times; from Gabby's lips to her hands, Nina kissed and kissed, and with each flurry, Gabby insisted there was no need for gratitude and praise, but if there was one person in this wide world Nina worshipped, it was her big sister.

Last night would have been well worthy of documentation even if I had not been working on the biography of a singer of note whose life had crossed paths with a novelist who managed a splash in certain circles. And since last night would stand as part of a "tell-all" biography—one that would see no identity spared (only Nina's and my name traveled beyond our clique) —last night's episode must have a dedicated chapter. Moreover, its recounting was shaping up as a poetic sexual odyssey grounded in pathos, ascending toward joy; the only question was placement. If inserted in the beginning—thus making Nina's biography a retrospective—such a racy opening could create the sort of stir sure to boost sales and please a publisher but risk cheapening a story whose crux is the transformative journey of a transcendent soul. Having Nina's story resonate in that fashion was always the goal, and with last night behind me, I was more guarded than ever against illuminating a figure of such complexity as Nina using a garish glare of light. I had to be wary of Nina's biography— a piece I was crafting with wistful elegance and literary prose—getting sucked into the mindless machines known as American and British pop culture, then featured on television shows hosted by morons giddily crooning, *Guess what?* or, *Stay tuned, you'll never believe it!* I would not let that happen, not if I could help it. Nina's story was too important, personal, and meaningful; it needed to be read and discussed by those able to ignore their appetite for the sensational and apply sensitivity.

Nina brought me fresh coffee. I reciprocated by handing over the pages I had thus far written.

"Shall I read them in front of you?" she asked.

"Not unless you'd be more comfortable elsewhere," I told her.

Nina opted for a spot on the bed. I could sense her delight and approval despite my not keeping an eye fixed on her as one might when anxious for a critique. I sipped coffee, captivated by the naked sun-kissed bodies of Gabby and Ursula as I had been many a Sunday. That I was well absorbed all morning with a literary honoring of last night was no reason for two oiled-up glowing forms sprawled on chaise lounges to have escaped my notice. In other words, the sun and other forms of nature were not their only sentinels; thus, the loveliness of Gabby and Ursula exposed as they were proved every bit as inspiring today as in the past.

When lying beside one another, slathered in oil and illuminated by rays of sunshine, a sense of playfulness and frolic was present in Gabby and Ursula. Naked or otherwise, this spontaneous air of excitement has become more prevalent in recent days but seems especially apparent when fully unclad. Moreover, when I am held captive by the frivolity and impulsivity that their synergy never fails to generate, laws of gravity seem to get obeyed with an accord analogous to planets and satellites, and which of these beauties assumes the role of planet or satellite is anyone's guess.

Once, Gabby and Ursula shared a chaise lounge. Lying on their sides, thus unable to prevent features of their frontal nakedness from touching, they took turns reading passages from a light romance novel they decided to share; the content caused them to giggle like

271

schoolgirls. And these sun-worshipping sessions never passed without a playful touch, impromptu kiss, or caress that would seem to any on-looker—or pathetic wanton pleasuring himself—unmistakably erotic. And not for a second am I convinced these sunbathing beauties are unmindful of the torture they levy upon poor Warren and me. More-over, when contemplating the potency of feminine charm, as Gabby and Ursula tend to wield it, "madness" and "distraction" are two words that come to mind, as does the phrase "pitiful bastards." For years, Warren and I were on guard, peeping from a favorite vantage point within our respective domains, and engaged in involuntary hand-hon-oring arousal—concerning the latter; I should only speak for myself—while wondering whether the delight of playful frolic would evolve into something more meaningful. About the matter: doubtless, these highly intuitive creatures were aware and amused—aware of their po-tency and amused by the madness it creates—though it was a subject never broached, not between Gabby and me, Warren and me, or when the four of us were all present and counted, which was often.

As I sipped coffee and Nina read silently, Ursula—the entire length of her willowy form—rose from her chaise with swanlike ele-gance and silkily settled herself at the foot of Gabby's chaise. At first, she sat straddling the elongated chair, then crisscrossed her legs to in-vite Gabby's feet onto her lap. The end of Ursula's sinuous arms fea-tured slender lovely hands: with how they undulated and swished through the air, one was helpless to honor them appreciatively. Unfurl-ing her arms, she reached under Gabby's legs and, with petrissage-like movements, kneaded her calves. Next, her fingers traveled the length of Gabby's shins on the way to her delicate little feet, gliding first over her well-formed arches, then pinching her toes: Not in the past had I regarded Gabby's feet sexually, my ignorance attributed to Gabby be-ing well-endowed in other areas; however, when observing the sensual manner Ursula's hands honored them, I sat pondering whether I had been missing out or, worse, failed to explore Gabby to an extent wor-thy of her assets. I began to suffer an attack of inadequacy stemming from the notion if awarded the chance, Ursula, whose femininity and understanding of women as sexual beings were unrivaled, could sur-pass what I, a man, could do for Gabby. I fretted over the dilemma should I feel threatened, or was I, as they say, making much ado about nothing? Next, I witnessed what appeared to be the manifestation of the devil flicker in Ursula's eyes. She raised one of Gabby's feet from

The Bohemian

her lap. I could feel my body drawn nearer to the window, not to improve my vantage point; my vision was unobstructed. But then the devil that resided within Ursula surrendered to the schoolgirl, and the result was her giving Gabby's big toe a playful love bite. Afterward, the two giggled as would pubescents on the threshold of discovery.

Next, I felt arms as slender and sinuous as Ursula's, snaking around my neck and slithering to my chest. In my preoccupation, I failed to hear Nina roll off the bed and steal up from behind me, yet there she was, her chin resting on my shoulder and whispering in my ear: "Why the consternation, Mitch? Girls will be girls."

"Is that so," I said, with more scorn than intended. It led Nina to intone, "Yes, Mitch, and should it evolve into more than that—if Gabby and Ursula feel driven to discover one another beyond 'girls being girls'—would it be so terrible? The last I heard, you and Gabby were hardly sharing what anyone would describe as a compulsory marriage, so whatever occurs between Gabby and Ursula, or, for that matter, you and I, if it can serve to take intimacy already dazzling to new heights, then I respectfully submit, what's wrong with that?"

Although a bit "sideways," as one might be inclined to describe her perspective, there was rationality to Nina's reasoning that should have resonated better than it had. Was I becoming, dare I admit, old-fashioned? Had I evolved into the sort of man who would deny his wife freedoms similar to the one I recently was granted with Nina or was long ago forgiven for with Molly? It bothered me to think of myself in that light.

"Here," said Nina. She handed back the reading material I allowed her to preview. "The words rival the experience; they leave me feeling fulfilled yet wanting more. I can feel proud that I was part of what happened between us last night and that it compelled you to express it as beautifully as you have. I cannot imagine my biography in more capable hands."

****

And so life went on amongst us bohemians and in a bohemian way. Then arrived the day when I spotted another envelope placed in the scaffolding of the olive hedge. Inside the envelope was a letter issuing the ever-predictable summons and that Jenny would make it a threesome. As I read on, it became clear that Jenny required my presence. "There are issues," Elizabeth urged, "that my darling great-niece wishes to discuss and believes you are the very person to impart her with wisdom." *Mmm,* I thought. A young, beautiful woman going through an "older man phase" seeking wisdom; how could I resist? Then, in a tempest-like manner, an idea brewed in my head; it prompted me to run straightaway to Gabby. Upon reading aloud Elizabeth's letter—it was no aberration: as heterodox thinkers, Gabby and I often ended up in the same place—Gabby conjured an irresistibly wicked scenario similar to mine. The following day, I made a point of waylaying The Canadian Elk Hunter before he managed to occupy his hands with a piece of manly equipment. Warren was curious about Elizabeth. And, if truth be told, it had become somewhat of a sore subject that I was the only one on the block with whom the eccentric old recluse had struck a relationship.

"I suppose you have to be a novelist to be considered worthy company for the old lady," Warren once groused. I did not bother to correct Warren by explaining: although Elizabeth may be an older woman, she would hardly strike anyone as an "old lady." But the real issue that got Warren all rankled? I was awarded time with Jenny by way of a request. With that in mind, for Warren's benefit, I manufactured a tale: I told him I made it clear to Elizabeth that Gabby and I "regrettably" had an engagement that "not for anything in the world could we break" and that Elizabeth was understanding concerning the matter. What's more, "Jenny would be just as interested in spending time with, and I quote, 'That rugged-looking neighbor of yours.'" A spark of interest flickered in Warren's eyes. "Is that so," he intoned with anticipation and incredulity. I warned Warren: "If you are so inclined, you must report at two o'clock sharp; Elizabeth Montague is a woman who clings strenuously to decorum: In other words, she isn't the sort to tolerate even a second of tardiness *and*, if you do manage to arrive on time, you need not bother knocking or ringing the bell; just walk right in; you'll find Elizabeth and Jenny seated in the second room on the left; you can expect tea and sandwich wedges."

Warren approached the big white house with confidence that soon gave way to trepidation. Perhaps the stoutness of a wrought iron gate that allowed one access to the other side of an equally impressive stone wall Warren never before ventured beyond was what transformed poise to the uneasiness and grimacing I spied when peeking through the blinds of a second-story window. Another consideration was the uninviting tangle of landscape through which one would need to negotiate.

The Bohemian

Warren lifted the latch of the near century-and-a-half-year-old piece of iron architecture and eased it ajar. He cringed when the groaning sound of old iron rubbing against old iron overpowered the gentle breeze rustling through the trees, the chirping of many birds, and the countless wings of countless insects that lend to summer its unbroken murmur. Oversensitive to what he alleged was an unwelcome stirring, Warren sighed when realizing nothing but a gate made to groan had altered; his presence had no appreciable effect on the ether or its occupants. Slipping through to the other side, Warren settled the gate back into place, disappearing into Elizabeth's tangled forest. Without making a sound, he gained entry into the big white house. Next, he reminded himself where Elizabeth and Jenny would be seated and waiting for him but discovered his feet frozen to the floor, eyes widening like one who had just stepped into a museum where opulent representations of antiquity were carefully preserved. It served to heighten his trepidation.

"Am I to take it that we're to move our humble get-together out into the hall?" The voice was jarring; its derisive tenor caused Warren to cower. He considered turning tail and running off before revealing himself the recoiling lump of humanity he was reduced to—besides, what had he owed the irreverent voice that echoed into the hall? —but managed a deep breath and puffed out his chest like a man who handled heavy equipment like children's toys. He was sure the derisive tenor came from a mature woman and thus belonged to the never-before-seen Elizabeth Montague, not her great-niece. Warren reminded himself the destination was the second room on his left, then pried his feet loose from the floor.

"Mitch, dear, the surgery worked like a charm; I can hardly recognize you!" Elizabeth's words were whimsical; her brows arched in irony when adding, "Oh, the capers we shall pull."

"Haven't you a package?" Jenny, who seemed unfazed, less amused by Elizabeth's humor, had asked. She was posed regally in her chair with one long aristocratic leg draped over the other. Warren's eyes were drawn to the glossy red polish made available by a thinly strapped white sandal; Jenny's pendulous toes, rotating ankle, and flexing calf muscle were both arousing and authoritative. Finally, she turned toward her great-aunt and asked, "Are not delivery boys instructed to leave packages at the door?"

"Ahh, dear niece," Elizabeth intoned," this one here is no delivery boy, not this specimen." With a finger placed at her chin, Elizabeth's assessing eyes made a thorough examination of Warren. "I know this fellow, although—her gaze shifted to Warren—you're a touch taller than I realized. Nevertheless, I suppose you've come to break the bad news of the unforeseen occurrence that caused our favorite novelist to be a no-show. How thoughtful of Mitch and you to do his bidding."

"If that is indeed the case, Auntie," Jenny chimed in before Warren could reply, "we mustn't discount that he is handsome, albeit in a brutish way, and also of a suitable age. I submit we ought to have him stay."

Warren stood in the archway dividing the room from the great hall, bemused by two women who persisted in regarding him as though he were not present, or worse, a mindless ornament or entity whose worthiness of their time and attention was up for debate. His eyes settled first upon Elizabeth, who, as was her custom, was attired in her white lacey dress and ballet slipper-style shoes. Next, they traveled to Jenny. To Warren's surprise—it had been years since he last glimpsed Jenny exiting a limousine dressed in a gown—she was rather skimpily clad in a summery outfit. It was a bizarre scene into which Warren had interposed himself, and his presence, if anything, served to augment its peculiarity. Of only one matter, Warren was sure, for by then, it was painfully clear: I had put one over on the Canadian elk hunter, having lured him into an ambush.

"Perhaps you're right, my dear," Elizabeth intoned. "We should have him stay. And who knows, it might prove fun. Oh, *do* sit down, Warren, won't you? I assure you we're not nearly as scary as we appear."

Warren did as urged; he helped himself to a seat. Before long, he found himself engaged in the offering of tea and a sandwich wedge. He even gawked at Elizabeth's impressive collection of novels but wisely—perhaps for fear of being tested—owned up to being a reader of nonfiction and magazines that celebrate all things outdoors. The admission caused Jenny to lurch forward in her chair with probing eyes; she scrutinized Warren using a compelling gaze that made it clear she suspected him of someone with little sophistication and limited intellect.

"Now-now, dear niece; we mustn't judge," Elizabeth warned. "It would be a tedious world if only filled with intellectual elites. There

The Bohemian

are numerous reasons man gets gifted a worthwhile pair of hands, and opening books represent but one. Thus, I can state with unshakable confidence that our friend, Warren, has put his hands to good use more often than most."

Warren did not dare puff out his chest to display that he had gained an ally in Elizabeth, where Jenny's haughtiness was concerned. In other words, whatever delight he may have taken in Elizabeth's philosophy that men celebrating their machismo were hardly buffoons, Warren remained staid if not wary, for looming larger than Elizabeth, or so it seemed, was the gorgonesque Jenny. And although no stranger to tall, beautiful women with minds of their own—aside from marrying one, numerous occasions saw Warren challenged by Molly, our clique's antagonist—he sensed Jenny was a different animal, someone representing unknown danger, a choppy sea to a novice swimmer; and be it Jenny's imposing posture that bordered on menacing, or her distressingly supercilious affect, Warren, his physicality notwithstanding, felt surprisingly diminished in her presence.

"Now, what shall we talk about?" Elizabeth brightly chirped.

As usual, Elizabeth relished the role of accommodating hostess and poured more tea; she hoped her obliging deportment would inspire a civil dialogue. Warren found it odd that a pending conversation—instead of evolving as they tend to—should come by way of selection but was not so bold as to dare instigate a topic: Warren chose, for he assumed it wise, to defer to Elizabeth and Jenny, which he would learn in due course was the same as yielding only to Jenny—it would be Jenny's version of "baptism by fire" that would prevail—thus what began as an approachable tete-a-tete based on the probability of blind patriotism breeding nationalism and ending in jingoism should the current administration prove too influential, got dumped in Warren's lap by way of Jenny's authoritative nod signaling he was permitted to share his opinion. Because of Warren's rugged appearance, Jenny guessed he was the type eager to carry water for the Bush administration; hence, the topic. Unfortunately, Warren would prove Jenny a good judge based on appearance. Jenny frowned that Warren had shown himself too hawkish concerning the subject; it led to Jenny accusing him of being aligned with "those dreadful neocons who would prefer to drive up the deficit to accommodate an unjust war rather than a comprehensive education bill."

Nevertheless, Warren doubled down on his position with what he assumed was suitable humility: First, by suggesting there was "too much indoctrination in academia;" second, by parroting some of the Bush/Chaney/Rumsfeld rhetoric disgorged liberally from the capital, which was gnawing away at a nation already fatigued with war. And gnaw it did, as Jenny was not the only one Warren made frown. Following the Iraqi bombardment—which, advisable or not, initially seemed to provide a well-engrossed majority pleasure—boots hit the ground, thus turning our Sunday soirees into respectably heated discussions over the justifications for war. Warren thumped his chest for what he deemed "a righteous cause" before adding: "Weapons of mass destruction or no weapons of mass destruction, the term 'moral relativism' cannot apply to the Saddam Hussein's of the world, or else we're a lost cause as a species." Molly accused Warren of being "the ultimate oxymoron," which she later clarified as having meant "Warmongering Canadian." Perhaps the term "respectably heated" was a bit generous.

"Is it not fascinating how 'Shock and Awe' and 'Operation Iraqi Freedom' got bundled into the mundane label 'The war in Iraq,'" Molly affectingly intoned. "What happened? It seems we were just yesterday waving pompoms and throwing streamers; now we're flapping our middle fingers and expressing distrust for our so-called powerbrokers for having sold us another regime change initiative. Indeed, it's quite fascinating how quickly sex appeal ends up in the crapper when it lacks substance and is spawned by bullshit ideology. However, I have to give credit where credit is due: Double-U truly believes his own bullshit, so, in a fucked-up sorta way, it makes the sonofabitch authentic."

"There's something to be said for authenticity," said Warren. "And we could argue justification until we run out of wine, but I believe in finishing what we started. And let us not forget it was the media waving those pompoms; you name an outlet, and it licked its chops over an opportunity to cover a war, but the minute matters went sideways, Lady Liberty went from a liberator to a colonialist."

Ursula gave a beautifully executed sardonic roll of the eyes before stating with an unmistakable appeal for forgiveness: "And here, all along, I thought I had married a Canadian." Warren, who was employing his considerable manliness at a sizzling grill, missed the irony entirely and whined, "I *am* a Canadian!"

The Bohemian

"But now he's a 'Bush-boy apologist,'" Molly sneered.

"He's not the only one," Real-life Harold chimed in. "This business in Iraq, I believe, will go down as the undoing of Tony Blair."

"Indeed, it will," Real-life Jane, who favored Tony Blair, gravely parroted.

"I was once told: it's not the bee sting that causes anaphylaxis or kills you, but the immune system overreacting to what, essentially, is a mild pathogen," Daddy Russ began. "Not that it was unjustified, but our overreaction to 9/11 was what put us on this path—a path that, if we're not careful, could lead to us cannibalizing ourselves and the many systems we depend upon." It was with an ironic shrug that Daddy Russ added, "I suppose that's the point of terrorism: to get a nation to doubt itself and begin a steady internal decay. And since we're a hierarchal structure, if we're going to assign blame for our current dilemma, it's got to start with the top: Bush and Chaney. I'd have no qualms seeing them tried as war criminals, but not until they clean up the mess they made."

The latter was why Daddy Russ voted the "Batman villains," as Molly referred to them, for a second term. "They broke it; let them fix it. Then we'll hang them; perhaps a public hanging. I'm thinking Time Square would be a nice touch, and before the bottom drops out, we'll have a weenie roast: hotdogs, beer, and a hanging. What could be more American!" As an afterthought, Daddy Russ lamented, "And poor John Kerry, marching around in that idiotic hunting outfit Teresa must've had overnighted from L.L. Bean. With a rifle on his shoulder, his aid marching behind him, carrying a dead goose he bought from the hunter who actually shot the goddamn thing; I'm sure the gun people and environmentalist were impressed. Christ, he looked dopier than Gary Cooper playing Sergeant York!"

"You'd have to go out of your way to lose an election to a sitting president as unpopular as Double-U," Molly crowed.

"I don't believe it was Kerry's ineptness as much as it was the silent majority not so hot-to-trot to see a changing of the guard during wartime," Gabby theorized.

"Precisely my point," added Daddy Russ.

Despite the tide railing against him, Warren, undeterred, clung to the notion that the capture and subsequent execution of Saddam Hussein, regardless of the faulty ideology that hastened it, should now and in the future be considered a worthwhile act of humanity. And so there we sat: four Americans, four Brits, and one Canadian sipping wine and sharing eight varying perspectives with room to evolve, and one unwavering one, on America's ever-growing presence in the Middle East.

Next, the challenging great-niece of Elizabeth Montague nimbly transitioned to another polarizing subject that has proven to create friction in each passing century: Faith. Given the present entanglement and America dubbed a collection of infidels, it marked an easy shift. First—breaking the cardinal rule of judging a book by its cover—Warren issued a partial truth or what he assumed Jenny wanted to hear. Though, to be fair, it was hardly a reach to imagine that Jenny—a fresh-faced all-American beauty and product of old-money suburbanites—was a Daughter of the American Revolution, thus an acknowledged Protestant, Presbyterian, Baptist, or Lutheran, despite academia guiding her epistemological compass toward relativism and skepticism. But Warren, as he tends to do, overplayed his hand. Assuming that Jenny's experience with revealed wisdom came from many years of Sunday school prompted him to claim he treads nowhere if not with Jesus, and nary a Sunday passed that he failed to occupy a space in the pew eager for evangelistic dogmatism. The former was fractionally true; the latter was bullshit. Next, Warren became familiar with the consequence of making assumptions. With fury, fittingly biblical, Jenny unleashed a categorical bombardment of religious fundamentalist movements and their crimes, beginning with the Muslim conquests of the Levant and the First Crusade launched by Pope Urban II, and ending with Joseph Kony, a Ugandan and leader of the Lord's Resistance Army—many of his conscriptions were abducted children—whose holy cause was to purify Uganda until transformed into a theocracy. The usual suspects, The Spanish Inquisition and Salem Witch Hunts were not omitted. Poor Warren grew wide-eyed and shrank in the face of Jenny's antitheist diatribe.

"Show me a holy man, and I'll show you a con artist," Daddy Russ somewhat whimsically maintained with a hand occupied with a California Shiraz under a setting sun. "Love God all you want; have at it, but we have a word for ideologues who claim to know what He intends: Charlatan. And believe me, I'm the first to admit that there resides a spiritual domain within human potential, but that's where yours truly draws the line, as should everyone if they have an ounce of sense."

280

The Bohemian

"Baghdad was once the cultural and intellectual center of the world until those who 'claim to know what He intends' came storming into town." Among us, Molly's education was the broadest, and like Daddy Russ, her intellectual curiosity was steep, and occasionally she would enlighten us with little-known knowledge. Then, abandoning her pedagogic tone, she added, "Down with the systems by which Aristotle reasoned and up with Jesus. Nothing can tarnish a legacy more than half-baked zealots acting on your behalf. Poor Christ."

"Faith, I'm guessing, was never meant to be a psychosis; unfortunately, for some, that's how it ends up," said Daddy Russ. "There must be something faulty about how we're wired because anytime a new dogma got introduced, it's led to centuries of con jobs and ass whippings."

Some of us were atheists; others were agnostic. Not Warren: he maintained that religion, for all its brutality and totalitarianism, was still a force for good in the world. Thus, the Canadian Elk Hunter would not go down without a fight and posed the sensible question: "Whenever science veers onto a crooked path, people manage to separate 'it' from malefactors with ill intentions; why is religion never afforded the same consideration?"

"Point well taken," Molly conceded. "But rarely, if ever, does science breed fanaticism."

"Not unless you take into account Al Gore," Real-life Harold managed to interject.

"Indeed, we must account for Al Gore," Real-life Jane parroted.

Next, to complete a trifecta whose initiative seemed the jugular, Jenny served up a heaping helping of twenty-first-century feminism. Warren, to his credit, was expecting the ambush. Unfortunately, his timely anticipation saw him froth with ardor by overselling his position. He began by claiming foremost among his routine endeavors was channel-surfing for WNBA games. "I prefer it over the NBA," he crooned. "And more than anything, I wish Philadelphia would petition for a franchise."

It was one matter to proclaim reverence for women; it was another to reach for the farcical. Surely, Warren was not so dunderheaded as to imagine patronization, as a tactic, would increase his chances with Jenny; such a notion would require him to believe there was a genuine opportunity upon which to build. And yet he was not through. Next, Warren gushed that his veneration of womanhood was based on universal attributes owning no alliance with beauty and sex appeal; he was beginning to sound like the hopeless racist who imbecilically boasts: *some of my best friends are black!* Thankfully, he stopped short of throwing his arms in the air and crying: *what are tits but unfortunate accessories women must endure for the sake of ogres?* Poor Warren: once the thrust of momentum was at his back, getting out of his own way was akin to dodging wind; thus, he continued beating the drum on behalf of feminism until his mouth ran dry—until Jenny was convinced he was a man worthy of her affections. Unfortunately, as he was pounding his way to a dry mouth, his leering eyes betrayed his words as they gorged upon the parts of Jenny left bare by a scant summer outfit.

The time had come for Elizabeth to introduce her "special truffles" into the conversation. Warren's eyes swelled over the unexpected delight as he continued to gush over the many praiseworthy aspects of Jenny's gender.

"I'm not much of a sweet eater," Elizabeth confessed. "And as for my dear great-niece? You know how it is with young women: counting calories and watching their figures is a way of life. But, Warren, don't mind us. Dig in; eat as many as you like."

Warren did as urged and popped one of the round chocolate delights into his mouth. Then, following a moment's deliberation, which indicated a favorable assessment, he ate another, then a third; he had barely allowed total ingestion before inviting another into his mouth. He assumed it was the sweetness—too much sweetness can produce a slight burning sensation in the throat—that caused the slurring of his words. But then mild confusion set in; thus, not only did his words come out slurred, but some were also uttered in the wrong sequence. His muddled state sent his mind racing, which hastened sudden bursts of anxiety. Finally, he tried to say *I should get going* but sent forth the near-inaudible and incoherent jumble, *"Uh-sooging."*

"I beg your pardon, Warren; I couldn't catch what you said." Jenny's polite tenor came across as abrupt and snapping. Elizabeth, whose concern seemed genuine, added, "Warren, dear, you're looking a bit peaked; would you care for a glass of water? Perhaps a cold rag?"

Elizabeth's words fell upon Warren's ears in an odd distortion of sounds that bore little resemblance to language, despite being right on the heels of Jenny's. Weakness and dizziness began setting in; thus, Warren's head grew hot, then hotter; in the chair, his body felt heavy, then heavier. The totality of his person saw its reduction to a slumped sack of potatoes owning no command over limbs or facility; for all intents, he was rendered immobile. He failed to notice either Elizabeth or Jenny shift, yet their proximity to one another seemed to narrow. Stranger yet, only their faces were visible. Moreover, their eyes bore in on him from the opposite end of something long and cylindrical; the experience was akin to the afflictions or overwrought sensations one suffers when stripped of fundamental freedoms afforded all humans and reduced to a lab rat.

"Are you all right, Warren? That glass of water won't be any trouble. Neither would the cold rag. It'll only take a moment." The assuaging words of the old recluse and her young great-niece came alternately. Warren heard both women offer utterances but failed to comprehend their words. Clinging to what little keenness remained, he sensed that the kindness flashing in their eyes was both mocking and insincere. Following a brief spell of acuity came hallucinations. In the first, Warren saw both women's faces orbiting one another, and the cylinder into which they peered lengthened. The macabre vision got interrupted when struck with a rush of abdominal pain—the twinges came upon him with sharp bursts. Between torrents came visions of Ursula and Gabby—transcendental and idyllic visions—the thrill of their oiled nakedness, the loveliness of their frolic, the sight of two bare beauties feeding one another grapes in a garden kissed with sunshine. Despite an unpleasant vicissitude, a sense of peace washed over Warren; it was the prevailing visions of Ursula and Gabby engendering the anomaly.

Although at times a Neanderthal, Warren was well aware of how fortunate a man he was and did manage, now and again, to credit Ursula for his enviable position. "He must have a herculean penis and a honey badger's stamina," I once told Gabby. She, in turn, replied, "Can't you get it through your bourgeois American head that two people, however ill-suited they may appear, can discover a beautiful and sustaining love."

Warren had just enough mind remaining to swear if he survived whatever it was inside those truffles making his viscera shrivel, he would make sure that Ursula, every day, would understand the true meaning of the word worship.

Michael De Stefano

The prevailing visions of Ursula and Gabby vanished when shooting abdominal pains traveled and became a sensation far more alarming: panic brought on by a constricting throat. It launched Warren, who all along sat pinned to a chair, to his feet; then, like a whirling dervish, he was sent spinning about the room before flinging himself to the floor. Gasping and convulsing, he crawled toward the hallway. If only he could reach the front door, he could will himself out into the open air and escape the slippery slope that had ensnared him, or so he believed. Along the way, the room turned sideways, then upside-down—the gallery and volumes were all ablur—then, by way of an abrupt clockwise contortion, the room righted itself. When Warren reached the hallway, he suffered one last violent spasm, then collapsed. Elizabeth glanced up at the clock. "Time of death: 4:08 p.m. Meanwhile, dear, we sit tight and wait until dark and try not to mind the mess in the hall. Then I'll call our dear old friend, Mr. McGruder."

Darkness fell; the night was quiet and still. Mr. McGruder—as a young man, he was befriended by Daniel Montague, thus became the only person to learn of Elizabeth's existence (A secret he vowed to keep) and promised, upon Daniel's death, to occasionally look in on Elizabeth (the oath provided a gateway to learning many mysteries concerning the big white house)—had a keen sense why his telephone was ringing so late in the evening. It was ten o'clock. Two hours later, at midnight, attired in dark clothing and a skull cap, he went creeping across the pike, slipped through the gate far more deftly than Warren had earlier, and disappeared into the tangle of overgrown trees and shrubbery. It would be a strenuous midnight ramble, Mr. McGruder realized. He wore old shoes—the ones he always reached for when his telephone rang so late in the evening. By the hands, Mr. McGruder took hold of Warren and dragged him down the hall, through the dining room, kitchen, and onto the patio. He managed to prop Warren up, underhook his arms, and instructed Elizabeth and Jenny each to grab a leg. Then off the three of them went, carrying the ill-fated Canadian Elk Hunter into the woods. Once a suitable burial ground was selected, Jenny dashed to the cellar and retrieved a shovel and lantern. Upon her return, Mr. McGruder began sculpting a subterranean hollow sufficient to accommodate Elizabeth and Jenny's latest victim.

And so that was Warren's demise: an episode more or less orchestrated by his friend, neighbor, and bike-riding partner—a person with whom he had, over the years, developed a bond. It should

284

be noted that the truffles were Elizabeth's idea, though someone must have put it into her head that Warren was never one to pass on dessert, no matter the time of day. And now, with Warren tidily out of the way—thanks, in part, to the ever-dutiful Mr. McGruder—Ursula and Gabby were free to delve further into discovering one another, and Nina and I could enjoy similar freedoms. That, after all, was the main objective of this complex scenario. And yes, I admit to being the primary orchestrator of what proved a convoluted affair. Moreover, dissuasion, where Ursula, Gabby, and Nina were concerned, if not nonexistent, was in short supply. In other words, no one's arm required any twisting, and obtaining the cooperation of Elizabeth and Jenny—two women who kill for sport—proved the easiest part of all.

****

"Mitch, I owe you an apology," Gabby began. "I was anything but encouraging when you first approached me with the idea of writing a serial killer spoof. I clearly remember telling you the concept was suspect at best, would never take flight, and that your most loyal readers would let you know it. Well, yours truly is prepared to eat her words: *Friends and Neighbors*, if held to its own standard, though it's likely one of a kind, could rate as your finest work. And though I wouldn't dare suggest you're not a man of wit or missing any appreciation for irony, I was skeptical of you applying those aspects as cleverly as a spoof would see them needed. I was never more pleased to be wrong: *Friends and Neighbors* is, dare I say, Hitchcockian! And, incidentally, it was a nice touch dedicating the novel to Warren: I'm sure he'll be appreciative; you might even consider allowing him to read the manuscript before sending it away; it's the very least you could do for killing him off."

Indeed, good ol' Warren is every bit as alive as real-life Harold—he persists as a genuine and viable piece of living, breathing nonfiction. When Elizabeth first gushed to me the concept of a serial killer spoof, I thought, why not use my friends and neighbors as characters? Hence, the unimaginative title. And I must admit not suffering a moment's compunction over exposing the numerous quirks of my peculiar friends and neighbors. And Warren—whom I suspected might offer an objection—bless his heart, had no qualms portrayed as the heel whose curiosity over a young woman, for whom he was terribly unsuited, led to his demise. And it was all quite ironic; for whenever

Warren got the sort of itch known to lead weak men astray, it was never to—I shall borrow one of Gabby's idioms—"play in the bushes."

"At least you didn't have me stabbed in the shower by a psychopathic transvestite or blindsided with a shovel," Warren said. "If one must get snuffed out, laced truffles would head a very short list of favorable methods."

It would have been the perfect time to remind Warren of his one-and-done novelist cousin from Canada and the story of the heroic dwarf with a speech impediment for which he seemed so proud, but why spoil the spirit of a kind moment? When a friend expresses gratitude, one should reciprocate with a show of appreciation. Later, Gabby and Ursula raised the suspicion that *Friends and Neighbors*—aside from a well-crafted serial killer spoof—was a cunning effort to encourage our sunbathing beauties beyond oiled nakedness and their usual titillating sense of frolic (the latter never failed to feature playful kissing and touching) to something more meaningful.

"A real sly dog, aren't 'we,' Mitch Morningstar?" What followed Ursula's playful accusation was a wagging finger to indicate she was owed an expression of shame. What followed my unsuccessful resistance to appear shamefaced was Ursula winking at me. I interpreted the gesture as a forewarning that two beautiful women discovering one another and other potencies rest on the horizon. However, it could be my cockeyed optimism leading me astray.

Where Elizabeth was concerned, there was a time when Gabby and I did suspect the possibility she was a deranged killer. But then time passed; we settled on the notion that one Miss Elizabeth Montague, aka Miss Havisham, was but a kooky, eccentric old recluse—given her childhood, it was a wonder that was all she became—with a less kooky and eccentric great-niece, who was not a recluse, quite a pleasure to look at, but, at times—her elitist educators must bear some blame—could be downright challenging.

"We all dream of greatness, Mitch—or, if not greatness, of being much more than we are," a near weepy Elizabeth told me one afternoon. "But those are just dreams. What we humans truly desire is an opportunity to matter. You gave a batty old lady a chance to feel as though she were truly collaborating with an artist."

I mean this sincerely: Elizabeth's words were worth more than the royalties.

The Bohemian

Life went on; our best days lie ahead. Molly evolved beyond the need for predatorial-type sexual escapades, maintaining that her only "real necessities" were the sensitivity and generosity of Daddy Russ, thus proving, once again, with age comes wisdom and self-awareness. She and Daddy Russ would eventually marry.

Real-life Harold and Jane continue to run their book club in London and visit whenever possible. Their asexuality aside, they remain a couple with worthy passions upon which they share with equal spirit. Who could ever have imagined, upon my first meeting them in Bloomsbury at Lord John Russell Pub, years of enduring fondness would follow. Surely, not I.

Whether or not *Friends and Neighbors* provided agency or proved instrumental—it is difficult to determine whether the project was motivated by a novelist's deviance or a genuine belief that Elizabeth Montague's brainchild was a worthy endeavor (I am not guarding secrets; some influences are subliminal)—the friendship of Gabby and Ursula would deepen to where discovery was inevitable. And for the record: this development did not levy me with bouts of inadequacy. Warren, to his credit, also avoided battling insufficiency. Where our wives were concerned, he and I were a unified front.

As for yours truly: I would manage one more serial killer escapade before completing Nina's biography titled *A Woman for all Seasons;* it was as well-received as Nina, years ago, had predicted. Moreover, another of her forecasts proved prophetic: the biography would further her considerable, and my far less notable, celebrity. In the future, Nina split her days between two continents: She used the Bloomsbury flat to rest when not in cities where her satiny and haunting contralto was in demand; the rest of her days she spent in a sleepy Philadelphia suburb, making up a third of what was evolving into an artful marriage.

"If one Norwich sister is good, then two must be better," Molly playfully intoned. It led to Elizabeth giving me the old finger-wagging tsk-tsk reprimand during one of our teatime engagements and labeling me a "metrosexual libertine." Anyway, an arrangement owning the potential to become unwieldy acquitted itself surprisingly smoothly. But then, to everyone's delight, Nina met a man; thus, our bohemian clique at long last rounded off to an even ten.

As for Mr. McGruder: the old curmudgeon was often seen glowering at the Papermill Tavern and popping off "How dare he" and swearing to bring litigation against me for having been made an accomplice to murder: "Defamation of character!" was what he grumbled to his regulars. Mr. McGruder had no legal leg upon which to stand. Nevertheless, and with an objective whose only intention was to extend an olive branch, I figured what had I to lose by paying him a visit. Moreover, I took no joy that one of the locals got rankled over a work I produced: I'm supposed to be the "serial killer guy" recognized by a Bert and Ernie cycling jersey, not an agitator, less a neighborhood provocateur. Mr. McGruder told me he would cease raising a fuss if I could broker a meeting between him and the phantom of the big white house. Tactfully, I explained Elizabeth's peculiarities and that although I would make every effort, I could not guarantee a result. And yes, I was perfectly aware that Mr. McGruder's threat to bring litigation against me was all a ruse and that my visitation left me open for a bribe. However, it seemed a small price to win over someone considered a pillar of the community.

During my next visit with Elizabeth, I explained the pickle, although my dilemma with Mr. McGruder hardly qualified as a "pickle," into which I had gotten myself. She brightened over the notion I was being bribed and readily agreed to a meeting with Mr. McGruder. *Friends and Neighbors* made Elizabeth feel daring and gave her the spark to end her days as a recluse. And while we are on the subject of sparks: I remained in the sitting room long enough to watch them fly between two people born seven decades ago, then made an unnoticed departure. How wonderfully strange is this unending experiment we call life.

I went home and found Gabby busy at her sketchpad. Looking over her shoulder, I saw Warren sprawled on the cold hard tile of Elizabeth's hallway. Jenny's glary expression implied that Warren's demise could not have been more deserved. Meanwhile, Elizabeth appeared as if the Canadian Elk Hunter's expiration was just another ho-hum affair. I remarked aloud the sentiment I pondered upon leaving Mr. McGruder with Elizabeth: "How wonderfully strange is this ongoing experiment we call life."

"It is as it should be," Gabby said with an air of indifference.

ABOUT THE AUTHOR

Michael DeStefano owns a hairstyling salon, where he has spent the past four decades beautifying the super people of Philadelphia. His past titles include the historical family saga *The Gunslinger's Companion* and the comedy/tragedy *Waiting for Grandfather*. Please forward any comments or criticisms you wish to share concerning *The Bohemian* to dtbhs62@icloud.com.